INTERCEPTION

Harness in hand, Jess picked up a thin sheaf of sealed pages in a waterproof cover at the duty room, signed out, and headed off to an empty stall to change.

There, she disrobed, and hung her human clothes over the stall door. She fastened the absurdly large harness around her neck and body, and took a deep breath, and—

Exhaled a noisy equine sigh of happiness. The previously merely lovely scent of hay and grain in the stall turned sharp and distracting. She yawned a huge yawn, and shook herself like a wet dog, settling the harness more properly in place.

Peacekeepers. Lady's ears tilted as though listening to someone on her back. That was the Jess-voice, deep in her head. The one she had to listen to, even though it was equally important to avoid the more complex concepts her equine brain couldn't process. *Deliver to the Peacekeepers*.

Lady snorted, pushed the unlatched door open, and walked out. She was on her way, out on the road, gearing up into a lope, snorting into the wind and letting out her speed, until she was galloping, tail flagged high and black legs flashing too fast to follow.

In a quarter mile, she connected with a main road and shifted into a trot. Ahead of her a man ran out into the road. Lady stopped short, ears clamped tightly to her skull, then charged down the road, not bothering to snap at the pinprick of a fly bite at her neck. Then she stumbled to her knees, tottering like a newborn foal. She snapped at a new fly on her shoulder, and received a surprisi

Manmade. Dart. Fury was

ing fear that followed her i

Baen Books by Doranna Durgin

Dun Lady's Jess
Touched By Magic
Changespell

DORANNA DURGIN

CHANGESPELL

A Baen Books Original

Baen Publishing Enterprises
P.O. Box 1403
Riverdale, NY 10471

ISBN: 0-671-87765-8

Cover art by Larry Elmore

First printing, February 1997

Distributed by Simon & Schuster
1230 Avenue of the Americas
New York, NY 10020

Printed in the United States of America

This book came from the summer of change,
and is dedicated to the man in the center of it,
my husband Matt.

Chapter 1

Jess leaned over the young bay gelding's neck, letting him run on this, their last outing together. The tree-lined road was wide and smooth, and empty of all other travelers at this early hour. Jess closed her eyes, riding the smooth, powerful surges of his body as though it were her own. The wind tore at her long dun hair and flattened her shirt against her chest; she flared her nostrils and drank it in.

Then, reluctantly, she sat back into the saddle and eased the bay down into a moderate canter, where the wind only tickled her nose. Their last run together, and then the bay, whom she was delivering to a small wizard hold on the edge of the precinct, would unleash his speed for someone else.

She would miss him. He was cheerful and easy to work with, and he loved to run. She could run without him, though, and would—on the way back. Human courier on the way out to Aashan's hold, she would make her way back to Kymmet Stables on her own feet—only then, she would be hooved and four-legged, a mare with refined features and an eloquent arch of neck. Dun Lady's Jess.

The bay slowed at Jess's request, moving out in a loose-jointed trot as she posted to his powerful strides. She hoped Aashan's courier, Willsey, truly did want the speed and power she'd admired in this young horse, and would not regret that he was not for a lazy rider. Jess had thought that question when Willsey had decided on the bay, but had not asked it out loud. A year ago, newly come to her human form, Jess would have blurted the query without hesitation. Now she was trying to learn tact, but kept getting tangled in the line between honesty and deception.

After another mile, she let the gelding walk, and dropped the reins over the blunt saddle pommel to gather up the hem of her loosely woven shirt and wipe her sweaty face on it. The shirt was a nuisance, but that was another lesson she'd had to learn: men could go without clothing on their upper body, but not women. Jess still didn't really understand that, but she didn't fight it, either, not when it seemed so important to Carey.

Carey. She thought wistfully of her former rider, and the man who was so important to her—even if both of them were still struggling to define their relationship. He'd turned cautious after he'd come to realize she was a person in her own right, and not just a horse in human clothing. Too cautious, Jess thought, frustrated. She wanted to explore the human emotions she knew were waiting for her—if only she and Carey weren't separated by distance and his concerns.

But the distance was her choice, as was her position as courier and trainer in a large stable, two days north of Arlen's hold. As much as she wanted to be with Carey, she wanted to discover *herself* even more. And doing so put her here, on the back of a sweating horse, turning onto a back road so little used that it didn't even have a protection spell over the surface. Tree roots were poking up through it, and miniature, rain-washed gorges peppered its length at every little slope—and there were plenty of those, since Aashan lived at the top of a long, low moraine.

Hmmph. If Willsey was going to be running one of Jess's horses over this road, the young courier was going to have to convince Aashan to lay a spell on the road—or buy one, if doing so wasn't in the wizard's repertoire.

You're just being crabby, she told herself. If she were a human woman, no doubt some man would make a snide comment about it being "that time," but so far, Jess's body had been too confused by the fairly frequent switching between human and equine bodies to settle into any cycles. Her fellow female couriers were sporadically envious; Jess wasn't sure how to feel about it. No, she was just plain crabby—hot in midday of the first truly warm day of the season, about to turn over one of her favorite horses to another stable, and missing Carey. She felt like kicking someone.

But even as Lady, she'd known kicking was not allowed. So she wiped her face again, resettled her polarized sunglasses—a gift from her friend Jaime, who lived in a place called Ohio, far from Camolen and Jess's world—and let the bay pick his own path up the wooded hill.

Willsey was waiting by the informal gate at Aashan's hold, her posture signaling her anticipation. When she saw Jess emerge from the trees, she waved enthusiastically—enthusiasm was Willsey's motto in life—and Jess could see the brilliance of her smile even with the distance between them. She took pity on the younger courier, who was practically hopping up and down in place, and asked the bay for a smooth canter. No Running Toward The Barn was another rule, but Jess pushed away her guilt with the knowledge that the gelding didn't realize this was *his* barn, not yet.

"Jess!" Willsey shouted, running out to meet them when she apparently couldn't stand it any longer. "I thought you'd *never* get here!"

"It's hot," Jess said, as she halted the bay. "There was no reason to push him." Except for that one run. But that had been *good-bye*.

"No, no, of course not," Willsey said, holding the reins

just below the bit while Jess dismounted. Jess forbore to tell her it wasn't necessary; the horse was better trained than that. After all, Jess had learned about training from the horse's side of it, first. *Crabby*, she told herself, and kept her mouth shut, her irritation betrayed only by the slight tilt of her head that said her equine ears would have been laid back. Only Carey would have noticed it—or perhaps her friend Ander.

And indeed, Willsey did not. "It's just that I've been waiting so long to get a new horse up here. Babe is good and steady, but you know how old she is." She gave the bay a longing look, her mostly plain features—mud-brown eyes, snubby nose, and rounded, undefined features, all saved by a beautifully shaped and expressive mouth—transformed by excitement into something shining and lovely.

She was doing her best to be polite, not to step on Jess's toes. The payment for this horse had already been exchanged, and now it was up to Jess to literally hand over the reins. Reluctantly, she did so. She stepped aside and offered Willsey the braided leather reins.

Willsey took them, grinning hard. "Thanks, Jess. I can't wait to give BayBoy his first good ride."

"He's already worked today," Jess said as the young woman mounted. She looked small up on the horse—but then, as most of the couriers, she was slight and wiry, a distinct contrast to Jess's lithe and long-limbed athleticism.

"Oh, I know. I just want to feel him out for a few minutes. Say, there's water waiting by the gate—iced!"

Jess barely heard the last words over the bay's hoofbeats. BayBoy's hoofbeats, she corrected herself, glad she'd never named him. She headed for the gate, and the water. That Aashan had bothered to ice it was quite a compliment; Jess knew the hold had no cookmages, just ordinary human help like herself.

Like herself. She snorted and flipped the long dun

forelock out of her face. It was streaked with a centerline of black, as was the length of coarse, thick hair that was tied off to fall in a tail down her back, tangling with the handful of tiny sapphire and onyx spellstones that held the changespell. Dun, with black points and a thick black line down her back. Not quite *ordinary human* at that.

❧ ❧ ❧

"Aashan taught me a little spell for bright days," Willsey said, squinting through Jess's sunglasses a moment before handing them back. "I don't know if I could get used to having these things on my face."

Jess pushed the glasses back up her nose—a nose that was a bit long, straight, and graced with cleanly defined nostrils. She and Willsey sat at the wood table outside Aashan's main hold, eating lunch. What Willsey ate, Jess didn't want to know—it clearly smelled of meat, and while she'd experimented with eating meat, there was very little of it she enjoyed. She took another bite of her buttered, honeyed bread and caught the overflow of honey with a quick tongue. "You should see Ohio," she told the younger courier. "Some people wear these all the time, to make their eyes good."

Willsey's own eyes widened slightly. "I never thought about what it would be like without vision specialists," she said. "I used to be farsighted, myself. Just took a couple of corrective spells when I was little."

Farsighted. Jess spent a moment playing with focus, near and far, all without moving her head. As a horse, she focused by bringing her head up so she was looking at an object at the proper angle. She still found herself surprised at how much of her vision was clear at one time, especially when she was startled—

Like now. Something darted past the corner of her eye; her head came up, her jaw stopped in mid chew.

"Relax," Willsey said easily. "Just that annoying little

dog Aashan's daughters keep." She bumped Jess's elbow with her hand. "Say, did you hear about that warning spell in the Lorakans?"

Jess shook her head, giving the dog one last look out of the corner of her eye. Just let it try to come over here . . . "Lorakans?" she asked.

"The mountains that nearly cut off those old coastal precincts," Willsey said. "Something triggered some old border spell—no one knows what it's about, though they all think it's some sort of warning."

Jess wasn't sure what kind of magic Aashan specialized in; she received so many private, courier-carried messages from the city that Jess wondered if she didn't, somehow, specialize in gossip. Then she'd decided that was nonsense, since no one could ever make a nice hold like this by trafficking in silly bits of news. She licked a drip of honey off her wrist and thought about Willsey's words. "Why don't they know what it's about?"

"Oh, it's old," Willsey said dismissively, waving Jess's question away with a gesture. "The people there don't really use the same kind of magic we do; they haven't, for centuries. It's clan magic or something. I don't really understand it." She grinned. "I didn't do very well in history class, in case you couldn't tell."

Jess waited, knowing she'd get to the point.

"Anyway, the warning spell's for *some*thing, so they're falling all over themselves trying to figure out what." Willsey grinned, glanced over her shoulder, and then leaned forward, lowered her voice, and said, "But the really interesting stuff is happening right here, in the middle of Camolen."

"Here in Kymmet?" Jess asked. She picked out a browning apple slice from the small ceramic bowl in the middle of the table, and let the treat sit on her tongue. Mmm, small, tart apple; it had always been her favorite. She spoke around it. "What?"

"It's not *in* Kymmet," Willsey said. "That's the thing. Just listen to this. At least three of the Council members have detected strong magic at work, and not one of them recognized the signature."

Jess frowned. "I thought the wizards who work strong magic are all . . ." she searched for the word, "*registered* with the Council."

"That's just it," Willsey said, sitting back on the bench with a *see there?* look on her face. "They're supposed to be. And even if they're not registered yet, by the time anyone can work really strong magic—which makes for loud magic—the upper level folk have learned who they are, anyway. But not this time. And not only that—now the magic's being *shielded.*"

Jess just looked at her.

Unlike most of the Kymmet Stables' customers, Willsey was never surprised when Jess came up lacking in the most basic of subjects. She never gave Jess strange looks because of her speech pattern, when her words became halting or got a little thick where vowel met consonant; because Willsey knew horses, she always understood what little thing had caught Jess's attention, and distracted her from the discussion at hand. Other people tended to think she was either stupid or rude.

Jess knew she was not stupid. And as for being rude . . . well, when she was, she was rude with her typical honesty, and there was no mistaking it.

"There's not supposed to be anyone out there who's strong enough to shield from a Council member," Willsey told her. "They're all desperate to find out who's doing it." She grew suddenly casual, playing with a bit of apple that Jess had not yet claimed. "They're also, uh, a little concerned that if people knew, they'd overreact. So don't tell just anyone, all right?"

"You're telling me," Jess said, making sure she had it right, "but I'm not supposed to let other people know."

She frowned, and pushed the sunglasses up on her nose. "Why is it all right to tell me?"

Willsey grinned. "Because you're my friend. And sometimes you just gotta tell *someone*."

Jess sighed. One more thing to remember. Maybe she'd ask Ander about it. He was good at explaining human vagaries to her; she thought he enjoyed helping her, though she wasn't sure just why. He didn't seem to help any of the other couriers quite so happily.

Ander. He would be waiting for her; they had to evaluate a courier applicant in the late afternoon. What the applicant didn't realize was that he would be tested by two Kymmet employees instead of one—the courier who watched him, and the courier he rode.

Willsey seemed to note her distraction. "Gotta get back, huh?" she asked. "You want to say good-bye to BayBoy?"

"I already did that," Jess said. She stood and picked up the tangle of leather beside the bench, looking down at the remains of the food. "Thank you. My favorites."

"I figured as much," Willsey said, looking pleased. "That was from the first shipment of apples this season; I had the cook hold one aside for you. Oh, no, Jess—you should do that in the barn."

Jess's hands hesitated at the snap to her breeches—another gift from Jaime, although she'd also advised Jess to wear a long tunic to cover her bottom, since Camolen hadn't yet developed stretch fabrics. Jess hadn't understood Jaime's comment—something about the fit being "too hot" for the unsuspecting men of the Camolen; Jaime had muttered something about good conformation and left it at that.

Willsey's concern was the clothes rule again, of course. Jess'd thought since they were out in this quiet courtyard, with no one but Willsey in sight—even the scruffy little dog was not to be seen—that it would be all right. Apparently not. "All right," she said. "The barn."

At the barn, Willsey was polite; she'd done this often enough to know that while Jess was casual about her nudity, she didn't like to be studied when she triggered the changespell to Lady. So, with Jess's gear hung casually over one shoulder, she stood beside the stall where Jess disrobed, and accepted her clothing piece by piece, starting with the sunglasses and ending with the lightweight bra that Jess despised.

In the dimness of the stall, Jess loosed the thick fall of her hair, and shook her head to settle it. Just behind her ear, next to the spot where Arlen's brand stained her skin, there was a long, thin braid; sewn to that was the dangling collection of tiny sapphire and onyx spellstones—the sapphire to change her to Lady, and the onyx to change her back. If, she thought with a determined little scowl, her equine form could ever learn to trigger the changespell on her own.

With the wood shavings of the stall crunchy against her bare soles, Jess picked out one of the sapphires and folded her hand around it, closing her eyes for the moment of concentration that allowed her to find that proper little niche in her mind, the one that whispered *LadyLadyLady* the entire time she was Jess.

And then she let it free. She opened herself to the sensations of the ground beneath hard, sturdy hooves, of the scents of grain and hay and the inevitable bit of mustiness that came with a barn, of sounds that caught in her mobile, finely shaped ears, and the feel of a tail whisking against sensitive skin. She let go of the well-ordered thoughts that dominated Jess. No sensible sentences in her head, no flashes of sudden understanding that came from putting separate bits of knowledge together.

No, Lady's world was made up of Rules and Carey's special Words, of sensations flooding her brain and leading to immediate, unthinking reaction. Jess's goals were translated into simple directives. Sometimes it was, Run to a hold she knew; this afternoon it would be, Do you like this rider? and for now, it was Go home.

In the stall, a dun mare snorted, shaking herself off with a decisive flap of her long mane. Behind her ear, a tangle of spellstones clinked against one another; one of them was newly dulled. Under her mane, along the upper curve of her fine, arched neck, Arlen's old brand traced his name in her dark dun hide.

She snorted again, and nudged the stall door open.

"All set then?" Willsey asked her. Lady ducked her head, and Willsey dropped her gear over it, pushing it down to her well-sloped shoulders. The pouch that held Jess's clothes and any messages settled into place high, behind her withers. Willsey snugged a supple girth in place behind Lady's elbows, and ran her fingers along the breast collar to make sure it was correctly placed, and wouldn't rub as the mare returned to Kymmet Stables. In the center of the breast collar, a finely tooled and dyed leather circlet held the Kymmet insignia; it was the best they'd been able to do by way of identifying Lady, though she still had to evade the well-meaning citizens who occasionally tried to catch her.

Willsey gave her a gentle pat on the neck. "You're all set," she said. With confident strides, Lady trotted out of the barn, out the open gate, and picked her way down the path to Kymmet.

❧ ❧ ❧

Dayna stared at her notes, frowning, and not really seeing the notes at all. After a moment she realized that, and shoved the notes across her desk, turning the frown into a truly impressive scowl.

The truth was, it was hard to concentrate, even for an important test, with all the whispering that was going on. And even though Dayna was in her own, small, private room with the door closed, she knew the whispering was still happening.

Study, she told herself, knowing it was not about to happen. She'd wanted to impress Chiara with this test, too—it was the most complicated spell she'd ever tried, and she had a history of losing hold of the complicated ones.

If only they'd let me work with magic the way I did when I first came here. That'd been a year or so ago, when she'd been dumped on this world of magic with Jaime and Jess, Carey and Mark—and Eric's still-warm body. Unschooled, unsuspecting, she'd immediately tapped into unstructured magic—raw magic, Carey had called it, and warned her off it.

But before their adventures had ended, she'd been pushed into using it more than once, despite the dire consequences of magical backlash when she had lost control. And that was how she had started studying under Chiara, the wizard Sherra's best advanced student. It hadn't been by choice, that was for sure. She'd wanted no part of the magic, and no part of this world.

Until she'd realized how rare her talent was, and just how good she could be, if she tried.

So here she was, trying. Starting over again at age thirty-two. Staring at the papers scattered across her scarred wooden desk, with her very own magelight providing light from behind, and the noises of Sherra's hold—the children, the goats, the birds, and especially that damn rooster, who obviously thought it was dawn all day long—sounding more like home than the silent little Ohio house she used to call her own.

The test was scheduled for this evening. Dayna was beginning to wonder if she should ask for a postponement; she was certainly not thinking about the disciplined mental process for turning water into an impervious hollow sphere. No, she was thinking of the rogue magic.

She wasn't really supposed to know about it. None of them were—but they'd all felt it. The others were all talking about it like it was some exciting new event, as though they had the chance to be in on the discovery of a great new talent.

Dayna knew better. She had not mastered control, but she had sensitivity in spades, and she knew just how powerful this unknown wizard was. She saw the worry in Sherra's eyes, the distraction in Chiara. Even Katrie, a friend among Sherra's private peacekeepers, seemed somber and preoccupied.

And Dayna had been there to see just how destructive a wizard bent on having her own way could be. The others were too innocent, young men and woman who had been relatively unaffected by Calandre's short and contained reign of terror during the previous summer; they assigned the unknown wizard benign motives, and made up heroic backgrounds—a man from the far east, self-taught and making his way to the Council House in Kymmet. A woman of desperate circumstances, keeping a low profile until she was certain of her welcome.

No, Dayna knew better. She knew any wizard who bothered to shield himself so thoroughly had nothing good to offer Camolen. She knew any wizard who *could* shield himself so thoroughly was a threat to Camolen. And she knew checkspells were nothing to a truly devious mind bent on creating damage.

Calandre had twisted spells to hurt Mark, and to try to kill Carey. Willand had twisted healing spells to torture Jaime. It didn't matter that there were checkspells on every malignant spell the Council had discovered, and that those checkspells underwent diligent monitoring in case someone tried to fiddle with them. Dayna had spent time thinking about the problem, looking into it; she knew how easy it was to turn a beneficial spell into something of horror. What if you applied the same spell that placed a protective barrier over her teeth to someone's nose and mouth? What if you took the same little spell that temporarily plugged plumbing leaks, and inserted it into someone's heart instead?

Those sorts of things didn't happen in Camolen, at least not often. And that was because each time a wizard used a spell, it left a signature, ofttimes a lingering one. Even when a spellstone was triggered, it left the signature of the wizard who created the spell, and the overtones of the individual who triggered it. In this magic-driven society, that meant a lot of noise in the background; Dayna had already learned to close most of it out.

But a wizard who could maintain a shield against even the Council members could do whatever he or she wanted, without detection. And a wizard whose signature had never yet been tied to an individual was under no threat of discovery. He or she had complete freedom to do whatever they wanted, for good or bad.

Dayna leaned back in her chair—a small one, sized to her own diminutive stature—and let her head fall over the back of it so her sandy, shoulder-length hair spilled down toward the floor, her throat as open and exposed as she imagined Camolen's to be.

Dramatic, Dayna. Really dramatic. She decided to raise her hands over her head and turn it into a stretch, instead.

And then she decided to go ask Chiara for a postponement. And while she was at it, it might not hurt to ask a question or two. Let the other students make up their romantic fantasies about the new magic. Dayna wanted the truth, so she would know what to prepare for.

Chapter 2

Lady's tail swished in annoyance—a sharp, constant rhythm that her rider would have done well to heed. The young man on her back didn't know when to leave well enough alone, and Lady, though obedient, had never been one to suffer fools.

She circled the far end of the large, covered arena, eyeing Ander, who stood in the center. She knew she was here to evaluate this rider. And she knew Ander had gotten her into it, had let the young man saddle her, interfering only when the saddle was placed so far forward it would have pinched her shoulders. He had *not* interfered when the young man had so abruptly jerked the girth tight, or when he had failed to lift Lady's tangled forelock from beneath the browband of her bridle, where the hair caught and twisted unpleasantly.

No, he had not stopped any of it. He merely stood in the arena and called out simple directives, things like, "I'd like to see you trot her now."

Bump, bump, bump. The applicant's heels banged her sides at every one of her ground-eating strides. There was never any change in Ander's voice—no surprise, no dismay. Lady knew well enough that this young man was not up to riding her. She snorted sharply, and loudly, and began to creep in on the circle, closing in on Ander.

"She'll do better than that for you," Ander said mildly, no doubt referring to the way Lady hollowed her back, turning her gait rough and uncomfortable. Another few feet closer to Ander as she circled him and she could find some excuse to stop. . . .

She nearly stumbled as her rider yanked her head to the outside; he'd noticed her shrinking circle. That was *it*, she wanted him *off*. She wanted to be Jess, who could yell at this oaf in ways Lady couldn't. The spellstone, the spellstone . . . she speeded up her trot as the man tapped her sides with his heels, and set her jaw against the reins he was pulling on, trying to get her into a nice headset. *The spellstone. Jess* could trigger it . . . Lady had some vague notion of how it worked, but could get no further than wanting it.

"Try a canter," Ander said. "She's got quite a nice one."

Canter? No. If she couldn't turn into Jess, if she couldn't break the Rules and rid herself of this clumsy rider, then she'd do the opposite. She'd do just what he told her. And right now, he was telling her a muddled combination of things, with his legs thumping indiscriminantly against her sides, his seat shoving into her back in some indecipherable and uncomfortable cue . . . she speeded up her trot, extending, creating her own breeze.

He could barely post her movement. "C'mon, canter," he muttered from behind teeth that sounded clenched. And canter she would—as soon as he cued her properly. She ducked her head and came behind the reins, her neck arched in a caricature of the noble headset he'd been trying to achieve all along. She rushed on, her equine thoughts falling into a rut. *The spellstone. Jess. The spellstone—*

Smack!

Lady leapt forward, mortified. The oaf had a crop! She'd forgotten he had a crop and he'd *hit* her with it! She was cantering already, startled into it; she could almost feel his satisfaction. But Lady had had enough. It was a spacious arena, plenty big enough for a good gallop. She bolted, almost leaving her rider behind. Clods of soft dirt flew into the air behind her, kicked up by her hooves. With her chin almost touching her chest, he had no control with the reins, and she certainly wasn't going to listen to his seat—assuming he found it again, instead of clutching her mane and sliding around in the saddle.

"Lady!" Ander shouted—as if Lady was going to listen now. She made two complete circuits of the arena at top speed, and then slowed with a series of jerky bounces off her front legs. When she was slow enough, she started to buck.

She wished he'd stayed on more than two jumps. It would have been a lot more fun. But the instant he left the saddle for good, she stopped and dropped her head, barely breathing hard, her face a study of stupid innocence and the reins laying so far up her neck they looped around her ear and crossed over her forehead.

Ander ran up to where the young man was getting on his hands and knees, spitting the carefully raked arena dirt from his mouth; nothing broken, from the looks of it. Hands low on his on hips, Ander said mildly, "Subtle cues. I told you, all our horses take *subtle cues*."

Lady stretched her neck to get a better look at the young man's face, and then snorted in it, the wettest snort she could muster. Ander, she could see, was hiding a grin—but he might as well not grin at all. She hadn't even started with *him* yet.

ଓ ଓ ଓ

"You *knew*!" Jess shouted toward the door of the stall. She jammed her head into the tunic and found the neck of it through brute force. "You *knew* he'd be like that! And you let him ride me!" No wonder Ander hadn't triggered the changespell when she'd returned in the early afternoon, hours before the ride. No wonder he'd kept her out grazing until just before saddling time. Jess ran her tongue over her sore gums and rubbed the hip that still stung from the young applicant's crop. Then she jerked the rest of her clothes on and stormed out of the stall to face Ander, who still hadn't responded to her.

He sat on the sturdy tack box that held Kymmet Stables' first-aid supplies, his long legs stretched out and crossed at the ankle. Broad shouldered, lean hipped—he was, like Jess, bigger than most of the couriers. But he was a consummate rider and trainer, and he'd gotten the job at Kymmet's prestigious stables despite his size—also like Jess.

But unlike Jess, he was fully human. And he was male. Sometimes Jess thought humans should come with the instruction books she'd learned to read—especially the men. For although Ander looked a bit embarrassed, he did not look truly chastised or abashed. In fact, she'd have to say he looked *satisfied* beneath that little shrug and grin of his.

She barely stopped before she reached him. Crowding him, just like she'd crowd another horse in the pasture. But no other horse would calmly put his hands on her waist and carefully move her to the side—and she was not sure Ander should be doing it, either. She tossed her head in annoyance.

"Relax," Ander said. "I didn't have any choice. The fellow was nephew to the senior man on the Precinct Lander Council. There's no way Koje could turn him away without the ridden interview. And you were the best horse for it—I knew I could count on you to respond in some appropriately spectacular manner."

Jess made a noise deep in her throat—certainly not agreement. "You should have told me."

"I thought it would work out better if you reacted more naturally." Unperturbed, he picked a wood shaving out of her hair.

Jess tilted her head back, more annoyed than ever;

she stepped out of his reach. He was making decisions for her again.

Unlike Carey, who was in his early thirties, Ander was nearer to what Jaime had estimated to be Jess's own biological age, in her mid twenties. He was also her first friend here at Kymmet, the largest public breeding and training courier stables in central Camolen. Jess'd arrived fresh from the conflict over the world-travel spell that had taken her—and Carey—from Camolen to Ohio, and turned her into a woman in the process. And she'd been more than a little frightened, walking away from Carey and her home to take a position in Kymmet.

But Jess was nothing if not determined, and during her first day here, the man who had started out resenting her because of her quick and easy hiring at Kymmet ended up supporting her when she'd refused to let a horse go on a run. The horse's assigned rider was an experienced one, and had turned furious fast. It was Ander who backed her when she said she saw signs of distress in the animal. And it had been Ander she'd woken when the horse became colicky in the middle of that night.

Friends, and friends fast and true. But did friends make important decisions for one another? Jess wasn't sure. She wouldn't have done the same to him, but she never knew if her innate reactions were the correct human ones. So she didn't call him on it. Instead, she said carefully, "This will not happen again. No one rides me as Lady who has not spoken to me as Jess."

Ander shrugged again. "All right," he said. He gave her a sidelong look and said, "But didn't it feel good when you dumped him?"

Jess snorted, but a smile tugged at the corner of her mouth. "Yes," she said. "It did." She finger-combed her long dun hair and searched in her pocket for the tie that held it from her face.

"Let me," Ander said, when she'd found it. She turned

her back on him and held out the tie, taking the grooming as she'd accepted such things from anyone who had handled Lady. He gently pulled her hair back, untangled the snarl he ran into, gathered up the spellstones, and tied it all away from her face.

Jess paid no attention. She was thinking back to the moments in the riding ring. While Lady was unable to think with all of a human's facilities, Jess was perfectly able to search her excellent equine memory, no matter what form she was in when the memories were made. And now she was thinking of the changespell, yet again, and Lady's unfocused efforts to do something with it. "If I'd been able to change," she murmured, not finishing the thought. It was clear enough to *her*.

And to Ander. "As if you haven't tried to do it before, and failed—over and over," he said. "Jess, I *know* it's important to you—but I hate to see you tear yourself up over it when it's not going to happen." He put his hands on her shoulders and turned her around, but Jess had had enough of handling for the day. She stepped back out of reach, nostrils flared; Ander knew her well enough not to push.

"It *might* happen," she said. "I do *not like* having to depend on you or Koje to spell me back." Carey could do it, if he were here, and Arlen, his friend—and the wizard who had created the world-travel spell—could do it without the spellstones. She even had a spellstone keyed for Jaime. Lady, though . . . It had been a year, and Lady had never shown any signs of success.

But she hadn't tried for months. "Things change," she told Ander.

"True enough," Ander said. He didn't say anything else for a moment, but regarded her, biting the corner of his lip.

The barn aisle stretched out behind him, and an equal length ran behind Jess. Beside them, there was a wide, short aisle connecting this side of the barn with the identical row of stalls parallel to it. The high-ceilinged structure echoed with the clop of hooves and the metallic ring of stall latches shoving home; the grooms were bringing the horses in for the evening feeding. Jess's stomach rumbled at the smell of grain; she ignored it. Ander had something else on his mind, she could tell.

"What?" she said, watching his handsome features, wondering again why they did not please her as much as Carey's, though the other female couriers made such a fuss over them. Jess liked his eyes best, which were light blue and crinkled at the corners from the frequent smile that touched them.

"Got a rider in from Anfeald today," he said.

"Carey? Is Carey here?" Jess straightened, perking phantom ears.

Ander quickly shook his head. "No, no—one of his riders, though." Carey ran Arlen's stable—a much smaller operation than Kymmet, but no less crucial to the wizard. "It's a message for you, Jess."

"What does it say?"

Ander gave another shake of his head, and a wry little smile. "It's written in English—at least, your name is. Just for you. But the courier said a thing or two he shouldn't have, so I've got an idea—no," he said, cutting her off before she could ask him. "I suspect you should read what the letter has to say, first."

Whatever it was, its security was important enough to have warranted a letter instead of the more efficient wizard talk. So many messages went through the wizards' magical message and communication service, the Mage Dispatch, that Jess still didn't understand how they didn't get all tangled and misdirected. But most of those Dispatch wizards were specialists, just like the ones who had fixed Willsey's eyes, and the ones who doctored Carey after he was so badly injured by magic the year before. There were wizards who specialized in manufacturing long-lasting clothes, like her stain-resistant tunic, and those who made sure the traffic in Kymmet's crowded streets moved smoothly. And then there were scholars like Arlen, powerful magic users who researched new spells, and who occasionally taught others to do the same.

Arlen could send a Dispatch message that practically no one else could decipher or intercept. But he had sent a letter to Jess instead, relying on the security of a courier who was probably mounted on one of Jess's half-siblings.

"Where is it?"

"With the courier," Ander said. "And judging by the time, he's probably eating dinner. Let's go find him."

Kymmet had on-premise housing for its trainers and couriers, even those with families; the stable was famous for being able to deliver a message no matter what time of day or night, or how busy the season. Along with the housing came overnight facilities for delivery couriers, and a well-staffed kitchen that served them all. Jess was not fond of the dining room—it was noisy, and filled with overwhelming smells, often of meat. She usually managed to slide in at the very beginning or end of a meal period, and the staff had quickly learned her grain- and fruit-weighted diet.

It was with some reluctance that she accompanied Ander to the dining room now, at its peak period; only the lure of Arlen's letter kept her from stopping at the threshold of the solid little structure. At least it was cool inside, and the thick flagstone floor felt good against her bare feet.

Ander stopped just inside the doorway, sliding aside so he wouldn't block it while he scanned the tightly spaced tables for Arlen's courier. Jess had him spotted first, someone she'd never seen before. He was a dark, wiry little man, with skin the color of the eastern lands people—making it almost the same toasty shade as her own. But his black hair was half the length of hers, and drawn into a short, dirty tail at the back of his neck. With the same quick judgement she'd used to assess humans all of her life, she decided she didn't really want to get any closer to him.

But he must be all right. He was Carey's man, and had ridden one of Carey's horses here. With Ander a startled step behind her, Jess headed for the courier's table.

Up close, he was no more palatable, but after a hot day like this, it was no surprise that he should still bear the sweat and dirt of his ride. He looked up at Jess as she came to a stop on the other side of the table from him, and after a moment the question on his face smoothed. "You're Jess," he said, and his voice was pleasant enough.

She nodded. "I have come for my letter."

His black-brown gaze flickered to the fine, supple leather of a courier's pouches, the scaled-down saddlebags that fit right over the top of full-size saddlebags, and then again settled on her, a moment longer than made her comfortable. "Jess," he said. He put down his split-ended spoon and drew the pouches into his lap. "Care to show me your brand? So I know it's you?"

Jess's eyes widened; her head raised, and Ander put a hasty hand on her arm. "This is Jess," he said, his voice hard in a tone he seldom used. "And that was uncalled for."

The man shrugged, undisturbed, and took a healthy gulp of his ale, dragging his wrist across his mouth; he did, at least, muffle his belch. "Interesting things happening," he said. "You can't be too sure about getting that sort of news to the right person."

"What does it matter, if you talk about it all along your route?" Ander said, his brow notched in a frown. "I don't expect either Carey or Arlen would be too happy about *that*."

"I'm not too worried about it," the man said, and his casual attitude made it clear that was true. "I'm filling in for them. More a favor than a job." That was no doubt the case. Carey was still trying to fill the ranks of his modest crew of couriers; Calandre had killed most of them the year before.

Jess sighed, an abrupt *whuff* of air, recognizing the mutual posturing for what it was, a human male thing. "I want to read the letter," she said, and thought she sounded reasonable enough, considering the chaos of the dining room around her and the attitude of the man in front of her. She'd seen it before, that slightly narrow-eyed interest that meant he was trying to find the horse in her.

He hesitated, obviously still looking, and not eager to give her the letter so she could walk away. Ander opened his mouth, his normally amiable features arranged in a scowl, and Jess casually, deliberately, stepped on his foot and shifted all her weight there.

It worked better when she had hooves but it surprised Ander enough to keep him quiet, and Jess held out her hand for the letter. The man gave a sudden little grin and shrugged, then reached into his courier pouch. "Here," he said. "Maybe I'll see you around Anfeald, eh?"

"Thank you," Jess said, closing her hand around the thick, tough paper Arlen used, doubting very much he would see her in Anfeald—or anywhere, if she saw him first. She left the table, and then the dining room and its unpleasant man, behind—and almost left Ander behind, as well. With long strides she crossed the short grassy lawn between the dining room and the dark brick building that held her small room, the sealed letter in her hand. She took the winding steps to the third floor two at a time, and pushed through the door, feeling the tingle of magic as it unlocked at her presence.

The room was purely Jess in nature, a combination of no-nonsense function and odd personal tidbits. She had a pair of saddlebags flung permanently over the plain headboard of the narrow bed; she'd been carrying them when she first arrived in Ohio. Separated from Carey and distressed at the sudden changes in her life and her very form, she'd clung to those saddlebags. Now, they were a reminder of the struggle she'd won in that bewildering world, and they bolstered her onward when she struggled in this one.

Besides, they were Carey's.

Jess tossed her sunglasses on the small dresser beside the bed; tacked to the wall over the dresser was a small row of ribbons, second and third—and one first—placings in dressage shows where Carey or Jaime had ridden Dun Lady's Jess. Next to them were photographs that never could have been made in Camolen—snapshots of Jaime on her Grand Prix horse, Sabre, and of her brother, Mark. There were photos of Eric, with his ever-distracted, gentle expression. Bittersweet photos, for Eric had been killed in the effort to keep Arlen's world-travel spell out of the wrong hands.

And there were photos of Jess, a newly human Jess, with an open, honest expression on her exotic features, but with large eyes that managed to convey the inner confusion of a mare who suddenly finds herself human and doesn't know the Rules.

She looked at that one a moment, and snorted. She still didn't know the Rules. Being a horse was certainly much less complex.

Ander cleared his throat from her doorway, a request.

"Yes," she said, and he came in to take the one chair in the room, a straight-backed wooden chair without padding.

"Nice fellow," Ander said, meaning the courier, and meaning he *wasn't*.

Jess shrugged. "I have the letter." She touched the hard seal, and it softened beneath her fingers. She peeled the seal off and looked at it a moment—Arlen's name, one of the few Camolen words she could read.

"Jess," Ander said impatiently, "don't you want to know what it says?"

Jess hesitated. "Change," she said finally. "It means change, whatever it is."

He looked at her in surprise, and ran a finger along his dark blonde mustache—it was thick, like his hair, but not the same sun-bleached gold. "I suppose you're right," he said. "But that doesn't mean it's bad."

Jess shrugged, unconvinced, and unfolded the thick paper. The letter was short, penned in Arlen's beautiful hand, with slanted lines and precise curves that were easy to read, even if Jess wasn't used to cursive. "We have found a man we think was a horse," he wrote. "Will you come tell us for certain?"

She looked at Ander. "It's not *good.*"

"What is it?"

Jess set the letter aside and went to the dresser to look at the picture of herself. Her long legs made Mark's old cutoffs look short, and her suntanned skin was not tanned at all, but its natural color. She looked at those worried eyes—eyes that had brown irises a bit larger than normal—and at the way she stood, poised to move at the slightest noise.

She'd made it. She'd found her way from Lady to Jess—and only later realized it was because she had Carey to focus on, and her complex and thorough training to start with. It didn't take much thought for her to know that few horses had the right nature and background to make that journey as she had. "No," she said. "This is not good."

❧ ❧ ❧

Ander patted his young mount and looked over at Jess; she was as endearing as ever, with those sunglasses and what she called a baseball cap. She'd pulled her long hair through the back strap of it, keeping the mingled dun and black strands off the back of her neck. Another sunny day for the heart of Camolen, and they were losing the shade of Kymmet's rocky woods as they moved into the more arable precinct of Anfeald. Jess caught him looking and gave him a little smile; it included that puzzled little overtone that meant she didn't really understand something human—probably, why he was watching her.

There was a lot she didn't understand.

She didn't, for instance, really understand why he insisted on coming with her to Anfeald, although she'd acquiesced without much fuss, simply because she obviously didn't think it was worth fussing over. As if there was any way he would have let her go alone, after hearing of the rogue magic she told him about. Not that she'd started that conversation with the need to pass on Willsey's confidential news—it had been an inquiry about confidentiality, and how could something be secret if everyone who heard it told just one friend? He didn't have an answer for her, of course. He seldom did. Watching Jess wrestle with human nature was just a reminder of how many odd and inexplicable things came along with being part of society.

Jess, for all her unique complexities, was as straightforward as they came, and that had spoken to a very deep part of him. When he'd seen her, literally trembling with the effort it took to speak up against a senior Kymmet rider to keep his horse off a crucial run, he couldn't help but back her—although up until that point, he'd felt nothing but irritation at her much-anticipated arrival.

Well, things change. Ander smiled to himself. And aside from keeping Jess company on this trip—two days on a seasoned horse, and two and a half on the young mounts they were conditioning—Ander thought this was the perfect time to let Carey know that fact. *Things change, Carey. I'm with her in Kymmet, and you're not.*

"What?" Jess said.

Ander blinked out of his thoughts. "Huh?"

"You were smiling," Jess told him.

"Just thinking, Jess," Ander said, and smiled again. "That happens, you know."

"Yes," she said seriously, and his smile broadened. She gave him a little frown, then clearly decided not to worry about whatever it was she didn't understand this time. The road ahead of them was clear for quite a stretch—a lull in the marketday foot and cart traffic between the small town they'd just passed and the small town they were heading for—and Jess moved her mount into a reaching trot, posting it with the same unselfconscious supple athleticism that permeated her every move.

Ander let his gelding fall behind a short distance, and then trotted out after her. On his back, his bow and quiver bounced in their harness, a gentle reminder that something was not quite right in Camolen. On the other hand, Ander practiced his archery almost daily, and usually brought the bow with him when he was out and about, anyway. If nothing else, he got Kymmet city-credit for any game he brought the stables.

Ahead of him, Jess abruptly stopped her mount, waiting for Ander to catch up. When he drew alongside her, she didn't waste any words. "We have the courier spellstones," she said. "Including the shieldstone." Each courier carried his own mix of spellstones—detection spells, mapspells, recall spells—but the stone they universally clamored for was the shieldstone, a complicated spell that prevented anyone from using magic directly against them. Not that that was any guarantee of safety from magic, but it helped. "I ride alone all the time. I can take care of myself—"

Ander didn't let her go any further with it. "Then why

am I here?" he said. "Besides the fact that this gelding needs the experience?"

"Yes." She nodded, turning to look at him; somehow Ander knew those large dark eyes of hers were trained right on his from behind the sunglasses. For a moment he thought she was going to add something else, but the moment passed.

When she gave him that particular look, there was no use for anything but the truth. "No good reason, Jess. Because I'd worry, knowing what you told me about the mystery magic, and knowing what you're going to face at Arlen's. Call it a favor—more to make me feel better than to make sure you're all right." *And to meet Carey*, he added silently. Telling the truth didn't always mean telling the whole truth.

She thought about this a moment, then gave a short nod. "That's all right, then." And she trotted off, this time a jog that was easy to sit.

There was nothing to do but follow her.

Chapter 3

Carey was Arlen's head courier, and had been for years. He had survived unexpected transport to another world, he had been the driving force behind the small, unprepared team that rescued Arlen from imprisonment at the wizard Calandre's hands—and he had survived a deadly spell thrown by that same wizard. But he knew when he was outmatched, and that time was now.

He had no intention of getting any closer to this strange, changed man that he, along with Jess—and her friend Ander, whom Carey had heard about but was not altogether pleased to meet—were here to see. He stood with them at the doorway to the small room, regarding its occupant with some trepidation.

"Burn off!" the man said thickly, his slurred words very much like Jess's first attempts at speech, coming from a tongue that was not used to talking.

"He seems to know that one pretty well," Carey said dryly. Looking at the little frown that drew Jess's brow together, and the utter concentration on her face, he wished again that he'd been able to talk her into waiting a few moments before visiting the man. After all, she and Ander had only just arrived from Kymmet. They were sweaty and smelled of horse—not that that could ever bother Carey—and he'd have preferred to sit Jess down in a dark, cool corner of Arlen's carved-rock hold, give her something cold to drink, and spend a few quiet moments with her.

But then, he hadn't been expecting Ander to arrive with her.

He needed some time to adjust to the man's presence, and hadn't protested too much when Jess asked to come straight to this small room. It was in the stable section of the hold, because they thought the changed man would feel more at home here, but their attempts to make him comfortable seemed to have made no impression on him. He was antagonistic and uncooperative, and difficult enough to approach that they simply had stopped trying.

Jess bumped his shoulder with hers. "Like me," she said. "But . . ."

"That's what I thought," Carey said. "I wasn't there when you first . . . became Jess, but there are still things about him that make me think of you—and things that don't. In any case, Arlen's spell to change you to Lady doesn't work for him, not even with fine-tuning for his sex."

"Did I hear you say he'd been . . ." Ander started, trailing off with a grimace that Carey could empathize with. It'd taken him some time to get used to the idea, as well.

"Yes," he said. "He's been castrated, though obviously not too early in life."

"Burn off!" the man said. He snorted, stamped his foot, and turned his back on them. His clothes were little more than rags, though a small pile of clean clothing sat untouched at the foot of his bed. His hair was unkempt, what there was of it—it was short and spiky in such an uneven fashion that it had to be natural, and though the man was clearly into his middle years, there was no gray in it.

Jess bumped Carey's shoulder again, but didn't say anything. It was reassurance she was after, he knew, and he rested his hand at the back of her neck, quietly stroking the fall of hair out the back of the black cap she wore.

In the corner of his eye, Ander shifted; Carey ignored him. "What do you think, Jess?"

She shook her head. "Like me," she repeated. "But not." He thought she was going to say something else, but instead, she took a deep breath and made a noise in her throat he could only call a nicker.

He was astonished when the man whirled around to look at her, eyes narrowed. Unlike Jess, he was not the culmination of years of careful breeding, if he was even a changed horse at all. His legs were a little too short, his belly a little too big. And his ears . . . well, somehow their generous size seemed to fit his strong-boned face. And the expression on that face as the man looked at Jess, the crafty intelligence as he sized her up and obviously realized what she was, was more than Carey had ever expected to elicit from him.

But that surprise was quickly followed by another. The man snorted, a loud sound accompanied by plenty of spittle, and rushed them. Astonished, Carey pulled Jess back, only to have her yank herself from his protective grip.

With a little squeal, she met the man, half-turning at the last instant and letting fly with a powerful kick that took him in the thigh—not only stopping him short, but knocking him back. He sprawled on the floor, his attempts to regain his feet hindered by his anger and his apparent unfamiliarity with those particular feet.

Jess followed up with another, less powerful kick, sending him scrambling backward, his long face more sullen than alarmed. She lifted her chin, eyeing him, balancing lightly on one leg while the other foot remained just off the floor. The man regained his feet when he reached the far wall of the little room, and he stayed there, watching her balefully.

Ears back—Carey knew *that* expression—Jess gave her head a little toss, turned on her heel, and left the room, pushing past where Carey and Ander shared the doorway.

"Jess—what . . . ?" Ander followed a step behind Carey, who ignored him. The doorway was spelled against the man, no need to worry about him, either. But Jess's shoulders were back and tight, her fury radiating from every line of her body. She swept by Arlen's new apprentice, Natt, who had unhesitatingly yielded the hallway to her despite his astonishment, and then yielded again to Carey—and presumably to Ander behind him.

Out past the stalls she went, and out of the stable entrance, into the bright sunshine of the hilly Anfeald fields. Carey had slowed by then. If she was still leaving them behind, it was because she needed the space—although Ander did not appear to appreciate Carey's hand on his arm when he would have gone ahead.

"Give her a moment," Carey told him.

Ander turned on him, frowning, the very set of his mustache full of challenge. "I know how to deal with her."

Something in the way he'd said it made Carey blink; he held up his hands, exaggerating the release of Ander's arm. "Fine. You deal with her, then. You want to push her, after you just saw what she did to that man? *I'm* going to give her a moment to settle down."

Ander hesitated; it was enough so Carey could leave him there, walking slowly out of the shadow of the hold after Jess—who was simply standing, looking out at her favorite old tree in the winter pasture. A breeze lifted the ends of her long hair and danced with them, a whimsical little motion at complete odds with her stiff anger.

What Carey wanted to do was walk up and put his arms around her from behind, nestle his chin at the side of her neck and whisper comforts into her ear. Maybe give that ear a kiss or two.

But Jess was still struggling with things human, and

she needed the space to learn how to handle them. Carey knew enough to give it to her . . . he glanced at Ander beside him and wondered if the same held true. He had the feeling Ander did a very good job of taking care of someone who didn't necessarily benefit from the help.

She knew they were coming; her head canted slightly to the side and then back again; he could see her shoulders lift in a sigh as he came up beside her and stopped. "Jess?" he said, after a moment of watching her watch the pasture.

She sighed again. "No kicking—I know."

Carey felt a grin lift one corner of his mouth. "I'm not sure that rule counts under these circumstances." He knew well enough that Jess—and even Lady—would break the Rules when endangered.

She nodded, and said firmly, "It shouldn't." After another moment, she sighed, and said quietly, "It's hard when I'm human but my body acts like a horse. Confusing."

"I know," Carey said.

"What did you think?" Ander asked her, moving around in front of her.

She gave him a little frown. "Not a horse," she said. "A mule."

Carey gave a short laugh, thinking back over the ten days since the man had been found wandering in the closest town. He'd been stubborn and uncooperative, but never stupid. He never did anything unless he saw a clear benefit for himself, and their handling of him had required the utmost tact. "A mule," he said. "That *does* make sense."

"He was rude," Jess said, the insult still audible in her voice. "As soon as he realized I was a horse—"

"A strange horse," Ander said. "Crowding him."

"Yes." Her mouth was tight; Carey flashed on the exact expression that would be on Lady's face, had she been in Lady's form . . . then stopped himself.

"Jess," he said, lifting his hand to touch her back and

then not quite doing it, "you've haven't even said hello to Arlen yet. How about we go back into the hold, and you two can have something to drink. There's plenty to talk about besides that mule. Did you know Jaime was coming in, tomorrow?"

"Jaime?" Jess demanded, turning to search his eyes. Then her own widened slightly with realization. "It's time for the hearing. For Willand."

Carey nodded.

"C'mon, Jess," Ander said, easily resting his hand on Jess's shoulder. "He's right. Let's take a few moments—get that mule out of your system." His hand tightened, shook her shoulder gently. "Not that he's likely to bother you again. He's not going to walk the same for days!"

Jess snorted, gave a little smile; her distant expression made it clear she was reliving the confrontation. When she looked at Ander, she'd gone a little shy—and a little sly. "I did show him, didn't I?"

"Not much doubt about that," Carey agreed. She was over it now, the conflict of behaving like a horse while in her human body, and it seemed to him she was doing better with such moments all the time. As they turned and walked back to the hold, he wondered if he might not have given her that kiss or two after all.

ઉ૪ ೫ ઉ૪

Arlen's hold was built into the side of a rocky hill. The lower levels were entirely within the hill, including the stables—which, thanks to Arlen's magic, were well-ventilated and well-lit.

The upper levels emerged about two-thirds of the way up the hill, and were built with excavated rock; they ended just before the crest of the hill. Most of Anfeald was cultivated in some fashion, although there were solid chunks of forest here and there where the rock burst through the soil, and an arid old riverbed gorge to the south. But from Arlen's rooms on the top level, the view was a pastoral panorama of fields and parkland, including the hold's vegetable garden and Carey's training corrals.

That was where Jess, Carey, and Ander found Arlen, with a tray full of refreshments on the low table between the scattered old chairs in his personal quarters. Arlen sat on the short couch with a small black and white cat on his lap, absently stroking it while he reviewed a thick manuscript.

"Arlen!" Jess cried at her first sight of him, scattering both cat and papers. She bounded in to greet him, giving him a horse-hug that meant leaning up against him with her head firmly against his shoulder.

"Jess," he said, amusement in his voice; he patted her back and said, "has it been that long?"

She pulled back and said seriously, "Spring is when everyone wants the new young horses ready to go."

"Well," he said, his mouth twitching. "I guess it's been quite a while, at that."

Jess looked at him a moment, suddenly realizing how much his hair had grayed since she first met him in her human form, barely a year earlier. His mustache—a thick thing that neatly obscured his slight overbite—was nearly all gray, despite the fact that he was only a few years older than Jaime. But he looked good, fit and dressed in a black, belted tunic over a pair of blue jeans—more of Jaime's handiwork—and fully recovered from his ordeal at Calandre's hands.

Calandre. Jess gave an internal snort. That one, the wizard now in permanent isolated imprisonment, would have been better off dead, after what she'd done to Arlen and Carey. It was easy for Jess to let her thoughts drift to anger at Willand. But what *did* the look on Arlen's face mean?

"Oh," she said. "I forgot. This is Ander. He's my friend."

"Yes, I believe I've heard the name before." Arlen

looked at the courier a moment, and then over to Carey; Jess couldn't fathom his expression, so ignored it. She stooped to pick up the papers scattered by her entrance.

"Thank you," Arlen said, accepting them as she stood. "Just part of the paperwork for Willand's supplicant's hearing. But we'll talk about that later. For now, there's plenty else to concern ourselves with."

"I didn't mean to scare the cat," Jess said, looking around for it; she liked cats, and always had.

"Never mind," Arlen said firmly. "She made it through last summer in better shape than any of us. She'll live through today just fine. Have a seat, Jess."

Jess sat where she was, leaving the chairs to Carey and Ander, and watching to make sure Carey *did* sit, and that he put up the leg that was always giving him trouble. Ander had to move Arlen's latest needlework project from the seat of the remaining chair, rather gingerly placing it in the little basket next to the chair. Jaime had the last one in her Ohio house, in a prominent place in the living room.

"Well?" Arlen prompted, once Carey had made himself comfortable and Ander, looking distinctly uncertain about meeting so casually before one of Camolen's most powerful wizards, had settled. The powerful wizard nodded at the tray of food and said, "Eat. And tell me what you think."

"I do not think," Jess said, eyeing the melon on the tray. "I *know*. The man was a mule, and not a very nice one." She pulled her cap off and shook her hair out, spreading the strands of her black centerline over the rest.

"No doubt he lacks the benefits of Carey's training," Arlen said, then raised an eyebrow at Carey's responding expression. "What is it?"

"*What* happened would be the better question," Carey said. "The fellow went after Jess when he realized what she was—and in his space."

"I took care of it," Jess said, matter-of-fact about it now, picking out a piece of the melon. "Arlen, where did he come from? Who did this to him?"

Arlen shook his head. "We don't know, Jess. It's one of the reasons I'm so unhappy that he showed up. It's important to help him get back to what he was, but it's just as important—if not more—to make sure this doesn't happen again."

Jess nodded, and was startled to hear Ander say, "Maybe he could learn to be human, like Jess did." For an instant, she just stared at him. She barely heard Carey's muttered, "Not good, Ander," before her scowl took over her face, and then she was up and on her feet, scattering Arlen's papers all over again.

"Easy," Carey murmured, but his old Word of command had no sway over her now. Ander, too, was on his feet, clearly trying to decide whether to approach her, when she stomped some of that anger out with the sharp thud of her riding boot against the thick old rug that padded Arlen's floor.

"No!" she said, and left the homey circle of chairs for the window. The cat was sitting on the long ledge that ran the length of the window and beyond, and she startled, scooting away until she recognized Jess. Then she sat primly at the end of the ledge, her tailed curled around her feet.

"No," Jess said again, clearly and decisively. "Turn him back. Turn him back as soon as you can." She swung around, staring at them—practically glaring at them. "And treat him like a mule until you do."

"All right, Jess," Ander said, giving Carey a bewildered look. Carey only shook his head.

"No, it is *not* all right," she snapped at him, her words stumbling a little over one another. "He is a mule, and being a mule is a good thing. Being human is not *better*."

"I didn't mean—" Ander started. He didn't have a chance.

"Do you think it was easy, trying to understand the world from a brand-new body? Do you think I was *happy* to be without my whiskers, my ears—my tail? It took a long time to learn about being Jess, and it was *hard*." Her voice cracked on the last word; she turned her back on them again and blinked fiercely at the green fields before her. She could just barely see her old friend, the big pasture tree; it was a blurry brown and green blob to her left. She swiped at the few tears brought on by the memories of those days, when she'd have given anything just to be a horse again, and took a deep breath. "I had Carey. He has no one."

Carefully, Ander repeated, "All right, Jess. I didn't mean to upset you. And I didn't mean that being human was better than being a mule—or a horse."

"Damn straight," Jess muttered. Distantly, she heard the challenge of the stallion, who was pastured around the curve of the hill. Her father. Her *father*. "Damn straight."

"Now that we have that settled . . ." Arlen said, and left the thought where it was. Jess heard him get up, rummage in the short chest against the wall behind her, and gently move in beside her.

"Here," he said, giving her a fine square of dark blue material. "Upset by seeing him, were you?"

Jess looked up at him, at the light brown eyes that were ofttimes hard, the eyes of someone who wielded immense power. Sometimes, especially when they were looking at Jaime, they twinkled a little, but most often, as now, they were simply somber. Somber understanding of her words, and concern for her. And she realized he was right—she'd been more upset than she'd thought, and it hadn't simply been because she'd run into a conflict between her human and equine behavior. "Yes," she said, and repeated: "He has no one. Maybe he doesn't even have Words to listen to."

"Maybe not," Arlen said. "But he's no doubt a crafty old fellow, and he's probably got a lifetime of outsmarting humans behind him. He did, after all, get away from whoever changed him. He'll be all right until I can get him changed back—which should be considerably easier, now that I know what he is."

Jess looked at the material in her hand; it was nicer than most of her clothes, an odd bit of luxury amongst Arlen's well-worn things. "Do you really want me to—"

"Yes," he told her, smiled, and returned to his seat. So she wiped her face and blew her nose, and left the material on the inner window sill. When she turned around, she found Ander still on his feet, watching her cautiously. Carey was still up, as well, but his expression was different, it was . . . *restrained*. Odd. After a moment he sat down again, and Ander followed suit. Jess decided to stay where she was, and was glad when the little cat oozed back in the window and whispered a mew of feline commentary.

Arlen said, "I imagine Carey's told you we know little about the man. We know where he showed up, so we imagine he's from someplace fairly close to us. Why he was changed, we have no idea. The only wizards with enough skill to create this sort of spell are on record as clearly opposing such inhumane experimentation. You can be certain we'll *all* be watching for more signs of this sort of activity."

Jess had only been to a few Council meetings—the Council of Wizards, a gathering of Camolen's most powerful wizards from each of its precincts—but she'd seen enough to know this was Arlen's way of saying they were through talking about the mule. That was fine with her. She scratched the cat's ears a moment, then realized it would be polite to pick up the papers she'd once again scattered.

And picking them up made her think about Willand.

She paused in the middle of the job and sat back on her heels near Arlen's feet. "Will Willand be freed?" she asked, point-blank.

"Who's Willand?" Ander said, as Arlen gave a sort of grimace, obviously searching for words.

Carey gave her a questioning glance, surprise on his face as he realized Jess hadn't told Ander of Willand. She just looked back at him, equally surprised that he supposed she *would* have. As if Calandre's young apprentice, and the things she had done to Jaime, were something Jess wanted to *think* about, never mind talk about.

Word of the previous summer's events had certainly been disseminated, through word of mouth, courier, and regional events centers—manned by wizards who specialized in a Dispatch level that handled nothing but important events. But the only names that came up in casual conversation were Arlen and Calandre—and, of course, Jess. Nothing about Jaime, Dayna, Mark and Eric—or Willand.

Jess twisted to look at Ander. No one else answered his question; they were all looking at her. So it must be her place to say the words, as reluctant as she was. "Willand is . . . *was* . . . Calandre's apprentice. Jaime . . ." she hesitated. Ander had heard about Jaime, and certainly saw evidence of her, in Jess's breeches and sunglasses and assorted Ohio-based belongings—but had never met her. And Jess did not feel right telling Ander about the things Willand had done to Jaime. Jaime was more than Jess's friend—she was the one who'd taken Jess in after Eric and Dayna had found her. Now Eric was dead, Dayna was in Siccawei studying magic, and Jaime was back in Ohio riding high-level competition dressage and dealing with the memories of what Willand had done. "Jaime," Jess said, carefully, "spoke against her in front of the Council, about the things Willand did with Calandre. Willand hates her."

Carey gave her a little nod. "Willand has a supplicant's hearing coming up—she's trying to convince the Council she's suffered enough, that she can be sufficiently monitored to assure her good behavior outside of confinement." His tone of voice made it clear what he thought about *that*.

If Ander heard the undertone of unspoken words, he let it pass without obvious notice. "And Jaime's coming tomorrow, right? It'd be nice to meet her."

"You'll be here, I assume," Arlen said, his voice matter-of-fact. "There's no point in having you turn right around and go back to Kymmet—besides, we may need Jess's help with our mule."

"Kymmet expects us back," Ander said, somewhat cautiously. "Can you clear it?"

Arlen gave the courier a tolerant look, and raised an eyebrow, as if surprised that Ander could doubt it. "Oh, yes," he said. "I can clear it."

Chapter 4

Jaime Cabot had her eyes closed and her teeth clenched, waiting for the inevitable disorientation of world-hopping from Ohio to Camolen, and triggered the spellstone Arlen had given her. Usually she ended up a foot or so above Camolen soil—and usually, she fell right on her butt.

That was why Arlen had set up an enclosed spell booth—so she could land on her butt in privacy. She and the few other people who were allowed to go from one world to another, for it took a special nullification of the checkspell that barred unauthorized use of Arlen's world-travel spell every time they visited. In a way, some small part of Jaime was glad for the supplicant's hearing, and the promise of more Council hearings over the years—otherwise, she wasn't sure she'd ever get to see Jess, or her friend Dayna, or Arlen.

But it was a very small part of her.

There must be something wrong with the spellstone. She was still standing on her own two feet, and not sprawled on the floor in some undignified and painful manner. She cracked her eyes open to the pleasant surprise of the stone spell-booth walls around her.

Arlen stuck his head in the door, looking about as mischievous as a forty-year-old wizard with the weight of a precinct's welfare and the responsibility of cataclysmic spells on his shoulders could look. "Welcome back!"

"Arlen!" she said. "What did you do?"

He invited the rest of himself into the room. "Fixed the glitch," he said. "Like it?"

"Do I *like* not arriving flat on my ass?" Jaime said. "I guess you could say that." She opened her arms wide and Arlen walked right into them; considering she was a compact and rounded person while Arlen was definitely in the tall and lanky mode, they fit together rather well. What their relationship would have been like if they'd lived on the same world, Jaime didn't know. What she did know was that after their time together under Calandre's cruel hand, they were irrevocably tied together, no matter how much time, distance, and . . . *whatever* separated them.

Arlen kissed the top of her head and pulled back. "I'm sorry you're here because of Willand," he said, "but I'm glad to see you. And Jess is waiting upstairs."

"Jess is here?" Jaime said, pleasantly surprised. Usually Jess was so busy in Kymmet that the two had little spare time to spend together, although they did the best they could. Jess was always eager for more riding lessons—and for more training as Lady, as well. The dun mare was built for endurance and agility, and did not have the scope or suspension in her gaits to make a truly great dressage horse, but she enjoyed it. And, she had confided to Jaime, she missed the close partnership of horse and rider she'd had with Carey—for Carey had not been able to bring himself to ride her since he'd come to accept and love her as Jess.

"Jess is here," Arlen confirmed. "I asked her down for another reason, and then . . . *convinced* Kymmet they could do without her for a while." He tucked his arm around Jaime and picked up the small suitcase she'd brought with her. "Not only is Jess here, but her friend Ander came with her. He and Carey are on shaky ground with one another, I think. So you should have plenty of entertainment while you visit."

Jaime raised her eyebrows. "Ah, is that the way it is? Jess has mentioned Ander, and I *did* wonder . . ."

"Jess doesn't see it yet," Arlen said. "And she's too distracted by the mule to see it now. No, never mind," he said, cutting off the question she'd opened her mouth to ask and guiding her out of the spell booth. "There'll be enough of that later. For now, come say hello to everyone—and I hope you have room for lunch."

"I'm ready for dinner, actually," she said. "But I'll take what I can get."

"It's one of those Earth things, that peanut butter stuff that Jess likes so much," Arlen said, correcting her with a firmer touch on her shoulder when she would have turned left instead of right—she wasn't sure she'd *ever* memorize the way from the secluded booth to Arlen's private floor. It was deliberate, of course, in case someone unauthorized arrived there despite safeguards. And Jaime didn't even want to *know* about the spells he had set up to catch the unwary in these hallways. But Arlen was still talking about lunch. "I've made sure there's some *real* food tucked away for those of us who want it. Nice haircut, by the way."

Jaime's hand crept to the nape of her neck of its own accord. She was long used to having a thick, short braid fall just to her shoulder blades, but last week, as she contemplated the prospect of facing Willand again, she was suddenly ready for a change. Now her dark hair was quite short up the back of her head, with a cap of soft bangs that, released of the weight from its length, had suddenly found a bit of curl. She'd wondered what Arlen might think—she hadn't seen any such hairstyle here in Camolen.

Of course, Arlen *had* spent some time in Ohio, even attended a horse show or two along with Jess and Carey. Now he was looking at her with a quizzical eye as they mounted the first set of stairs—Jaime almost thought she knew where she was. "Lost in thought there, weren't you?"

"There's a lot of that happening lately," Jaime admitted. "Arlen—"

But her words were lost in Jess's cry of greeting from two floors up. "Jaime!" she said, bounding down the stairs and into sight, her movements as light as ever. Jaime exchanged a glance with Arlen, a grin of affection at which he only shook his head.

Jess came around the stairwell before them at some speed, and almost instantly stopped short, staring at Jaime. Jaime bore the silent inspection without comment, knowing that the importance of immediately checking out New Things was one of the equine attributes Jess still carried with her.

It only took a moment, and then Jess said, "It's good," a note of surprise in her voice. Then she nodded to herself, and added, "I like it. Welcome back!"

"Thank you, on both counts," Jaime said, grinning. "Have you been practicing?"

Jess rolled her eyes. "Nothing but young horses all spring," she said. "I asked Koje for a horse to work with; she says maybe after the rush."

"Well, maybe Carey has a horse or two we can use for lessons while I'm here," Jaime said, taking the hand Jess held out to her, as Arlen let her slip out from beneath his arm.

"That would be good," Jess said. "As long as it's not my brother. He's so stubborn." She gave Jaime a quick glance as they walked up to Arlen's floor. "Don't say it runs in the family."

"Wouldn't think of it," Jaime said hastily, not bothering to cover her smile.

"How is Sabre?" Jess said. "And your new horse, the little black gelding?"

The top floor was all Arlen's—first his main workshop

off to the left, and several little ones off the other side—where his apprentices worked, when he had them. At least one of them looked to be in use, so Jaime figured she'd have someone new to meet. "The gelding? He's getting better," she told Jess absently—absently, because she'd caught a glimpse into Arlen's room, and seen parts of Ander—a booted foot, a lower arm with dirt smeared from wrist to elbow—whom she'd long been curious about.

Absently, because Carey was there as well, and the tension between them reached all the way out into the hallway and piqued Jaime's interest.

They were both standing when Jess and Jaime, followed by Arlen and her suitcase, entered the room. And Jaime understood immediately why Carey was uptight. Where he was lean, a perfect rider's build, Ander had an extra few inches on the breadth of his shoulders. Where Carey's head barely topped Jess's, Ander could look down on her. His blond hair was striking, his eyes were beguiling, and his mustache perfectly suited his features.

Jess, Jaime noticed, was looking at Carey. She hoped Carey had noticed, as well.

"You must be Jaime," Ander said. "It's nice to meet you after all this time."

"Likewise," Jaime said, nodding her head politely, as she'd never figured out just what greeting gestures belonged in what social circles. The nod seemed to work all right. To Carey, she gave her hands and a smile; he took them, and held them a moment, ever aware of her restraint toward him.

When she'd met Carey, he was a desperate man on an even more desperate quest, and in his attempts to fulfill it, he'd endangered her entire barn full of horses. She'd never quite been able to forgive him for that, as much as she truly did care for him, and she was sure he knew it. It showed in that look in his eye, the one that was grateful she tried, as he squeezed her hands and released them.

"Nice haircut," he told her.

"You're looking pretty good yourself," Jaime said, and it was true. He looked less stiff than the last time she'd been here, when she'd begun to wonder if he'd ever fully heal from the damage Calandre had done him. "How's the leg?"

He made a face. Still some problems after all, it seemed.

"Jaime," Jess said, circling the room to scoop up Arlen's cat, "did Arlen tell you about the mule?"

"Arlen hasn't had much time to tell her anything," Arlen said, tucking the suitcase away inside one of the two small rooms—aside from the bathroom—off to the right of the entrance door. "Except hello, nice to see you—or did we even manage that much?" he asked her, raising an eyebrow.

Jaime smiled. "We did, more or less," she said. It was so easy to forget Arlen's considerable status here, and how much magic he could wield, when he turned on the charm. "I was too busy being pleased I didn't land on my butt."

"He fixed that?" Carey asked, surprised.

"The *mule*," Jess said, insistence creeping into her voice.

Jaime surrendered. She flopped down on the short couch, never minding that it was still warm from somebody else's bottom. "Tell me about the mule."

Jess came to the end of the couch and knelt, the cat still in her arms, purring madly and not minding that it had twisted itself nearly upside down. "Someone changed a mule into a man," she said intently, her dark eyes holding the confidence that Jaime would understand the importance of the statement.

Jaime did. The foot she'd been in the act of crossing over her knee hit the floor again instead. "You're sure? Who did it?"

"Yes, and we don't know," Arlen said, and the light

tone was gone from his voice as well. He sat down in the chair by his needlework. "He escaped from whoever it was—or they turned him loose."

"Considering how difficult he is to handle, I wouldn't be surprised if they turned him loose," Carey said, shaking his head.

"If we'd been paying attention, we might have felt it." Arlen meant the Council, Jaime decided. "But we weren't, and it takes a mighty powerful magic to get someone's attention amidst all the other chatter that's going on out there. If I didn't have a low-level filter around this hold, I'd probably be insane by now."

"Some of us have our doubts, anyway," Carey said, a twist at the corner of his mouth. "Considering the spells you insist on investigating."

Arlen's reaction was mild. "Better for me to discover the dangerous things before someone else." But Jaime saw a little wrinkle over his eyes, and knew there was something Arlen was leaving unsaid.

Jess had come to attention, clearly struck by some thought; the cat leapt lightly from her arms and padded over to Arlen, who stroked her absently while she decided if she would jump in his lap. "The mule would be big magic," Jess said. "And you already said no one you know would do it. But there was that magic, the strange magic, and no one knew who did it. Maybe *they* changed the mule."

Arlen's eyebrows went from concern straight to astonishment. "How in the Ninth Level did you hear about *that*? That's strictly Council—oh, hold on. You make runs out Aashan's way, don't you?"

Jess looked suddenly stricken. "I wasn't supposed to—I . . . I thought it would be all right to say it, because you'd already know."

Arlen shook his head. "Never mind, Jess. You're right. I already knew."

"But my friend—"

"It's all right, Jess," Arlen repeated firmly. "Your courier friend never took a Council Oath, and she can't be held to someone else's. Don't worry about her."

Jess subsided, not looking entirely convinced. Jaime decided it was about time to move on, and Carey apparently had the same idea.

"And what *big magic* is it that Jess isn't supposed to have heard about? You might as well tell us all, now. Although," he glanced at Ander, "not all of us seem surprised to hear of it."

Jaime gave Ander a hard stare, willing him to keep his mouth shut. No point in stoking Carey's little fires of jealousy into something bigger.

Arlen apparently felt the same, for while Ander was looking blankly at Jaime, probably wondering what he'd done to deserve her censure, the wizard gave a grumbling sigh, entwined his fingers together, and settled them on his lap above the cat. "The big magic," he said, "is somewhat of a mystery to us all—although I think Jess is absolutely right—it's connected to the appearance of the changed mule."

"What's the problem?" Carey said. "If it was such a concern, didn't you track it down?"

"*That's* the problem," Arlen said. "And the reason we're truly quite alarmed about it. We *can't* track it down. Whoever generated the unfamiliar signature managed to shield themselves a short time afterward, and we haven't heard a peep from them, since."

That sounded like something that needed attention all right, but Jaime looked at Carey's somber expression and knew she wasn't getting the implications of the statement. "That's bad, then," she said, looking for confirmation.

"That's bad?" Carey repeated. "I'll say. The wizard who can put up a shield that even the combined members of the Council can't break through is one hell of a powerful wizard. We're not talking about the sort of physical shield that Calandre put up when she occupied this hold. We're talking about something . . ."

"Much more subtle," Arlen finished as Carey hesitated. "Much more difficult to create, much harder to keep control of. It totally erases all signs of the magic. None of us have felt a trace of that unfamiliar signature since the first incident—which, I might add, the majority of the Council wizards detected without even thinking twice about it—and we certainly don't believe they've stopped using magic, whoever they are."

"How could anyone *that* powerful just pop up?" Jaime said doubtfully. "I mean, they had to *learn* somehow—and you'd have felt them, then."

"Exactly the point," Arlen said, and leaned back in his chair, stroking the cat. "Exactly."

Ander, who'd been quietly listening, asked just as quietly, "And what's the Council doing about it all?"

Arlen regarded him a moment, until Ander looked like he wished he hadn't asked. Then he said, "I've already told Jess I'll be looking for a way to change the mule back to his natural form. The Council as a whole, of course, is on highest alert, searching for any sign of the strange signature. Other than that, there is little we can do."

"You mean," Jaime said, realizing the extent of the situation for the first time, "that they could be doing *anything*, wherever they are, and you won't know about it until it's too late?"

"Anything our checkspells won't keep them from doing," Arlen said, and nodded. "Yes."

And Jaime knew from firsthand experience how destructive a determined and powerful wizard could be, checkspells or no.

ꕥ ꕥ ꕥ

Jess peeked around the half-closed door of Arlen's main workroom. She'd never interrupted Arlen at work before, but if she didn't talk to him soon, it might be too late. There he was, his back to her, sitting on a stool in front of a long worktable that was snugged up against the room's widest window. She liked this room, even though she'd only seen it a few times; it was an asymmetrical wonder of odd corners and crannies, with five walls, an assortment of windows, and book-lined shelves. In a pot next to him were simmering fragrance herbs, which smelled to Jess's sensitive nose as though they were starting to singe.

And strewn out on the table before him were papers. Endless papers, in stacks and layers and piles. He was making some notation or other as Jess waited, hoping he would pause so she wouldn't be quite *so* interruptive—but it was Arlen who spoke first. "What can I do for you, Jess?" he asked, without turning around.

"Oh," she said. "You have a spell or something?"

"To figure out who's peeking in my door?" he said, and gave a low chuckle; the warmth in his voice made Jess a little bolder. "Do you think I would sit with my back to the door if I didn't?"

After some thought, Jess decided not. "Did you, before last year?"

He twisted on the stool to give her a thoughtful look. "I suppose I wasn't quite as careful about that sort of thing, no. But it's live and learn—or quit living."

"Yes," she said. That much, she had always known. Even a foal growing up in Arlen's stables knew that particular Rule.

"So," he said, leaning his elbows back on the work table. "Now that you have my full attention: what can I do for you?"

Jess eased in the doorway. "Your herbs are going to burn."

"Ah." He gave the pot a look, and the mageflame beneath it winked out.

Jess leaned against the wall beside the door and gently bumped her bare heel against its stone. "Jaime is giving me lessons, but no one here has asked me to do anything else. I can ride for you, Arlen. Until I have to go back to Kymmet."

He gave her a look of genuine surprise. "You said that like you think I need someone. Do I?" He looked down at his hand, his fingers moving; Jess realized he was doing something as mundane as listing his couriers on his fingers. "Carey's almost up to speed," he added, re-counting.

"He still looks stiff when he stands up, and when he first mounts a horse," Jess corrected him. "And his gaits are off. Why can't the healers get that one leg right?"

"I don't know," Arlen said, looking somewhat bemused at her immediate dissent.

"Would you be using that courier who came to Kymmet if you didn't need help?" Jess asked. "He spoke when he shouldn't have, and he was rude."

"Was he, now?" Arlen said, giving her an evaluating look.

Jess was suddenly uncomfortable. "Have I done something wrong, Arlen, to tell you?"

He rubbed a finger down his nose, and gave a sudden little smile. "Well, Jess, some wizards might take offense at the suggestion that they didn't know how to run their own holds. But as it happens, you're right on this one. Carey took him on because he *is* an excellent rider. But he's definitely got what I've heard Jaime call 'an attitude problem.' "

"Then let me ride for you, Arlen. If Carey tries to take too many rides just so that man won't go on them, he'll never get well."

Arlen looked away for a moment. Behind him, a warm breeze ruffled the scattered papers, bringing a touch of the scent of summer hay to the cool stone hold. "Jess," he said slowly, "you have to understand something. Carey is as healed as he's going to get. He was badly hurt, and his healers are surprised he's done as well as he has. Riding a moderate number of jobs keeps him from getting too stiff, and he's perfectly able to keep up with the breeding and training."

"You mean . . ." she said in a small voice, "he's really never going to get any better than he is?"

Arlen gave a short nod. "He's grateful for what he's got. He's accepted what he'll never have again. But he's been afraid to let you know; afraid it would upset you. It's important that you think about this, Jess, before you say anything to him."

Jess just blinked a moment, taken aback. Then she took a deep breath. "Well," she said, "he still doesn't need to have that man riding for him. So do you want me to ride instead?"

Arlen's grin, with his slight overbite, had always been a particularly engaging one to Jess; she seldom saw it. He nodded his head and said, "Of course, Jess. He's been riding by the job instead of on salary, and we'd be glad to pay you the same way. I'll have to clear it with Carey, of course, but I doubt he'll have any objections."

"No," she said. "Kymmet pays my salary. For Carey, for you, I ride for free."

He looked at her a moment, and gave another short nod. "That's a generous offer."

"It's for *Carey*," Jess said, as if that should explain everything.

"Yes," Arlen said. "I know." And then, when Jess still hesitated, missing that moment when she knew she should have left, biting her lip and looking at Arlen through the ends of the long bangs that had fallen in her eyes, he said gently, "What else can I help you with?"

"Jaime!" Jess blurted. "I mean—Willand. Does she—

can't she—" She took a deep breath, closed her eyes, and said, "Does she have to face Willand again? She did it last year, and it was so hard for her . . . can't you fix it, Arlen?"

"I'm a member of the Council, not its boss," Arlen said, but if he meant the response to be reproving, it lacked force. He gave her a pensive look. "Maybe there's a way, Jess. I'll see what I can do."

"You can do it," she said positively. "Especially for Jaime."

He raised an eyebrow at her. "Yes," he said quietly. "Especially for Jaime."

ଔ ஐ ଔ

Carey was feeling good; good enough to go down the stairs two at a time, like he used to. Every morning, after checking the horses, Carey went to the top floor of the hold and checked in with Arlen—and today, that had meant receiving several pleasant surprises. Arlen, it seemed, had been quite busy. He'd managed new arrangements for Willand's hearing, and although Jaime was still traveling with Arlen to Kymmet City as planned, she would not have to face the Council in the presence of Willand; they'd all been a little worried about that, and Arlen seemed quite pleased about the accomplishment.

It was merely a warm-up for the next announcement—that Jess would be riding with Carey for the short time she was here; by then, the new courier from Siccawei should be at Arlen's Anfeald hold—all of which meant Carey had been able to tell the job-rider, Shammel, that his work here was over. It had been quite satisfying to stroll into the couriers' quarters on the second floor and inform the man he could grab himself some breakfast and go.

Carey was just coming from breakfast himself, after a routine check-in with Arlen's resident healer. He fully expected to find Jess in the stable area, where he could hand over Shammel's ride for the day and know it would get done quickly and properly. The only thing that could possibly make this day better would be to discover the weather-sighting wizards were wrong, and that their dry spring was finally coming to an end with some rain.

Whoops. He hit the bottom of the stairwell to find Ander lingering in the doorway, exchanging comments with one of the young grooms. It was Klia, the adolescent niece of his newest rider, and wouldn't *he* be pleased to find the girl making eyes at this visiting courier. So there was indeed *one* other thing that would improve this day—but Ander seemed likely to be here as long as Jess was.

Well, it was more than an even trade. It'd been half a year since Carey had an extended amount of time to spend with Jess.

He stopped just before the doorway, intending to stay only long enough for the meaningful look he gave Klia—but he spotted something down by the tack room that made him stop and stiffen. Ander followed his gaze, reacting likewise.

Jess was at the end of the hall, coming out of the tack room with a bridle in her hand, holding it out to straighten its tangled straps. She was concentrating utterly on her task, as she was wont to do, though never to the exclusion of an awareness of her surroundings. When Shammel came striding down from the overflow tack room with his own gear, she saw him coming in plenty of time to step aside.

But he didn't simply pass her by. He stopped, and he crowded her, turning on Jess in a movement precisely timed to startle her. Carey couldn't hear what he said—Shammel's voice was low and meant for privacy—but it surely wasn't pleasant.

"Ninth Level damnation," Ander growled, and started off to intervene.

Carey's hand landed on his arm—not gently—stopping Ander short.

"What's your problem?"

The young groom, seeing Ander's expression, scurried behind Carey to get on with her duties. Ander scowled at Carey only long enough to get the point across before turning his gaze back to Jess and Shammel.

She was responding to the job-rider, without any attempt to keep it private. "You were rude. It's your own fault."

"Leave her be," Carey told Ander. "She can handle this."

"She shouldn't have to!" Ander shot back, as surprised as he was angry. At the end of the hall, Shammel crowded Jess even closer, and his words came back at her fast and hard, no doubt unpleasant.

"It *is* my business," she responded to him, her back against the stone wall and the bridle down at her side, her fingers clenched around it. "You were making trouble for Carey."

Carey moved around between Ander and the scene at the end of the hall. "Maybe she shouldn't, but she needs to learn she *can*," he said intently. "If you protect her from everything, what's she going to do when she runs up against someone like this and you're not there?"

Ander hesitated. "Fine," he said. "She's dealing with him. Now can we go put a *stop* to it?"

"Leave her be," Carey said, making a wall with his voice, keeping Ander where he was. Behind him, he heard Jess's anger growing.

"You have no Words for me," she said, in the tone that meant she knew she was perfectly right, "and you don't even know your human rules. Leave me alone."

What she did then, Carey didn't know. Shammel's muffled oath made her effectiveness clear enough.

Ander's gaze flicked back to Carey for a moment. "She's

not your horse anymore," he said, anger in his low voice, sparks in those bright blue eyes. "She doesn't belong to you."

Carey glanced over his shoulder. Jess was standing alone at the end of the hall, looking at them. Her hair, as often happened, was coming loose from its ponytail; her chin was up and her eyes, their expression dark and fastened on Carey, seemed to hold some edge of hurt. She hefted the bridle, shifting in her grip, and abruptly turned away from them, heading for the spot where the hall turned to barn aisle.

She was all right, then. Disturbed, as she ever was at this sort of conflict, but all right. Carey turned back to Ander, and said softly, "She doesn't belong to you, either."

Jaime thought she should feel better than she did. She'd testified in front of the Council again, hadn't she? She'd never counted, but it seemed there were at least fifty of them, wizards of all ages seated in staggered tiers of long, gleaming hardwood tables amid all the pomp and presence one might expect to find in Washington, D.C. She knew some of their faces, by now, and even had some friends—like Sherra, of Siccawei, with whom she'd hardly had time to do more than exchange a greeting.

She should definitely feel better. It was over. Willand's request had been, as expected, denied. She hadn't even had to look at the petite blonde wizard, with the Gidget-cutesie features that almost—*almost*—managed to make you forget the harm she'd caused, and the look of gratification she'd had on her face while she'd tortured someone.

No, not *someone*. Jaime. While she tortured Jaime.

It's over, she told herself. Willand wouldn't be allowed another supplicant's hearing for three years. And Jaime . . . well, Jaime had best get her mind on the lesson she was trying to teach. "Jess," she said, "you need a deeper seat there. You're losing him right before you try the flying change, because you're lightening your seat in anticipation. Give him the support he needs."

Jess's only response was to nod; she seldom came out of her deep concentration to say anything during a lesson. Despite the problems she was having, Jaime thought Jess was doing beautifully—she'd only ridden the horse for the first time the day before, and while it wasn't Jess's first go at flying lead changes, the gelding was clearly uncertain about the whole affair. Done right, the flying change looked like a light, balanced skip in midair. Done wrong, it turned into a muddle of trot and canter that made no one happy.

"I'm beginning to think we should go back to simple changes for another day," Jaime called to Jess as she approached center ring at a canter and the gelding's expression grew anxious. "He's not as ready for this as I thought he was."

Without comment, Jess dropped the horse back into trot for three strides, then picked up the canter on the opposite leading leg. She cantered once around the ring, Carey's biggest training ring, then quietly brought the horse down to a walk and let him have a long rein. After a few moments, she came to a halt beside Jaime at the long side of the ring and said, "He was too tense."

"I agree," Jaime said. "No point in pushing him so hard he decides lead changes are a bad thing." She leaned against the fence, wishing she'd borrowed a hat and brought some water. The ring was dry and dusty, and even though they'd started this lesson early in the day, it seemed far too warm to be standing around in the sun. "Maybe you should take him on one of the trails, let him cool off that way." There was a patch of woods not too far from here, behind Arlen's hold.

Jess made a face. "Deerflies," she said, and that was

enough. Even though they weren't exactly the same kind of deerflies Jaime dealt with in Ohio, the Camolen fly was just as nasty.

"Just walk him out here, then, I guess." It was hard to give lessons on someone else's turf. You never knew when you might be interfering with established regime.

But Jess didn't respond to her suggestion; she sat on the gelding with her eyes focused well behind Jaime, her posture alert. Her expression had turned to one of curiosity by the time Jaime caught on and turned around.

Arlen? Arlen had left the hold for the late morning heat to find them? For there could be no one else to find, not here. This training ring was a quarter mile from the hold, and was isolated from all the activity of the hold by the thick, green—thanks to vigilant watering—vegetable garden between them. Tall bean trellises, tall rows of something Jaime couldn't help but call corn, even if it wasn't—from here, all you could see was the very top of the hold hill, and the road that passed by on the way out of the hold. Opposite them was pasture, brittle-looking grass that the horses had spurned to rest under the few shade trees that dotted the rolling field.

And here was Arlen, in a black outfit Jaime would have called a martial arts uniform if she'd been in the States. Or on Earth, for that matter. "What's up?" she called to him, hearing the doubt in her own voice.

He lifted a hand in greeting, obviously not willing to shout about whatever it was. And then Jess made a little noise, and her attention shifted up the road; Jaime knew enough to follow her glance. In a moment, one of Carey's duns cantered into view, with Carey sitting relaxed and easy in the saddle—but he was cantering in the heat, and he was cantering toward the barn, and he wouldn't have done either without reason. Jaime found her own trepidation tightening around her.

"Arlen," she said, "something's happened."

"Yes," Jess agreed, dismounting behind Jaime. Jaime heard the sound of the stirrup leathers being run up, the creak of the girth being loosened. The lesson was over, even the cool-down.

Arlen walked right up to her, unhurried, and gave her a smile of greeting. Jaime wasn't sure it was convincing, and was about to say so when Carey pulled up in front of them, creating little whirlwinds of dust.

"What's up, Arlen?" he asked. "It's been a while since you did the old summoning trick." He flashed his hand open in a gesture that meant nothing to Jaime until she remembered that Arlen could call Carey through the ring he wore, creating an insistent tingle that wouldn't go away until he was in Arlen's presence.

Jaime turned a no-nonsense stare on the tall wizard. "Yes, what's up, Arlen?" Behind her, the training ring fence creaked as Jess leaned against it, no doubt echoing the question with all her body language.

"It's not good, as you've probably guessed," Arlen said. He ran a hand down the back of his head, smoothing shaggy, gray-shot hair.

"You've never been much good at this sort of thing," Carey said, as his horse shifted and snorted beneath him. "Just *tell* us. It's kinder that way."

Arlen opened his mouth, hesitated, shrugged, and said, "Willand has escaped."

Jaime felt the world crowd around her like a tunnel, closing in her shock, closing out the noise and colors of the world. Then Jess's strong hands grasped Jaime's shoulders from behind in a comforting grip.

"I'm not sure that was such a good idea," Arlen was saying to Carey, his voice a wry mutter. He took her hands and said, "Are you all right, Jaime?"

Jess behind her, Arlen before her . . . she was, at least, not going to fall down. Jaime opened her mouth, but was unable to voice anything.

Carey managed quite nicely. "Burning damnation, Arlen, *how*? That little bitch was closed up in a null-magic facility, with wards that should have held *Calandre*, for Pete's sake!"

That was his time in Ohio, showing in his speech again, Jaime thought distantly.

"In a minute, Carey," Arlen snapped—*snapped*, a reaction Jaime had never seen in him before. "Jaime," he said gently. "Are you *all right*?"

"I really don't know, Arlen," she said, her voice much more calm and reasonable than she expected. "She . . . escaped?"

He nodded, a grim gesture. "She did. Dayna's being told right now, and I don't envy Sherra the task. And you and Carey and Jess—we're the only other ones who had a direct hand in bringing her to justice with Calandre."

Thank goodness Mark was at home. At least one of them was safe. "Maybe she won't come after us," Jaime said, hearing her own voice as she spoke, sounding dull and unconvinced . . . Willand had threatened retribution often enough, during the trial. And Willand . . . *enjoyed* retribution. Jaime rubbed a finger along her slightly crooked nose, broken in an attempt to escape Willand. It hadn't been Willand's fault, though. Mere physical brutality was a boring option to someone with that much magic.

"Arlen," Carey grated.

Jess spoke up from behind Jaime, her voice low, and the words a little thicker than usual. "How, Arlen. Tell us how."

Arlen gazed at Jaime, his eyes worried. He released her hands for her shoulders and drew her in; Jess let her go. Jaime let herself rest against the black shirt, staring at the fancy stitching over Arlen's collarbone, black on black. "I wish we knew," he said, and his chest hummed against Jaime's ear with the words. "Carey's right. The wards should have held her, and easily. To say the Council is in an uproar is an understatement."

"That's *it*?" Carey demanded. "No one knows *anything*?"

Jaime felt the motion as Arlen shook his head. "Not quite true, but even that is not good news. At the time of her escape, we—every single one of us on the Council, and who knows how many other wizards besides—felt the magic that did it. It was powerful—and it was unfamiliar."

"The same magic I heard about?" Jess asked.

Arlen said flatly, "No."

"Shit," Carey said.

"Yes," Arlen said. "Well and concisely put."

Jaime pulled away from him, and looked directly up at him. "I want to go home," she said. "I'm not doing this again. I want to go home *now*."

Arlen looked down at her and hesitated, just long enough for Jaime to know what the answer was, and her fear flared into temper. "Why *not*? Arlen, I came here to testify for your Council, and now I want to go home! Getting me out of the way of that sadistic little valley girl is the least they can do!"

"Jaime," Arlen said gently, "it's not going to happen. There's no way they're going to lift the checkspell on the world-travel spell while Willand is on the loose. We have no way of knowing just how much of that spell she learned with Calandre—even if those two didn't have it completed, she's smart enough. She can get there. And . . . she obviously has someone very powerful on her side."

"What about Calandre?" Carey asked, sounding like he didn't really want to know the answer. "Is she . . . ?"

"Safe and sound in her own little confinement," Arlen said. "She's isolated except for approved visitors. She hasn't been in good health of late, either."

"What a shame," Jaime murmured, struggling with a wash of fear and loathing that she simply wasn't used to feeling—as well as a surprising dose of anger at Willand. Damn the woman, anyway! "Let me get this straight, Arlen. You're saying I'm not going to go home until Willand is back in custody."

Arlen hesitated again; he obviously didn't want to *say* it at all. But finally, after Jess's gelding had snorted a great belly snort and shook like a dog until the reins flapped against his neck, after Carey had nailed the big green horsefly that was plaguing his mount, after the tickling trickle of sweat had run down Jaime's chest between her breasts, Arlen nodded. "That's what it looks like," he said. "And it's not just Willand. There's someone out there—at least two of them—and now we know they're not necessarily interested in playing by the rules. We've got a mess on our hands, Jaime—and once again, you're right in the middle of it. You and Jess and Carey . . . and me."

"Then," Jess announced, as if it was obvious and she didn't understand why no one else had said it yet, "we will have to find Willand, and her friends. We have to stop them."

Jaime turned to look at her—they *all* looked at her—and found only what she'd been expecting: the same sort of determination that had carried Jess through her change from horse to woman, and helped to save a world while she was at it.

❧ ❧ ❧

After Arlen took Jaime inside, Jess sponged the gelding with cool water and turned him out in the pasture; Carey, after handing over his courier pouches to Arlen, did the same with his dun mount. They said little to one another as they worked; Jess, who was not prone to idle conversation, was too filled with the grim reality of Arlen's news to even discuss the situation.

Find Willand. She'd said it herself—it had to be done.

How was something else entirely, and if the Council couldn't do it, she really wasn't sure how one horse, practicing to be human, was going to be able to help. She only knew that it was she and her small group of friends who had made the difference the last time Willand and her mentor caused trouble.

But as she and Carey walked back from the pasture together, he offered her his hand, and somehow that made things a little better.

At least, until she realized that Arlen was waiting for them at the entrance to the stables. He and Jaime—and Ander, who'd probably just wandered up, since he did seem to have a knack of finding the excitement wherever he was—were standing in the scant noon shade offered by the open stable door in the base of the hill, and they were clearly waiting. Jess tightened her hand on Carey's, and took heart from the squeeze he gave her in response.

Was there something else, then? Jaime's face was still hard and cold, but there seemed to be an added dimension to her expression now, signs of perplexity and concern around her eyes that were clearly visible now that she'd removed her sunglasses.

Jess stopped a little short of the trio and said, "What?"

"What *else*?" Carey added.

"I need Jess's help again, I'm afraid," Arlen said.

Jess felt a small cold fist of dread. "There's another changed animal."

"West of us, just over the line into Sallatier Precinct."

"Not exactly in our backyard this time," Carey said.

"They still need our help," Arlen said. "Except for Dayna, we're the only experts there are."

"Experts," Carey snorted. "Right. We're making it up as we go along."

Jaime gave Arlen a look that said she was prepared to do battle. "I'm going with you."

"Good idea," Arlen said. "I don't want to leave you alone here right now, anyway."

"I have the feeling," Ander said, sounding a little resentful, "that there's something else going on here I don't know about."

"And you're right," Arlen said immediately. "Carey, I've informed Cesna and Natt" —*his apprentices*, Jess remembered— "of the situation; they'll be maintaining a low-level web around the hold, and can reach me at any time. I'll be taking Jaime and Jess—if she consents to help—to Garwicke for the afternoon. If you had another run planned, give it to someone else. I don't want you out today." He paused, and gave Ander a look—Ander, who was obviously trying very hard to sit on his impatience to know what was going on. "Feel free to let Ander know the details about Willand. He may want to return to Kymmet."

"We're going *now*?" Jess asked.

Arlen looked briefly at her dirt-smudged breeches and boots. "I'd like to know what's happening as soon as possible. But if you'd like time to change, I'll wait."

Jess thought about the feeling within her, the distress she felt over the prospect of another changed animal. Freshening up just meant she'd have to wait that much longer to discover what had happened in Sallatier. She gave her head a quick shake. "No," she said. "I want to go now."

Arlen wasted no more time. He took Jaime and Jess up to his workroom, and to the small room off the end of it that was clearly marked to keep the casual visitor away.

Jess felt only a slight *shift* in the air around her, much less of a disturbance than going from Anfeald to Ohio. The travel room here was slightly larger, the walls made of pale wood instead of stone, the floor carpeted instead of bare. "We're here," she said, sounding surprised even to her own ears.

Jaime, who had traveled to Kymmet by similar means just the day before, nodded like she was an old hand at the procedure. "We're here," she agreed.

"And lucky that a small town like this has an established booth at all," Arlen said, stepping out of the little room. Jess followed him, and discovered they were at the back of a coach station.

There weren't many of those, either. In Camolen, people of importance, or those who had to travel long distances, paid for mage-travel. Otherwise, travelers walked from place to place, or hired horses, if they didn't have their own. Only the larger towns tended to have coach stations for horse-drawn, well-cushioned travel.

This station wasn't particularly full, at least not at the moment—though the facility looked well-used, and had the particular smell of a place that saw many people through its doors. No matter what cleaning magic the maintenance people used, they would never hide such hard use from Jess's nose.

Arlen caught her eye. "The town was basically built on the fact that it's a natural split in the road from Sallatier City to Anfeald and Kymmet," he said. "It's got an unusual combination of amenities. And, occasionally, oddities. At any rate, I've let Forret—he's the closest thing they've got to a wizard—know we're here; someone'll be along shortly."

While a young boy in tunic and trousers detached himself from his distracted mother and eyed Jess in her breeches, a man breezed through the swinging door, stopping just inside to let his gaze wander the room. When he saw the trio, he headed toward them without hesitation.

"Forret sent you?" Arlen said, a hint of suspicion in his voice. Jess thought again that Jaime was not the only one with scars from the previous summer.

"I'm Crait," the man said. He was shorter than both

Jess and Arlen, and built round. Jess thought he would make a stout cob horse, if horses came in that peculiar bronze carroty color, with freckles amassed so closely upon one another. "I'm Forret's assistant." He glanced at Jess. "I take it this is the horse?"

All three of them opened their mouths at once, but it was Jess's voice that spoke out, low and clear, and unable to hide the hint of disdain she felt for this human who had no manners. "Jess," she said. "I am Jess. And I am here to help you." Just in case he'd forgotten it. Beside her, Jaime winced.

"Right, right," he said, walking up to her and then around her. She didn't bother to turn to look at him. "Forret's is only a short distance from here, which is good, considering the heat this afternoon. We sure could use some rain."

Weather talk. Jess had learned by now that it usually meant nothing, just words to fill the air. When Arlen headed for the door, she followed.

The pinch came suddenly, like a bite on her haunch. Jess reacted instantly, not thinking, just moving—her leg flashed back and connected solidly; she whirled to face whatever threat had sprung up behind her—

There was nothing. Just the freckle-spattered man on the carpeted floor, clutching his thigh and rocking back and forth, moaning. She gave him a puzzled look. Against the wall, the young boy's mother watched with an expression of surprise that turned to an odd smile of satisfaction, while Jess tried to figure out what had happened.

"Jess? What on earth—" Jaime said, as Arlen realized there was a problem and came up behind her.

"What happened?" he asked, not sounding as angry as Jess thought he might.

"I don't know," Jess said. "Something bit me." Mortification was setting in. "I didn't mean to kick him . . .

I thought . . . it felt like . . ." A bite. An unexpected bite that any horse would have kicked at. What . . . ?

"I thought—" the man said through clenched teeth, "this . . . *woman* was supposed to have come from well-trained courier stock."

"Something bit you?" Jaime said, and gave the man a sudden hard look. "Jess, just *where* did this something bite you?"

"Right on the—" Jess was about to use Carey's word for it, and then glanced at the young boy. She wasn't used to the young humans, but knew enough not to say *that* word. Instead, she pointed at the offending spot, on the curve of her muscled bottom.

To her surprise, Jaime scowled at the man. "Do you do that to all the beautiful young women you meet?"

"No, I—"

Jess was beginning to understand. There was no threat. There was just this freckled man. "*You* did that?" she said, incredulously. On the other side of the room, the boy's mother was nodding, as if she'd become part of this. "But *why*?"

The color was returning to his pale face; he opened his mouth to answer and Jaime didn't let him. "Because," she said. "Because you're lovely, and he felt he just *had* to handle you." She walked closer to the man, until she was standing over him; his pained outrage had faded completely, and he gave Arlen a beseeching glance. Arlen was standing well back, his arms crossed, a mere observer.

"Tell me," Jaime said, glowering at him so hard that Jess finally realized this outrage was on *her* behalf, that this man had done more than just handle her without permission. "*Is* this how you treat all the women you're introduced to, or just the ones who used to be horses?"

"No, I—" he said, stopping as Jess moved in to stand on the other side of him from Jaime. "I—figured she'd be used to it! Any courier's horse is used to being handled by people!"

Jess's eyes narrowed. "No," she said. "If I were a horse, you would have no Words for me. I never listened to those I did not respect."

"And she's *not* a horse now," Jaime said. "She's a woman. Too bad. If she were a horse, she would have broken that leg for you instead of just making you limp for a week." She looked at him a moment longer, muttered, "Microcephalic oaf." Then she turned her back on the man and marched right out the door.

Jess was left to stare at him; he seemed to be going from unusually pale to a shade of bright red. "If you ever meet me while I'm Lady," she said, "don't do that then, either." She leaned over him a little; he shrank away from her. She glanced up to meet the gaze of the woman across the room, who was clearly too far away to follow the conversation, but nonetheless had been watching it unfold. She gave Jess a firm nod, one that made Jess give her a tentative little grin in return.

As she, too, turned her back on the man and walked for the door, she heard Arlen say in a deceptively conversational tone, "And did Forret send you out here with the intention of insulting the friend of a senior Council member? I thought not. Better see if you can walk on that leg. I think we've wasted enough time here."

And Jess smiled again, this time inside. But it didn't last long. She knew she was seeing a side to humans that would crop up again and again, as she encountered more of the world outside of Kymmet Stables. And she knew it was something that would affect every animal the powerful, unknown wizards changed.

Chapter 5

They ended up in the town house of one of Sallatier's biggest Landers, a man who had been on the Lander Council a long time. His name was Chesba, and he was an older man with long white hair that was tied at the base of his neck as if defying the wide bald area on top of his head.

To Jaime's surprise, she found the style suited this man well. Despite his age, which she estimated to be at least sixty, he was straight-shouldered and trim, and he carried himself with a precision that was also reflected in his words—and in the house he ran.

He met them at the door on the heels of a manservant, and after introductions, led them into a room where Forret was waiting, explaining the situation as they negotiated narrow, well-lit hallways, with Arlen in front and Crait trailing them, limping well behind Jess.

"We found her near the Land house," Chesba said. "We were hunting bear, and the hounds flushed her out. She ran, but not far; she's in poor shape. We were lucky to pull the hounds off before she fell; they'll chase anything that runs from them, you know." He stopped by an open doorway and gestured them in; as Jaime passed him, she saw he was eyeing Jess. Unlike Crait, Chesba's gaze was a sharp one, and Jaime had no doubt he was analyzing the small differences in Jess's appearance, trying to relate them to the woman he'd saved.

There was a man waiting for them in the small room; he wasn't all that much older than Crait. He was still fighting the remnants of acne, which even to Jaime said much about his ability as a wizard—for this was, she assumed, the wizard Arlen expected to meet. Arlen confirmed it by giving the man a nod. "Forret."

"Nice to see you, Arlen," Forret said, and Jaime figured it cost him plenty to keep his tone that casual, considering the fine beads of sweat on his forehead. Forret was obviously trying to impress this Council member—not easy, considering Arlen had been called in when Forret couldn't handle the situation. "Crait, what happened to you?"

"That's a matter for another time," Arlen said, at which Crait looked much relieved. Arlen looked around the room with an obvious gaze that Jaime followed, wondering if he saw anything more than she did—a small room with one high window and not even enough chairs to seat them all, though there was a petite round table with a pitcher and fine glasses, stained in the multihued colors Jaime was beginning to recognize as magical in origin.

"This was once the sitting room of a nursery," Chesba said. "Of course, even my grandchildren are beyond that stage now." He nodded at the door in the corner of the room. "She's in there. We thought a smaller room would suit her; she was traumatized by the transport here, for which we had to tie her."

Arlen raised an eyebrow at him. "Indeed?"

"No way around it," Chesba said, shaking his head with regret. "My healer simply couldn't understand enough about her to tranquilize her, and while Forret has been what help he could—contacting you, for instance—he hasn't been able to puzzle her out, either. In fact, I'm afraid we've been able to do very little for her. As weak as she is, if you touch her, she strikes out. We haven't been able to feed her at all—and though I've had fresh food and water in with her at all times, she hasn't partaken of it. I'll be surprised if she lives out the day."

Jaime watched Jess, certain of the distress this would cause her. But Jess said nothing, merely listened to Chesba while her dark eyes examined him, sifting through the clues of human expression and behavior. When those eyes flicked briefly to Jaime, Jaime lifted her chin in the barest of nods. *I believe him*, she said in answer to that question, and Jess went back to watching Chesba—with an occasional sidelong glance at Crait, who was still keeping his distance.

"I'd tell you what *I* think about our find, but I'd prefer for you to form your own conclusions," Chesba finished, moving for the door. "Don't worry; she's usually in the back corner, and won't react to you unless you move in too close. I'll warn you before you reach that point."

"Ready?" Arlen asked Jess.

Her gaze rested briefly on Crait. "He stays out," she said.

"We're *all* going to stay out," Arlen said. "I'll watch from the doorway, and Jaime as well. We're not going to push this woman by marching in on her in numbers. Just you, Jess. Until you think you've got her figured out."

"*If*," Jess said, and left it at that.

"Just do your best," Arlen agreed quietly.

Chesba gestured at the door. "It's not locked from this side."

Jess put her hand on the door and paused, just long enough to look at Crait again. Then she slowly pushed the door open. Jaime moved in close, craning to see around her. Let Arlen fend for himself; he was much taller and could see over her head.

Jess hesitated in the doorway, and even Jaime could understand why. The room smelled, a combination of equally strong odors—disinfectant, body wastes, and a distinct animal odor that Jaime was unable to place. The woman was curled up on herself in the far corner of the room, and dressed only in a tattered, stained tunic; the emaciated lines of her hips and bottom were clearly visible.

Her arms were curled up under her chest, and her head rested on the floor, facing them. The room was well-lit by both window and magelight, and it was easy to see her features. They were finely cast, looking too small for the face that held them, especially the nose. Her eyes, though, were another story; though closed above her slightly twitching nose, they were large, and set off the delicacy of her features even further. Her hair was fine and silvery, and varied in length, with an even mix of short, fine hair and longer hairs that reached to her shoulder.

"Not horse," Jess said, ever so softly. She'd gone tense as soon as she'd entered the room, more than the trepidation Jaime had seen on her face earlier.

"No," Jaime murmured in agreement. She was sure Jess wanted nothing more than to turn around and leave that room forever. "Not horse." She inched into the doorway and stopped, not willing to crowd Jess any further. From there she could see the neat spread of old papers in the corner, where some despairing soul had tried to protect the floor in what was obviously the woman's chosen toilet spot. It was on the opposite side of the room from where the woman herself still lay curled, thin and pathetic, her breath coming in rapid, shallow little whispers.

Not too far from her was the food, but Jaime was inclined to agree with Chesba. The woman was not likely to live long enough to accept it.

Jess made a noise in her throat, a low equine murmur of greeting. The woman's eyes opened, and Jaime couldn't stifle her swift intake of breath; they were beautiful, luminous green, dark rimmed and almond shaped. The large pupils quickly shrank to pinpricks as the woman lifted her head from the floor—a movement which seemed to take some effort. She made a face—a strange grimace—and then returned Jess's greeting with one of her own, one that despite her weakness managed to sound less than benign.

Jaime made no sense of it, but Jess immediately backed away, glancing over her shoulder with eyes that showed an unusual amount of white, and with the frown of effort she wore when she was human and trying not to let her equine self take over. Jaime wasted no time getting out of her way, pushing Arlen back with her shoulder.

Fortunately, Arlen complied quickly and quietly, and within seconds they were all on the other side of the closed door again, where Jess looked at Arlen with eyes that were still too big and said, "She is one of the eaters."

"Eaters." Chesba repeated the word without understanding, while Arlen regarded Jess with the small frown that meant he was thinking hard.

"Eaters," Jess said impatiently, and then made a visible effort to relax. "Big cats."

"Mountain lion?" Jaime guessed. "If you have them here, that is."

"Not by that name," Arlen said, his expression clearing. "But we do have a large creature which is very feline in nature—and they do occasionally band together for attacks on outlying farm livestock."

"The pursan," Chesba said. "Of course. We've never had one this far into Camolen, at least not in my lifetime. But they have that silvery fur . . ."

Jess addressed Crait directly for the first time since they'd left the coach station. "You better not handle *her* bottom."

"What?" said Chesba, startled. Jaime could see he was about to put it together when Arlen spoke.

"Never mind," he said firmly. "I don't want to get distracted from the business at hand; Forret and I will be discussing *that* matter after we're through here. Chesba, I think you should send to Sherra; she has the best healers in Siccawei, and has worked with Jess. I don't think there's much chance of saving this woman—and I'm not sure what we can do with her if we *do* save her. At this point, the only thing that's clear—and painfully clear—is that someone is doing extensive experimentation with changespells, and they're not too terribly concerned with what happens to those results that they can't handle." He shook his head, adding in what was more of a murmur than a comment, "It's too bad the Council is so distracted by—" and then he glanced at Forret and Crait, and finished, "other things. This deserves a full-blown investigation."

"Let the Council do what it can," Chesba said. "I'll see about getting Sherra's best healer here."

Jess, almost as if she couldn't stop herself, put her hand on the doorknob and slowly turned it, until the latch released and she could peek in, just like a child fascinated with horror. Her own worst enemy, in a different form but still just as quintessentially pursan as Jess was yet Lady. But after a moment of watching, Jess turned away and pushed the door all the way open. "Never mind," she said, sorrow in her voice. "You cannot help her now." And she looked at Crait and added, "I think maybe it is better this way."

* * *

"Dayna, are you in here?" Chiara's call was startling against the quiet of Sherra's library.

Dayna struggled to replace the heavy text on the bottom shelf in the back corner. She'd been reading up on shielding, and Chiara's call wasn't a welcome interruption. "Back here," she answered, following it up with a grunt of effort as the book finally edged into place.

Chiara's steps mapped her progress to Dayna's corner. "Dayna, didn't you get the summons?"

Dayna gave her a blank look as Chiara came around the end of a row of shelves, standing and dusting off her loose slacks. "Summons?" she said. Come to think of it, hadn't she heard that tiny mental knock a while ago, when she was in deep concentration? "I was reading," she said, apology in her voice. "I'm sorry. Did I miss anything important?"

"No," Chiara said, exasperation tingeing her voice. "Not really. I'll just have to explain it to you, too."

"Who else did you summon?" Dayna asked.

"Just one of the entry-level students," Chiara said. "He's going as an assistant. But you they want for what you've done. It's quite an honor, actually."

Dayna felt a prick of irritation: "What are you talking about?"

Chiara said evenly, "If you'd paid attention to the summons, you'd already know."

Dayna just crossed her arms and looked at the woman. Flatly, she said, "Fine. You're right. Do you want to tell me now?" It wasn't like she'd been goofing off, even though shielding research wasn't on her assignment list for the week. But if there was some wacko out there misusing shielding, Dayna wanted to know all she could about it.

Chiara sighed. "Just pay attention next time, all right?" She didn't bother to wait for Dayna's nod, perhaps having finally learned the depth of Dayna's stubborn streak. "You've heard of the changed animals they found in Anfeald and Sallatier?"

Of course she had, and she'd found out all she could, though people were being as tight-lipped about that as they were about the strange signatures. Out loud, she merely said, "Yes, two of them. A mule and, just recently, a pursan, whatever that is."

"A big predator," Chiara said absently. She ran a hand down the shelf at her elbow, making a face at the dust there, and then continued with her own thoughts. "The Council isn't so distracted by finding the wizard—or wizards—who are causing the trouble that they aren't going to do something about the changing spells. They've put together a team to come up with a broad checkspell—and you're on it."

"Me?" Dayna said, in true astonishment. She looked down at herself—a first-year student, currently dressed in dust-smudged clothes she'd earned by providing a Siccawei tailor with some easy spells to protect his cloth. She wasn't even from Camolen, for Pete's sake, and despite her ability to manipulate raw magic, she was far from outstanding in her grasp of the layered, complicated spells.

"You're too hard on yourself," Chiara said impatiently, as if she'd read Dayna's thoughts. She tucked a few strands of curly brown hair behind one ear. "You've had to learn twice as much as any new student here, and you're still not behind schedule."

Dayna said, "That's not enough to put me on a Council committee." What was she getting into? A committee where she'd probably be ignored, was all, and something that would take her away from the project she'd assigned herself.

"No, you're right. It's not. But you're one of very few people who have actually invoked a changespell. That counts for a lot."

Incredulous, Dayna said, "I was desperate! I just *did* it!" She could still feel that desperation, as she thought of it—trapped in a small niche of rock while Dun Lady's Jess, injured and pushed beyond her limit, fought to stay on her feet. Lady was frantic, hurting herself with her own spirit, threatening those who loved her. Those hooves had been so close—

"And now that you have some training in you, you can use your memory of what happened to try to reconstruct the spell the way it *should* have been done," Chiara said.

"You'll have plenty of guidance, don't worry. Rorke is just going to fetch and carry and take it all in—but you're going to be right in the middle of it."

"Wonderful," Dayna said.

Chiara eyed her. "Better take care of that attitude before you get there," she said. "This is an opportunity, not a punishment. You're going to be where things are happening, and you're going to be part of it. The rest of us are just going to hear about it."

Dayna smoothed her tunic down, brushing at the remaining dust as though she were already under the scrutiny of the more experienced team members. That was true enough. She wanted answers . . . well, they could hardly keep her out of the flow of information when she was right there—wherever *there* was going to be.

"Then I'd better throw some things together," she said. "Where am I going?"

"Anfeald," Chiara said.

"Why didn't you say so?" Dayna said. "I've been trying to figure out a way to visit Jaime for days!"

❧ ❧ ❧

Jess dangled her new spellstones before her, letting them catch the sunshine and throw facets of early afternoon light onto the dry, yellowed grass of the pasture. *Rain*, she thought, with the memory of drought-grass taste in her mouth. She plucked a long, crisped seed stalk from the ground beside her. *We need rain*. But it wasn't what she was really thinking about, sprawled here beneath her pasture tree.

The spellstones. Arlen had made up a new batch for her, sapphire and onyx. She'd grown used to the subtle clinking in her hair, grown fond of it, even, just as she'd liked the occasional ceremonial bells Carey added to her saddle.

She just wished she could trigger them both. Here

she was, about to go on a run as Lady, and knowing once again that she'd have to depend on someone else to change her back to Jess. Feh. She caught the spellstones up in her hand and rolled over on her back, putting her forearm over her eyes to block out the sun.

She'd had to fight for this run as it was. There they'd been, Carey and Ander and Arlen, all discussing—no, be honest—*arguing* over her decision to continue making runs for Arlen.

It wasn't as if Carey and Arlen didn't need the help. With the obvious lurking presence of the two unknown wizards, Willand's escape, and the new checkspell team ensconced in Arlen's third floor, the percentage of secured courier messages had gone up again. Important communication—words that needed to be absolutely private—no longer went by the wizard Dispatch. Jess's help was no longer a luxury; it was a necessity.

And there was Ander, saying she couldn't possibly ride, not when Willand was free and eager to cause trouble for Jess. Not when someone was out there fooling with changespells, spells that Jess would be especially vulnerable to. And Carey, his face stubborn, hands on hips, telling Ander to let Jess make her own decisions. She'd been wistful at that, watching from the door of the courier duty room where the jobs were posted—and where no one had noticed her yet. She'd wondered why Carey didn't try to protect her, too, and then she'd wondered why she wanted him to.

Arlen hadn't said too much, only that he was perfectly willing to accept whatever Jess decided. For her part, Jess wished Jaime had been there, with her common sense and her unerring ability to strip a discussion to the heart of the matter. But Jaime was visiting with Dayna, who wouldn't have much free time once the last members of her team arrived, later today.

So Jess had ended the argument by walking into the

middle of it and declaring her intention to go. She'd been posted to ride to the local peacekeeper hold, where they'd recently and inexplicably lost several pairs of patrolling officers; the peacekeepers had been exchanging messages with Arlen for a number of days now. In fact, Jess had gone there two days ago, which was how she knew it was a rough ride, and that it would be much easier for her to negotiate as Lady. She'd told the three men as much, and then she'd left them to come here and think it all over.

Ander tried to make decisions for her; she didn't like that. Carey refused to help her make decisions, and she wasn't sure she liked that, either. And she didn't understand why he'd mumbled and stuttered and given some obviously fabricated excuse when she playfully lured him into the stall next to where hers used to be, where he'd occasionally brought women on his own before he ever knew her as Jess. She was still learning about human emotions, but she knew how she felt about him. And even though he'd been so ill he could barely stand after Calandre hurt him, he'd still managed to find her, to comfort her, and to make sure she knew he loved her. She wondered if he'd changed his mind.

"Feh." She said it out loud, spitting out the hayseed stalk she'd been chewing on. She'd never figure people out, not really. So she might as well just get on with the business of being Jess. And Jess was born to run, not to hide from people like Willand. It was time to change to Lady and get this human stuff out of her system for a few hours.

She walked the dusty road back to the stable, noting that even Arlen's road surface spells weren't keeping the dust from puffing up at each step she took. She absently greeted Roj, one of the other riders, her mind on her route and what would be the kindest to her feet—for although she had tough hooves, this kind of weather made the ground especially wearing, and she wouldn't be shod. She never was, anyway, there was no point. She'd only lose the shoes as soon as she turned from horse to human.

Lost in thought, she was deeply startled when she went past the courier duty room and nearly collided with wiry Shammel, the job rider. She nimbly avoided him, but not his unpleasant grin. "You'd better watch where you're going," he said, and then laughed, heading for the main stable door.

She just stared at him, frowning, and by the time she thought to demand what he was doing in Arlen's stable, he was almost out the door. Eventually she shrugged and went on to the tack room, where Lady's special courier harness was stored. Maybe Shammel was hoping Carey would reconsider hiring him, now that the pressure was on—but she was confident Carey would not, so she wasn't going to bother worrying.

Harness in hand, she picked up her cargo—a thin sheaf of sealed pages in a waterproof cover—at the duty room, signed out, and headed off to an empty stall to change.

There, she disrobed and folded the clothes, hanging them over the stall door. She fastened the absurdly large harness around her neck and body, and took a deep breath, and—

Exhaled a noisy equine sigh of happiness. The dim corners of the stall brightened around her, the lovely scent of hay and grain turned sharp and distracting. She yawned a huge yawn, and shook like a wet dog, settling the harness more properly in place. Good. Sometimes it didn't settle, and she'd have to find some human who understood what the problem was.

There was that grain smell again. Had some careless horse spilled his portion? Lady snuffled in the bare corner beneath the grain box, sensitive lips easily able to sort the grain from the other nonsense there. She whiffed a few breaths at it, blowing away wood chip dust. Ah, there—grain.

Peacekeepers. Lady stopped lipping at the spilled grain, her ears tilting as though listening to someone on her back. That was the Jess-voice, deep in her head. The one she had to listen to, even though it was equally important to avoid the more complex concepts her equine brain couldn't process. *Deliver to the peacekeepers*. Lady snorted. So much for finding the last bits of grain.

She pushed the unlatched door open and walked out into the aisle. Several of the horses nickered at her, surprised at a horse walking around unescorted—and wanting to be out there with her. One of them called to her, a demanding neigh she might have answered if she hadn't been on duty. At the main stable door, she had to wait patiently for someone to come along and undo the chain that stretched across the opening, a precaution against loose horses. *Other* loose horses. Klia found her there in a few moments, her first encounter with Lady. The girl awkwardly patted her shoulder, unlatched the chain, and stepped to the side.

Lady trotted out without hesitation. *Peacekeepers*. She was on her way, with the kind of freedom that Lady without Jess had never been given. Out on the road, gearing up into a lope, snorting into the wind and letting out her speed, until she was galloping, tail flagged high and black legs flashing too fast to follow.

When she slowed, it was to prance, full of herself, knees lifting high in the natural passage Jaime had taught her how to sustain. Her head was high, too, until she snorted again, a high, resounding noise that was meant to warn off pursan or bear, but that also served to announce her presence to the world.

No one answered, of course. There was no one else in sight, although she'd passed several hikers and one six-horse coach on the way out. After a few moments she dropped down to a walk, shook her head so her mane flapped against her neck—she was barely damp, even in this heat—and heaved a big sigh. Then she was back on the job, trotting toward the turn-off to the peacekeepers with a brisk, businesslike tempo. She'd take advantage of the road while she could. Soon enough, she'd find Carey's shortcut, and that was a strictly walk-and-scramble operation.

She had her mind on an upcoming creek by the time she crested the shortcut's jagged, crumbly overhang. In another quarter mile, she connected back with a main road—smaller than Arlen's, but well-maintained nonetheless—and shifted into a trot, already smelling the water ahead of her.

That was when she caught the first flutter of motion from the corner of her eye, downwind and definitely not the flash of bird wing. She slowed, lifting her nose to the wind—there was nothing but water and dried out foliage on its eddies—and turned her head, searching the dusty-looking fields along the roadside. The fields were ditched against runoff into the fields, and the ditches were lined with thick head-high meadow growth, rustling in the hot breeze and obscuring her view. Nothing.

The Jess in her didn't like it. There'd been *something*, she knew there had, and it made her tense. Lady increased her pace, and then she saw it again—someone running in the ditch, a flash of dark material between the lighter-colored meadow growth—and instantly shifted to a canter.

Ahead of her, someone else charged out into the road, arms waving madly in time to their wild whooping. Lady stopped short, ears clamped tightly to her skull, dancing between threats until the danger by her side overcame her hesitation and she charged down the road, not bothering to snap at the pinprick of a fly bite at her neck. She didn't want to run the man down, she knew better than to run anyone down, but— She stumbled as the ground swooped wildly before her hooves, then plunged onward, her movements growing uncoordinated and exaggerated.

Run! Both the Lady and the Jess inside her flared into fear, desperately trying to get past the man who now stood in the road, hands on hips, looking small and wiry and . . . *Shammel*, said the Jess voice, and Lady felt a flare of honest equine hatred as she stumbled to her knees. Furious, she snapped at him, though he was clearly out of reach—laughing. Unable to reach him as she lunged back to her feet, tottering like a newborn foal, she snapped at the new fly on her shoulder, and received a surprising mouthful of feathers. *Man-made. Dart.* Fury was replaced by a blinding, searing fear that followed her into darkness.

ଔ ଔ ଔ

"What do you mean, she didn't make it?" Carey asked flatly. Covered with dust and sweat, his eyes stinging with it, he turned from where he'd been blinking at the job board—where, in fact, he'd been checking to see if Jess had signed in and he'd somehow missed it.

"Just what I said," Ander spat at him, his bright blue eyes full of anger instead of the charm that so easily drew women to him. "She should have been there long ago. Jaime just asked me to find you—Arlen got something from the Dispatch saying she wasn't there yet."

"It's a rough road, and a hot day," Carey said automatically, knowing instantly that Jess had certainly had time to get there and back again. It was past dinner, and she'd left right after lunch. Lady, unhindered by a rider, easily could have been there in an hour. Should have been.

"Horseshit," Ander said. "You wanted her out there. You wanted her to make her own decisions. Now you've got what you wanted, all right, because someone's got *her*."

Carey said sharply, "Don't jump to conclusions," but

at the same time felt a pang of fear knot his stomach. "Someone might have caught her, all right—thinking she was a stray. It happened once before. We had her back before nightfall."

"Was Willand on the loose then?" Ander said, moving in from the doorway to stand close—too close, looking down on Carey at a distance that emphasized his own height. "Were there rogue wizards out messing with changespells?"

Carey looked up at him, and fear made way for anger. His voice intense and low, he said, "Back off, Ander. I didn't shove her out there. I left her the freedom to make the choice."

Ander laughed, entirely without humor. "Right, Carey. And if a parent gives a one-year-old the choice to do just what she wants, is that the responsible way to care for her?"

"Jess is far more than a one-year-old child!" Carey said, and felt his grip on his temper slipping. "Dammit, Ander, you know that! I can tell just *exactly* what you think of her by the way you look at her!"

Ander stayed where he was—too close; his voice grew cool. "She has a choice, Carey. That's what you keep saying. It's true as regards us as well—she can choose what she wants."

"Not if I—" Carey started, completely forgetting the difference in their sizes, and the new limitations on his body, as his temper, fueled by worry, flared and overcame common sense completely; he reached for Ander without completing his sentence.

"Boys." It was Jaime, her voice flat with disapproval. "If there's anyone acting like a one-year-old, it's you two. And yes, everyone in the stable could hear you. So you want to break it up, and try approaching this again? Try to use your brains, and see if you can do Jess some good."

Carey's hands fell to his sides. Without the anger, he

was suddenly acutely aware of the worry, and the pain at the thought of going on without Jess. He shook his head. "If those wizards have Jess, there *isn't* anything we can do that will help," he said. "It's up to Jess."

And Jess was stuck inside Lady, unable to change herself back.

ꕥ ꕥ ꕥ

The smells were the first thing Lady noticed. Moldy straw, close to her nose. Old wood. And above it all, a mixture of animal scents. Some were horse; most were not. They were wolf and the wolf cousin, cairndog. There was the scent of pursan, and at least one earthy badger. And, of course, the ammonia smell of old urine, overlaid with the pungency of carnivore excretion.

It took her dulled brain a moment to realize her danger. There were eaters here! Lady's legs flailed without coordination as she sought for purchase in the scant straw beneath her; chunks of dirt thunked off the sides of the enclosure around her. Eyes rolling with fear, she at last managed to fling her unnaturally heavy head up off the ground, getting her legs beneath her so she could rise.

And, that accomplished, could do no more than stand there, trembling unsteadily, swaying and barely able to catch herself. She lowered her head and braced her legs, breathing hard enough to scatter the straw beneath her nose.

She stood, wanting nothing more than to run, knowing she was stalled, and that her body was for some reason failing her. Dimly, the Jess-voice trickled into her awareness. *Don't panic*, it said. *Easy. Don't panic*. Sweat trickled down her flank and neck. It was closed-in here, hot . . . and she was thirsty. Very thirsty.

Water, then. She smelled water. She raised her head, and took her first good look around in the dim light. She was in a stall, all right. An old stall, with one board missing between her and the occupant of the next stall over—another horse, but that wasn't her main concern, not with thirst nagging her. Her stall door was chest high; it'd been higher at one time, but it, too, was clearly missing a board.

Water. It was here somewhere. Carefully, Lady stepped forward, almost falling when her leg hit the ground a few inches below where she'd thought it should. The next step was better, and just a few more got her to the door. Cautiously, she put her nose over it—just far enough for her widened nostrils to investigate what else there was to smell, just for a moment. Then she pulled back, making little *huffhuff* breaths, to think about it. A persistent fly buzzed around her head.

Horse to the left of her. To the right were all the carnivores, and across from her were stacks of cages—rabbits, ferrets—even rats. Lady gave a snort of disgust—the smell was almost stronger than that of the eaters. But nothing moved in response to her appearance. Nothing seemed to care. She took another step, exposing her whole head.

There they were, the eaters. Down at the end of this barn, with one short row of stalls and the rest of it full of half-walled, partially torn out sections that held cages. Closer to Lady, the cages held a wolf and a cairndog. At the far end of the barn, the cages were taller, and held . . . she wasn't sure. They were human, at least partly human, and partly clothed. But they were on all fours despite the height of their cages, and as she watched, one of them snarled a lazy snarl at her.

That one turned in its cage, circling itself—and revealing that it also had a tail. Lady snorted loudly and withdrew into her stall. She had not seen water; she had not seen a way out. The barn's only light—fading evening light—came from gaps between the boards; no doors, no windows.

She snorted again, moving uneasily, checking out each corner of her stall. The horse next to her stuck its nose through the missing board, exposing a questing black muzzle. Lady ignored the black's overtures as her anxiety rose again. No water, no food, no fresh air, no human she could trust. Unless she could call them, unless there was someone in earshot. She lifted her head and neighed her distress to anyone who could hear her.

No one came.

Carey crouched by the side of the narrow road, scowling. His fingers crumbled the small chunk of dry, clay-heavy dirt that had edged a hoofprint just a moment before. Lady had taken his shortcut, all right. He stood, trying not to let Ander see his stiffness, and squinted up the hill, his reins trailing out of one hand.

"Did she take it?" Ander said impatiently behind him.

Carey waited another beat before answering. He hadn't expected Arlen would let him take this ride alone—but he hadn't expected Jess's unwelcome friend Ander to be the one who went with him, either. "Yes," he said, after just long enough. "She went this way." He slapped the reins lightly against his leg a few times. "I wish we'd been out here sooner."

"There wouldn't have been any point to trying this in the dark," Ander said, though an unhappy note in his voice said he was really agreeing. They'd left just before first light, knowing they'd have daylight by the time they really needed it. "For once, at least, we can be glad we didn't get rain overnight."

Carey snorted. "As bad as we need it, you're right." He flipped the reins over his horse's head—it was Lady's dark dun half-brother, a horse who, like Carey, had nearly been ruined by Calandre's use—and mounted up, ignoring the pain that shot through his leg. Too stiff from the early hour, too tired from a ride, too tied in knots by the weather—it was always something these days. There was no point in paying any attention to it. He settled in the saddle and glanced behind to find Ander waiting.

Ander. Carey turned the gelding up the hill, grabbing a chunk of mane and leaving the reins loose so the horse could do his own navigating on the rough climb. Jess's friend Ander. He was a hell of a rider, if nothing else. And even if he did try to protect Jess too much, he obviously cared about her. Carey thought he might even like the man, under different circumstances.

But now, having finally seen them together, he begrudged Ander all the time he'd been with Jess—although he had a strong feeling Jess wasn't picking up on Ander's possessiveness, and the reasons for it—and he especially begrudged missing out on the little discoveries Jess was making about being human.

He could see them in her, each time she visited. A little more confidence in her voice, a little more surety in her choice of words. And somehow she still remained Jess, with all her little Lady-driven quirks and her deep honesty.

He'd wanted to let her discover what she could be—so he knew if she kept coming back to him, it would be because she chose to, and not because it was the only thing she knew. Surely that had been the right thing to do.

Beneath him, the gelding labored. The slope turned suddenly steeper, and rose above them with a short, almost perpendicular cut; above that, it would level out, but until then, it was time to walk. Carey kicked his feet out of the stirrups without stopping the gelding; a glance behind told him Ander had done his own moving dismount.

Carey grabbed onto a stirrup and let the gelding help him up the steep incline, until they were almost at the top, where he stopped the horse and carefully climbed ahead, using Jess's dug-in hoofprints to place his feet in. Once up, he urged the gelding to follow, then moved out of the way for Ander.

He'd wanted Jess to choose. He hadn't wanted to confuse her by pushing too far, too fast. Now, walking the gelding a few feet further from the edge to give Ander room to make it over, he wondered if he hadn't made a mistake.

❧ ❧ ❧

Lady called throughout the night, taking restless little naps between, and yearning for the water she could smell in her neighbor's stall. By morning she was bleary-eyed and thirsty enough her tongue wouldn't work properly, and her belly was cramped and empty. Added to her discomfort was an odd itch of a feeling, an internal want that was building to need. She was standing listlessly in the back corner of the stall when she heard the scrape of a sagging door against the ground.

The barn erupted into cacophony. The eaters, changed and unchanged, barked and howled, some of them pacing at frenzied speed, and some merely snarling a softer and more ominous note. Beside Lady, the black gelding nickered hopefully. Lady, as starved as she was for water, was suddenly more cautious. She stayed in the corner of the stall and waited.

A man walked by, dragging something heavy and muttering. Lady didn't know half the words he used, but she knew discontent when she heard it, and the smell of fresh blood when it was under her nose.

And grain. There was grain. Lady couldn't help but prick her ears up, but she stayed in the corner. The noise from the end of the barn faded, exchanged for the equally grisly sounds of rending flesh and chomping jaws. After a moment, the man returned to the door and retrieved two buckets of grain—a mere handful each. He put one in each stall, then threw in hay as well, not paying any attention to the fact that he hit Lady in the face with some of it.

But it was not hay or grain that Lady really needed. It was water. She waited in tortured impatience while the man slopped buckets of water into the cages, never getting quite close enough to the cages to be entirely efficient. Then the black horse . . . Lady's nostrils twitched, widened, drew in the scent of fresh water so close—and at last the man appeared in front of her stall.

He was the enemy. And while Lady's earliest lessons had drilled certain Rules into her—no kicking, no biting—she also knew there was a different set of rules for the enemy.

And she wanted that water.

The broken door was low enough that he easily leaned over it to place the bucket in the corner. Lady let him come, ears perked, attention focused on the water. He released the bucket handle and stood, his face expectant. "There you go. You're the new one, the one who's been changed before. They went to a lot of trouble for you—too much, I think. That new wizard . . . *she's* the trouble. She'll make us lose sight of why we're—"

But Lady didn't care for his words. She had her food, she had her water. Her ears went from perked to flat against her skull as she lunged for him, teeth bared. They snapped together, a loud, angry sound, in the place where he'd been loafing an instant before. The man staggered backward, trying to catch his balance and tripping over the black's empty water bucket. When he finally caught his balance, he just stared at her a moment. Then the cursing began, words Lady recognized, even in the harsh mutter he used. "Shit," he said, and, "Ninth burning hell!" and then, "Damned bitch mare," which he liked well enough to say twice.

She watched him with her ears back, her head high and her chin lifted; when he took a step forward to retrieve the bucket, she shook her head at him, and struck the stall door with her hoof.

"I'll set the new wizard on you," he said balefully. "Then you'll see."

But Lady, secure in the knowledge that she could have bitten him if she'd truly wanted to, shook her head again, her eyes rolling white at him. She knew which one of them had come out on top, this time.

She didn't even wait until he was out of sight before plunging her muzzle into the bucket, halfway up her face in water. She drank greedily, the cold water sliding down her throat like a balm, while the Jess-voice nagged at her—*not too much, not too much*! and the water level dropped steadily. She would have downed the whole thing at once if she hadn't had to raise her head so she could breath. But when she dropped her lips to the water again, this time for a more fastidious approach, the Jess-voice thundered in her head. *No more*!

Vexed, Lady bobbed her head, dragging her lips across the water and then snorting the moisture out into the stall. The Jess part was adamant, and seemed to be thinking of a big bellyache. With her ears canted back in annoyance, Lady went to investigate the grain. For the moment she wasn't thinking about where she was, or how badly she wanted to be back at Arlen's, with Carey, or even the nagging itch of *need* inside her; she just thought about the hollow ache in her stomach.

For the moment.

* * *

Jaime looked up from her lunch to see Carey walking into Arlen's modest second-floor dining room, Ander behind him. He looked awful, she thought. His face was tight, as if he let his expressions out too freely they might get away from him. Up until this point, she'd thought he'd looked pretty good this visit—without the pinched look chronic pain had often brought to his features over the last year—and moved fairly easily. His hair had been cut short for the heat, aside from a longer forelock which usually managed to fall into his face in a manner even she had to admit was appealing.

Today, it only served as contrast to the look of loss in his eyes.

He dropped a small, brightly colored bit of something on the stone table between Jaime and Arlen. "We found it on the road."

Jaime reached over her lunch plate to pick it up, but the quick lift of Arlen's head stopped her, and she let her hand hover a moment above the object while she looked at it more closely. Almost immediately she found the wicked metal tip, and she carefully picked it up by the other end, by the tips of the feathers that made up the bulk of it.

What on earth? She glanced at Arlen, seeing by the grim look on his face that he immediately knew the significance of it. "It's no great surprise," he said to Carey, and to Ander, who came around the square little table to sit next to Jaime. "We knew they'd gotten her somehow, and they couldn't use magic against her. Not with the shieldstone she had."

Carey's hand went to his chest, where his own collection of spellstones lay beneath his shirt; they were nothing but a small lump under the cloth. He, too, had a shieldstone—and so did Ander, Jaime supposed, just as she had been given one for the short time she rode courier for Sherra. She knew from personal experience that they were no guarantee of safety.

"I'd hoped—" Carey started, and hesitated. He sat down beside Arlen and rubbed a hand over his face, then said more briskly, "I'd hoped she'd simply gotten a stone in her hoof, or pulled a muscle . . . but we rode on to the peacekeepers, and there was no sign of her. Nothing but these—there were several of them—in the road." He dropped something else on the table, then—a thin courier's pouch. "We picked up on the run for you, as long as we were there."

Jaime didn't care about the run. She looked at the object dangling from her fingers and said, "A dart? Is this a dart? They drugged her?"

"That's certainly what it looks like," Arlen said. He pushed away what remained of his lunch. At the other end of the room, a handful of wizards from the changespell team rose from their own meal, and headed out of the room. Behind them, one of the two boys from the kitchen quickly moved in to clean up the area. It took Jaime a moment to realize that Dayna had peeled off from the group, and had come up behind Arlen; she was a small and subtle figure at his shoulder, and Jaime was more concerned with the expression on Arlen's face than anything else.

He was holding out his hand. "Let me see that," he said, even as Dayna leaned forward.

"What's *wrong* with that thing?" she asked.

"You feel it too?" he murmured, though not as if he expected an answer. He took the dart Jaime proffered and set it carefully in the middle of the table, then gave Jaime an intent look. She felt a sudden warm flush—and while that happened sometimes, it wasn't when he was looking at her quite so somberly. She frowned at him, but he gave his head a slight shake and she subsided, waiting. "Do you have any more of these?" he asked.

"All of them," Ander said, sounding puzzled. "We didn't know what might help. . . ."

Arlen said, "Give them to me," and there was no request in his voice. Ander, after casting a doubtful glance at Carey, reached into the small leather pocket hanging at his belt and carefully produced the darts—two more of them.

Jaime knew Arlen well enough to know it was no idle request; a glance at Carey's alert reaction confirmed it. "What's wrong?" she asked warily.

Arlen held up a finger that meant he wasn't going to answer just yet. He put the three darts together in a close pile, and held both hands above them as if sheltering them. After a moment, Dayna said, "Oh!" and that was the only warning they got before the darts gave off a sudden *poof* of smoke and collapsed into a blackened heap of ashes.

"Hey," Ander protested. "We could have used those darts. We could have found out where they were made, maybe even who they were made for."

Jaime gave him an incredulous look. "Ander, my child," she said, "when one of Camolen's most powerful wizards invokes magic, you can be certain he does it for a good reason." As he blinked at her, she added, "In other words, shut up."

Carey was good—or he tried to be, anyway. When Jaime looked at him, his grin was restricted to a small quirk at the corner of his mouth.

"Always nice to have a champion," Arlen said. "These darts were tagged, Ander. Whoever used them on Jess knew that Carey and Jaime were likely to be handling them. They were set with a tagging spell—one that wouldn't have triggered the protection of the shieldstone. I'll have to remove it from both of you."

"A tagging spell?" Jaime said. "So someone could track us?"

"Possibly . . . but I doubt it. This one didn't have an easy to read marker. Unless I'm wrong—" and he looked at Ander and said dryly, "—which I doubt—these tags were tied into other spells."

Jaime had to ask, although she wasn't sure she wanted to know. "And the point . . . ?"

"It's meant to try to get past shieldstones. As soon as

Carey took his off—to bathe, to exchange a used spellstone, whatever—he'd be hit by whatever spell this was tied to."

Jaime felt a trickle of fear invade her chest. "But I'm not even wearing—"

"It's all right, Jay," he said, as if he knew using her nickname would automatically take the threat down a notch. "I've got you shielded. You're safe, and I'll get that tagging spell off you immediately. And *then*," he added, under his breath, "we'll make you a shieldstone. I don't know why I didn't do it when you first got here, even if you *aren't* riding courier this time out. You've been involved in enough controversy to have earned that protection."

"I . . . I guess I thought I was safe here," Jaime said. This was Arlen's hold, the most secure place in all of Camolen for her. And there was Arlen, across from her, dressed in black as usual, today with the black jeans she'd gotten him. He still looked as solid and as eminently proficient as the wizard she'd come to know. She thought of him as her champion, simply for the care he'd shown last year when he'd been fighting for his life, and she'd been caught in the middle. There'd always been an unspoken understanding between them, that he would never let anything touch her like that again.

But he wasn't a god. He was a man, in a land that didn't even have gods to turn to, but instead had guides that took them to whatever Level of the nine heavens and hells they had earned in that particular life. He was a man, and now he was looking at her from brown eyes that knew her fears and clearly spoke of his own failure to protect her from them.

So Jaime shook off her numbness and took a deep breath and said, "Well, I should have asked for a shieldstone right away. It's not like you don't have enough to think about." She paused, thought a moment about the sequence of events they'd all just experienced, and suddenly realized how lucky she really was. She recalled the flush of warmth, and knew then that it was the shielding spell she'd felt.

Dayna must have been thinking along the same lines. "I can't believe you moved fast enough to protect her from the tagspell," she said, wonder in her voice. She, apparently, had at least heard of the business of tagging people for spells. "Too bad we couldn't have it to tag something else, and try to trace the secondary spell back to it . . ."

Arlen shook his head. "There was another spell on those darts, as well. I have no idea what it was, but I suspect it was for me, in case I tried to fiddle with them. No matter. I would never take such chances where Willand is involved."

"Willand," Jaime repeated, her voice faint.

Carey's voice was much harder. "Willand," he said. "Willand's signature was on those darts?"

"Not exactly. It was someone else's signature; someone else's actual working. But it was the same person who helped her escape—I've no doubt Willand was involved. And whatever spells she was directing . . . well, I'd characterize her as a little too ruthless to take chances with."

"And she has Jess," Carey said. He looked away from them all, the tension in his jaw evident, as was his difficulty in swallowing. "She has Jess."

Chapter 6

Lady circled the limits of her stall, damp with sweat in the afternoon heat, and thirsty again. No one had been in to check on the animals and changed humans confined in the barn today, aside from a brief visit by two women who quickly sedated and removed one of the smaller cairndogs. They didn't even glance at Lady's flattened ears as they walked by with their living baggage.

The gelding beside her made occasional overtures of friendship, and his whiskered black muzzle still appeared in the gap between boards every now and then. But Lady, irritated about so many things already, was coming to understand that it was not a gelding she wanted right now.

It was a stallion.

She hadn't been in season for over a year, not since the first change to Jess had disrupted her system so thoroughly. Now, it seemed she was adjusting . . . or that she'd been trapped as Lady—three days, now—long enough for her body to take advantage of it, and with a vengeance. It took her barely tolerable situation and made it intolerable, and she wanted nothing to do with the gelding, the barn, the humans, or the heat that created her thirst. She wanted out, and she wanted it *now*. She wanted something else, too—but she was confused about that, because the thought of a stallion kept mingling with the thought of Carey, which had never happened before.

She'd just snapped at a big fat green fly on her side when she heard the first voice, and her ears flew forward, for it was a familiar one.

Familiar didn't necessarily mean good, and she certainly wasn't happy about this particular voice, even though she wasn't sure just who it belonged to—not until the small group of people came inside, and she saw the man who'd been talking. Small, wiry, his black hair drawn into a tail at the nape of his neck, he stopped in front of her stall and looked at her with distinct satisfaction on his face. Shammel.

"Too bad she was a horse when you took her," he said, crossing his arms and standing hipshot just out of reach of her teeth. "The woman could have been made to talk."

"I'm not concerned about that," said a woman in the group, and Lady suddenly realized who she was looking at. Blonde, her ample curves gone a little angular from her time in prison, her pert features more gaunt than they'd been when she'd helped Calandre launch her attack against Arlen and Anfeald, Willand's expression yet remained the same. Calculating and cold. "Whether she's here as horse or woman, she's still accustomed her body to the changespell, and it'll be easier for you to analyze the elements of the spell than it would with any old horse. *Then*, I can force her into that nag shape forever, and let her pull carts the rest of her life. She'll help us figure out the changespell whether she cooperates or not. *But*," and here she turned to look at another member of the group, the man Lady had launched herself at earlier that day, "according to Benlan, she can't be handled, and I need to get that shieldstone from her, as well as her other stones—there might be a changespell with them."

"Let's just dart her again." This was said by one of those who'd taken the cairndog earlier in the day, a tall and lanky woman with pale skin and thin pale hair cut in a short cap.

Willand turned on her. "Don't be an ass," she snapped. "Do you know how lucky we were that the darts didn't kill her in the first place? We were expecting a human, not a horse, and we don't have a drug that's *meant* for a horse." She turned her back on the woman and considered Lady another moment, then looked at Shammel. "But we do have you. You're a courier—you handle her."

Shammel shook his head, but it wasn't refusal. "She's bluffing. She's a well-trained mount, one of Carey's horses—and that means something, whether you realize it or not. I'd say she's just smart enough, with whatever human is left inside her, to know what sort of trouble she's in." He looked at her, shaking his head again. "Any of you can handle her. You just have to make her believe it."

Lady watched the group—there were several others besides the ones she already knew—and retreated to the back corner of her stall. She wasn't sure what all their words meant . . . she recognized some of them, and understood the tone of most of them. But she'd also learned that the Jess part of her *would* understand them, once Lady was in human form again. So she listened, and she watched them, and she knew deep inside herself that she was in dire trouble.

Shammel looked at the group beside him, whose faces bore nothing but skepticism—aside from Willand, who clearly wanted the whole thing handled, and handled now. He shrugged, and said, "Watch—and learn. I can't come back here again like this. That groom saw me at Arlen's, and if she ever wises up enough to mention it, they might come looking for me. I'm on my way north for a while." He glanced around the dim interior of the barn and finally spotted and retrieved a decent length of rope. He tested its strength, tied a knot at the end, and let it dangle beside him as he approached Lady's stall.

Lady wanted nothing to do with him. As he pulled the door open, she moved her front feet restlessly, looking for some way around him; her haunches tucked slightly, ready to pivot away from him. He didn't seem the least concerned, but when she flattened her ears, he gave her a sharp command. "None of that!" he told her, coming inside the stall. She presented him with her haunches, tail clamped, ready to let fly with a kick that would—

The rope whistled through the air, whipping the knot into her rump with a loud *smack* of assaulted flesh. She grunted, kicking out of reflex, but the swing of her leg was jerky and aborted. *Smack!* The rope landed again, splitting the flesh over her hip, and she bolted up against the corner of the stall, panicked, brainless, and searching for escape.

Shammel stood quietly until she stopped driving herself against the splintered wood boards. In the next stall, the gelding snorted anxiously, his movement rustling straw. Finally, Lady stopped, and turned to face this human and his rope. After a moment, Shammel stepped forward.

Lady snaked her neck out, not charging him, but not about to let him close. The rope was a blur as it landed on her cheek, and then twice more on her neck; she half-reared, but Shammel was standing quietly again. To the group behind him, he said, "She makes a threat, you nail her. Don't push her too hard—give her a chance to think about it, or she'll break her neck trying to get away from you. She knows she's supposed to stand and let you approach her. It won't take much to convince her."

As if to prove his point, he took another step closer to her. Ears flattened, head raised, quivering, Lady let him do it. And she let him take another, and another, until he was beside her, and had slipped the rope around her neck just behind her ears. A coil of it went around her nose and through the neck loop, and she was standing haltered. Back hunched, tail still clamped—but standing.

He turned to the team behind him. "You see? Now come on in here and take her, so she understands you're going to handle her."

In that instant, Lady thought about taking the biggest chunk of his shoulder she could, driven by her fear and the overwhelming revulsion the Jess part felt at being handled by this man. But he still had the rope, and the knotted end still dangled free.

She stood for him.

Benlan came forward, prodded by a look from Willand. "All we need is the shieldstone," he said. "Then we can hold her with magic."

Shammel shrugged. "You need to know how to deal with her," he said. "Come hold her. I'll get your shieldstone."

With obvious reluctance, Benlan entered the stall. But Lady had no desire to protest, not even when Benlan took Shammel's crude halter rope and Shammel himself started to run his hands over her. "She's in heat," Shammel said, amusement—and a little something else—clear in his voice. "Too bad you can't change her back now. I'd like to see what that's like, to have a woman in heat."

"You're disgusting," Willand said, as Shammel ran his hand down Lady's tail. "Quit toying with her and get the stones. They're right up there in her mane, as any idiot can see."

"Bitch," Shammel muttered, then said, "Give a man a break, will you? How often do you think something like this comes along?" But he was back by Lady's neck, his fingers sifting through the hair at the crest of her neck and coming up with the strings of spellstones. "They're not coming out easy," he told the wizard. "She's got them sewn into a braid, and she wasn't taking any chances when she did it. You'll have to cut them out."

"Then do it." Willand made an impatient gesture. "I have work to do, and you're wasting my time."

Shammel smiled at her, a slow, lazy smile. "Got a knife?"

Lady knew the word. She knew Shammel would have one, because a courier never went anywhere without at least a small pocketknife that could cut tangled reins, splice broken leather, and pick stones from a horse's hoof.

"Someone must have one," Willand said, as Shammel turned his back on the team to fuss with Lady's mane and run his hands down her spine. She tilted her head to watch him, eyes rolling, causing Benlan some concern. He had a knife, all right. His face held a quiet, secretive smile—the smile of a man who likes his petty revenge. Revenge against Jess, for taking his place at Arlen's. Revenge against Willand, for insulting him. It amounted to nothing but delay, but his satisfaction, until he wiped it off his face and turned to face the wizard again, was evident.

"I think we're going to have to go get one," said the tall woman. "We're all a bit spoiled by being able to cut things magically, it seems."

"This is ridiculous," Willand said. "I've got better things to do. One of you find a knife and get those spellstones, and bring them to me when you're done. I'll be in my workroom." She turned on her heel and left, her blonde hair bobbing on her shoulders as though for emphasis.

Shammel appeared to have been waiting for it. "Sorry, friends, I've got to go, too. I detoured from a run when you gave me that lovely little magical tap on the shoulder. You shouldn't have any problem with the mare now." He gave Lady a pat on the neck, just below the swollen lump he'd created there. She didn't even flick an ear at him; it was the closest to an insult that she could come.

The courier left the stall without looking back, and the remaining wizards simply stared at one another a moment—except for Benlan, whose expression as he watched Lady was somewhat more wary. Carefully, he removed the rope from her head, and backed out of the stall.

"I dunno, Ben," one of the men said. "She looks safe enough, I suppose."

"Well, she wasn't *safe enough* this morning, I can tell you that," Benlan said fervently, closing the stall door. He left the rope coiled carefully by the side of the door, and joined the others.

Lady didn't move. Her welted flesh throbbed with heat and pain, and she was more than a little stunned by the turn of events. Deep inside her, the Jess-voice seemed stunned as well, and was silent, letting the equine part of Lady deal with the aftermath of Shammel's rough handling.

The group before her didn't seem any happier than she was. "I don't know why she thinks she can treat us like that," said the shorter woman. She was middle-aged and stocky, with plain features and brown hair she'd drawn tightly back from her face to fall in a thin braid down her back. "Dayton brought her into this *after* all the rest of us, and it's not like she's even working on the main project."

"That's supposed to make a difference? She's ruthless, Renia, and we're not," Benlan said. Beside him, a portly, balding man nodded, his eyes worried.

The tallest man in the group shook his head. "Speak for yourself," he said. "You're fooling yourselves, thinking you're going to present Camolen with a squadron of advanced workers—wolf-guards, badger-miners, meek little rabbit-servants." He laughed, and even Lady could tell he was laughing *at* them, though she had no notion why this little group before her suddenly seemed to polarize into two distinct parts. "By the time I'm finished, your little production line of workers won't be worth talking about."

Lady snorted, starting to relax a little, and to realize that whatever dangers this place meant to her, no one was going to come back into her stall, not for now. The tall man looked at her. "If revenge is what keeps that woman going, more power to it," he said. "She's the best thing that could have happened to us—she's got more drive than the rest of you put together."

Renia looked more than a little uncomfortable. "But this isn't just an animal any more, Jenci. She's been human for too long not to treat her as such."

"Shammel didn't have any problem," Benlan said wryly, leaning on the truncated stall door to regard Lady. A short while earlier, she would have flattened her ears at him. Instead she ignored him, not acknowledging him in any way. "He's seen her as human, and look how he treated her."

"Shammel isn't someone I'd choose to model my behavior after," Renia said, disgust in her voice.

"Don't get righteous on us," said the tall woman. "They're all animals, and we treat them like animals. Look how hard it's been to train that one cairndog bitch we changed. She'll stand guard all right, but damned if she doesn't steal something every time we turn our backs on her. She is what she is."

"Exactly why I'm coming at this from a different angle," Jenci said. "You'll see. In the end, it'll be my work that's valuable to us."

This started another round of argument, and Lady, despite the fact that she knew she should listen for what Jess might be able to make of it later on, turned her back on them as they headed for the door. She heard the groan of its stressed old hinges, and the scrape of it across the ground, and then turned her attention inward, to the throbbing of her wounds and the jarring memory of Shammel's assault on her.

He thought he'd had her cowed, but she'd merely been stunned, surprised by abuse she'd never endured before. Abuse she certainly wasn't about to let happen again.

ଔ ଔ ଔ

"As far as anyone can tell, the peacekeepers are just disappearing," Arlen said.

Some moments after the wizard had spoken, Carey realized what he'd said. He stirred from his spot by Arlen's biggest window in his workroom, where he'd been staring down the hot, painfully dusty road that Lady had taken.

Arlen was staring at him with a pensive and worried expression. He opened his mouth as though he was going to say something reassuring, reconsidered, and merely shook his head, slowly, as if to himself.

Carey knew why. There was no point in reassurance. No one had seen any sight of Lady, and Arlen had utterly failed at his attempts to locate her—just as the rest of the Council failed to find Willand, or any trace of the wizard who had been scattering pathetic changespell victims across central Camolen. At least the new changespell team housed at Arlen's had managed to turn the mule back to his natural form—although the animal had proven to be completely unmanageable, and had been magically transported to a high northern pasture where no one would ask anything of him again.

"I don't know how the peacekeepers can be *just disappearing*," Carey said, finally wrenching his thoughts back to Arlen's initial comment. "They've got spellstones to trigger if they run into trouble, not to mention the shift wizard who keeps track of them all."

"And don't think those things haven't been remarked upon," Arlen said. "But it's clear there's something going on. Two more went missing this morning."

Carey gave him a swift, questioning glance, well aware there had been no incoming couriers from the peacekeepers, and that he hadn't sent any out to them, either.

"I set up a cipher," Arlen said. "Simple enough. All the peacekeepers are concerned about is word of this leaking to the general population of Anfeald—you know there's always some young wizard lurking in the Dispatch and nosing about where he doesn't belong, just to prove he—or she—can do it."

"Hackers," Carey said.

Arlen repeated flatly, and without comprehension, "Hackers."

Carey was back to looking out the window. "That's what Jaime called them earlier today. Has to do with computers, and people who break their security."

"Ah," Arlen said, his voice significant. He'd been to Ohio several times himself, and his introduction to Jaime's computer had not been a total success. After another moment of silence, in which Carey thought, for the hundredth time that day, that they'd better get rain soon or there would be no second cutting of hay, and then wondered if that was really a dark cloud just off to the west, Arlen said, "In any case, the point is, despite all the precautions you mentioned, something—or someone—is getting hold of the peacekeepers—and without any apparent motive."

"Blame it on the mystery wizards," Carey said absently.

"As a matter of fact, we are." Arlen paused, watching his courier for a moment. Carey knew he was being less than conversational, knew Arlen had better things to do than explain this sort of thing to him, knew he should be down in the barn, checking the job sheet and ensuring Klia wasn't too busy making eyes at Ander to get her stalls cleaned.

For his part, Ander, frustrated at the apparent lack of effort to find Jess, was keeping his distance from Carey, and making sure the two young mounts he and Jess had brought from Kymmet were ridden each day. As far as Carey knew, Ander was getting all his information from Jaime; an accurate enough source when you considered the time she spent with Arlen.

Carey wished Ander would simply return to Kymmet,

though he knew it would never happen. If Jess came back—*when* Jess came back, Carey didn't want Ander around, spouting his strong opinions about what Jess should or shouldn't do. Even in silence, Ander was a constant reminder that there was another way Carey could have chosen to approach his relationship with Jess—and a reminder that maybe Carey's hadn't been the *best* way.

"She's only been gone a few days," Arlen said gently, breaking through Carey's thoughts. "Give her a chance, Carey. She'll do her best to help us find her, somehow. She's not a quitter. You said that from the very start."

From when Lady had been born, Arlen meant. From those first wobbly steps, taken an astonishingly short time after the Dun Lady had given birth to her. The Dun Lady had another foal by her side this season, a dark bay with deep black points and the same grit and spirit shining in her eyes as Dun Lady's Jess had shown in her early days. Carey had high hopes for her . . . but he'd had higher hopes for Jess, and more personal ones.

"No," he said to Arlen. "She's not a quitter." He glanced away from the heat-distorted fields and into Arlen's concerned brown eyes; the wizard was stroking the side of his mustache as he leaned back in his chair before his worktable and watched Carey. "I think I'll go for a walk," he said.

Despite the fact that it was clear lunacy to leave the stone-and-magic-cooled rooms of the hold, Arlen merely nodded. "I'll call you if anything comes up."

* * *

The spellstone. Lady thought about being Jess, and how Jess's clever human hands could unlatch this stall door and allow her to escape. She tried her best to stop thinking *stallion*, and grasped futilely at the concept of the spellstone, searching for the feeling that Jess experienced when she triggered the stone to change to

Lady. Motionless, eyes half-closed, an observer might have supposed she was sleeping. But she was working harder than she had in her life—and failing.

There wasn't even a trickle of magic in the air—nothing but oppressive heat and humidity, and an empty water bucket. The black gelding had knocked his over, and was bumping it around his stall in a hopeful way.

Spellstone. Jess.

Nothing.

Nothing but the muted rumble of distant thunder. Lady flicked her ear at it. The pastures were so dry they crunched, whether beneath Lady's tough hooves or Jess's equally tough bare feet. Rain. She lifted her nose to the scent of water in the air, and to the rising breeze that slipped through the gaps in the side of the old barn. She'd like to be out in it, with the drops drumming on her back and trickling down her sides, browsing on tender, water-soaked leaves to slake her thirst.

Spellstone!

Lady snorted in irritation as nothing happened, and then fell silent, ears pricked, at the sound of human voices. Benlan and Renia. *Spellstones*, said the Jess-voice from within, coming alert for the first time in that long afternoon, spent hurting and desperate for freedom. But it wasn't a suggestion, or a push at Lady to trigger the changespell. Lady remembered Shammel's hands on her neck, separating the spellstones from her mane and tugging on the braid they were sewn into. They wanted her spellstones. Her protection. Her chance to escape.

And Benlan would have the rope.

Lady turned her rump to the stall door and waited. In between rumbles of thunder and one distinct flash of lightning, the two wizards scraped open the door to the barn and walked up to her stall.

"I hate this," Benlan grumbled. "She could kick my

brains out. Look at her, she's got those back feet ready to go."

"I don't like it any better than you do," Renia said. "I still think there was a better way than whipping her . . . but I doubt you're going to get in there now, without following Shammel's advice. He said she was in heat, and I think that's supposed to make them a little difficult to start with."

Lady stood, her tail clamped and her head raised, turned just enough so she could see the rope in Benlan's hand. She didn't give him a chance to use it. Her leg flashed out, slamming into the stall door as Benlan reached for the latch. Renia gave a startled little scream, jumping back from the stall; the black gelding neighed a low, anxious question. *Wham!* she kicked the stall again, even as she saw the rope making a less than authoritative stroke at her haunch, one that wouldn't have even hurt if it hadn't landed on the lump Shammel left behind.

Outraged, Lady spun in the stall and charged the door, ears flattened and neck snaking, sending Benlan stumbling backward. She half-reared before the shortened stall door, and the Jess-self kicked in—insistent and urgent, fighting Lady's every inclination. *Jump it!*

Jump it, and be free. Jump it and run right over the man staring at her, jaw agape. Jump it, spellstones intact, the way home clear . . .

Lady settled onto her haunches, her front feet dancing as she battled between Rules and freedom. And then, every muscle in her back and haunches bunched, her front feet tucked tightly to her chest, she flung herself over the door from a standstill, her back cannons scraping along the splintered wood even as she landed lightly in front. Renia screamed again, throwing herself against the gelding's stall. He dashed from side to side within its walls, calling after Lady as her back feet touched down and she scrambled for footing, her hooves skidding on the rock-hard packed dirt of the barn floor. Benlan had fallen before her, his arm raised as though it could protect him when her hoof came down hard on his thigh as he rolled beneath her.

She ignored his scream, and Renia's cries, and bolted for the exit. Closed, it was closed! *Go!* demanded the Jess-voice—along with every instinct Lady had. *Go!*

She charged it, slamming into it with her shoulder and taking it right off its damaged hinges. Thunder rolled in counterpoint to the noise of her escape, followed by another flash of brilliant, too-close lightning. Lady charged down a rutted, weed-festooned lane, past a precariously tilted chicken house and along a half-fallen zigzag of a stacked-wood fence. Lightning splashed white light off the old farmhouse she raced by, and by the time anyone within it roused to her escape, she was almost too far away to hear their shouting.

She swept out onto the main road, startling a man who'd stopped his cart to get out rain gear—though the clouds were producing nothing but ominous darkness and blinding flashes of light, followed close on by claps of air-rattling thunder.

Lady ran from it. She ran to Carey and Arlen and home, stopping only once to drink far less than she truly wanted at a creek that was running muddy from hard rain somewhere upstream. She found the shortcut down the hill and all but destroyed the overhang, recklessly flinging herself over its brim and down the steep hill. Trees brushed hard against her side; their limbs stabbed at her, taking hair and flesh from her hide.

She felt none of it. *Carey. Home.* Run. After the hill she had to slow, and shifted to a ground-eating trot, maintaining the pace while the storm followed her and the first hard drops of rain hit her back, shockingly cold against her sweat-soaked skin. She stopped, then, and shook herself off, and simply stood. She wasn't far from home, now, but she was tired, and she needed the moment to gather herself, to simply stand there with her nostrils flared wide and her sides heaving.

After several moments, she shook off again, snorted softly to herself, and walked on. She even paused to snatch a mouthful of grass here and there, ignoring the rain that dripped off her forelock and down her long, fine-boned face.

Without warning, the storm opened up around her. Stinging rain bounced off her back, sparking renewed pain in her bruises, and she bolted a few thoughtless strides at the white flare of lightning nearby. Thunder followed instantly, and Lady turned her bolt into a steady gallop, her ears flattened and her neck stretched out. Water splashed up on her legs and belly from a road too dry to accept the sudden deluge, and she rounded the bend before Arlen's hold at full speed, intent on the sight of the pastures before her.

She almost missed the lone figure walking along the side of the road, head up as though the rain didn't even exist. The drum of rain and constant rumble of thunder obscured the sound of Lady's approach, but he didn't have to turn around for Lady to know who it was. She skidded to a stop and called to him, then trotted forward to meet him even as he turned, squinting through the rain.

Carey. Of course it was Carey. Walking alone and in the rain as if it suited his mood to do so. Lady trotted right up to him, shoving her head against his chest and nickering, gravely inhaling the scent of him, gently lipping along his arms and shoulders and the nape of his neck, while he laughed out loud at her and ran his hands along her arched neck.

"Lady," he said wonderingly, and laughed again; lightning played across the sky behind her and flickered against his features. "No, you're no quitter." He lifted her forelock and planted a kiss at the little cowlick at its base, and suddenly Lady had had enough of waiting to change to Jess. She bumped her head against him, rubbing the braid and its spellstones along his arm. *Jess.*

"*Here?*" he said, looking around them and blinking as the rain hit his face and eyelashes. It was lifting some, with a break in the clouds moving in from the south, and the sky was no longer so imposingly dark.

She shoved him with her head, not quite as gently. He frowned at her, and said, "No, not here. Come with me."

She stood for an instant, looking at him and his slightly off-kilter gait, then jogged after him. She realized where he was headed right away—the small tack shed between the training corrals. Halfway there she overtook him, flagging her tail at him on the way by. When he finally reached the shed, she snorted resoundingly, an impatient noise, and stretched her neck out to present the spellstones to him.

"All right, all right," he said, but there was still laughter in his voice, and relief on his face.

When Ander did this for her, he politely turned his back, releasing the spellstone as it was triggered. Usually, Carey did pretty much the same. But now, rushed, trying to wipe the rain out of his eyes and clearly as impatient as she was, he simply took hold of the stone and triggered the spell.

The feeling of being Jess flooded over her. She closed her eyes and threw back her head and felt the blur of changing, the way her feelings and thoughts and sensations tangled together, until suddenly she was standing, barefoot and nude, with her wet hair streaming against her back and rain washing the sweat from her upturned face.

"Jess," Carey whispered, as if he was seeing her for the first time.

She looked at him; blinked at him, still feeling the transition. Then abruptly she was feeling something else, something unfamiliar and hot and driving. She threw her arms around him and kissed him—not the gentle touch of lips that Mark had once used to introduce her to the idea, nor the tender kisses Carey frequently planted on her cheekbones and forehead, but an embrace driven by passion.

Startled as he was, Carey instantly responded to her, tangling his hands in her black-streaked dun hair and pulling her closer, spreading his kisses to take in her jaw, her neck, and the curved line of her collarbone, never minding that she had pushed him up against the shed. Any vestige of rational thought deserted Jess, and she was lost in the same unthinking reaction that drove Lady when she was frightened or angry—or in heat.

Beneath her lips, Carey's mouth began to move in something other than desire. "Jess," he said, as his hands stopped pulling her toward him and started instead to gently push her away. "Jess, this isn't—*Jess*."

She acquiesced to the pressure on her shoulders and moved back—but not far, staring into his eyes from inches away, panting from the effort of her run and her fervor. "Yes," she said, and reached for his mouth again.

Breathlessly, Carey said, "No. Not *now*." He managed to gain another couple of inches between them, inching along the shed.

"Yes, *now*," she said, frustrated, tossing her head to get her wet black forelock out of her eyes; the rain had eased to a sprinkle. "Why not now?"

Carey closed his eyes and took a deep breath. "You think I've been raising horses this long and can't tell a mare in heat when she trots by me?"

"There is nothing wrong with being in heat," Jess said, moving up against him again.

"No—I didn't mean there was—I mean—" Carey covered his face with his hands and groaned. "Damn, you've made it hard to think."

"Then don't."

"That's just it!" Carey burst out, coming out from behind his hands. "You're not! I can't let you do this now, when it may not be what you really want!"

Of *course* it was what she wanted. It was what she'd wanted for a long time. She frowned at him, but he didn't let her get any words out. "Look, Jess," he said, talking fast, his bright hazel eyes fastened on hers. "Take my word on this. You don't want to do this now, when later you might wonder if you truly wanted to, or if it was just because . . . Lady went into season."

Jess hesitated, and took a small step back. "I don't wonder. Do you?"

He shook his head. "I care too much about you to let you make a mistake about something this important. It's important to me, too."

"But those women you brought next to my stall," Jess said. "You didn't stop *them*."

His eyes flickered away from hers, and closed momentarily. He took another deep breath and looked right at her again. "That wasn't the same," he said. "You—*we're* . . . you're far too important for *me* to chance making a mistake."

Well, then. Jess looked at him for a sad moment, recognizing that not even Carey, who'd been human all his life, could always be certain of just what he should do. "It's easier with Rules," she said. "You're the only one with Words for me, Carey. You should never doubt *that*."

He just looked at her, his expression puzzled. His were the lips that had uttered her Words from the very start—Whoa, Easy, Stand . . . and her very favorites, Words she seldom heard as Jess—Braveheart, and Good Job. But from the way he looked at her, with that little furrow between his brow and his deep-set eyes puzzled, he didn't understand what she meant. She sighed and shook her head, and he smiled at her. "It's all right, Jess," he said. "We'll get it worked out."

She just nodded, and gave a little shiver, suddenly chilled from being soaked after her long run. His smile faded. "Stay put," he said. "There's bound to be a blanket in the shed."

He slipped away from her, and opened the door with a hand on the lock that accepted only his touch. She stared after him, starting to process the things she'd experienced as Lady, the words that suddenly made sense and the expressions that just as suddenly had more meaning, most of them caught by her excellent equine memory. *You're no quitter*, Carey had said to her, just moments ago. She looked after him with thoughtfully narrowed eyes and said, "Damn straight."

❧ ❧ ❧

Jaime moved idly down the stairs from the third floor, where she'd been discussing—*no*, bitching—*let's be honest with yourself*—to Dayna. She frowned despite the strange look one of the hold's few children gave her on his way up the stairs. Yes, bitching. As much as she enjoyed time with Arlen, he was hardly able to play the host while trouble of such nebulous origin stirred through the precincts of Camolen. And she'd only ever meant to stay for a week at most—it was twice that, now, with her highly trained dressage horse on furlough all that time, and for who knew how much longer. She'd already forfeited the entry fees to the show she'd meant to attend at the end of the month—even if she got back in time, Sabre wouldn't be fit for it.

You're kidding yourself again. The real problem wasn't so much that she was missing home, as irritating as that was. The problem was that she was sitting around Anfeald, a great big target just waiting for Willand to cause more trouble.

The damn woman. Jaime thought she'd dealt with this, and put it behind her. She'd *thought* she was ready to move on in her life. And then she'd come here, testified against Willand, and known better. She'd thought herself lucky when Arlen arranged for her to testify without Willand's presence—although her little inner voice knew she'd never get past the fears and renewed nightmares until she faced those fears head on. Faced Willand.

And now it seemed she might get her chance. Not that Arlen wasn't doing his best to make sure it didn't happen. She had a shieldspell, and every day he personally checked her for tagspells and assorted other magical gimmicks he wouldn't elucidate to her. Meanwhile, she wasn't doing anyone any good. She wasn't running messages for him—too risky, with her shallow knowledge of the surrounding precincts—and Carey was too ragged to bring her up to date on his training projects so she could help out. Dayna was practically a nun, closed away with her team members to create the details of various changespells.

Jaime was reduced to such tasks as inspecting equipment for wear and weakness and making sure the horses had enough water in this entrenched draught—for the rain she'd just noticed out the single window of the stairwell would hardly make the thirsty ground damp for more than an hour or so. At the moment, her big project was choosing the contrast color for the decorative lacing on the bridle she was having made for Sabre.

She was even on the verge of asking Ander if she could help exercise the horse Jess had left behind. She shook her head, sorting through the lengths of soft leather lace in her hands, a rainbow of colors. She didn't have anything against Ander, not really . . . he just had a way of getting on her nerves sometimes. Too much self-assurance, perhaps—it verged on the cocky, and that made her want to take him down a peg or two.

The problem was, he *was* a good rider, and an extraordinary archer, to boot. And he was handsome and healthy, and almost never without an admittedly charming glint to his blue eyes. Except for the last several days, of course, when his bleak expression came close to rivaling the misery in Carey's eyes.

Jaime hit the bottom of the stairwell and moved into the well-lit stable hall, holding the lacing up before her to compare the scarlet with a slightly deeper, scintillating shade of red she'd never seen before.

Abruptly, her focus snapped beyond the lace, to the two figures coming up the hall beyond it. "Jess!" she gasped, fumbling the laces, grabbing at them, and finally snatching them out of the air to stuff into her pocket. By then they were upon her. Jess and Carey, he looking distracted and somewhat bemused—not what she expected—and Jess very much the worse for wear. Jess, in the dry clothes she'd been wearing the day she changed to Lady, but her wet hair soaking her tunic, her face red from effort and exhaustion, her eyes wary and hurt. And her face . . . on the angle of her jaw, halfway between chin and ear, there was a bruised, split lump of almost as many colors as Jaime's lacing samples. Nothing but brutality had cause *that* injury.

"Jess!" Jaime repeated, and threw her arms around her friend, not surprised at the sudden rush of tears to her eyes. But even as she blinked them away, as Jess's arms came up to clutch her in a grip of near-panic strength, she realized she wasn't the only one crying. Jess sobbed almost silently into Jaime's shoulder, and Jaime's surprise was no less than Carey's, who looked at her over Jess's shaking shoulders with astonishment in his eyes.

"She was fine a moment ago," he said, his voice low, his hand hovering and then finally landing on the back of Jess's neck. "Her feisty self, I would have said." Gently, he massaged Jess's nape, to no effect.

Jaime said, "Go check the duty room. If there's anyone in there, clear them out."

After an instant of indecision, his reluctant eyes filled with concern, Carey nodded and went back down the hall to see to it. Jaime made generic soothing noises, stroking Jess's back with some care and the thought that the one bruise she'd seen might not be the only one there was, until Carey appeared at the intersection in the hall, gesturing her forward.

Jaime guided Jess down the hall and around the corner, catching her when she stumbled and glaring off Roj's curious hesitation. When they finally made it to the duty room, where Carey hovered by the job board, she balanced on one foot and used the other to shove the door closed behind her. Then she thought better of it and looked at Carey, gesturing with her head—her arms were still full, and Jess, as lithe as she was, was a solid package—at the door.

"What?" he said. "No—"

"Git," Jaime told him. "Go tell Arlen she's back, but don't you dare bring a crowd back down here!"

Carey still hesitated, his expression a mixture of irritation and reluctance. Jaime didn't blame him—it was his stable, and Jess was . . . if not exactly *his* anymore, still closely tied to him. But Jaime was the one Jess had chosen, this time. Carey looked at her; she no longer sobbed so openly, but still hid her face in Jaime's shoulder. "All right," he said. "I won't be long."

At last. Alone in the small room, Jaime led Jess to the small desk and sat her at its chair. Jess sat quietly, sniffling, not looking up at Jaime. Finally Jaime sat on the edge of the desk and asked, "Do you want to talk to me? Or have you got it all out of your system?"

Jess flashed her a miserable look. "I don't know. I don't know why I cried so hard. I thought I was happy to be back, and I . . . I was happy to be with Carey. But when you . . . all of a sudden . . ." She bit her lip, and looked away again.

"It's all right," Jaime said, as matter-of-factly as she could. "You've had a terrible experience, I imagine. It's normal to cry, even when you don't expect it."

Jess looked up at her again, her expression pensive behind her reddened eyes and runny nose. She was, Jaime knew, thinking of the time when it had been Jess who'd found Jaime crying in the aftermath of her experience with Willand.

At the memory, Jaime couldn't help but ask—even if she didn't really want to know the answer. "Jess . . . that mark on your face . . . they didn't . . . I mean, did they—"

"Mostly they ignored me," Jess said, although her eyes took on the spark of a darker emotion. "It was Shammel who betrayed me, and Shammel who beat me—beat Lady."

"There's more than just your face, then," Jaime said, her heart sinking. There was so much of Lady at the heart of Jess, and to beat a sensitive, intelligent horse . . . there was no *good* result. Sometimes the horse was ruined. Sometimes it nursed hatred and anger. *And sometimes*, she told herself, *a good horse can recover and get past it*.

Jess's hand went to the juncture of neck and collarbone, hovering over the material there. Without saying anything, Jaime reached to pulled the tunic down, letting her hand hover above it until Jess met her glance and nodded. There would be no *handling* Jess, not now.

She let her breath out at the livid bruising she found, suddenly aware she'd been holding it. The wounds were split and seeping fluid, but not as swollen as they might be, and the fluid was clear. Still . . . Carefully, she released the tunic, reclaiming her seat on the desk. "Did Carey see that?" she asked, wondering if the man would think to bring something to soothe the angry marks. Jess mutely shook her head. Well, surely Arlen could provide something. "What did Shammel use?"

"It was a rope," Jess said, anger sparking in her voice. "He knotted a rope. And if he gets near me again—"

"I don't imagine he ever will," Jaime said, before Jess could finish the thought. "Carey changed you, didn't he? And he didn't notice those? Are there any more?"

Jess nodded, but her thoughts seemed to be elsewhere. "It was raining," she said. "And he was . . . distracted." She looked away again, and Jaime realized with surprise that there were fresh tears making their way down her cheeks.

"Jess, what? Did he say something to you? What happened?"

"There are so many human things I cannot understand," Jess said, her voice breaking. She took a deep breath and looked right at Jaime. "I know the things that should happen between a man and a woman who love each other—who *say* they love each other. But Carey—" she shook her head in frustration. "Why does he stay so far away from me?"

Ah. So Jess *had* noticed. Carey, for once, had abandoned his headstrong, achieve-the-goal-at-all-costs attitude, and was instead being too cautious. Neutrally, Jaime asked, "What happened?"

And Jess spilled a torrent of words about being Lady for too long and going into season and finally escaping and finding Carey and *wanting* him and being pushed away and was there something wrong with her and—

"Whoa, Jess!" Jaime laughed, and then shook her head when Jess did just that, accepting the Word for what it was and stopping short. "Jess, I—well, I think I have a couple of answers for you. One is that Carey is trying very hard to do what's right for you, and I imagine it's the first time he's truly put so much thought into this particular issue. He's fumbling a little, I think. The second thing is that in this case, he may be right. When someone's been through what you have, and especially if they're in the, um, physical state that you are, it's easy to let your emotions get confused."

With a touch of irritation, Jess said, "I'm not confused. I know what I want."

"Good!" Jaime said. "Then go after it!" *Sometimes the man deserves to be shaken up a little, so he doesn't think he knows everything*—but then she had to be fair, and add, "But do it when *Carey* can be sure it's for the two of you, and not because of anything else. You have to think about how he feels, too."

Jess blinked a moment, and reached a decision. "That makes sense."

"I'm glad," Jaime said, though she couldn't help but feel there was something yet untouched, something lurking in Jess that she hadn't faced yet. Jess, however, was trying out a tentative smile, one that turned into a wince as it stretched her jaw—and then Carey was knocking, suddenly and loudly, at the door, calling to them.

Jess stiffened at the sudden noise, her head raising a notch in her ears-back gesture. Jaime pretended not to notice. No point in making a big deal out of it—several leased and flighty Arabians had taught her that too in the early days of her riding career. "We're fine," she said, shifting on the desk. "Come in."

She'd expected Carey and Arlen, but had somehow completely forgotten about Ander. Damn. Neither she nor Jess needed to deal with the way these two couriers prickled at one another. She gave Ander a clear, stern look he glanced at and ignored, pushing by Carey to reach Jess.

It was the wrong thing to do, Jaime knew it instantly, knew it by the expression on Jess's face. She flung her leg up to block Ander's way and snapped, "Give her some room!"

Carey must have seen Jess's wild-eyed expression as well, for his hand landed on Ander's arm, then fell away at the look the taller man gave him. "You all right now, braveheart?" he asked Jess.

Jaime didn't pretend to understand the painfully wistful expression that crossed Jess's face, but it was enough to make her speak up, gather their attention to her instead of examining Jess like some sort of specimen, as well meaning as they were. "She's got some terrible bruises," Jaime said, a no-nonsense tone. "Shammel beat her—or, at least, beat Lady."

"Shammel," Arlen repeated in surprise. "Well, that's one piece of the puzzle, then. He had no great fondness for her."

"He hated her, you mean," Carey said, his voice hard. "I should have made it clear to him that he would have been dismissed regardless of her offer to ride for me. He was trouble from the start."

"Klia said she'd seen him," Ander said thoughtfully. "It was a couple days ago. I just figured he was hunting for work, but if he got a look at the job board—"

"He'd have known she was taking the peacekeeper run," Carey finished, exchanging a look with Ander.

"I should have—" Ander started, but Carey cut him off.

"There's no way you could have known it was anything other than what it looked like," he said. Ander gave him a surprised and grateful look, and said nothing.

Arlen held up his hand. "I appreciate that this is something we all have a stake in, and we all want to talk about it," he said. "But I'd really like to simply listen to Jess tell us what happened, as best as she can translate the experience into human terms." He cast a gentler eye upon Jess. "And then, dear, we'll have Cesna take a look at you. She may be my apprentice, but she has a better feel for the subtle spells of healing."

"No," Jess said, surprising them all. She looked at Jaime a moment, as if hoping Jaime would explain it to the others, and then simply said, "The bruises will be as spurs, to do my best to help stop them."

"Whatever you'd like," Arlen said, though Jaime thought the split wound on Jess's face might scar, and winced to think of it. But Arlen was moving onward. "Can you tell us, then, what happened? We know where you were taken, and how. But we don't know where you ended up—or with whom."

"The changespell wizards," Jess said grimly. "And . . ." she looked at Jaime, "Willand."

Jaime nodded, just as grim. "We figured that. She let us know she was involved in her own darling way."

"Details, Jess," Arlen urged her. "The best details you can give us."

So Jess told them, and in the end Jaime found herself astonished at how much Lady could retain for Jess to later interpret. She thought she saw surprise on Ander's face, too—but mostly they were caught up in Jess's description of the barn and the animals within it—and the obvious disregard for their overall well-being.

And then Jess got to the period of time when she was simply trapped in the dirty stall, waiting, impatient and angry. And there she stopped, and gave Arlen a purely miserable look. "I couldn't work the changespell stone," she said. "If I could . . . I could have gotten away. I could have learned more about them, or . . . or freed the others. But I *couldn't do it*. I was . . . I was helpless."

Jaime felt a strong, resonating twinge of inner pain. *Helpless*. She'd been helpless, too, when Willand revelled in tearing her apart from the inside out. How had Sherra finally explained that spell? A healing spell to stimulate nerves?

And now Jess had felt it. She was staring at the floor, as though her helplessness had somehow been her fault, and Jaime could see the flush of emotion on her light nut-brown skin. This was what was behind the heart-wrenching depth of Jess's tears, and what Jaime had sensed lurking, unsaid, between them. No wonder Jaime's embrace had undone Jess, who was, more than anyone else besides Arlen, aware of what Jaime had been through.

"Jess," Jaime started, but didn't get the chance to finish. Jess raised her head and looked at Arlen.

"I need a changespell Lady can trigger, Arlen," she said firmly. "I want no more of being chased by farmers who think I have run off from you, and no more waiting until someone finds Ander or Carey when I return from a run. The change must be my choice."

"I agree with you completely, Jess," Arlen said, but Jaime heard the caution in his voice. "I'm just not sure it can be done. I can try a cascade spell, but often those end up requiring more power, if less thought."

"It *has* to be done," Jess said, desperation edging her voice.

"We'll work on it," Arlen said. "I'll mention it to the changespell team, as well. But I won't make you false promises, Jess. It's a complex spell, and highly individualized."

But Jess seemed satisfied. "Truth," she pronounced it, nodding to herself. She took a deep breath and closed her eyes, and related what of the farm conversations she'd been able to hold on to and process.

It was harder to make clear sense of these than of the physical descriptions Jess had given them. Frowning, Jaime finally had to close her eyes to divorce herself from Jess's expressive face, and the distraction it lent her words. When Jess finished, and waited in silence for their reactions, Jaime took a deep breath and opened her eyes, fastening her gaze on Arlen. She wasn't the only one. Clearly, his was the next move.

He, too, took a deep breath, rubbing the bridge of

his nose with his thumb and forefinger. "I still have no idea who these people are, aside from Willand, or who's driving them. It's got to be a third party, or they wouldn't have been so unhappy with Willand's presence."

"Dane," Jess said suddenly, and frowned. "No, that's not right. It was like Dayna, but not."

"Don't try too hard, Jess," Arlen said. "If it comes to you, it'll be when you're not thinking about it."

But the frown remained in place, deepening the wrinkle between her dark brows. Then, abruptly, she shook her head. "I can't. I must not have heard it right when they said it."

"You can be that certain?" Ander said, his eyes widening a little. "You remember things that clearly, even after you change?"

Jess gave him a patient look, and a wry expression crossed Carey's face. He murmured, "Never underestimate her, Ander."

But Arlen was moving on. "So far, this group is nothing but an ethics problem," he said, "though I've no doubt they could create a market in the highly landed for the specialized workers they're developing. The Council will certainly not tolerate their dabbling with the lives of others, be they animal or human. But that one man . . . I wish I knew what he was up to."

"Jenci," Jess said. "I didn't like him." She considered a moment, and added, "I didn't like any of them. But him, less."

"And there's Willand," Carey said, voicing Jaime's thoughts. "She's already proven she's far worse than an ethics problem. These wizards must've broken her out of confinement somehow, and they wouldn't have done it if she wasn't going to be of use to them."

"You've forgotten something important," Arlen said. "Willand was allowed no visitors with magical skills above the level of your average citizen—say, what you and Jaime can do. And the signature was different from the early one we detected. That whole incident is still very much a mystery."

"We've *got* to learn more about them," Carey said, while one hand absently rubbed along his hip. Jess watched him, quiet concern in her eyes, obviously distracted, for the moment, from her recent experience and the pain she still felt.

"True," Arlen said. "I imagine they're already packed and out of the site where Jess was, but we need to get a look at it."

"That's easy enough," Jess said, looking away from Carey to meet Arlen's eyes, and surprising them all. She gave a small smile. "Did you think a horse who found her way home couldn't find her way back out again?"

Chapter 7

Dayna sighed, shifting in the saddle and thinking about how fast things could happen. Two days before, Jess had been missing. Between now and then she'd come back and then gone right out again, guiding Arlen to the farm where she'd been held. They'd returned to the farm less than a day after Jess's escape, but the place was, not surprisingly, abandoned.

Not for long. Now Dayna's team was on their way, escorted by peacekeepers—two pairs of experienced protectors who rode with the group of uneasy wizards and their companions. That made a group of Arlen, Jess, Carey, and the changespell team, watched fore and aft by four peacekeepers. Dayna made sure she was near one of them at all times, not completely reassured by Arlen's presence and promise of protection. She'd have felt better with Katrie, Sherra's woman, whom she'd come to trust.

They were, after all, dealing with a handful of wizards who had already done plenty of things they shouldn't have been able to do. Even if Arlen was right with his speculation that some of the small, power-flouting crew—most notably, the ones who objected to Willand's presence and who were developing the changed, specialized workers—weren't as dangerous as they were deluded. What difference did it make when Willand was with them? She'd already shown herself to be preoccupied with revenge. Just look at the tagspell Arlen had intercepted—and what had been done to Jess.

Just what *had* been done to Jess during her captivity, Dayna didn't know. She'd seen her friend shortly after her return, and had instantly divined the difference in Jess, a difference that went beyond the appalling bruise on her face and into a deeper part of her.

She reminded Dayna of no one more than her own self. Dayna knew what she was, that she was easily threatened and had spent her life looking for ways to feel safe. She didn't need a lot of expensive psychobabble to know it was the result of her unusually petite stature and her unusually abusive father, and she didn't think it was necessary for her to get herself "fixed." She lived her life in ways that made her feel safe—except when she was out riding in plain view on the way to the enemy's den—and she was satisfied with that.

But it didn't belong on Jess. Even when Dayna and Eric had first found Jess, newly human and lost on a strange world, she had still had an inner confidence—something Dayna and Eric had not been able to shake, despite their disbelief that Jess was not a horse. Jess had known certain things—her Words, her Rules, and the behaviors that lay at the root of all horse/human interactions, and she'd never doubted them.

When Dayna had looked at Jess's face the day of her return, she saw the repercussions of shattered Rules. Her eyes were wary when they settled on someone she didn't know, and she was far more jealous of her personal space. Even Ander had earned a quick glare for coming up on her too fast.

Dayna, recognizing the threatened, had no problem. She moved slowly near Jess, and waited for that moment of subtle acceptance before getting too close. She knew she didn't want to be around when someone finally ignored those subtle keep-your-distance signals once too often, and Jess exploded on them.

Dayna shifted in the saddle, wishing once again for the smooth-gaited little bay mare she used when she was at Sherra's, the one Mark had laughingly dubbed Fahrvegnügen. Of course the name had stuck, just one more piece of evidence that Jaime's brother would never completely grow up.

"Not used to the riding, huh?" Carey asked, moving up beside her on a dark brownish horse that reminded her of Lady. He sat in the saddle with ridiculous ease despite his permanently lingering, magic-induced injuries. She just scowled at him. "I thought so," he concluded, giving her a crooked grin. "Too bad you wizards never learn to ride properly."

"As if there's any need," Dayna grumbled—though she, too, understood it was best not to shout out their activities with the magical signature of so many wizards taking mage-travel to the little farm.

Carey's grin faded. "Do you think you'll really be able to find anything at the farm?"

Dayna grimaced, thinking of what she'd seen the evening before—Arlen's magical recordings of the site, and the animals that had been abandoned there. "Nothing obvious," she said. "Arlen would have spotted it yesterday if there was. But he did put a stasis spell on the dead woman they left behind, and there are a couple of sickly animals we can work with. If we can figure out how they're refining their spells, we have a better chance of creating an effective changespell." She blinked, and made a face. "I said that like I'd lived here all my life, didn't I?"

"That you did," Carey agreed. They rode in silence for a few moments, while Dayna dropped back slightly so she could watch Carey watching Jess. She'd been wondering why Carey was along—she knew he was understaffed, and that drawing a ride out like this one—three-quarters of a day instead of the three or four hours it would take a fast courier—was hard on him. But the reason, of course, was obvious. Jess.

He caught her eye. "I can't let anything happen to her," he said. "Not now. There's too much . . . going on." He looked at Jess again and added, "Or *not* going on," but that last was a mumble Dayna didn't think she was supposed to hear.

"As I understand it, Jess was the one who wanted to take the run," Dayna said, her voice taking on the slight edge it got when she thought someone was bordering on dramatics. "She told me so herself. She makes her own decisions, Carey. No need for you to beat yourself up over it."

But the look he gave her wasn't drama, it was true misery. "I could have at least said something," he said. "She might have decided differently, then. Or maybe not—but at least I wouldn't be watching her now, wishing I'd at least *tried*." He patted his horse's shoulder, a gentle, wistful motion. "This is Jess's brother, you know. Well, her half brother. Last year, Calandre's people nearly ruined him. Hard riding . . . worse treatment. It's taken a long time to get his confidence up again." He nodded at Jess. "She always had more grit than he did. She's the kind of horse who'll turn hard, and kick back."

"She's more than a horse, now," Dayna reminded him. "She'll get through this."

Carey sighed. "I know. She can be one of the strongest people I know. But at the same time . . ." He shrugged, and didn't continue for a moment. Finally, he said, "I wanted her to learn she *is* strong. I thought it would be best if I let her make her own decisions. I think I stepped back too far."

Dayna's response was as perspicacious as ever. "Then maybe you should try just being your normal cuddly and lovable self, and quit trying to orchestrate how her life should go."

He gave her a surprised look. "Careful, Dayna. Someday, someone's going to figure out that you really care."

She didn't manage to come up with a retort for that one before he nudged his horse into a trot, moving up beside Jess with an ease that renewed the scowl she'd given him before. Bad enough he wasn't getting saddle-sore—he had to get the last word, as well?

❧ ❧ ❧

Jess was back at work. She needed it, needed its distraction and needed the reassurance of doing something she was good at. She stood at the top of the shortcut, well away from the steep bank Ander was struggling to climb over. Yesterday, they'd had to take the long way around, knowing the wizards in Dayna's changespell team would never navigate this section of the shortcut. Hard to believe she was out here again already, once more about to ride past the place she'd been ambushed, on route to the peacekeeper hold she'd never reached the last time. Well, Kymmet had wanted some miles on these young courier horses, and when Jess and Ander returned to their stable in the next few days, it would be with two newly seasoned, ready-to-sell horses.

With Ander at the top and flashing her a grin, Jess mounted up again. She didn't feel quite ready to leave Arlen's hold for Kymmet, and she definitely wasn't ready to leave Carey. There were too many unspoken, unfinished things between them, things she couldn't stop thinking about—things she didn't *want* to stop thinking about.

But Kymmet wanted them back. And Arlen reluctantly decided Jess might actually be in more danger *here*, closer to the nucleus of changespell activity, and the focus of Willand's attention. He hadn't wanted Jess to ride any more courier runs here, either—including this one—but Jess could be as stubborn as anybody; and she could *see* as well as anybody, too—which meant she could see Carey needed the help as long as she was able to give it.

Besides, she had to ride this stretch of road again. She had to prove to herself that she could. She knew it was the Lady in her that made her heart beat so fast, knew that this facet of equine memory would be hard to overcome—but overcome it, she would.

Her gelding started to jig beneath her as it felt her tension. Jess narrowed her focus to breathing, deeply and slowly. Here was where she'd first seen the threat. Here was where she'd felt the sting of the first dart. Here. Here was where she'd fallen. *Breathe*, she told herself.

"Jess?" Ander's horse nudged her own; the geldings exchanged a quick conversation of flattened ears and snaky-necked threats, and Jess moved away from Ander, but not without turning to wordlessly ask why he'd created the problem. He grinned. "I thought that would get your attention."

She snorted and turned away, but it was with a small smile. Ander's grin was hard to resist; always had been. Maybe that was why she let him get away with so much. Beneath her, the gelding snorted too, mouthing the bit in the aftermath of his crabby spell.

But Jess's diversion from her tensions was fleeting; ahead, on the long, straight stretch of field-edged roads, there was movement. She stopped the gelding with a shift of her weight, hesitating, tipping her head so the black brim of her baseball cap shaded her eyes.

"Other people use the road, too," Ander reminded her, his voice low and calm. "You know the outlaw wizards aren't going to be anywhere near here—they're slinking around Sallatier Precinct somewhere, most likely."

True, she thought, raising her head for better focus even though these human eyes didn't need her to. Even so . . . Then she caught the flash of color, consistent on each of the several figures she could pick out. Red and white, the uniform of the peacekeepers.

Ander must have seen it at the same time. "They're just out on an exercise," he said. "Bet if we hang around, we can catch them teaming up for stalking games. I don't blame them. With all the trouble they're having, I'd sharpen up my skills, too." He ran his hand along the strap of his quiver.

Jess didn't blame them, either, considering she was riding to pick up the compiled statistics of peacekeeper losses for Anfeald and the surrounding precincts. They'd be high—she knew that much. Among the wizards at Arlen's hold, it was commonly accepted that the outlaw wizards, the same ones who'd captured her, were responsible—though no one was venturing just how or why. She looked at Ander's bow and quiver, and wondered if he could get his hands on the bow, and nock and aim before feathered little darts took them both down.

Probably not. So she'd just have to keep her ears and eyes and phantom whiskers on alert at all times.

They rode single file past the large group of marching men and women, exchanging greetings all the way down the line. And then, despite the heat of the late morning, Jess moved out in front of Ander at a canter, more than ready to be at their destination and knowing the turn-off was less than a mile down the road.

They were greeted with the sort of pleased enthusiasm that results from anxiety. "Glad you're here, glad you're here," said the middle-aged man who was posted at the gate. "After what happened to that one courier, well . . ." he trailed off and shook his head, obviously unaware that *that one courier* was right there in front of him. He made a quick gesture, and spoke into a small black square painted on the door frame of his small shelter. "Arlen's people are here," he said.

Jess started when the door frame spoke back to him.

"Should be two, man and woman. She's supposed to show you a baseball cap." The voice added less brusquely, "Don't ask me what *that's* supposed to be."

Jess pointed to her cap. "This," she said, frowning down on the man. Clearly, although important information wasn't going between the peacekeepers and Arlen via the Dispatch, there was still an exchange.

"Confirmed," said the man into his black square, then looked up at Ander and Jess with an apology riding his shrug. "We're being pretty careful these days."

"Yes," Jess agreed, glancing at Ander. "So are we."

The man waved them in, and they trotted into the peacekeeper yard, a dusty expanse with shriveled plantings lining the front of the huge stone main house. There was a hitching rail on the shaded side of the house, and Jess aimed her horse at it, reflecting that there was little point in hobbling him to pick at the crisp grass. It would take more than one storm to overcome the effects of such a dry summer.

They were met at the door by a young woman in black trousers and a red tailored and belted tunic. She wore a white armband, and Ander leaned in close to Jess's ear and whispered, "Youth Corps. They must really be hurting to have the Corps working the main house."

The young woman said nothing but, "This way, please," and led them down a long hallway. Jess had made this run once or twice before, but never had there been such solemn ritual involved. They were deposited at the open door of a large office, in which a woman and two men spoke in low tones.

Jess glanced at Ander and saw he was going to wait for her—after all, he'd never done this; he couldn't know how much things had changed, and that she was just as uncertain as he for the moment. She resettled her saddlebags on her shoulder and stepped into the office. There she saw the painted black square on the largest of two desks there, and pointed at her hat again. "Baseball cap," she explained. "This is for the Baltimore Orioles."

The man sitting behind the desk just grinned at her. "Glad to know it," he said.

At his casual response, Jess relaxed. "I thought we did something wrong."

He made a sour face, which was an interesting sight when combined with his oversized nose and narrow eyes. "Things have changed. Formality encourages alertness among the newer recruits, and the Corps. Didn't mean to get you caught up in it unaware."

Beside Jess, Ander relaxed as well. "Does that mean we have a chance of getting lunch around here?"

"Indeed!" the woman said. She must have been about Jaime's age, but looked older, with lines of worry and fatigue around her eyes. "In fact, I think we owe your companion two lunches, unless I'm wrong about who she is."

"Jess," said Jess, without hesitation. The woman nodded, and Jess saw the little glimmer that meant the woman knew—really *knew*—who she was.

"We appreciate your effort in getting out to us," the second man said. He was a big man, with the pale lines of a recently shaved beard. The heat, Jess thought, he'd only now just shaved from the heat. That made him about as stubborn as she could be.

"Obviously," said the woman, "someone around here is intent on causing trouble for us. We're just grateful that whoever it is hasn't expanded their attention to the general population."

"No," said Jess. "Just you. And *us*." The woman was trying to make conversation, and Jess knew from Ander's surprised glance that her slightly prickly reaction wouldn't be understood. She didn't like it when people *tried* to make conversation, just so they could talk to her. And now the woman was staring at the fading, scabbed bruise against Jess's jaw, which was no better.

"Now, then," said the man behind the desk, breaking through the undercurrents as he reached into a drawer and dropped a thick, wrapped stack of paper before them. "Here it is. Let me get a leather folder for it, and we'll head off to that lunch."

Ander's stomach growled, right on cue, but Jess suddenly wasn't hungry any more. She didn't want to eat with this woman. Still, she accepted the folder and slid it into the saddlebags she carried, listening to introductions—First Level Commander Jep, and the woman, Friedan, and the large Karle, both second level commanders. Ander picked up the conversation with the standard topic of late—the weather—and smoothed out the rough spot Jess had created.

The dining room was in another building, just off the side of the main house. Jess had expected to find a scene reminiscent of Kymmet's dining room, but while the room's structure and furniture were similar, the activity within was not. There were too many empty tables—*the peacekeepers we saw on the road*, Jess reminded herself—and even given the occupants who were there, the room was quiet. Tense. As they stood in the doorway, Jess glanced to see if Ander had picked up on the atmosphere.

He shrugged at her. And the woman was talking—*had* been talking—through it all. Previously it was something about the day's menu; now it was a comment on the state of the dining room, by which Jess learned there was more than one company out playing stalking games today.

She listened with only part of her attention, devoting the rest to sorting out a table that she liked and leading the others toward it, not caring if they had their own favorite spot to eat. She just wanted to eat and move on—behind her, Ander was making sure someone would be offering their horses hay and water—and she was suddenly realizing that taking this run maybe hadn't been the best decision after all. She'd done what she needed to do, she'd forced herself past that spot in the road, but being here, with its loud and constant reminders of the strange and dangerous time this had become, was only making her nervous.

Friedan wasn't helping any, either, her slightly false-edged tone of voice reminding Jess of how *different* she was, how her almond brown—*dun*—skin and two-toned hair made her stand out even in a country of people with a variety of shades and forms, none of which quite matched her own. Jess just hoped Ander had caught her mood and was willing to—*quick movement, rushing up from behind—danger*! Jess shifted into instinct, throwing her head up, shifting her weight, her leg free and chambering to kick—

Ander stumbled into her, catching himself with hands on her shoulders, forcing her to step heavily on the leg that was about to deal out a damaging blow; his embarrassed laugh of apology was just so much confusion to Jess, and she twisted to free herself of his weight, panic edging her thoughts.

Ander's hands tightened on her shoulders. He pulled her back toward him, back against his chest. His voice in her ear was low but intense. "Easy," he told her, as much of a command as anything he'd ever said to her, a deliberate invocation of one of her Words. She stopped pulling against him, a battle which had been apparent only through the whiteness of his knuckles and the indentations of his fingers in her shoulders. But her eyes were wide and she trembled against his grip, the need to strike out and run still strong within her.

Ander turned so she could see the threat. The young woman who'd met them at the main house door, her face flushed with running. She was tugging her uniform back into place, and straightening her shoulders, her attention on the three ranking peacekeepers.

"That was quite an entrance," said Jep, both eyebrows raised above his narrow eyes, which held disapproval.

Ander invited himself into the conversation. "Especially when you consider how tense things are around here," he said, and though he kept his voice lighthearted, Jess heard the irritation in it, and knew it was for her sake. She took a deep breath and relaxed against him so he would know she was calm now, and not about to kick anybody into next week's dinner.

"A good point," said Karle. "Once you get into further training, Lydda, you'll think twice about running up behind someone who spends as much time in the field as I do." The young woman's face flushed even deeper, this time from obvious embarrassment.

They hadn't seen her, Jess realized. Ander had been between herself and the peacekeepers, who were strung out in a diagonal line behind her as Lydda had run up to Jep, behind Ander. They hadn't realized she almost took down one of their own. She wouldn't have to explain, not with Ander's quick thinking to hide her reaction. She took another breath as Ander released her, and rubbed her shoulders in a quick apology for that bruising grip.

"But the shift wizard—" Lydda said, stopping as it became apparent from Karle's darkening expression that protest wasn't the path to take. She tried again, and spoke more humbly this time, her gaze fixed firmly on her toes. "I'm sorry," she said. "It won't happen again." Then she looked up, and some of the excitement returned to her voice. "Falcin sent me—he's lost contact with one of the companies at the stalking games!"

"He's tried to reach the second in command?" Jep asked sharply.

"Which company?" Friedan asked at the same time, while Karle's expression darkened.

"Gestan's," Lydda said. "And yes, but he can't reach her! He can't reach *any* of them."

Jep's expression had turned grim. "Is that the extent of Falcin's message?" At Lydda's nod, he dismissed her. Without hesitation, he turned to Ander and Jess. "I'm sorry," he said. "I'm afraid I'll have to see to this." Then to Friedan and Karle, he added, "Eat. I'll need you later, and I don't want you hungry."

Neither of the two looked happy at that, but neither did anything more than nod. They proceeded to Jess's chosen table in silence, at which point they had the menu to talk about, and the problem to solve of what they could offer Jess. Peacekeepers, it seemed, were fond of meals based on meat, which Jess had never learned to stomach—aside from the occasional Ohio fast food meal, which failed to strike her senses as true hamburger.

Eventually they had the head cook combine all their fresh greens with fruit preserves and crackers on the side, and Jess found her appetite had returned by the time she was served. Unlike the Kymmet dining room, the ranking peacekeepers were served where they sat, a luxury they more than earned today by spending the meal in intense conversation about the new situation.

Jess said little. At least Friedan was no longer trying to force conversation, and she herself had little to add to this one—aside from a glance or two at Ander as it became obvious that the Council wizards had not told the peacekeepers everything that was happening, including the mystery wizard development. Jess would have wanted to know, in their situation. But there was, she supposed, nothing they could do about it anyway, aside from getting upset about it. She was not in the least tempted to tell them. A courier didn't, not if she wanted to keep her job.

She ate quickly and ended up waiting for Ander to finish; Friedan and Jep, who had done more talking than eating, both stopped their conversation when they realized the two couriers were finished.

"I'm sorry," said Friedan. "We weren't very good hosts. We did want you to know how much we appreciate your work on our behalf."

"No apologies necessary," Ander said. "I hope your company is all right. Glitches happen, even to the best of wizards."

Her mouth crooked in a wry smile. "Not likely, with Falcin. But thank you for the thought."

"Hate to be rude," Ander said, "but we're expected back . . . and our people have reason to worry, too."

Karle nodded. "You'd better be going, then," he said. "Do you need a guide back to your horses?"

Ander looked at Jess and grinned. "No," he said. "It's straightforward, and Jess's got a pretty fair sense of direction."

For the first time during the meal, Jess grinned at him, and didn't point out that they hardly needed a sense of direction, since the horses were visible from the dining hall and they had no intention of winding their way back through the main house again.

They left their dishes in a neat stack and walked to the horses in silence; neither of them spoke until they were retightening their girths. Then Ander said, "She would have startled anyone, Jess. Don't worry about it."

"She was stupid," Jess said immediately, making sure her saddlebags and their contents were secure. "She would have deserved it." And then she stopped, and blinked, and said, "I don't know why I said that."

"She *was* stupid, to go pelting up on someone like that." But Ander's expression held reservation, and he looked a little startled besides.

"Yes. But . . . it was a mistake." She frowned down at her fingers as they rebuckled the flap on her saddlebag. There was no point in being so angry at someone for a mistake. Jess made enough of those, herself.

"Well, I don't think she'll make it again. Karle and Jep

didn't like it any more than you did," Ander said with assurance, leading his horse away from the rail and mounting up.

Foot in the stirrup, Jess hesitated. "Do you hear . . . ?" she said, but then couldn't hear it herself any more, and mounted up. Just a breeze knocking branches together, or an approaching rider. Or . . . several of them?

"What?" Ander asked her.

She shook her head, but before they reached the gatehouse, she stopped her horse. Then Ander heard it, too, the sound of many dozens of hoofbeats, but not shod, not heavy horse hooves. Lighter steps, ticking and pattering against the hard road in such numbers as to create a minor alto rumble. Ander threw a puzzled look at Jess as the man in the gatehouse stepped out into the middle of the road, where his view was much better than theirs.

Just as fast, he ducked back into the gatehouse, and shouted something incomprehensible into his little black square. At least, Jess thought it was incomprehensible. She couldn't really have heard him yelling about sheep, could she?

"Maybe we'd better move," Ander suggested, his blue eyes changing from puzzled to alarmed. And then it was too late, and there was nothing to do but hold their horses and wait it out, as a large herd of sheep hit the entrance, bottlenecked briefly, and poured through.

They ran into the yard without slacking speed, until the bulk of the herd was in, milling around with a cacophony of unceasing and angry-sounding bleats. There were rams and ewes in equal numbers, and the rams seemed willing to go head-on with anything in their way—each other, a tree, part of the fence . . . A surprised looking ewe came out of the gatehouse at the pointed end of the peacekeeper's boot; Jess saw his mouth moving, but couldn't hear his voice any longer—nor did she have attention to spare, for her horse, tail clamped and back humped, quickly had his fill of the large wooled creatures and ducked his head to buck his displeasure.

Jess got him sorted out in short order, and was relieved to see his little temper tantrum had at least earned them some space, if not any quiet. But Ander's expression didn't reflect any relief at all—in fact, it was downright grim. She put her face into a question mark and when he caught her eye, he simply shook his head and pointed.

There, caught around the neck of one of the ewes, were the remnants of a red and white peacekeeper uniform.

Chapter 8

Dayna went out to the barn and sat just inside the doorway, where she'd put down an old feed sack to keep the barn's accumulation of grime, crud, and . . . *muck* from her clothing.

From there, she could see it all. She could watch the empty crates at the far end of the old building, and imagine them full of animals—pacing, snarling, angry. The way the remaining crates were arranged made it quite clear there had been more of them, but there were enough left to give Dayna some idea of the scope of this operation—and to give her the shudders, as well.

To her right were the stalls—two of them, both filthy. One had the broken door Jess had described to her. To her right, one broken small-animal cage, and generous piles of odoriferous droppings.

All in all, a thoroughly disgusting place. But inspiring. Far more inspiring than the old farmhouse and the comfortable if not luxurious accommodations it gave them. The farmhouse was huge, and had obviously been a multiple-family dwelling; there was plenty of room to house the people Jess had described, and to give them several workrooms, as well. The kitchen had probably taken some fixing, but Dayna's team had arrived to find it in working condition, with the cooler spell still functioning and provisions still stocked within.

The changespell team had settled in quickly enough,

even though Rannika hadn't been feeling well. With Rorke to do most of the mundane chores—magically insuring the plumbing pumped them hot water, the food stayed properly preserved, and the house was lit at night—there was little to distract the team from their job of creating the checkspell. They had, in fact, come up with one, and were fine-tuning it to exclude Jess, but Dayna didn't think it would work. It was too broad in scope.

The fine-tuning was being done without her, which was as it should be. She was there, after all, for her ability to take her desires and distill them into action through magic. Doing that let the more experienced members of her team follow along, and pick apart what they'd observed into the component parts so they could duplicate it.

Raw magic, that was her strength. And now, for the first time since she'd set foot on this world, it seemed to be failing her. Trying to use it did nothing but set up a discord in not only her own efforts, but those of the entire team, and Hastin, not of the most generous nature in the first place, was quick to let her know when it happened. Suddenly Dayna was realizing just how often she cheated and used raw magic when she was supposed to be memorizing spells instead. Subtle things, like little shortcuts within legitimate spells.

Frustrated and embarrassed, she'd come out here to the barn, hoping for more inspiration. Last night, thoughts of the barn had gotten her through the evening's tedious work. All she had to do was think of Jess in that stall, or picture the dead woman—a woman even more petite than Dayna herself—as the gentle and finely furred rabbit she'd once been. Probably died from fright, Shandy, who was farm-bred, had said. Rabbits did that, sometimes. And the thoughts made her tuck away the tired, whining voice in the back of her head, and get back to work.

Not today, though. Not when the interference of her

raw magic had increased so much she was being more of a hindrance than a help. Instead of returning to the farmhouse, Dayna stayed where she was, and practiced.

She ran through some spells she knew by heart, rigorously screening out her tendency to slip into the raw magic. She tried a handful of training spells, and made the surprising discovery that once she eliminated all traces of raw magic, the spells came to her more easily than ever before.

She called water up from the underground well, and then shaped it into a perfect sphere instead of her standard lumpy Play-Doh shape. She lit the barn in a handful of colors, and then blocked out all light to make it darker than night. Disgusted with the smell that suddenly seemed more obvious in that darkness, she proceeded to clean every inch of the barn without lifting a finger—and without a mistake she commonly made, which was to take a thin layer of the original material along with the dirt. Had she done that in this wreck of a barn, it probably would have fallen in on her.

And after all that, she wasn't tired at all. She stared at her hands, her nimble, obliging fingers, which had happily gestured out the elements of the spells as she'd been taught—was it this easy? Had this been the answer all along, that her raw magic was confusing the structured spells? Did she merely have to make the effort to separate the two?

Cautiously, Dayna reached for the raw magic, shaping her will to accomplish nothing more complicated than spinning a breeze down the center of the barn. Instantly, a grating noise filled the inside of her head—and almost as quickly, Shandy, the small, elderly lady whose patience with Dayna had been extraordinary during this tense project, snapped a silent, direct, "That's enough of *that*, young lady!" just barely cutting through the noise.

Which was odd enough, considering Shandy's easy

proficiency with personal messages. Dayna released the gathered raw magic in a careful trickle, no happier about the result than Shandy. Whatever the noise was, it obviously extended to affect the wizards in the farmhouse.

Then something chimed; Dayna stiffened in surprise. It was a pleasant, melodic chime, from nowhere and everywhere at once. Then, from the top of the newly pristine barn, a flutter of *something* drifted downward. The chime sounded again, and on its heels came a distorted voice, as though Dayna was listening through water. "Found you," it said, and then drawled out her name. "Daaaaayyna."

Dayna jumped to her feet, her mouth hanging open and her eyes wide and horrified. Instantly, she threw a shield around herself, but as the object dropped steadily but serenely towards the floor, impulsively dropped the shield and threw her magic—*structured* magic—at the traces of the message she'd just received.

She caught it, latching on to the whisper of a distorted laugh, racing along the lines of its origin, perceiving a blur of forests and fields and then, suddenly and painfully, crashing headlong into a sturdy, impenetrable shield.

Dayna opened her eyes to find herself on the barn floor. Her stiff body proclaimed that she'd been this way for some time, awkwardly folded around herself. Groaning, she pushed herself up, some small, wry part of herself noting that at least she'd cleaned the place up *before* she'd smeared herself on the floor.

In the center of the spotless barn lay that bit of . . . something. Not quite ready to get up, Dayna dragged herself over to it, wary despite the utter lack of magic around her. Black and green, feather and metal . . . it was identical to the darts that had taken out Jess.

Willand. Dayna's breath caught in her throat. Willand had found her.

And she had found Willand . . . hadn't she? She'd traced

that spooky message right back to its source, or as close as she could get. Hadn't she? Dayna smeared her hand across her eyes, suddenly unsure. There was no way that she, neophyte wizard, could have traced a message that far, that fast . . . especially not the message of a wizard as powerful as Willand, since Willand no doubt would have taken precautions against just such activity.

Or maybe not. Maybe she'd led Dayna along, spreading bread crumbs to keep the less accomplished wizard on her trail. Maybe she'd *wanted* to be found. And if that was the case, there was nothing but trouble in it—especially if Dayna told the others.

Carefully, Dayna got to her feet. And carefully, she aimed a small spell of incineration at the dart. In a moment, it was nothing more than a bad odor lingering in a clean barn. Dayna wasn't sure what had just happened . . . and until she was, she had no intention of mentioning the incident to the other wizards on her team.

ᴗ ᴗ ᴗ

Jaime scowled. Trust that *she* would be the one out by the gardens, stealing sweet peas from the vines and looking around the drying pastures, wondering if a rain dance would work here in Camolen, when this woman walked by. And of course, it had to be Jaime that the woman approached, first asking, and then insisting, that Jaime take her to Arlen.

The woman was Jaime's age, but heavy, and carrying most of it in her hips. Her face was plain, with small eyes and a thick, doughy set to her features. Her hair, pulled tightly back into a thin braid, did nothing to improve her looks. Neither did her attitude, which Jaime was rapidly tiring of.

"I'm *not* going to take you straight to Arlen," Jaime said. She'd tried to handle this politely and diplomatically, but those qualities were exasperated out of her, now. "I don't know you, and I'm not even going to take you into the hold, not until someone else clears you first."

"Don't be an idiot," the woman snapped. "Every moment you stall me adds danger for the both of us, no matter how well shielded you think you might be." At Jaime's surprise, she added, "Yes, I'm a wizard, and I can certainly tell an augmented shieldstone when it's in front of me. That probably means you've had trouble lately, which also probably means that Willand has a soft spot in her heart for you. Now stop playing games, and get me into that hold!"

Jaime snorted, knowing she should probably be afraid of this woman, but finding that she wasn't. "After what you just said? You've got to be kidding. I'll take you there, but you'll damned well wait outside until I get you cleared!"

"My luck to have chosen an imbecile," the woman snarled, more to herself than to Jaime. Readjusting the tight waistband of her trousers, she turned away from Jaime and headed for the hold, her steps fast and determined.

Jaime laughed. "You've got to be kidding," she repeated, easily catching up. "Which one of us do you think will get there first?"

To her astonishment, she discovered there were tears in the woman's eyes. "I don't care, as long as I *get* there," the woman snapped, as though there wasn't suddenly fear in her eyes. "I've got to get to safety, and if that means being greeted by Arlen's personal peacekeepers who want to wrestle me to the ground and slap null-magic bonds on me, then that's what I'll do!"

For the first time, Jaime hesitated. "Convince me," she said. "The hold is half a mile away. Convince me, and I can have Arlen here in seconds."

The woman was already panting. She slowed, giving Jaime a look as suspicious as the majority of the ones

Jaime had bestowed upon her. "You cause me any extra trouble, and it won't just be Willand you have to worry about."

"Threaten me, and I leave you in my dust," Jaime shot back at her.

They glared at one another a moment, and then the woman seemed to shrink into herself. She broke eye contact and said, "And there's enough dust around this place that you could do it, too."

Jaime snorted. "Just tell me what's going on."

"Well," the woman said, "I don't know who you are, but if Willand's been giving you trouble, you probably know as much about this as anyone. My name is Renia, and I'm seeking sanctuary from Willand and . . . well, another wizard you won't have heard of. Yet." The sound of hoofbeats, the three-beat rhythm of two horses in a slow and easy canter, interrupted Renia—or, rather, she interrupted herself when she heard them.

Jaime shook her head. "Couriers," she said shortly, and then suddenly hoped she was right. If this woman was on the run—but no, she was running from Willand. Willand wouldn't bother with horses.

But the woman had darted off the road anyway, and into the garden. Jaime put her hands on her hips and said, "Oh, come *on*. What are you, a rabbit?" and then couldn't account for the strange and astonished look that crossed the woman's features.

By then, the riders were coming up on her—Ander and Jess, whom she couldn't have been gladder to see. "Jess," Jaime said, as they pulled up before her. Jess's responding hail was distracted and anxious, but Jaime ignored it as something to be sorted out later, since they were clearly fine, though covered with sweat and dirt. "Grab someone at the hold, will you, and have them come down here for this—"

"You!" Jess said, her distraction turning to fury in a

heartbeat, and all the focus of that fury on the woman who was standing half hidden in the corn. Utterly astonished, Jaime stood and gaped as Jess kicked her horse forward, aiming him straight at Renia.

"Jess!" Jaime cried. "Not in the *garden*!"

Renia gave a thin scream and bolted, but Jess plowed through the corn and cut her off, her horse's hooves digging up great clods of dirt and roots as he sat on his haunches, responding to Jess like a cutting horse as Renia dodged through the garden.

"Jess!" Ander's puzzled cry echoed Jaime, but Jaime wasn't frozen stupid any more. She darted into the garden to join the fray, and was treated to several moments of blundering through the loose, fertile dirt, her vision filled with whipping cornstalks and grunting horse and screaming Renia. At last Jaime snagged Renia's sleeve, and in the next instant, got Jess's reins with the other hand.

Just pray they don't take off in opposite directions, she told herself, stretched out between them, gasping with the exertion of it all.

"She was *there*," Jess said, and her face was full of thunder. "She was one of them!"

"Burning hells," the woman gasped, astonished realization on her face. "*You*—you made it back!"

"Burning hells, *nothing*," Ander yelled from the middle of the road. "If you three don't get your dainty little feet out of that garden, *Arlen*'ll roast you without the benefit of the hells!"

Jaime looked around the ruin of the garden. "Damn," she said, then gave Renia and Jess equally stern glares. "Do I have to drag you out of here, or can I trust you to make it to the road without starting up this little war all over again?"

The woman shook herself free as Jaime slowly released the gelding's reins. Neither of them said anything; Jess restricted herself to a glare of impressive expressiveness, and the woman strode through the loose, deep dirt of the garden with as much dignity as she could muster.

Once they were all out on the road again, Jaime stood between them and gave Jess a wary look. "What's this all about, then? Who is she?"

Jess's gelding flipped his head up and down, ready to run after all the excitement. She gave his shoulder a pat without easing up on her glare and said, "Her name is Renia. She's one of the wizards who kidnapped me."

"I was *there*," Renia spat at her. "I didn't have anything to do with it."

"You didn't stop them," Jess returned without hesitation. "You let them beat me."

"What makes you think I could have done anything about it?" The wizard flipped her thin braid back behind her, and squared her shoulders. "I was *there*," she repeated. "That's all."

"Fine, you were there." Jaime stepped into the confrontation with very little patience for Renia—or for anyone who ducked responsibility so . . . airily. "What the hell are you doing *here*?"

"Running," Jess said derisively. Renia only stared at her, and didn't respond—and Jaime suddenly realized that was because Jess had responded for her.

"I've had enough of this," she decided. "Let's go. Arlen's going to want to talk to you, all right."

"That's what I was trying to tell you in the first place," the woman said, resuming her march along the road. She cast an uneasy glance around, as though expecting the sky to fall on her.

Jaime gave the woman's back a scowl, heard Jess's snort of disdain, and looked up to exchange a shrug. "Be interesting to hear why she's shown up here," Jaime said. "But I don't think she should go in the hold before Arlen checks her out. She could have some sort of tie to the other wizards who took you."

"My thoughts exactly," Ander said.

Jess held out her hand to Jaime, and kicked her foot out of the stirrup. "Then we'll get there first."

Jaime mounted up, settling in on top of the saddlebags and shifting around until the buckles weren't sticking into her knees. She wrapped her arms around Jess's waist and the gelding's haunches bunched beneath her; Jess had cued him straight to a canter—a slow, relaxed canter that nonetheless quickly passed and then left the woman behind, though her dogged little jog never faltered. Ander cantered beside them, looking over his shoulder to watch Renia.

Jaime noticed his frown as Jess halted the gelding in front of the hold, then forgot to see what it was about when she realized Arlen was waiting for them.

He stood at the entrance to the hold, the separate door from the stables that was mostly ignored and seldom used. Hands on hips, eyebrows raised, explanation clearly expected. When Jaime—and everybody else—just looked at him, he said, "I do have windows in my workroom, you know. The garden is well within sight."

Now this was what a wizard should look like, Jaime thought. Arlen wore black trousers and a deep, clear blue tunic with finely embroidered sleeves and collar, somehow understated and impressive at the same time. And he'd just had his hair cut, she thought, and the full mustache trimmed. That mustache twitched, now, and Jaime suspected it hid a smile—and figured Jess and Ander must be wearing the same expression of stupefied guilt as she was.

He shook his head and held out his arm, and Jaime took it, sliding to the ground as gracefully as possible. "Never mind the garden," she told him, turning back to the road. "There's this woman—good god, what's that?"

"I thought I saw—" Ander started, as Jess swung her horse around; Jaime's attention was riveted on the road.

The wizard was running now, or running as best she could—but Jaime didn't think it was likely to be good enough. Behind her, bringing its own dark cloud of dust and debris, a wall of wind roared down upon her.

"Get inside," Arlen ordered them, as the first wisps of a breeze plucked at Jaime's hair, making the short strands at the nape of her neck stand on end with the realization of the unnatural power that was bearing down on the hold. "I don't know if I can stop this—"

"She'll never live through it," Jaime whispered, watching the woman. Renia had been terrified that Willand would find her, that Jaime's intractability would cost her more than time. And she'd been right.

Jaime hadn't thought anyone heard her horrified realization—not above the rising sound of the winds, or the shouting that was coming from the stable. But Jess had heard, and suddenly her gelding was charging down the road, closing in on the wizard and the savage windstorm that rushed them. "Jess, no!" Jaime cried after her, knowing it was useless. There was hardly time for the cold fear to hit her stomach, before, suddenly, Ander was galloping out after Jess, bent over the saddle to duck the winds.

And Jaime just stood there, unable to do anything else. Arlen's eyes were closed in concentration; there was no way she was going to run inside and leave him here—someone had to drag him back if he sunk so far in effort to stop the wind blizzard that he lost sight of his danger. Squinting against the wind, pushing herself into it, she watched as Jess reached Renia, barely in control of the gelding. The woman reached for Jess's hand, tried to get her foot in the stirrup as Jaime had done only moments before, but the gelding skittered around in the wind like a leaf about to lose its grip on a tree, and Renia was simply too heavy, too tired, to keep up.

A section of road, sucked up by the vacuum of abruptly

changing wind, popped out of the ground some distance behind them, spattering them with dirt and stone, and the gelding reared. If the full strength of that storm reached them—Jaime snuck a look at Arlen, whispering, "Oh, Arlen, hurry—" even though the words were snatched out of her mouth before they made it into sound. Something pelted her—a rock, a small stick, who knew—and she cringed, unwilling to leave Arlen, and unwilling to drag him away from his efforts while Jess and Ander fought time and wind.

Ander had reached Renia, had flung himself from the saddle and choked his reins up brutally short to hold the horse while Renia tried to mount. Ander gave her a healthy shove and she plopped into the saddle; he released the reins and smacked the horse, and it bolted for the stable.

Jess's hair was whipping in the wind; her cap was between her teeth. Ander managed the mount Renia could not, and Jess let the gelding go. The horse galloped for the stable, its neck outstretched and its ears pinned back, staggering once when a substantial piece of debris bounced off his haunches. The road exploded behind them again, closer, and then Jaime couldn't help it, she was screaming at them, "Run, run, *run*."

Someone—*Arlen*—snatched her arm and dragged her away, and the wind buffeted her until she literally fell through the doorway. Arlen dove in behind her, slamming the door and sealing it with a quick gesture and a flare of power around its edges.

"The stable," Jaime said hoarsely, and he didn't so much as nod before sprinting down the hallway, bumping his shoulders as he tried to regain his own windblown balance.

She wobbled after him and soon got her legs sorted out. Deep in the hold she couldn't hear or feel the wind, but she *knew* it was there, and she threaded the hallways to the stable at a dead run, not even pausing after the near collision at one of the corners.

The scene she found, when she finally ran past the duty room and into the stable proper, was nothing like she'd expected, and it stopped her short.

She'd thought she'd find chaos, and wind damage, and injured and panicking horses. Instead she found silence, and Arlen facing off against Renia. Jess stood aside, alone, from the remaining cluster of Carey, Ander, the two geldings, and several others—couriers, grooms, who knew what. The stable door was closed and secure, and Jaime didn't think Arlen had had the time to do it. Renia, then.

Jess had a peculiar look on her face, perhaps just now realizing how much she'd risked for this woman who'd participated in her captivity; she was watching Renia and Arlen like she hoped to find out if it had been worth it.

But it was Arlen's expression that drew Jaime in; she saw the glitter of his anger, and a stiffness in his shoulders that said he'd been somehow offended. And there, in his eyes, in the quizzical, miniature lift to his brows, she saw that he wasn't sure who, of the two of them, would come out on top if he pushed his anger past Renia's breaking point.

Jaime wanted to run and throw her arms around him, as if she could make everything all right. It would, of course, be the worst thing in the world, so instead she just stayed where she was, feeling the surprise that lingered on her own features.

Renia flipped her braid back over her shoulder and tugged at a tear in her blouse so it didn't gape quite so widely over the slope of her ample breast. "I tried to get here before something like that could happen," she said, as though continuing a conversation in progress, although Jaime had the impression no one had yet said anything. She glanced meaningfully at Jaime. "I was delayed."

Jaime kept her voice level. "I had no intention of bringing you into this hold until Arlen said it was safe to do so. It was the right decision, and I'd do it again."

Arlen nodded. "So it was. And since—thanks to Jess and Ander—you're here despite that little windstorm, I think you'd better start explaining yourself. That storm was shielded, or I would have detected it long before it became such a problem. And there's only one group around here with the ability to shield major magics."

"Here?" Renia said, glancing around the stable with a touch of scorn. "You want me to tell you *all*? Here?"

"No," Arlen snapped. "I want you to dig deep and find the manners your mother taught you, and then I want you to follow me."

Jaime had to suppress a smile at the look on Renia's face—which wasn't hard, when she thought of how close Jess and Ander had come to being hurt or killed along with the rude new arrival. She glanced at Arlen, wanting very much to be included in the discussion to come, although it was clearly Council business.

Arlen nodded at her, the slightest tilt of his head, but his wary attention remained on Renia—and would, Jaime suspected, as long as the wizard was in his hold.

❧ ❧ ❧

Arlen and Renia stared at one another. Both were windblown—it would take more than the quick pass of Arlen's fingers through his hair to tame it, and Renia's wind-burned cheeks flushed red in her otherwise pale face. Her blouse was torn in several places and not nearly the quality of Arlen's tunic to begin with—but if she was intimidated by her poor presentation, her face didn't show it. Her face held the look of a wizard who's neatly outperformed a colleague.

That's not how Jess thought of it. Arlen could have done the same, if he'd been in the stable instead of at the side entrance. She sat on the floor in front of Carey as Renia looked around the meeting room and said, "We might as well have had this conversation in the stable, for all the privacy we've got here."

They were on the third floor, in one of the rooms that until recently had been utilized by Dayna's team. Not Arlen's private workroom or one of the cozier meeting rooms on the top floor. But Jess knew this room could be sealed and isolated from the rest of the hold, and wondered if Renia could tell.

Renia was too busy looking around the spartan room, with its no-nonsense furnishings—a long wooden table and lightly cushioned, straight-backed chairs, walls bare of decoration save a stylized version of Arlen's name, identical to the brand that curved behind Jess's ear and the seal that secured all of Arlen's messages. It was clear that Renia had expected more from the hold of a top Council wizard like Arlen, just as it was clear she resented the presence of Jess, Ander, Jaime, and Carey.

"Thanks to Willand's activities, they," Arlen nodded around the room, "know as much about what's been happening in Camolen lately as anyone. And," he added pointedly, "they're my friends, not to mention the people that saved your life. Strictly speaking, they may not belong in this conversation. But it's my call, not yours." He leaned back in his chair at the head of the table and said, "There will be two more. I've called my apprentices, and we'll wait until they get here." He reached to the center of the table, where a pitcher of cold tea and neatly arranged glasses had been waiting for them, and poured several servings, pushing one of them at the wizard. "You must be thirsty after your run. Help yourself after you finish this."

Without acknowledging his comment, Renia took the tea, downing half of the glass without pause. Jess leaned against Carey's legs and gave the woman a hard look, hoping she'd hear enough here to make her impulse to ride into the winds seem like a good one. Behind her, Carey pulled the metal comb he'd snagged from his room on the way up, and ran his hand over Jess's hopelessly tangled hair. The wind had turned it into a snarl made of snarls, and he leaned over to murmur in her ear, "We may have to cut it, Jess."

"No," she told him. She'd been in worse shape, especially that time when she was a yearling and had rolled in some burr bushes.

She heard the rustle of material that meant he'd shrugged. "All right," he said. "I'll try not to pull, but . . ."

Jess didn't say anything. Having him groom her in human form was a luxury, whether he was pulling at tangles or not. And it was the one time he seemed perfectly willing to touch her—because, she thought, he always seemed to be distracted by something else—and simply let his hands do what they wanted. What they *should*, as far as she was concerned.

Natt hustled into the room, looking more than a little harried. He was old for an apprentice, from what Jess had seen—he was in his twenties, and his features and demeanor held an air of maturity that Cesna lacked. "We saw it coming," he told Arlen, after a quick glance at Renia. "We tried to seal off the workroom, but there's going to be some picking up to do. Cesna'll be right here—she's getting damage reports from other parts of the hold." He stopped, obviously thinking about the windstorm, and shook his head. "What was that all about, anyway? I've never even heard of a spell like that—that powerful, and on that large a scale."

Arlen said, "Check your history. There were plenty of them set out in the border wars between Therand and Solvany, before they became precincts. It's just that folks have been too civilized of late to use them."

"No doubt you have spells for air circulation that make

checkspells for that sort of thing impossible," Jaime said dryly.

Arlen gave a regretful nod. "We use one in this hold, as a matter of fact—in the stable area, especially."

Jess winced as Carey's comb snagged in a tiny little tangle, nodding at his murmured, "Sorry." She glanced at Jaime and her recently shortened hair, and wondered, for a moment, what such a style would look like when she was Lady—then decided she didn't want to find out.

Cesna strode into the room, closing the door behind her with a series of clicks—one from the door, and one from the magic that now sealed them all in. Renia glanced at the door with a startled look, as if she hadn't counted on Arlen to be so cautious. She was trapped here, now, until he decided to release her.

"The hold did pretty well," Cesna said without preamble. She stopped next to Jess and Carey and sat in the chair Jaime shoved over to her. "The garden is completely destroyed, of course. And Carey . . . they got the stallion in before the storm, so he's all right, but half his fence is down. And I'm sorry to say one of this spring's foals was killed by flying debris—the groom who was trying to get him in was hurt, too, but she'll be all right."

Carey's hands stilled a moment, hesitating in the midst of a tangle. Jess heard the small noise he made in his throat; after a moment, he cleared it and said, "Thank you, Cesna. It . . . could have been worse."

"It could have been better, too," Jaime said fiercely, looking at Renia through suddenly reddened eyes. "Why are you here? Why is Willand after you? And why do you have such a goddam bad attitude?"

Yes. Answers Jess wanted, as well.

"That's an earth expression, I'd guess," Renia said coolly, "and undoubtedly not a pleasant one. I didn't come here for abuse."

Arlen rubbed a finger down his mustache and said quietly, "What *did* you come here for, Renia?"

His tone of voice made it as much of a threat as a question; for a moment, no one said anything, completely focused on Renia's answer. She looked back at them, resentful; Jess thought she saw a spark of fear in the woman's small eyes, as well. Good.

The silence stretched out a moment; Carey's fingers worked through Jess's hair, a touch more intimate than she'd ever felt as Lady. Cesna, glancing at his difficulties, rested her hand on top of Jess's head a moment, and suddenly the comb met less resistance; Jess glanced up her thanks and discovered Renia watching, her expression an unpleasant mixture of envy and resentment. Jess returned her gaze, a hard, unyielding look; it was Renia who looked away.

"I'm not sure anymore," Renia said, sounding like a sullen child as she finally answered Arlen's question.

"Let me guess," Arlen said. "I've seen what you can do—it was no small thing, closing that stable door against the wind and then shielding it. And since I know everyone in Camolen with that sort of power, and I *don't* know you, you must be in with the group that's been hiding itself from the rest of us. The ones who took Jess. She had a reason for going after you in that garden."

Renia just looked at him, and Arlen stared back for a long moment, then continued. "The fact that you're here means you had some reason to leave them—not a friendly one, or we wouldn't be spending the next week making repairs from that distinctly unnatural windstorm. And I suppose you thought you'd arrive here and receive great welcome, and all sorts of gratitude from us that you'd come to help explain what's been going on." He leaned over the table, weight on his elbows. "The thing is, we've already pretty much got it figured out. And we're really not very happy about what you've been up to. So this little reception of cheery, grateful faces is about as good as you're going to get."

They pretty much had it figured out? That was news to Jess, who tilted her head to look back at Carey. The glance he gave her was eloquent in its hard, silent request—*say nothing*. Jess thought about the peacekeeper sheep, but did as Carey wanted.

Arlen tapped the corner of his mustache, eyeing Renia's continued silence. "You wouldn't have left without some damn good reasons. Which means you had something to gain by coming here. What is it you want, Renia?"

Renia stared another moment and then said abruptly, "Sanctuary!"

"In exchange for?" Arlen's voice was as hard as Jess had ever heard it. Renia fell back into silence, hesitant this time. "Did you think it would come for free, after all the trouble you've caused?"

She looked at him, looked away, bit her lip, and started to cry.

"Oh, stop it," Arlen said. "You got yourself into this. You broke some of the most stringent Council rules to do it." His voice was brusque, but this time Jess heard a note of sympathy in it. "Let me make a suggestion. You don't have much of a bargaining position if you really want sanctuary here—we have witnesses to your crimes, and we also already have a pretty good idea of what we're up against, should your friends *really* decide to come after you. I have no intention of telling you what we do or don't know, and giving you the chance to confirm it. *You* tell *us*—and you tell us everything. You can leave things out, you can lie—but you'll never know if *I* know better." He leaned back in his chair, fingers laced in front of his hips, and said matter-of-factly, "Of course, if you do lie, and I do happen to know better, that's the end of sanctuary."

She hesitated only a moment. "All right," she said. "I intended to tell you everything, anyway, so that's not much of a concession. But I want your word that you won't suck everything you can from me and then toss me back to the others when things get a little tough. They didn't think much of me; they may not bother with more impressive attempts to do me in. But if they do, I want to know you won't betray me. I want your official oath on it."

Carey's hands stopped moving through Jess's hair, which was nearly combed out, anyway. Arlen's eyebrows disappeared into his grayed-to-steel hair a moment, and Jaime gave him an uncertain look. "I take it that's pretty serious stuff."

Arlen nodded. "It is. Usually it's a ceremonial thing. To be done under these circumstances is . . . a tad insulting. But I can't say as I blame her. You have it, Renia. When we finish here, we'll go up to my workshop and take care of it—assuming we don't have to reconstruct the room first. But I want you to start talking *now*."

Renia shook her head; her voice was tight. She was, Jess realized, truly frightened. "The oath."

Arlen didn't look the least bit concerned. "I don't think so. Not until I get a flavor of what you've brought us—and how truthful you're going to be. Not everything, don't worry. Just a taste."

Renia hesitated, but everyone in the room knew she had no choice at this point. She knew it, too. "All right," she said again, sounding weary. "Let's talk."

"The sheep," Jess said suddenly, startling them all and drawing Arlen's sudden frown. "Tell him about the sheep first."

Renia's eyes widened. "He did it?" she said, sounding aghast.

Jess nodded, and said, "Tell him."

"Yes," Arlen said, pouring himself some more tea, though his gaze never left Renia. His voice was uncompromising. "Tell me about the sheep."

Chapter 9

Renia, Jaime thought, was the classic whiner. She made decisions in life that created trouble for herself and every one around her, and then felt unjustly persecuted when everybody else objected, and even perhaps let Renia know they resented her actions.

Jaime had no patience for it at all. Not when it was Renia's people who were keeping her here, with horse shows approaching and her careful training plan going awry. And yes, it was nice to have an extended visit with her Camolen friends, but enough was enough, and with Willand on the loose and everybody she knew looking over their shoulder, it wasn't exactly a relaxing vacation.

Jess, at least, had had to get on with her life here. Kymmet Stables wanted her and Ander back, and though Arlen offered to speak up for them, Jess had decided to go. She'd left that morning, her face and neck still marked by fading bruises—that whip cut on her jaw was certainly going to leave a scar—and her expression uncertain despite her determination to lead her life normally regardless of the outlaw wizards.

Renia had found it hard to believe she had been considered outlaw from the start. "Plenty of wizards go into seclusion when they're working on a new spell," she'd said the day before, after she'd finally begun to talk. "So what if a group of us got together and did the same? We weren't working on anything forbidden."

"How do you know?" Arlen said. "There's a procedure for developing major new spells, and it involves running a prospectus through the Council. In fact, the Council hasn't—or *hadn't* yet made up its collective mind regarding work on changespells, beyond Jess. You may or may not have been given permission, depending on your goals and procedures."

Renia's pallid face flushed deeply. "We were a bunch of lower-level wizards, and the Council always made sure we knew it. Any application we made would have been dismissed on those grounds, and you know it. We never would have had a chance to try it *your* way."

"You might have tried," Arlen said mildly. He glanced at Jess, and his voice hardened. "You might have gotten some helpful guidance on what is and what is not considered humane treatment of experimental spell subjects."

"What, *after* they turned us down?" Renia said. "I don't think so. Look, all we wanted to do was spell an effective changeover in certain animals—the ones that would be especially suited for some of the occupations normal humans are doing now. Once trained, they'd be twice as good at it. And they wouldn't require the same sort of compensation."

Jaime's temper, already at its edge, flared high, but when she turned it on Renia she found her voice was lost in similar protests from Carey and Ander. At once, they all realized that Jess, the voice that should have been the loudest, was silent.

She was sitting beside Carey, and the look in her dark eyes as she regarded Renia was cold enough to give Jaime a chill. Deliberately, she got to her feet, every movement full of the lithe athleticism that proclaimed her *other*. She looked down on Renia, flipping her head back in the short, abrupt gesture that was equine disdain and objection. The black stripe that was mane and forelock in Lady's form spread out over the dark dun color of the rest of her hair, and her nostrils flared slightly in what was yet another loud equine statement. She was, Jaime thought, as much horse as anyone in human form could get. She flaunted it before Renia, and stamped it with her pride.

And then she turned to Arlen and said evenly, "I saved her life because I was human enough to do it. I came here to find out if *she* was human enough to have deserved it, and now I know. I would like to leave now."

Good for you, Jess, Jaime thought. *You can show her what it means to be humane better than we can ever tell her.*

"Of course, Jess," Arlen murmured, gesturing quietly at the door. It not only unsealed for her, it also opened. And after Jess had taken leave, it closed and sealed again. Arlen turned to Renia and said, "You *will* watch what you say in this hold. I have sworn to protect you from without—but not from within."

Renia clearly didn't quite get it. But she was wise enough not to protest, and not to say anything that made her shortcomings any more obvious. She glanced uncertainly around the table, finding nothing but hostility; when she looked at Jaime, Jaime gave her a cold, mirthless little smile that clearly declared her position.

"Let's forego discussion about your goals," Arlen said. "I'd like to know how you were accomplishing them. For a group of lower-level wizards who were so certain the Council would ignore you, you seem to have done quite nicely."

He did not, Jaime noticed, acknowledge the fact that he'd seen Renia accomplish that which would have tasked him. She knew enough about the situation to know Arlen was playing a brilliant hand of poker with this woman—and so far, he was winning. He was getting information from a wizard who was—somehow—probably powerful enough to resist any magical persuasion the Council was willing to apply.

"We found a way to combine our abilities," Renia said vaguely, and then immediately changed the subject. "But none of this is relevant to why I'm here, and that's the only other thing I'm going to tell you before I get that oath." She waited for Arlen's nod, and even then seemed to hesitate. "About those sheep . . ." she started, and stopped.

Arlen looked at Ander, which was all Ander needed. "The peacekeepers were running stalking games today," he said, staring hard at Renia, and Jaime thought the tone of his words was more suited to a different sentiment altogether, one that gave Renia precise instructions on what anatomically impossible functions she could perform. "And it looks like one of the companies figured out what was happening with all the missing pairs. Every last one of them returned to the hold as sheep."

Arlen literally choked in horrified astonishment. "*Sheep?*"

A self-satisfied little look crossed Renia's face. "It looks like you didn't know as much as you thought you did." At the collective expression of anger that turned upon her, she cleared her throat and started again, her tone much more humble. "It's Jenci. He's been with us from the start, and he's been playing with his own experiments all along, but once Willand got there, he . . . changed. He said our goals weren't impressive enough, and that we need *more*, something that would help protect us when the Council got jealous of our accomplishments. Before we knew it, he was in the advanced stages of work on the reverse changespell. It seems to suit his odd sense of humor to pick the peacekeepers out as his . . . experimental victims."

And that was all they got out of her. She'd claimed to be tired, and hungry, and not about to reveal anything else without Arlen's official oath. Well, Jaime had believed the part about being hungry and tired—*she* was, and heaven knows Ander had to be, after the run to the peacekeepers. So they'd disbanded, and gone their separate ways. Now Jaime was helping fix the stallion's enclosure, and Renia was in a safe room while Arlen met with the Council. Jess was on her way home—and Carey had gone on a morning run, still wearing the same expression Jaime had seen on his face as he watched Jess and Ander riding away together.

He'd noticed Jaime watching, managed a grin of sorts, and said, "Opportunities not taken," and walked away. She didn't suppose he imagined she knew what he was talking about. Sometimes she felt like the only one who *did* know what was going on between people.

She certainly knew what was going on with herself. She had nothing more than mild curiosity over how Willand had gotten involved with Renia's group, or who had managed to free her from confinement. She wasn't interested in the details Arlen was even now hashing out with the Council, on how they would protect the peacekeepers until they pried the outlaw wizards' location from Renia—assuming it was still accurate—and how Renia was to be treated in the interim. She didn't care about the strategy for rounding up the outlaws when they were found. All she wanted to know was that Willand was caught, and that Jess was safe from her *and* the changespell wizards. And then she wanted to go home.

ઉ ઈ ઉ

Lady cropped angrily at Kymmet's freshly—magically—irrigated grass, the only green pastures for miles around. The snorts she made were nothing less than equine curses, and the spellstones jingling pleasantly by her ear only underscored that she was, in fact, still Lady.

"Jess, I know there's some part of you in there," Ander said, leaning over the fence of the small, isolated paddock Lady had occupied for far too long. "You've been in there for five days now. Let me change you back."

Deliberately, Lady turned her back on him, placing the spellstones well out of his reach. She tore the grass off in vicious little snatches, not paying half enough attention to what was going into her mouth—so when she discovered the sour little yellow hops clover, it had already fouled everything in her mouth. She spit it out and headed to the small water trough in the corner. Ander might as well not have been there.

"Jess, enough is enough," Ander said, trying the Stern Voice. It wouldn't do him any good; Lady had a sterner voice in her head.

Jess had made a decision—to change to Lady and to stay that way until Lady changed herself back. Yes, it had been five days. And yes, she wanted to be Jess again, to take up the responsibility of her job as her boss Koje wanted her to. But more than that, she wanted *control*—over her life, and her form. Jess had been thinking very hard about that as she changed to Lady, and Lady was nothing if not persistent, especially not with Carey's *you're no quitter* echoing in her memory.

Ander sighed, loudly. He pinged a small pebble off Lady's side, next to the strip of flesh healing from Shammel's whip. She laid her ears back at him and returned to the grass. "All right, look," he said. "I didn't want to do this, but you're not exactly making it easy. Koje's riding me pretty hard, got it? Willsey's having some trouble with the gelding you delivered a while back, and Koje wants you to go straighten it out. I've held her off for two days now, but I can't do it any longer."

Lady raised her head and looked at him, pulling out the meanings of a handful of words but relying more on the new note in his voice. No cajoling, no urging, no *give up, Jess*. This was Ander needing her—needing Jess. And Koje's name, she knew well enough.

Swallowing the grass in her mouth, Lady walked over to the paddock gate, where Ander met her, his expression full of relief. "It's about time," he said. At his tone, Lady's ears canted back a notch. She wished nipping wasn't against the Rules—but there were other ways. She greeted Ander with the enthusiasm of a horse that needed its own personal face-scratching post, and slimed him from shoulder to elbow with watery green spit.

⁂

Jess rode for home, her thoughts hopping back and forth between Willsey's problems with her BayBoy—which were, indeed, Willsey's problems and not the horse's—and the most recent news from the Lorakan mountains.

She'd been right to have concern over Willsey's choice of the gelding; his natural power and speed meant he was good for the short runs she usually took, but it also meant he needed a rider who could handle his big gaits. Willsey had been trying to smooth her rides, but instead of encouraging him to move in a more balanced frame, which he was certainly capable of doing, she had only choked him back, tightening on the reins until the unhappy gelding took to head slinging and occasional fits of crow hopping.

Jess made Kymmet's standard offer—she would take the gelding back, minus a fee for the retraining he'd need, or Willsey was welcome to come to Kymmet for several weeks for a personal clinic, and learn how to handle him properly.

Willsey was so pleased at that prospect that she let Jess in on the latest from the Lorakans, even as she admitted that Aashan had been *spoken to* about keeping Council business to herself. After all, Willsey said, Aashan wasn't getting her news from Council sources, so how could it be strictly Council business?

Jess didn't bother to untangle that bit of human rationalization. What interested her was the mage lure.

The old border warning spell that Willsey had told her about had been triggered by the presence of mage lure crossing from Therand to Loraka. Mage lure, Willsey told her, was hardly more than a myth as far as the rest of Camolen was concerned, and all she knew was that it used to be a drug, and that wizards had once taken it, though at some risk—why, she couldn't say. Willsey had laughed about it. She was sure that if such a thing still existed, *everyone* would know about it by now.

But Willsey hadn't been captured by a group of shielded outlaw wizards. And Willsey hadn't outrun a windstorm even Arlen couldn't tame. Willsey, who always knew so much about the little juicy details of high-level Lander life, seemed to be completely blind to the bigger things happening in Camolen.

Jess hadn't been about to tell her. She made arrangements for Willsey to come to Kymmet, and she left. And now she was trying very hard not to push her mount in the afternoon heat just because she was eager to return to Kymmet.

Dark clouds dogged her all the way home, threatening rain but offering only humidity. Despite her care, she and the horse both arrived in Kymmet sweaty and tired. Hurried or not, she gave him a cool sponge bath before turning him out to pasture, and then wiped down her arms and bent over and flipped her hair out of the way to squeeze the sponge over the back of her neck.

That's when Ander showed up, of course; he was standing there, waiting, when she straightened, with little rivers of water running down her back and plastering her tunic to her chest. Ander looked away, and commented only, "You made good time, considering the heat. The gelding all right?"

"BayBoy," Jess said, using Willsey's name for the horse. "She needs a personal clinic. I knew he was not right for her. I should have said no."

Ander shrugged. "It's not only your decision, Jess. Aashan liked the horse, too—he's flashy, you know, suits her style just fine. And the Kymmet Landers liked the price she offered."

"Still," Jess said, and that was all. She dropped the sponge back in her bucket and picked it up, heading for the barn.

"What's got you all fired up?" Ander said, following her. "It's hot. It's almost dinner time. Slow down or you'll melt before you get it. Or," he added suddenly, as if in sudden inspiration, "are you still upset about that changespell thing?"

Jess didn't slow, but did throw a frowning glance at him. *That changespell thing.* How neatly he wrapped up something so important into three little words! "I have not given up."

He caught up with her, mostly because she'd slowed to carefully tip the remains of the bucket back into the water cleanser the stable wizards had created—this season, no one simply *threw out* water. "I don't like to see you getting so fixated on it," he said. "I can't believe you stayed a horse for so long this time—what's so bad about having Koje or me change you back?"

Jess left the bucket inside her tack stall and slammed the bolt home to close the stall door. "You aren't always there," she said simply. "I don't like to *depend*."

Ander frowned. "There's nothing wrong with having to depend on people, Jess. We all do, for one thing or another. To tell the truth, it's kind of nice to know you depend on me for *something*."

She did stop, that time, right in the middle of the door

that aimed her at the courier quarters. "I depend on you for friendship," she said. "I don't understand—" but she cut herself short. She didn't understand why Ander *wanted* her to depend on him so much, but she suddenly realized just how much that was true. It was why he tried to make decisions for her—and why he was always there to help when he thought she needed it—whether or not she really did.

She shook her head, disregarding the puzzled look on his face. This was nothing she wanted to take the time to understand now. "I have to go to Kymmet."

"Why?" Ander said, alert.

She said simply, "Come and find out."

Kymmet had a spell booth set permanently to a public city receiver, as well as its own receiving site. The couriers were allowed a modest number of free uses, and Jess always had a generous number of transfers accrued in her favor; the city seldom lured her in, save for the library—and even then, she usually walked. She signed off for a two-way use and then signed off again for Ander, who was more likely to be short on transfers. He saw her do it and just grinned thanks at her.

From the city receiving booth center, it was only a few blocks to the library, and Jess stretched her legs, ignoring the stream of people around her, and the occasional look she drew—even after she realized it was because she'd forgotten to change her damp tunic.

Kymmet was full of people doing important things and thinking important things and trying to make themselves look even more important than they'd been the day before—or, that was what Carey told Jess when she'd wondered why they spent so much time in such an unnatural place. At least the tall buildings around them offered shade, although they also cut out what little breeze the day offered. The city was neat enough—at least, this section of it; there were others that Carey warned her from and Ander wouldn't take her to—and the buildings were surrounded by tiny little islands of greenery and boasted the occasional fountain. Jess wasn't fooled—this was a place of brick and stone, not a living area like Arlen's hold.

Except for the library grounds, which were the Higher Level university's frontispiece to the city. Higher Level priests staffed the library, and while they never offered her conversation—Ander had once told her it wasn't anything personal, they were just like that—they were pleasant enough if you had questions to ask.

Someday Jess would ask them what the Levels were all about, anyway, aside from something for people to use in cursing. Jaime had said it seemed like Hinduism to her, but then had been vague in explanation. As far as Jess could tell, most of the people in Camolen seemed to accept that when you died, you went to one of the Nine Levels of either heaven or hell, depending on how you behaved in life. But only the priests seemed to spend a lot of time thinking about it.

She stopped before the library, in the spot where she always stopped, never failing to think about the library Eric had first taken her to in Ohio, and how he'd helped her learn to read. That always meant a moment of sadness for Eric, but they were moments she'd learned to treasure, because it was when she always felt closest to him, as if he hadn't died at all.

Ander misinterpreted her hesitation. "They're still open," he said, pushing through the token gate and into the lush gardens. Alongside the brick paths, the ground was covered in dense, short vines, impossibly tangled in one another and endlessly flowering. They set the stage for the patches of flowers, shrubs and small trees, all of which housed a noisy diversity of birds.

Normally, Jess took her time here, trying to sort the birds and seeing if she could spot any new flowers—

those were all Eric things to do, too. Today, she gently set her Eric thoughts aside, and followed Ander to the library itself.

The library building was surprisingly short, just a quiet stone structure in the gardens. Jess entered with Ander behind her—for once, he was not the one who knew all about their task. This was Jess's domain, not his. She took him to the big circular desk in the middle of the open hallway that made the single room of the first level, and told the priest there what she was looking for.

He raised an eyebrow at her, but said nothing; after a moment's consultation with his logs, he wrote out the location of several books for her, and told her to come back if she needed more.

"I'll never understand why you come here as often as you do," Ander said, his voice hushed as she took him down the stairway to the first sublevel—for all the library's shelving was underground, and the books spelled against damage and time. "It always gives me the urge to shout."

"Shout what?" Jess asked, consulting her list and deciding to go all the way downstairs and work her way up.

"Just shout," Ander said. "All this . . . quiet."

She said, "I like the quiet. And I like the books. They're different from the books Eric gave me . . . but when I read them, they answer questions for me." She glanced at him, and saw he didn't truly understand. "I have a *lot* of questions," she told him, leading him through a maze of shelving to reach the book she wanted.

He grinned. "That much, I know," he said, accepting the book she gave him. They'd have to get one of the priests to release its binding spell so they could open it, but there wasn't any point in that until she had them all.

Eventually, they ended up in the study area that took up the entire sub-four level, a stack of books spread out before them. Together they flipped through them, checking for references to mage lure. And when they pushed the last thick, stiff-paged book aside, Ander looked at the notes Jess had made in her careful printing and made a face. "There's not much *anyone* seems to know about this stuff."

Jess picked the page up and ran her fingers across it, enjoying the smooth feel of the paper, and the texture her printing gave it. "No," she agreed. "I think they all wanted it forgotten."

Ander shook his head. "That's no way to keep it from becoming a problem again," he said. "And I can sure see why they'd—wizards—consider this a problem."

Jess looked at the notes and nodded. Mage lure. Almost instantly addictive, often fatal over the long run with side effects along the way, fatal if discontinued without treatment . . . it also boosted a wizard's ability to channel magic many times over. There were no references to it in the recent past; all the information they found came from books several hundred years old, chronicling what at that time was recent history, and the apparent victory in the fight to eradicate mage lure altogether.

It'd been made on the southeast coast of Camolen, in Therand—when it was still a separate country instead of a precinct. Even then, very few people knew of the drug's existence—only those high-level wizards who manipulated its use. It was derived from a native plant, which none of the books would name, and several hundred years earlier had been considered obliterated—the underground distribution destroyed, the production sites razed, the recipe wiped from the minds of all who'd been involved.

And that was it.

"Jess?" Ander said, and his voice had a strong edge to it. Jess realized she'd been staring at the notes for some moments, and set the page down.

"Do you think the old border spell was right?" she asked.

"After all this time?" Ander shrugged. "Old spells decay and lose their precision. The thing could have been triggering at headache powder for all we know. I'm sure they've checked that possibility. I'm *not* sure Aashan had all the facts, or if she did, that Willsey remembered them all."

"Willsey usually gets it right," Jess said. "It's part of her job to remember details about her runs for Aashan."

Ander snorted. "That sounds right," he said. "She'd probably want to know just how her messages were received." He shook his head. "I dunno, Jess. This stuff sounds pretty powerful, and hardly worth playing with. The science of wizardry has come a long way since it was last in use—who knows if it would even work as well with today's methods. But . . ."

"Those outlaw wizards," Jess finished.

"It's a pretty strong argument," Ander agreed. "What do you want to do about it?"

Jess blinked. She hadn't thought about that. Slowly, she said, "I don't know . . . Arlen needs to know. But that won't be good for Willsey."

"Arlen already knows," Ander scoffed. "You don't think Aashan could scare up gossip this important all by herself, do you? She's just the only one who stoops to passing it on to high-level Landers who like to think they're more important than they are."

Of course Arlen already knew. They hadn't really accomplished anything here—except now *they* knew, and understood, what they were up against in the outlaw wizards—and in Willand, who had made it no secret that she wanted to get her hands on Jess, to trap her in equine form forever. If she truly had access to mage lure, Jess wasn't sure there was anyone who could stop her.

What do you want to do about it? Ander had asked. Jess pulled half the stack of books toward her and shoved the other half toward Ander. "I have to teach the Lady in me to trigger that changespell."

Ander groaned—but it wasn't as heartfelt as it might have been, and this time, Jess thought, there was a glimmer of understanding, and fear, in his eyes.

❦ ❦ ❦

"Drugs?" Jaime repeated, looking from Natt to Cesna to Arlen. "This is about drugs?"

"I don't know that I'd put it that way," Arlen said. "Most certainly mage lure is involved, no matter how much Therand protests the idea. But this is *about* power and greed."

"No, it's not," Jaime said, closing her eyes and very deliberately clenching her jaw in lieu of, say, screaming. In her mind's eye she saw herself and her friends moments after their unexpected travel to Camolen from Ohio. Jess, in equine form again after months learning to be human, down and in deep shock. Her brother Mark and herself, slowly beginning to realize what had happened. Carey, numbed at finding Jess a horse, when he'd only just realized how much he loved her as a human—and Dayna, crying out her anguish over Eric's still-warm body.

And then, some distance from the grieving friends, the stumbling figure of a two-bit hood from Ohio, the man Carey's enemy Derrick had chosen to help him in that new land. The man with the unlikely Sesame Street name of Ernie—and the man who had killed Eric. Transported here along with the rest of them, and running free.

Dayna would have killed him then, with her grief and her innate and ignorant use of raw magic, but Carey—who knew the dangers of uncontrolled raw magic—had stopped her. And Ernie had disappeared into the nearby woods. After that, in their struggle to survive, none of them had given him much thought.

It had, Jaime realized, been a mistake. She opened

her eyes to find all three wizards staring at her. They were in Arlen's rooms, where he had chosen to reveal the news of the mage lure to his apprentices, and where Jaime had been sitting, thinking—no, let's face it, moping—about the disruption in her horses' training. Now she carefully stroked the little cat in her lap and said again, "No, it's not. It's about drugs, Arlen. Deep in the heart of it, it's about drugs."

He was wearing that same deep blue, embroidered and satiny tunic he'd had on when Renia had joined them. He ran his fingers along the embroidery in absent thought. "I'm sure there's a reason you think so," he said. "Care to share it?"

"Ernie," Jaime said, and then got impatient when they remained obviously unenlightened. "Think, Arlen. Remember what came out at the hearings? When we first got here, we had another man with us, the one who killed Eric. He ran off, and we never gave him another thought—we figured he'd have enough on his hands, just trying to adjust and survive in this world on his own. We should have known he'd find the right layer of societal slime to thrive in."

"Forgive me," Arlen said, "but I don't understand why you're so sure this man has anything to do with our situation."

Jaime took a deep breath. "You've been on my world enough to have at least heard a reference to the drug problem there." She glanced at Cesna and Natt, adding, "Recreational and mind-altering drugs that pose dangers to the users, and are illegal. There's an entire class of people who specialize in dealing in those drugs. I don't know for *certain* that Ernie was one of them, but I'd stake anything on it."

"You think Ernie got his hands on some mage lure and became involved with Renia's group," Arlen said, trying it out for size.

"For all I know, Ernie *heard* about mage lure and spent the last year finding someone who could recreate it for him," Jaime said bitterly. The cat, disturbed by her tension and anger, finally gave up on her and jumped to the floor. "Once he had it, it would have given him more than just profit. It would have given him the means for revenge. Do you suppose it was just coincidence that the outlaws chose to work on the changespell? And that Willand, the woman who sweetly declared revenge on us all, was the one who escaped from her prison?"

Arlen looked at her for a long moment. "No," he said. "When you put it that way, I don't think it was coincidence at all. But I know how we can find out."

"Assuming Renia feels like talking today," Natt said, frustration evident. "I can't help but wonder if she's *really* been sick since she got here—or if she's still trying to protect her friends."

"She didn't look very well to me," Cesna said. "Not that she's exactly cooperative, mind you, but considering the protection the Council has offered if she talks, I'm inclined to think she'll talk soon enough. After all, she *did* tell us about the illicit travel site she used to get here. We're a lot safer now that you've destroyed it."

Jaime frowned. "Arlen," she said, "what was it you were saying about that drug? How it had so many drawbacks that it never did achieve wide usage, even before it was eliminated?"

Arlen looked at her in alarm. "Dangerous drawbacks," he said. "Withdrawal problems—fatal ones."

"Renia," Cesna whispered, looking suddenly horrified.

"Oh, Burning Ninth," Natt groaned. "But you'd have thought she'd have done something to protect herself—"

"What if she doesn't *know*?" Jaime said. "No pusher is going to talk about drug side effects."

"Even I had to look up the details," Arlen said. "I only

knew the drug had existed, and that it enhanced a wizard's ability with magic. There's no reason to think Renia knew any more—if that much."

Jaime stood up. "When was the last time anyone actually *spoke* to her?"

Natt and Cesna exchanged glances, and Cesna said reluctantly, "Yesterday evening. I checked to see if she wanted to eat with us. She arranged to have breakfast in her room this morning—"

"And now it's just past lunch," Arlen said. He shook his head, and his voice didn't hold much hope. "I think it's time to check in on her."

Jaime didn't bother to ask if she was invited; she was as much a part of this as anyone, and she invited herself. Renia's assigned and secured room was on the third floor, and Jaime followed the wizards down a back stairway from Arlen's bedroom that she hadn't even known about; no one said anything as they poured out into a corner of the third floor, so recently occupied by Dayna's changespell team and now mostly vacant—except for the one room they converged upon.

Arlen was knocking at the door before he even came to a stop. "Renia? We need to talk!"

The answer was slow in coming, and barely audible. "Go. Away."

"That's not going to happen," Arlen said, not hiding his urgency. "Renia, I know you're sick—and I know why. If you don't open the door, I'm going to do it for you."

"Try." As weak as it was, there was challenge in her voice, and satisfaction, as well.

"Don't be ridiculous," Arlen said. "You don't think I'd give you a room where I didn't have an override built into the door, do you?"

Behind him, Cesna and Natt exchanged a glance that made Jaime think Arlen had done just that. *Was* there any such thing as a built-in override for magic? Jaime didn't know.

"Wait!" Renia said, and there was more life in her voice that time. "I need to . . . I'm not presentable."

"I'll give you a minute," Arlen said. "Or, if you prefer, you can just open the door when you're ready."

"Just wait," Renia repeated. From within the room came the noises of someone bumping around.

"Arlen," Natt started quietly, his expression still puzzled, "about the door—"

Arlen held up his hand. "Not now, Natt."

Arlen! Jaime thought. *You're bluffing her out* again, *you sly thing*.

The faint sound of running water filtered through the door, and then there was an augmented click of released locks, both magical and physical. Renia cracked the door; she was leaning against the doorframe and she looked . . . Jaime glanced away. She looked like she was already dead, and just didn't know it yet.

Renia looked past Arlen to the three behind him with pointed surprise. "You didn't mention you brought a party with you."

"No, I didn't," Arlen said, pushing the door open and walking in past Renia.

Jaime was the first to follow him, and she came up right next to him and murmured, "I'm going to have to teach you how to play poker sometime."

Arlen gave her a brief quizzical look, and left it at that. "Sit down, Renia. We have to talk, and I don't want you falling down while we're doing it, in case that stimulant spell you just used wears off before you expect it to."

"Thanks for your concern," Renia said, and sat on the small bed to the side of the room, where the rumpled covers proclaimed her recent occupancy. The rest of the room was modest but comfortable; there was a small dressing table and one padded chair. Renia had brought nothing with her, but had nonetheless managed to give the room a used look—as well as the slightly sour odor of someone who's been in bed and in the same clothes for days, although an open closet showed that Arlen had offered her alternatives along with the room.

No one made a move to sit in the single chair. Arlen stood in front of the bed and said, "We *are* concerned, Renia, and we have good reason to be. What can you tell me about mage lure?"

Renia flinched. After a moment of hesitation, she put on a weakly arrogant expression and said, "What do you want to know?"

"Just exactly what I asked you. What do you know about mage lure?"

She frowned, clearly trying to understand his intent. "It's a drug," she said slowly. "It enhances a wizard's ability to use magic. And," she added, making a wry face, "it's very expensive."

"More expensive than you knew, if you're telling me the truth," Arlen said quietly.

"Ernie gave it to you, didn't he," Jaime said, unable to hold the question inside even though she knew she was lucky to be in on this, and ought to keep her mouth shut.

Renia shook her head, and then glanced quickly at Arlen, as if wondering whether she'd given herself away by failing to hotly deny the whole idea. Then she seemed to give up; she gave a little shrug and said, "No. It was Dayton. And believe me, I paid for it."

Dayton. Jaime looked at Arlen in triumph, only to find his frown. "Dayton, Arlen," she said. "Dayton, *Ohio*. He's played around with his name, is all. Probably dumped 'Ernie' the first chance he got, just like all first semester freshmen college boys grow beards and mustaches."

Understanding crossed Arlen's face, lighting his brown eyes; he gave Jaime an apprehensive nod. To Renia, he said, "Was it Dayton who arranged for Willand's escape?"

Renia made a face, which hardly improved the expression she'd already been wearing. "Yes, though it would have been better for all of us if he hadn't. But it was so easy . . . all he had to do was visit, and slip her a little mage lure. A couple of doses and she just walked right over the spells that were supposed to keep her there." She shoved her arms behind her and propped herself up on them. If anything, her bloodless face paled even further, and Jaime wondered if she was going to pass out on them.

"Told you that spell would wear off sooner than you expected," Arlen said. "You don't have much of the drug left in your system, I'd say. Your spells aren't as strong as you've grown accustomed to."

"You seem to think you know a lot about it," Renia said.

Arlen said, "I know enough."

Cesna glanced at Arlen. When he nodded, she asked, "Do you have any more of it, Renia? The mage lure? Can you get it?"

"No, and no," Renia said bitterly. "It doesn't matter. I wouldn't give any to you, anyway, and I expected to lose my power when I left the group. I just couldn't be part of what Jenci was doing."

"It does matter," Arlen said, and his voice had turned compassionate, the same voice that had soothed Jaime after the humiliation and torture Willand had exacted on her with Arlen as an unwilling witness.

Renia took it suspiciously. "Why?"

"Can't you feel what's happening?" Arlen asked. "I can, and I only wish I'd known about the drug sooner, or I might have been able to do something to ease the damage. We'll call for Sherra, but—"

"What?" Renia said, irritated. "What are you talking about? What damage? Get to the point, would you?"

"I doubt Ernie mentioned it," Jaime said, though she,

like Arlen, couldn't quite bring herself to tell the woman she was going to die. "Or Dayton, or whatever you want to call him. It might have kept you from joining his little group in the first place."

As if in reply, Renia bent double in a sudden fit of coughing, covering her mouth with her hand, while Jaime winced at the deep, rattling sound of it. When she straightened, she was looking at her hand in alarm. It was covered with bright red flecks of blood. "What the Hells is going on here?" she whispered, looking at Arlen with a face that had suddenly lost all its arrogance and turned beseeching.

"Mage lure," Arlen said, hesitating a moment, "is a dangerous drug. Not everyone can take it; it has side effects and some of them kill. But the most insidious part about it is that you can't simply stop taking it. Renia, you're not sick. You're dying because you quit taking mage lure."

"I'm *what*?" she said, and it came out in a gasp of disbelieving laughter. "You must be kidding. Dayton would have—" but she stopped short, suddenly realizing that no, Dayton *wouldn't* have.

"I've only read vague references to the problems of the drug," Arlen said. "But watching you over the last few moments lets me know just exactly what's going on. There's magic trickling through your body, Renia, uncontrolled magic—magic you *can't* control anymore, but had gathered to you with the strength the drug gave you."

"It can't be true," Renia said, sounding less than convinced. "We'd have known about it. We'd have heard it."

"I'd never heard of the drug at all, until after I got here, and was looking through Arlen's library," Natt said. "And I went to a damn good primary institute before my apprenticeship."

"They may simply not have known, back when the drug was previously available," Arlen said. "We've certainly come a long way since then—and the drug was manufactured in a country whose inhabitants practiced a less structured form of clan magics. I doubt they had the skills to deduce just how it worked."

"I don't *care* about any damn clan magic," Renia cried. "I don't want to die—not for *this*!" Her emphasis put her into another coughing fit, and when she was through she smeared a bloody hand print across the material covering her ample thigh.

"I'll call Sherra," Arlen said. His eyes went distant for a moment, while Renia cleared her throat in an effort not to cough, her arms wrapped tightly around herself as she rocked slightly on the bed. There was a barely noticeable tremor in her movement, and in the corner of her mouth, a small pool of bloody spittle collected.

Jaime blinked at that, and looked again; it seemed to her that Renia's face was a little lopsided, that the whole right side of it was slacker than the left. *She's bleeding inside*, Jaime realized. *Not just her lungs . . . everywhere. She's had a small stroke and doesn't even know it.*

Arlen came back to them. "She'll come," he said. "As quickly as she can. Cesna, would you meet her, please?" Cesna nodded, but there was no hope in her face—or in Arlen's. Jaime didn't quite understand it—Sherra had, after all, healed a major brain injury for Jaime herself, after Jaime had ridden Lady full tilt into a gate they both expected to be open. So there must be something more to it than the actual damage. She moved up next to Arlen, putting her back to Renia, and said, "It's the magic, isn't it? The uncontrolled magic in Renia—it won't let Sherra do her healing magic, will it?"

Arlen gave her a surprise look. "I anticipate some interference," he said, but the look on his face let Jaime know it was an understatement.

"If I'm going to die, at least don't be rude about it," Renia said. When Jaime turned back to her, the wizard was wiping a tear from her eye with a shaky hand. The gesture left a streak of a bruise across her face.

"Here," Jaime said. "Let me help you lay back in bed. There's an extra cushion on the chair . . . it might be easier for you."

"Oh, go to Hells with your pity," Renia snapped, but wobbled in the process.

"Get the cushion, Jaime," Arlen said. "Renia, you've got one chance at revenge. We need to know everything we can about Dayton and the other wizards. But if you tell us nothing else, tell us where they *are*."

Renia gave a short laugh. It wasn't pleasant, and as Jaime shoved the cushion behind the bed pillow, she wasn't sure if it was even entirely sane. Renia eased herself back against the pillow, turning into something limper than living flesh should be. She laughed again, a quiet little laugh to herself, her eyes closed. Natt made an uneasy movement near the door.

"You don't have to stay," Arlen told him, and didn't wait for a response. "Renia. Tell us. Tell us *now*."

The quiet laugh, repeated, ended in a little sob. "He got in touch with us individually . . . he must have done his homework . . . had us all pegged. Nothing but mid-level wizards, never going to be anything more. I *tried*," she said, opening her eyes to look earnestly at Arlen. "I really did try. But I never made it . . . too proud to be a vocational wizard . . . left me with nothing, really. Old clothes, friends who weren't friends at all, just other wizards who couldn't make the level. . . ." She blinked, then blinked again, hard. "Can't see you anymore, Arlen. Better not be pity you have on your face. Better not be."

Compassion was an entirely different thing from pity, Jaime thought, looking at Arlen. She moved in next to him, and he took her hand to give it a brief squeeze.

"Where are they, Renia?" he said, softly but insistently; he moved away from Jaime to sit on the edge of the bed, careful not to touch Renia, who had mottled streaks of bruising moving up her arms. "We can get Dayton, if you tell me where he is. Let us be your revenge."

Renia gave a short laugh. "Not with Willand there, Council wizard. Willand on mage lure . . . not something you want to see. She's been quiet, except for that one windstorm . . . doesn't want you all to know just how strong she is . . ." She was silent a moment, and then whispered, "That's why they never sent another storm, another anything. Dayton must have told them not to. He must have told them I'd die . . . I wonder if he told them just *why* . . ."

Where is *he*, Jaime wanted to scream, and bit her lip instead.

"Willand will kill you all . . ." Renia said, her sightless eyes wandering the room and making Jaime's skin crawl. "After she gets that *horse* . . . after she makes you pay . . ."

"Where," Arlen said, his voice no louder than hers but much more urgent. "Renia—"

Too late. Renia gave a cry of pain and snatched at her head, and seconds later, her body arched into a seizure. It was brief, just a few seconds of clawing fingers beating at the bed sheets while Arlen jumped to his feet to get out of the way—and then the woman went limp. A thin trickle of blood worked its way down from her nose to her upper lip, and stopped.

Arlen said softly, "Natt, go intercept Cesna and Sherra. Let them know there's no hurry."

Natt, decidedly pale, wasted no time; he was out the door before he finished nodding.

Jaime stared at the body in a sort of horrified fascination, but Arlen was frowning. "That doesn't make sense," he said. "She's right; they should have been trying to retrieve or kill her; they had no way to know she was stalling us, still hiding their location. Even if Dayton—or Ernie, or whatever you want to call him—knew that she'd die within days, they had no way to know she wouldn't talk during that time."

But Jaime was thinking of Renia's last words. Of Willand on mage lure. Of Willand . . . *after she makes you pay* . . .

Arlen regarded the body, and his frown deepened. He moved to Renia's side, sweeping his hands through the air an inch away from her body, until, in midmotion, he abruptly froze. "Shit," he said, so entirely uncharacteristically that Jaime just blinked at him. "Get out!"

"Wha—*Arlen*!" Jaime yelped the protest as Arlen shoved her at the door, hard enough that she stumbled to catch her balance and failed, sprawling on the hard stone floor beyond the room. Arlen came out behind her so fast that he tripped on her, and fell on top of her—but he didn't waste time in apologies. He twisted around to face the room, still on top of Jaime and grinding her hip painfully into the floor.

A gesture, and the door closed; a flare of light and it was sealed, then sealed again. Arlen's eyes narrowed in concentration, and his hands moved in a complex dance. The walls of the hallway that were common to the room fairly shimmered with light; Jaime twisted to see what was happening, trying not to disturb Arlen, whatever he was doing—

Whummp! Instinctively, Jaime threw herself down again, covering her head with her arms, cringing with the anticipation of the violent, flying debris from that explosion.

Nothing. Arlen rolled off her back and onto his knees, where he sat back on his heels, rested his hands on his thighs, and tipped his head back to breathe deeply.

It must be all right. Jaime let her hands fall to the side of her head, her cheek resting against the cold stone. "And what," she asked, as calmly as possible, her words blurred by the way the skin of her face stuck to the stone, "was that all about?"

"They must have suspected," Arlen said. "They must have been prepared. Smart, very smart. They didn't want to give away anything more than they had to."

"Tell me," Jaime said, a quiet but implacable demand.

"They seeded her," Arlen said. Then, realizing that had no doubt made little sense to Jaime, he took one final, deep breath and said, "The button on her trousers had been spelled. No doubt all of her trousers had been tampered with. They were listening to everything we said within earshot of Renia. They could have killed us all at any time—but as long as she wasn't talking, or wasn't saying anything they couldn't live with, they had a chance to learn what we knew about them, and what we were doing about them—and there was no point in revealing just how strong *they* are." He shook his head. "A listening spell right here in my own hold, shielded so well I couldn't tell. It must have been very frustrating for them when she sickened so quickly."

"I don't understand." Jaime hitched herself up on her elbows. "Couldn't *she* have found it?"

Arlen gave her a long look. "Just because she had the strength doesn't mean she had the years of schooling in how to use it."

She heard the note of hurt in his voice, knew he'd perceived her belief that Renia had been the stronger wizard, without the distinction that she wasn't necessarily the *better* wizard. "Oh," she said, her voice rather small.

"I'm not sure why they triggered the thing at all," Arlen went on, as if the unspoken subtleties of the conversation hadn't happened at all. "I should have ended up on top of you in the hall and feeling quite foolish when nothing happened. Renia was dead. There wasn't much we could learn from the body—at least, not much that would affect them, although it probably would have told Sherra a great deal about what happens when you withdraw from mage lure."

"I know why," Jaime said grimly. "Willand lost her temper, that's why. She doesn't like it when the game doesn't go her way." In her mind, she heard Renia's last words. *After she gets that* horse . . . *after she makes you pay* . . . "Willand's not going to like this—she's not going to like it at *all*." *After she gets that horse* . . . "We'd better warn Jess."

Chapter 10

Jess pushed her sunglasses back up her nose and turned her horse away from the low morning sun. Now that Jess was devoting a significant amount of time to working with Willsey, the only way to meet Kymmet's training commitments was to crowd the day. That meant either working through the hottest part of the day, when it was hard for horse or rider to concentrate on anything but the heat, or rising early.

Jess decided to nap through the heat and work through the dawn. Ander invited himself along, refusing to let her leave Kymmet alone. And as much as she wanted her independence, Jess understood his decision. She guessed she really didn't want to be out alone, anyway.

Besides, it gave her someone to commiserate with in moments like these, when her young mare refused an obstacle in the training course she'd been scrambling through since she'd started serious work under saddle the fall before. It was a combination of steep bank and a deep narrow stream, once natural and now deepened for drainage—not that it was needed this year—and just wide enough that jumping it wasn't practical or the least bit safe. Today the mare had decided she was having none of it.

Jess, hot and red-faced after several moments during which the mare's refusal turned into a short bucking fit, wished she was Lady, so she could bite this mare's rump and drive her over the bank. Instead, she sat on the tense creature and asked her for nothing, backing off. After a moment, when the horse seemed unlikely to explode again, Jess turned her away from the stream and started back for the stable.

Ander shook his head as he came up beside her. "I never was too sure about her," he said. "She's capricious. She might do for light-duty work, but I'd never place her in a stable where she'd have to come through in a pinch."

"I know," Jess said, unhappy to admit it. The mare *was* unpredictable, had always been that way. She'd hoped to work through it. "Koje won't like it."

Ander snorted. "You told Koje last fall that this horse was iffy at best. It's not your fault you couldn't shake her out of it. You should know as well as anyone that horses are like people—sometimes, you run into one that you'd do just as well without."

"Yes." Jess gave the mare a single, quiet pat, then asked her to relax her neck and bend it first right, then left, feeling the tension ease out of the blocky sorrel body moving beneath her. "This, I think, was her last chance."

"I'll back you on it," Ander said, shifting his quiver strap on his shoulder. He never rode without it these days, and while before it had simply been habit, and a chance for fresh game or target practice, now it was a deliberate and somber choice. "We've got far too much work to accomplish without wasting time on that horse. Koje will just have to sell her to someone who only does road riding."

Jess nodded, and turned back the way they'd come, back into the low sun. Ander didn't even squint—he'd recently learned the spell that shaded his vision, and Jess felt the tiny whisper of magic as he invoked it. She knew she ought to learn it, too, as well as the spell that protected her skin from burning, but stubborn equine habits were hard to break, and she had learned about sunglasses and baseball caps long before she knew of spells for her eyes.

They had several miles between here and Kymmet; for now, it was rough scrub meadow combined with the fallow and active fields they had permission to ride beside. Then a long stretch through Kymmet-owned woods, and . . . and what was *that*?

"Ander," she said uncertainly, eyeing the fallow field ahead of them. The ground seemed to be writhing. Another moment's examination showed the sky was doing the same. That was when Jess realized the whisper of magic from Ander's spell had not faded, and had, in fact, increased.

"What?" Ander followed her gaze, frowning. Like Jaime, he rarely felt the touch of magic from a spell.

"Magic," Jess said, and pointed, though by that time, the effects were obvious. Something was pulling itself out of thin air before them, something large—something Jess felt was hardly likely to be friendly. Hating to take her eyes off it, she twisted in the saddle. Nothing behind them. "Maybe we should go back." They could cross the stream and pick up the looping, longer route back to Kymmet.

"It might not have anything to do with us," Ander said. Jess gave him a look, and he shook his head. "No, I don't believe it either. I just don't know if I want to turn my back on it . . . we're not all that close. Let's just—*whups!*"

Jess's ears popped as the spell before them abruptly solidified, and then it was all she could do to stay on the panicking mare. As the horse whirled and fought Jess's attempt to calm her, she got only a glimpse of what had happened on—and to—the field; her nose told her a better story. Sharp acrid smoke hit her lungs; her eyes watered, barely seeing the bright glare of flames on the quickly ignited dry and fallow field.

"Jess!" Ander's voice, breaking through the chaos of

movement from the mare—whirl and rear, plunge and rear again. "Jess," he bellowed, "let her go! It's *moving*!"

Of course it was moving, fire always moved, but if she let the mare go in her panic, there was no telling—then another bellow cut through Jess's struggle of thought, and this time, it was not Ander. It was deep and booming, and its thunder blasted hot air across Jess's skin. She made a noise of profound surprise and released the mare from reins and seat.

They shot forward with the drive of the mare's bottled rage and fear, and Jess instantly realized she was only along for the ride. The horse plunged through a field of stunted crops, galloping at top speed and leaving Jess nothing to do but ride it out, the reins flapping loosely and the horse's mane whipping back on her hands and creating a tangle of fingers, mane, and rein.

Ander rode beside her, urging his horse on, fear on his face. It made Jess twist in the saddle, and then she was desperately sorry she had, for the magic was as much creature as it was fire, and it flowed after them with sinuous serpentine grace, leaving spatters of fireballs behind. Smoke rose from the fields as fire spread in the drought-primed ground and quickly fanned itself to strength in the draft of the fire snake.

They were supposed to outrun *that*? Jess turned forward again and stood slightly in the stirrups, going from passenger to jockey. How long before the horses gave out? How long would the fire snake last? She snuck another look to see they were actually gaining distance on it, but it was all she saw before Ander's cry of warning brought her whipping back around.

The creek. Of course, the creek. They had to slow down to take it, there was no way the mare could do it at this speed—but her head was in the air and the bit meant nothing to her; a blob of foam whipped away from her mouth and landed on Jess's face. She left it there, sawing cruelly on the reins, trying to at least *turn* the runaway and abruptly realizing that if she was going to live through this it would be by going along with the mare, urging her to her best effort *over* the creek.

Ander fell behind as he successfully brought his horse down to negotiate the bank, and Jess forgot about him, concentrating on that one spot on the *other* side of the bank, that sweet spot where the mare's front feet would have to land to carry them both to safety, and then they passed the place where the mare should have been gathering herself to jump, and the horse gave a sudden wild shy, realizing where she was—and then tried to make the jump anyway.

Jess lost her seat in the first frenzied bounce sideways, clinging to the horse only by dint of her grip on the mare's mane. She sunk her heels low and found the saddle just in time for her mount's futile leap. The opposite bank loomed fast and high, and the mare's flailing forelegs hit and snapped as the weight of her body drove them forward into stone and hard dirt. Jess catapulted off the horse and landed hard on the spot she'd meant for the horse.

All the air left her lungs, and her sight went black; she rolled with what was left of her speed and momentum and came to a sprawling, ungainly stop in a flop of limbs and streaming hair. It took several tries to pull air back into her lungs, and when she did, the pain of the fall flooded in as well. She was still too dazed to see when she heard Ander shouting for her—and heard the crackle and spit of the approaching fire. Then he threw himself down next to her, his hands on her face, turning it so he could look into her blinking eyes. The sunglasses hung brokenly across her face; he tore them off and threw them away.

"Jess," he said, his face so close the puff of his breath made her blink. "Jess, come *on*, we've got to—" his eyes widened, and he suddenly threw his body over hers; Jess felt more than heard the hoofbeats of Ander's horse as it scrambled up the bank and galloped past them. "C'mon, c'mon," he said, backing off and shaking her, not gently. She could do no more than make a noise at the pain it caused, and then Ander glanced quickly over his shoulder and looked back at her, his face suddenly hard and determined.

He jerked her body up and snatched a grip around her ribs, pulling her in against his chest as he dragged her backward, back to the creek. The heat sizzled off her exposed skin and crisped her eyes as he released her only long enough to jump down. Then he grabbed her tunic, tugging her back until she slid off the bank and landed heavily on him, splashing them both down into what remained of the drought-dried creek.

She cried out then, and suddenly found herself able to struggle, even though not everything was working quiet right.

"*No*—" He grunted and flung a leg and arm over her, weighing her down into the water along with him, so it flowed sluggishly around her head, tickling against the sides of her face and the corners of her eyes. She would drown, she would die in the water, and she reared—she tried to rear—the roar of fire passed above them, dribbling sparks and flame to hiss in the water. . . .

Ander's lips were against her ear. "Easy, Jess," he said, his voice soothing and as cool as the water on her skin. "Shhhh," he said, blending with the roar of the fire. "Easy."

Some trace of sense trickled into her head. She'd fallen from the mare. She was in the creek with Ander. The fire snake had just passed overhead, blindly missing the deep, narrow cut of the creek. Fire crackled along both sides of the banks, but they were safe, submerged in the water. She was not going to burn . . . and she was not going to drown. But she hurt. She wanted to tell Ander she understood all these things, as she stopped struggling beneath him, but instead she just whimpered, a sound that caught in her throat.

"Shhh," he said. "All right. You going to stay there?" He waited for the faint nod she gave him, and then made sure she wouldn't flounder underwater when he released her. Then he crept to the bank, cautiously climbing it until he could just see over the edge.

"It lost us," he said. "It's . . . I think it's following my horse." He slid back down and turned his back to the bank, leaning against it, his face bleak, his eyes touched with horror. "Everything's on fire . . . it's just sweeping across the fields."

"Fire watch," Jess managed. The fire watch—for there was one, and had been, ever since the extent of the drought became evident—would make sure the fire was extinguished. They were probably already on their way here.

"Yeah, right," Ander said, and gave a shaky laugh. "They'll put it out. And they'll find us, too. It'll be all right, Jess."

"Okay," she said.

"Okay," he echoed, although the foreign colloquialism sounded odd coming out of his mouth. He stood, and he looked as shaky as Jess felt. "Let's get you out of the water—or as out of it as we can, considering there's no way you're going back up this bank, at least not yet. Can you move?"

Jess considered it. "I think yes," she said, after wiggling her toes in her wet boots and gingerly flexing her legs. She tried her shoulders next and was rewarded with sharp stabbing pains through her body. "Ow!" she said, almost as if in wonderment. The water had buffered and soothed her, and shock had made her forget the wrongness she felt after the fall.

"Let me help," Ander said, and carefully sat behind

her in the muddy creek bottom and helped her, ever so slowly, to sit. Together they scootched back along the bank, and then simply stayed that way a moment, while Jess panted from pain and effort.

Ander ran his hands along her shoulders, a light, careful touch; Jess allowed it. She allowed it when he inspected her ribs, and that was all he could reach. "Collarbone's broken," he said. "A rib or two. Anything else, I can't tell."

"I rolled," Jess observed. "That's better than bouncing."

Ander's chuckle bumped against her. "Definitely better than bouncing."

"The mare—"

"She's dead," Ander said flatly. "I expect the same of the gelding, if that . . . *thing* kept following it."

"I could be dead, too," Jess said, suddenly realizing it, and then realizing exactly what had happened in those moments she lay dazed. Ander had successfully negotiated down the bank, and stopped in the creek with his horse, where he was safe—and then come out again. "You should have stayed in the creek, Ander. That was crazy, coming after me."

"Jess," he said, and held her a little tighter. After a moment, he said it again. "Jess. How could I *not*?"

It hit her then. Finally she understood. Sitting in Ander's arms, her head leaning back on his shoulder and his voice and breath in her ear, she felt from him the same quiet intensity that pervaded Carey when he thought he'd almost lost her to Derrick and Ernie at the midnight parking lot in Marion—when he first told her he cared for her. That he loved her.

But this time, it touched nothing deep inside her except surprise. He was her *friend*—wasn't he? Wasn't that the way it was supposed to be, with humans—one love, and many friends?

In a new kind of daze, Jess rested against Ander and

said nothing. Out in the middle of burning Kymmet fields, sitting in the muddy bottom of a sluggish creek with the black banks rising high on either side of them and her broken bones grumbling a rising complaint, she let him hold her, and wondered what she was supposed to do when the time came to ask him to let go.

ꕥ ꕥ ꕥ

Dayna sat in the big kitchen of the farmhouse—complete with ancient but working plumbing, a big wooden table made from thick hardwood boards and smoothed from years of use, and a stove that was only appropriate for the most basic of heat spells. Despite his inexperience, Rorke had taken the kitchen spells easily in hand—in fact, Dayna had had to squash more than one moment of extreme envy at how easily he'd handled his assignment here as general gofer for the changespell team.

Although the truth was, since she'd worked so hard at eliminating the habit of raw magic from her spells, Dayna was doing pretty well herself. Keeping away from raw magic hadn't turned out to be much of a problem, either. She'd developed a reaction to using it, and found it gave her an immediate headache and low-grade aches and pains for hours, never mind the fact that it fuzzed up and ruined whatever spell she was working on, and then kept her from returning to it for some time.

Well. She traced her finger along the distinct pattern of wood grain in the table and decided that maybe, just maybe, she had really gotten a handle on how magic was supposed to work in this world. Unfortunately, that didn't mean she had any more of a place on this team. She was here to analyze the evanescent *feel* of a spell—be it a changespell, or the checkspell they were working so hard to develop.

Her efforts had been a considerable contribution, and

she'd saved them quite a bit of time; they were preparing a spell to present to the Council, one they hoped would protect at least the herbivores. Of course, she couldn't do her part until the spell was done, and she checked it out. That meant she was on her own for a large part of the day, waiting out the gaps between their need for her.

She wondered where Rorke was. Usually he was hanging around the kitchen, snacking, fiddling with some new recipe to see what he could coax out of the old stove—whatever it was last time had failed, judging by the faint odor that hung over the kitchen. He should have cleaned up after himself a little better.

Really, Dayna thought, he belonged in a vocational chef school—not that he couldn't do more esoteric work, but there were obviously culinary talents trying to come to the fore. She bet that Sherra would gently point him in that direction before another month was out.

She rested her hands on the table and her chin on her hands, staring at the mug of tea she'd just cooled, remembering when she'd so envied Sherra's ability to casually cool her own drink, and feeling just a bit like a bored kid during summer vacation while all the grown-ups were off doing something interesting. Feh.

She closed her eyes and cast the spell to bring up the latest information on the public news Dispatch. No, they were still broadcasting the same story, the fires in Kymmet. The flames had been contained with considerable effort and no human casualty, although the loss of crops and woodland had been considerable. There was still wild speculation about the cause, and some reports of a magical, flying fire snake, but Dayna dismissed them. *Yeah, and Bigfoot lives, too*. The ground was so dry this summer, the only surprise was that this was the *first* big fire.

The sound of hoofbeats broke through her less-than-perfect concentration, and she cut the connection to the Dispatch. They weren't supposed to get a courier here until late afternoon, but maybe Arlen had gotten anxious for the spell. It didn't really matter—*any* distraction was a welcome one, this morning. As long as it wasn't a repeat of Willand's little greeting, which Dayna had been half expecting.

When she reached the porch off the kitchen, Carey was coming up to the hitching rail there, swinging off his horse before it even stopped, as though he didn't think twice about such a thing. *Carey*? He wasn't supposed to be making this run—and Dayna saw why, too, after Carey took one easygoing stride toward the porch and came up short. He came the rest of the way in a much more conservative gait, and Dayna thought he'd have been limping if she wasn't watching.

"What're you doing here?" she said, wrapping her arm around a porch column and leaning into it.

"Just the sort of greeting I've learned to expect from you," he replied, but the grin on his face was genuine enough. "Arlen sent me, of course. Wanted me to let you know what had really happened up in Kymmet. I'll stay overnight and take your work back tomorrow—don't worry, no one expects your spell to be ready early."

Dayna just stared at him. *What had really happened in Kymmet?* "It was *Bigfoot*?" she blurted.

Carey gave her a pointedly blank stare, and started again. "Arlen sent me," he said, deliberately slow with his words. "They're trying to keep this thing quiet, and since I was already in on it because of Jess—"

"What about Jess?" Dayna interrupted.

This time, he stopped long enough to give her a curious and somewhat amazed look, and asked, "Haven't you been tapping into the wizard-level Dispatch? You really don't have any idea what I'm talking about, do you?"

Dayna shook her head, not trusting her voice, which was sure to snap something angry simply because she felt stupid. No, she'd just been skimming the public layer of the Dispatch. It hadn't occurred to her that the Kymmet disaster was something that merited more—after all, the outlaw group was here in this area, somewhere between Anfeald and Sallatier, and she was right in the middle of that. No need to check wizard gossip, right?

Apparently not.

"Does *any*one here have the slightest idea of what happened in Kymmet?" Carey asked, his incredulousness tinged with irritation.

"We're busy," Dayna said archly. "So do you want to come in and tell me about it, or do you want to stand out in the heat?"

Carey shook his head. "I knew there was a good reason I started hanging around wizards," he said. "There's always a cool room around, even in the middle of summer. Yes, I'm coming in. I need to take care of the horse, first."

"Oh, Rorke'll do it," Dayna said. "You look—" *worn out*, she was going to say, but stopped herself at his sudden sharp look, and finished, "like there's a lot for us to catch up on. And I want to know what Jess is in the middle of, this time." She invoked the simple spell that would tap Rorke on the shoulder and let him know he was wanted, and where.

"Nice save," Carey told her. "But you're right, I'm tired. Give Rorke a call."

"I just did," Dayna said, frowning. The youth had just learned the response spell, and was using it at every opportunity—but this time, he hadn't answered her request. "Give him a minute, I guess."

But the minute passed, and then another, and Carey shook his head. "Might as well go ahead and do it myself," he said. "I'll be back in a moment. If anybody else is free, have them join us. There are bound to be questions, and I don't want to spend the rest of the day answering them." He returned to the horse and mounted up, riding down the farm lane to the barn while Dayna scowled and tried to get some sort of response from Rorke. Where *was* he?

She did a quick search through the house—but it was a large house, and she spent most of her time trying to get some of the others to join her in the kitchen with Carey. None of them had seen Rorke, either, and she could get only Rannika to pry herself away from the spell.

"I thought it was finished," Dayna said, as they entered the kitchen and she hunted up a mug for Carey, filling it with the last of the tea in the cooler. She frowned at that, too, because it was Rorke's favorite drink other than the evening wine the outlaws had left them, and he never let it get this low without brewing more.

"I thought so, too," Rannika said, wrinkling her nose slightly, and looking around to find the source of the odor Dayna had noticed earlier. "But you know Hastin—he looked at the section that protects Jess from the checkspell, and decided we'd tied it in all wrong. Alsypha insists it's fine, and they've got the whole thing torn apart again."

"*Again*?" Dayna said, astounded and dismayed. "Good god, Rannika, it's just a prototype. You don't think the Council's going to invoke it without going over it, do you? Someone needs to kick Hastin in the butt."

"I said as much," Rannika agreed, rubbing her hands over the sallow skin of her face; she hadn't been looking well since their arrival here, and today she appeared exhausted—although Dayna knew she'd gone to bed several hours early the night before. "You'd have thought that whoever picked the members of this team would have known better than to put a perfectionist in at this stage of the process. Bet anything it was a political appointment. What's 'god'?"

Dayna made a face. "Something I should remember not to say around here." Movement on the porch caught her attention and she called, "Come on in, Carey. Knock the mud off your boots, first."

"Ha ha," Carey said, opening the door and throwing himself into one of the wooden chairs around the table. "I could *do* with a little mud right now, myself."

"This is Rannika," Dayna said, without prelude. "So tell us what's going on."

Carey downed the tea in one long draught, his throat bobbing and a few drops of tea making its way around the edge of the glass to trickle down beside the corner of his mouth. He wiped it away with his wrist and slouched back in the chair. "Got you interested now, huh? Well, you ought to be. There's a lot going on out there."

"Just *tell* us," Dayna said, starting in on a good glower.

Carey preempted it. "If you've only been listening to the basic level news, you probably think the fire was natural—flared up, spread fast, and was put out. But it wasn't—it was just what some people claim to have seen—some sort of fire construct, created with a rudimentary search spell tacked on. No one felt the magic, so you know what that means. The Council's clamped down pretty hard on the news, though—even on the wizard-level Dispatch, you wouldn't have heard it straight out. People who know enough can figure out it, and that's it."

"Then how come *you* know?" Dayna asked bluntly.

"Dayna!" Rannika said, looking at her askance.

"It's all right." Carey gave Rannika a tolerant grin. "I'm used to her."

It was meant to be a poke, and Dayna knew it. She countered by sticking her tongue out, but didn't let the subject stray long. "How come?" she repeated. "Arlen could have sent this on paper."

"Because," Carey said, and his eyes grew sober fast, although she could see he was trying to keep it light, "the spell was after Jess. She and Ander were in the middle of the mess."

She's all right, Dayna told herself sternly, controlling

her reaction. *If she weren't, he'd be with her.* So it was Rannika who got to the question first, her exhausted eyes a mirror for her concern. "Is she—"

Carey shook his head. "She's all right—now. And so is Ander. They were out on a training ride. It got pretty wild . . . they lost both horses, and waited it out in one of those deep-cut creeks they favor in Kymmet farmland. As soon as they're fit to travel, Jess is coming back to Arlen's. It was a mistake to let her go in the first place. I knew it then . . . I should have said something." Something in his expression darkened, but he cleared it away and looked up at Dayna. "She had a few broken bones . . . Kymmet Stables has some good healing wizards, though, so I wouldn't worry about it."

"*I* would," Rannika said. "So far, those outlaws have been pretty quiet—keeping a low profile, at least until they took Jess. But a fire construct was a damn noisy thing to do, and a much greater threat than turning a few animals to people."

"Oh, I don't know," Carey said dryly. "The thought of being turned into a sheep isn't very appealing, either."

"But that woman—Renia—said it was only one wizard who was doing that, and that he was bucking the others to do it," Dayna objected. "Maybe it was just one—" but she stopped. The thought that a single wizard could pull off something like the incident in Kymmet was hardly comforting. "Never mind," she said. "I don't even want to think about that."

"That's another thing," Carey said. He got up and moved stiffly to the sink, where he drew a glass of water and handed it to Dayna; she cooled it for him and set it down in front of his seat. This time, he only downed half of it at once. "Renia's dead."

"She's *what*?" Rannika said.

Dayna repeated flatly, "Dead. What happened, Carey?"

"A couple different things," he told her. "The outlaws

are on mage lure, and Renia died from withdrawal. It's bad stuff, and is supposed to have side effects, as well. Arlen didn't learn much from Renia before she died, but we do know that Ernie—yeah, *that* Ernie, though he's calling himself Dayton—is the one who gathered the outlaws together, offered them mage lure, and started them working on the changespell." He shrugged. "Willand tried to kill Arlen with a spell she had seeded on Renia—it was a little temper tantrum of sorts. When that failed, she went after Jess. At least, that's what Arlen figures."

Rannika leaned back in her chair and let out a slow breath. "Mage lure," she said. "That certainly answers some questions."

But Dayna's thoughts were whirling. Ernie, back in their lives again? She should have killed him in the first place, and *damn* Carey for stopping her, anyway! And what did this drug have to do with anything? It didn't answer any of *her* questions. "What the hell is mage lure?" she demanded.

Rannika looked very tired indeed. "Supposedly, just an old story. It's a drug that enhances a wizard's ability to control magic. I doubt the others on the team have even heard of it."

Suddenly Dayna understood. "That's how they're doing all those things they shouldn't be able to!"

Rannika nodded. "For all I know, it changes a wizard's signature, too—which is why no one on the Council recognized it—or recognized Willand, for no doubt she broke herself out of confinement. It certainly couldn't have been anybody else."

"Wait a minute," Dayna said slowly, thinking hard, thinking about how she'd traced Willand's ominous message, and how she hadn't dared to tell the others of it, because she shouldn't have been *able* to. Thinking about all the little spells she'd finally mastered, believing it was because she'd eliminated her penchant for raw magic. "It enhances a wizard's ability . . . oh, god." She buried her face in her hands, and muttered through them, "Shit, shit, shit."

"Dayna, what's wrong?" Carey's alert concern was almost worse than no concern at all, for it only convinced her she was right.

But no . . . maybe she wasn't, she couldn't be. *The wine, they'd been drinking stocked wine.* No, not that much wine. Just a small glass in the evening, aside from Rorke, who had several. And no one else had mentioned anything about a change in their magic, had they? Besides, Carey had said there were side effects, but they were all fine. Weren't they? Dayna half lowered her hands to free up her eyes, looking at Rannika's inexplicable exhaustion. "Shit," she repeated, turning it into a mantra. "Shitshitshit."

"Dayna, *what*?" Carey said, and some of his concern had turned to exasperation. Then suddenly he was looking between the two of them, because Rannika had caught Dayna's eye, and her jaw dropped slightly. She shook her head, not wanting to believe.

"Rorke," Dayna said abruptly, still holding Rannika's eye. "Rorke had more than any of us—and I can't find him. He doesn't answer a summons, he wasn't in his room—"

Carey shifted, moving to face Dayna directly without moving the chair with him. He hooked his hands around a juncture of chair seat and legs, and pulled Dayna closer with a jerk. "*What*," he said, "are you talking about? What's the problem here?"

Close enough to see the dirt smeared across his face, and the way it caught on the stubble he should have shaved this morning, Dayna looked into his clear hazel eyes and said simply, "We've been drinking their wine."

"Shit!" Carey said explosively, throwing himself back into his chair.

"That's what I've been saying," Dayna told him, scowling.

"We have to tell the others," Rannika said, her voice low. "I . . . I've felt some changes since we got here. But they've been so small . . . and it's not like I've been trying to do anything I found particularly difficult to do before. This checkspell stuff is more about detective and detail work than it is about *power*. And if our signatures modified slightly over time . . ."

"We didn't have that much," Dayna said, out loud this time, and knew she sounded like she was trying to convince herself.

"I think you'd better try to find Rorke," Carey said. "He's young, he hasn't begun to explore the range of his power yet, and he's been at that wine."

"The wine," Dayna said, feeling suddenly savage. She wanted to pour it out on the ground, all of it. But just what Carey had said caught her attention. *He's been at that wine*. What if it was more than just extra glasses in the evening, which he drank as though it was Kool-aid? He never seemed buzzed, and she never smelled it on his breath, but it'd only taken one alcoholic in her life for her to know how well they could hide the drinking. "The wine!" she repeated, and catapulted out of her chair and past Carey, straight to the closed and latched pantry door. *Of course he would have closed it behind him—even latched it. So no one would know—*

She invoked a glow spell and jerked the door open at the same time, but somehow, she already knew what she would find—and she did. She made a strangled noise and turned away, putting her back to the edge of the open door. *I should have known*. She tipped her head back and said it out loud. "I should have known. I should have known it didn't stop at the evening wine."

"Rorke?" Rannika whispered.

Dayna nodded, her eyes closed, the edge of the door

digging into her spine. She turned back to Rorke. It couldn't have been an easy death. The smell of it was hitting her strongly, now—a mixture of vomit and feces, which he'd smeared into the floor with the convulsions that had left him stiff and twisted, his back arched, his face distorted into a grotesque mask.

"Side effects," she said, her voice hardly louder than Rannika's had been. She looked at Carey, and saw a reflection of her own stricken expression in his face. "I guess we don't have to wonder any more." Mage lure, in her system. Mage lure, which had killed Renia in withdrawal. "The question is . . . what do we do now?"

଎ ଍ ଎

Dayna. Jess. Arlen. Carey. And Jaime herself. Willand was doing it again—changing their lives, threatening them, putting them through experiences they wouldn't simply be able to walk away from, but would have to live with for the rest of their lives. Jaime heaved a forkful of manure at the wheelbarrow, hitting dead center with some satisfaction. Some people kneaded bread to work out their frustrations, and some people cleaned stalls—although Carey's regular grooms looked at her askance when they thought she wasn't paying attention.

Well, perhaps this new mage lure thing wasn't entirely Willand's fault. It had probably been Ernie who'd suggested leaving that drugged wine there, just because it pleased him to think of the possibilities. He probably hadn't anticipated just how damaging the wine would be—and if he'd found out about it, was no doubt gloating in a big way.

The entire checkspell team had been transported to Sherra's hold the previous day, along with what remained of the wine. For now, they were still drinking the drugged wine, although Jaime doubted they were enjoying it anymore. Sherra had grilled Arlen on what he'd observed in his short time with Renia, and was trying to construct a withdrawal treatment based on that, and whatever her assistants, frantically scouring libraries across Camolen, could come up with on mage lure.

Jaime could well imagine Dayna's fear and anger. She wished she could visit, but Arlen suggested it wait until Sherra had things under control.

Another forkful hit the wheelbarrow with a satisfying splat. Jaime only hoped Sherra accomplished her usual miracles, and soon. Otherwise, she thought she might go crazy here, wondering how Jess was healing and when she'd get here, wondering how Dayna was handling things, worrying about what they'd be facing *next*.

The Council, at least, had taken the checkspell team's work, and was analyzing it even now. Before Arlen had left to join the team early this morning, he'd allowed hopes they'd invoke the spell before the day was over—he, too, seemed to be getting impatient with his fellow Council members. If it worked as well as hoped, there would be no more innocent animals dragged into the outlaws' games. The problem was, Jaime didn't think anyone was truly concerned about the animal changespells anymore; they had merely been symptoms of a bigger crisis. They were concerned, suddenly, about being turned into sheep.

And Jaime's problem was that she was tired of being the one who waited, while her life in Ohio went on without her and the threats escalated around her. She raked the shavings with the manure fork, looking for clods she'd missed, and redistributed the shavings—a fragrant bedding made from one of the few trees that Camolen had and Earth did not. Her movements, she realized after a moment, were just a hair too vigorous to do the job well. Pent-up frustration and a growing need to *do* something kept trickling out of her—and she had a suspicion that trickle was going to grow.

Working it out on dirty stalls wasn't going to take her very far.

ઉ ઙ ઉ

No one had wanted Jess to ride back to Anfeald. Koje, who'd immediately realized Jess was suddenly more of a liability than a help even if it *was* the busy season, urged her to use mage-travel.

But Jess had wanted the privacy of the ride, the time to think. The thought of going straight from hovering healers to concerned and questioning friends was too much to take. On top of her recent experience at Shammel's hands, it was simply intolerable. She was tired of being on edge, of being surrounded by people who moved too fast around her. Privacy and quiet—that's what she needed.

She'd argued for the ride. They'd argued it was dangerous and too physically taxing. She'd turned stubborn; they'd gotten frustrated with her. It was Ander who pointed out that the real danger—another magical attack—could be avoided. For the four days a slow-paced ride would take, it was easy enough—and took less magical energy than mage-travel—to simply shield her from prying eyes.

And he, of course, could come with her.

Jess had really wanted to be alone . . . but Ander learned fast enough that she wasn't in the mood for chatter, and if she ached far more than she expected from even the leisurely ride, she wasn't about to admit it.

She spent her time thinking about the changespell. She'd already gotten past one recent hurdle—the new checkspell invoked by the Council just the day before. As soon as she'd heard it was in effect, she'd gone off to see if she could change to Lady. It did, she discovered, take a slightly different twist of effort, but was no more difficult than it had been before.

Of course, she then had to run and find someone to change her back. It was only in the course of moving around that she discovered what she should have known, if she'd thought about it—horses have no collarbones, and therefore not only was her movement unimpeded, it was free from the discomfort of the healing fracture, although her ribs made her gaits stiff and graceless.

It would have been so nice if she could change to Lady for a little relief, and change back again without having to find someone to do it for her. She was not yet willing to accept Ander's conclusion, that it was simply beyond the capacity of a horse, even a horse with a human alter ego. So while Ander gave her sidelong glances he thought she wasn't noticing, Jess tried to decide how to teach her Lady-self to trigger a complex spellstone.

By the time the morning of the fourth day rolled around, Jess was ready to face the world again, and they rode into Arlen's hold at noon, on a day that wasn't so much overwhelmingly hot as simply resigned to be without rain again.

They were beset with questions about the fire snake and much curiosity about the mad sprint for safety that had only coincidentally brought them to the ditch. Arlen speculated about the low quality of the search spell that must have been tuned to Jess, but hadn't managed to find her in a dimension where it might normally not be necessary to look—beneath it.

It was nothing Jess hadn't heard before. She ate a noisy lunch with Jaime, Arlen and his assistants, and two of the couriers—Carey was off on a run—then ducked away from Ander, who had reacted to the scare with the fire snake by becoming markedly reluctant to let her go off on her own.

She went out to the old pasture tree, and sat with her back to the trunk, gazing out on the struggling grasses. There'd been rain not too long ago, but it was short and light, and had dried off before there was even a chance for it to soak in. The same rain had been through Kymmet just a day before the fire, and had done nothing to alleviate the damage.

Jess closed her eyes, thinking about her foalhood in this pasture, as she often did when she was here. There was a certain . . . innocence to those days, before she'd learned the tricks of a top courier horse—a horse who often carries secrets others will kill for. But even after she'd learned to shoulder the enemy's horses off narrow cliffside trails to their deaths, to drop flat and lie quiet, to charge through areas with deadly footing by dint of sheer repetition and her knowledge of just the right place to put her hoof . . . even then, she had been full of innocence, compared to what she was, now.

But not too full of reminiscing to miss Jaime's footsteps coming up the lane behind her. She tilted her head to the side, just enough to let Jaime know Jess had heard.

Jaime checked the ground beside Jess for stones and knelt, sitting back on her heels. Not relaxed, then, Jess decided, or she would have simply sat down. She was in shorts, a style becoming popular in Kymmet City, but so far worn only by children out in Anfeald—and no doubt causing a bit of a stir here in the hold. Jaime said nothing at first, just ran her hand through her hair to lift the soft cut of her bangs from her forehead.

After a moment, she said, "You asked about Dayna at lunch. It was hard to get a word in edgewise, though."

"Yes," Jess agreed.

"Sherra's decided the problem with going off mage lure abruptly is that it's similar to experiencing a magical backlash. All that magic in their systems, and all of a sudden they don't have control over it anymore. She's got them all on steadily decreasing doses of the wine, and they're being monitored around the clock, by someone who has the ability to channel the freed magic into something more harmless. Everyone seems to be doing pretty well with it . . . but the wine supply's going to be a little tight, if you'll excuse the expression."

Jess gave her a blank look and Jaime waved it away. "Never mind. A pun. They're going to run out of wine just before they're through needing it. They're hoping things will be under control by then. Arlen seems to think that even if there's damage caused, everyone'll live through it. I'm sure Dayna's not taking it that lightly."

"No," Jess said, emphatic as she thought of Dayna. "Dayna would not."

"I was thinking . . ." Jaime said, giving Jess a sidelong look, "we should try to visit her. I haven't had any luck—everyone's too busy to take the time to get me there. But if both of us started pestering Arlen and Natt—he can do the mage-travel spell, too, at least the one to Sherra's—maybe we can get there."

"We could ride," Jess offered.

Jaime hesitated, then shook her head. "No," she said. "I don't think so."

Jess didn't try to convince her. "I'll pester," she said. "I want to see Dayna. I want to know more about the changespell." What she really wanted to know was if the team had found any more victims of the changespell, but she thought Jaime would understand that. In fact, Jaime was the one who would understand about her own personal changespell, as well. "I can't change yet," she said without preamble. "I mean, Lady can't change yet. Someone else has to do it. Ander doesn't understand why I want to be able to do it all myself, but—"

"But you need the control," Jaime said simply. "I understand. And Ander . . . has his own reasons for thinking what he does. I'm not sure they're right, but . . ."

"I know about them," Jess said, surprised at the sad tone of her own voice. She thought of how reluctantly Ander had released her to the fire team who'd found them, and how he'd taken opportunities since to lean against her, to touch her in ways that could have been meaningless, but weren't.

"You do?" Jaime sounded surprised, herself. "Well . . . that's good. Carey knows too, you know. That's why he's such a pain in the ass around Ander."

"Yes," Jess said, and sighed. Doing something about the way somebody else felt didn't seem . . . like it would work, even if she tried it. "The changespell," she started again. "I was thinking . . . because I can trigger it now, I felt I should be able to do it as Lady, too. But when we train horses to do a flying lead change, we don't just suddenly ask them for it. We start with simple changes."

"You can't break down a changespell to its simple elements," Jaime said, doubtful.

Jess fished in her tunic pocket for one of the stones she tended to carry with her as human, but which was no use to her as Lady. It was a spell she should learn for herself one day—Carey could do it, and so could many other couriers. Invoked, it identified a stranger as friend or foe, though it wasn't terribly precise and only picked up on enmity if it was clear and purposeful. Jess dangled the rough stone before her and said, "There are spells that are *already* simple." And with a spell this elementary, it was possible to put several of them on the same stone. Plenty to practice with.

"Jess, that's a great idea," Jaime said, a touch of enthusiasm touching features that had been all too serious of late.

"I want to try it," Jess said. "Without Carey or Ander. They have too many opinions about it. Yes I can, no I can't—you'll just try to help, and that's all."

"Do you still have that spellstone Arlen made last year sometime?" Jaime asked. "The one I can trigger? And . . . do they last that long?"

Jess shrugged. "I have it, yes. If it doesn't work, we'll get Carey. But we can try."

"That we can," Jaime said, and she sat a little straighter. "How wonderful it'll be if this works! It's about time I had a chance to help with something around here."

Jess didn't answer, simply started to remove her tunic. Then she stopped and glanced at Jaime. "No stall to hide in," she said apologetically.

"Never mind," Jaime said. "That rule's mostly for in front of men, and women you don't know. If anyone sees you from the hold, well, they'll just have to wonder."

Jess gave her a sudden grin, and pulled the tunic off, and then the snug, supportive half-top beneath it, and the trousers over her bare feet next. She dropped the identifier spellstone in Jaime's hand and said, "Give this to me . . . after. Sometimes it's hard to remember, right after I change."

Jaime just nodded. Then Jess closed her eyes and cleared her mind, standing tall and still, unmindful of her nakedness as a feeble hot breeze blew over her body. She recalled and concentrated on the feel of triggering the identifier spellstone, and tucked it away in the part of her thoughts she reserved for giving herself directions once she was her Lady-self.

Then, lifting her head to catch what little of that hot breeze she could, Jess touched one of the spellstones that fell from her braid—the longer ones were always the ones that took her to Lady, and she didn't even have to check anymore—and triggered it.

And then Lady was standing with her nose to the wind, taking in all the smells that the Jess-self had missed. Maiden-tear flowers were in bloom at the crest of the pasture, tasty little treats that made her ears swivel in that direction with interest. They swiveled again at the sounds of the hold behind her, the cleanup work from the windstorm. There was the clatter of wood being moved, the grunts of human effort—and then somebody dropped something into a wheelbarrow, something solid and big enough to make a loud hollow clank, and it was all the excuse Lady needed.

She bolted away from the tree, snorting wild dramatic alarm, and tore off through the pasture, her legs a blur and her tail flagged high. She galloped great sweeping circles, charging in toward Jaime and then veering off in time to brush by, while Jaime laughed at her. Lady lowered her head for a threat shake that neither of them took seriously, and geared down into a springy trot, her nostrils flared.

Only then did she feel the ache of her ribs, and she turned from her circle and walked back to Jaime, who was waiting with her hands on her hips and her smile intact. As Lady drew near, Jaime held up her hand and let an object dangle from it.

Lady sniffed at it. She sniffed it with first one nostril and then the other, making a great show of investigating it.

"You're pretty full of yourself," Jaime said with amusement. "I'm going to tie it to your mane." Lady stood for her as Jaime fussed with her long black mane at the withers; she could feel the stone resting against her skin when Jaime stepped back. She twitched her skin as though twitching off a fly.

"That won't do it," Jaime said. "Give it a try, Lady. See if you can trigger it."

Lady snorted loudly in resignation—time to work—and hunted for the remnants of Jess that would tell her what to do. She swung her head around to look at the spellstone, reaching for that feeling, that *twist* that would free the stone's spell.

And started wildly backwards when Jaime suddenly glowed bright blue, snorting and checking the scent of it with quick whuffing breaths.

Jaime laughed with delight. "That's *it*, Lady, you did it! Way to go!" The blue light faded and left Jaime just as she'd been, while Lady shook off her startlement and felt pleased with herself. She'd triggered a spellstone, at last. She could *do* it.

So she did it again, and this time gave a little prance when it worked. Jaime, grinning, gave her shoulder a couple of quick, hearty slaps, and then hung her arm over Lady's neck.

Movement caught Lady's eye; she raised her head to focus on the gate, and discovered Carey and Ander—together?—entering the pasture. She felt Jaime turn against her, and heard the sigh when her friend realized they were no longer alone. "Boys," Jaime said. "Some days, you just feel like they're full of cooties. Ah, well, I don't suppose we could have kept this from them long, anyway—but it would have been nice to practice a little more before they found out about it." She put a hand on the bone of Lady's nose and turned her head so Jaime could look her in the eye. "You are *not* to try the changespell, do you hear? It's too soon; you'll get discouraged. Don't feel pushed, just because *they're* here."

No spell to Jess. Lady got that part clearly enough. But it wasn't enough to keep her from showing off; she cantered up to the men, and when Carey put out a hand to greet her, to run along her shoulder and neck so she'd stop, Lady gave a burst of speed and circled behind them, making the little twist in her mind—

There! They glowed brightly, the two of them, and stopped short in surprise. Lady came back to face them, giving the high-stepping little dance of a trot in place that served as exhilarated laughter.

"Lady!" Carey said, and then laughed himself. "If you aren't something! Good job!"

"She did that?" Ander said, looking a little dazed.

"She sure did," Carey said, lifting his hand in greeting

to Jaime, who was walking to meet them. "You've got to start somewhere, eh, Lady?"

"You think . . . what, you think she's going to work her way up to the changespell?" Ander reached over to pat Lady's shoulder, but he was frowning.

"I expect that's what Jess thinks," Carey said. Lady nuzzled Ander's arm, then moved in close to Carey, putting her broad forehead and straight nose against his chest.

"I can't believe she'll ever do it," Ander said, his face all but shouting his doubt.

"Don't put limits on her," Carey responded, and the touch of anger in his voice didn't come through to his hands, which were gently stroking the mane up high on Lady's crest. "I did that, once . . . and it was a mistake."

Chapter 11

"I'm okay," Dayna said, sounding muffled through Jaime's fierce hug. "Really, Jay. I'm okay."

Jess, who decided from Dayna's voice that it was true despite the tension and fatigue she'd seen in her friend's face when they first stepped out of the spell booth into Sherra's hold, spared her the full-blown greeting and merely grinned at her when Jaime finally stepped back.

"Oh, I know you're all right," Jaime said. "I just felt so helpless, sitting there in Anfeald and knowing you were going through so much!"

Dayna made a face. "That's another goal down the tubes," she said, and must have quickly realized she'd need to explain. "One thing I swore to myself, way back when I was a kid—I'd never get hooked on anything. No drugs, no booze—*I* was going to be the one in control."

"It's not exactly like you had a choice," Jaime said.

Dayna shook her head. "You're right, but . . . I should have realized something was up when I was happy enough to have the wine every evening. I've never liked wine much, though I've learned to appreciate it since it's more common here. And then there were the—well, come on, let's go sit down in the garden. We'll pick up something to drink on the way."

They left the small room, and Dayna led them through the unpredictable, narrow halls of the long addition off the back of Sherra's log-built hold.

"I remember when we first got here," Jaime said. "Before I'd ever been to Kymmet, or realized that Siccawei was about as remote as a major hold can get in Camolen. I just sort of assumed that this place was backward, compared to home. I still think there are some aspects of it that are badly behind the times—ours *and* theirs—but I sure was wa-ay off on that one!"

"And you figured this out before or after Sherra did major brain surgery on you out by the gate?" Dayna asked, amused.

Jaime shrugged, following Dayna down a short flight of wooden stairs that echoed their steps through the stairwell. "It took a while, Dayna. No engines, no electricity . . . it's not obvious at first that they've got magic for most of those functions."

"Hey," Jess said, suddenly realizing, bringing up both the rear of the group and of the conversation, "*I* was the one who ran you into those gates. They were *closed.*" She still felt the surprise of that discovery, could feel Jaime's weight leaving her bare back as Lady frantically tried—and failed—to avoid the crash.

Jaime snorted. "Yeah, they sure were."

They left the building for the bright light and shadow patterns of Sherra's garden, and Jess moved out from behind Jaime, nearly stepping on Dayna's heels when the smaller woman moved in the same direction.

"Geeze, you're bouncy today, Jess," Dayna said, glancing back at her. "You get into some high-test grain or something?"

"No," Jess said, just as pleased to have Dayna ask so she could tell her the news. "I triggered a spellstone!"

This stopped Dayna short, to give Jess a deliberately and dramatically baffled look. "And?"

Jaime grinned. "She means *Lady* triggered a spellstone, Dayna. And she did, too—several times."

Dayna's eyes widened in a very satisfying way. "No kidding?"

Jess nodded, and she moved to the shaded garden bench, realizing only after she got there that she was, indeed, bouncy today. "But I need more practice, with different stones. I don't want to ask Arlen . . . I don't want Carey—or Ander—to find out how much I'm working on it. Can you make them?"

"She only needs simple ones, Dayna," Jaime added hastily.

"Good thing." Dayna snorted. "Simple ones are the only ones I can make. And I hope you have a few days . . . I can't just whip them up, you know."

"We have time," Jess assured her. "We have lots of other things to talk about, too."

"I'll say," Dayna muttered, her expression darkening. "It'll be nice to talk to *some*one I know will believe me."

Jaime's eyebrows went up. "Gonna tell us about that?"

"Unless you run off," Dayna said. "We forgot the tea, didn't we . . . I'll get it in a minute. Look, I'm really glad you're here, because the Council is up to it again."

"Up to what?" Jess asked.

Dayna gave her a look that Jess hoped was being used to express Dayna's opinion about the Council, and not about Jess's question. "You were a horse the last time we went through this with them. They're so damned conservative! No offense to Arlen, Jaime . . . Sherra's part of the Council, too. But if they're speaking up, it's not loud enough to make a difference."

"Facts, Dayna," Jaime said. "Give us some facts."

"You know how last summer, they were so keyed into working on the defensive that it took them forever to realize someone needed to go out and *stop* that woman, even if there was a cost to doing it?"

"You were in on that more than I was," Jaime said. "Calandre got her hands on me somewhere in the middle, after all. But I get the gist of what you mean. You, Jess?"

Jess wasn't sure, but shrugged. She'd learned that

sometimes if she just let people go on talking, she could figure it out.

"They're doing it again." Dayna hesitated, then turned and plopped herself down on the bench. Jaime sat next to her. "When I was at the farm, Willand sent me a little love note. I decided to trace it. I never expected to be able to actually *do* it—but the mage lure, you know . . ."

"You *did* it? You know where they are?" Jess said, wide-eyed, bouncing slightly on her toes as if her body was ready to run right off and do something about it if Dayna *did* know where the outlaws were.

"I know the general area," Dayna corrected her. "I'm not even sure how big a *general area* that might be. But the Council searched it—magic, of course—and found nothing. They even sent out a few peacekeepers, who also found nothing. Furthermore, they all came back, which the Council doesn't think would have happened if they'd gotten close to anything."

"Even Willand in a temper tantrum would know that to mess with those pairs would paint a neon arrow in her direction," Jaime said, frowning.

"Exactly. But since the Council couldn't find anything, either . . . they decided that, 'in my inexperience,' I was mistaken. Pretty patronizing, actually, considering that if they were able to locate the shielding without a trace to follow, they'd have done it already—the fact that they can't do it now doesn't mean a thing, as far as I'm concerned. But they've settled on another tactic—they're installing a full blockade, magical and physical, of all the passes between the Lorakan mountains and the coast. No more mage lure, no more problem. The outlaws will surrender so they can be treated for withdrawal, and the crisis is over."

Jaime snorted skepticism. "Yeah, right, just like America's been able to stop the influx of cocaine. These people obviously aren't used to policing drug dealers—or drug addicts, when they get desperate."

Dayna nodded, tugging at the sandy hair that almost reached her shoulder. "Just like last time. Stick to defensive tactics—until the problem's too big to ignore. The only thing they've *really* done is have Sherra work up an antidote—it's in solution, and it's triggered by body heat—works something like null wards. But even *that's* no good if a wizard's got personal shields up—no way to introduce it."

"Bureaucracy," Jaime said. She ruffled the bangs off her forehead and sat back.

"What do you want to do?" Jess asked, still standing beside the bench. Bouncy. Dayna wanted to *do* something, it was clear enough to Jess. And Jess, flushed from her small victory with the spellstone, wanted to do it too, whatever it was. What she really needed, she decided, was a good long Lady run. But her ribs weren't up to that, not quite yet.

Dayna gave her a humorless little grin. "I'm not usually the *doing* sort," she said. "I'm the stay-in-the-theater-seat-and-see-how-the-story-turns-out sort. But . . . this time, I have some ideas."

Jaime didn't look enthused. "I've been feeling like I wanted to *do* something, all right. It's been frustrating sitting around waiting for things to happen so life can get back to normal—and *I* can get back to Ohio. But this is no small thing you're talking about, Dayna. Going against the Council that now has jurisdiction over you is the least of it."

Dayna made a face. "No kidding," she said. "But just listen. You know I mess around a lot with raw magic—and how everyone hates it. They've been trying to stomp it out of me. Well, when I was under the influence of the mage lure, the slightest hint of raw magic was like getting hit with a big dose of internal static, volume on high." She looked at Jess, who was trying to decide what static was, and then at Jaime, who merely looked blank.

"Don't you get it? It's a weapon against anyone on mage lure! Ask the others on the team—they got feedback every time I slipped up and used it."

"If it's such a great weapon, why isn't the Council considering using it?" Jaime asked.

"They're afraid of it," Jess said suddenly, recalling that every reference to raw magic she'd ever heard had reflected the dread of its uncontrolled backlash. Every reference, except those from Dayna.

"Exactly." Dayna nodded in satisfaction. "Of course I mentioned it to them, and they believe it, especially with the word of the other team members to back me up. But they say the amount of raw magic necessary would just be too dangerous."

"And you don't think so?" Jaime gave her friend an incredulous look. "These are powerful people talking, Dayna. They didn't get on the Council with a lottery ticket."

Dayna made a rude noise. "That's right, but not one of them has used raw magic as an adult, I'll bet. People around here scare it out of their kids practically before they're old enough to walk. That's why I'm such a frustration to them."

"Look, there's a lot more to this whole idea than just saying you want to do something, and you want to use raw magic." Jaime shook her head. "We can't do anything alone, just the three of us. We need horses, we need provisions, we need to have some *faint* idea of where we're going—" Her voice rose, until she was almost shouting—and then she cut herself off. After a moment, she said, "Well, you get the picture. It's not so simple."

"All I know is, *we're* the ones who made the difference last time," Dayna said. "Sure, we can sit around and watch this happen—but is it going to be over before Willand does something horrible with a changespell, and traps Jess as Lady forever? Or before she gets her hands on one of us? She's made her intentions pretty clear—she wants revenge. And so does Ernie, or he wouldn't have recruited Willand in the first place, and set the outlaws to working on changespells."

"This is true," Jess said, speaking up fiercely for the first time, a startling contrast to the moments when she'd done nothing but listen. "Willand has tried to kill all of us, with her fire and her darts. She was happy to watch Shammel beat me." Jess fingered the dark scar on her jaw. "She will not stop coming after us—unless someone stops her first."

"Or until she's successful," Dayna said darkly. "Look, Jay, it's a lot to think about. I've had plenty of time here to do it, what with being the convalescent and all. You're going to be visiting for a few days anyway, right? So let's forget it for now. Let me get that tea I forgot, and let's talk about something else—like what sort of spellstones would be good for Jess. Or men, or shopping, or *any*thing."

Jaime nodded. "That makes sense. Okay with you, Jess?"

Jess looked at the two of them—Dayna, ready to take action for once, and Jaime, hanging back, her fear of Willand evident. She wondered what they saw in her, and whether they could look beneath the enthusiasm with which she had greeted this visit, and the conversation, and even the garden, and if they could see past it to the determination beneath. Then she nodded. Let them think about it. Her mind was already made up.

❧ ❧ ❧

"Come on, Lady, you can do it." Dayna knelt in the soft moss, waving away the gnat that circled her face. "You did so well with that glow spellstone . . . you know what you want. You just have to hold it all in your mind, just for a moment. . . ."

Resting on the ground beside Dayna and Jaime, her

feet tucked neatly before her chest and her tail flicking against her haunches even in repose, Lady snorted wetly. Dayna flinched back with an expressive noise of distaste, and was not amused when Jaime chuckled.

Ostensibly, they picnicked. It was, of course, an excuse to get them out of Sherra's hold, so Jess, as Lady, could work on the spellstones Dayna had made for her. But they'd lingered after lunch, a pleasant interlude in the shade of the woods, in a spot Dayna had found last fall. The creek ran nearby—a trickle, this year—and though there was a nearby thin spot in the woods to let the light through, this particular spot was mossy and shaded, and as cool as any place outside Sherra's hold was likely to get.

It would probably be the last day of their visit, since the nearly recovered members of the checkspell team would be going back to work, this time on the reverse changespell—after they figured out how to restore the peacekeeper sheep. Right now, Dayna's team had all the experience. So this was Lady's last chance to figure out how to trigger her spellstone back to Jess.

She'd done fine with a new identifier spellstone, even though Dayna made one a little more complex than the simple spell Lady had first triggered. And the glow spell had only taken a few tries to master. The changespell, though. . . . Dayna waved at the gnat again, thought about renewing her bug repellent, and waited.

Jaime shook her head. "She's done so well . . . but I don't think she's going to get it. Not today, anyway. You're sure you can change her back? I want to save that spellstone for when we're back at Arlen's. I'm sure she's going to want to try this again."

Dayna laughed. "Jaime, I'm part of the changespell team. Of course I can change her back. There are a lot of spells on that level that I can't begin to tackle, but that one? Yeah, I can do it."

Jaime looked a little embarrassed. "Sorry," she said. "I don't get to see much of you in action. I've known you for quite a few years, and most of them have been without magic."

"It's all right," Dayna said, grinning. "Still takes me by surprise sometimes, too."

"You seem to be happy enough with it," Jaime said, almost as if she was asking a question.

Dayna hesitated, her life in Ohio flickering through her thoughts. It'd been a good enough life. But this was better. "I *am* happy with it," she said. "Too bad this is the most you've seen of what I'm doing, and here we are in another crisis."

Jaime's mouth twisted, a wry expression. "Calandre and Willand are, no doubt, two of the biggest pains in the ass that I've ever run across. And that *includes* that guy south of Columbus who thinks he's riding Grand Prix on those great clods of horses that lurch around the ring."

"Worse than that, eh?" Dayna said, amused.

Jaime blushed. "Well, yes."

Lady chose that moment to snort again, giving Dayna a miniature shower. "That's enough of *that*," Dayna said. "Time to look like Jess again. Get ready."

Lady understood well enough. She threw her weight back so she could get her front legs beneath her, and then braced them against the push of her haunches as she stood. She shook off the bits of bark and leaf that clung to her sides, and then waited quietly, watching Dayna.

Dayna reached for the spell, running through the words of the first of it—a complex recitation dealing with muscle and shape and substance. Halfway through, she cheated, and triggered a flow of raw magic, shaping it more with her will than her intellect. The magic swirled around them, flickering through Lady with the effect it always had—look straight at it, and you couldn't see a thing.

Watch with the corner of your eye, and you might get a glimpse of hair settling back into place, or of Jess as she straightened and stood. But for Dayna, the spell wasn't over; the raw magic had gathered, and was waiting to break loose and wreak havoc.

Dayna took a deep breath and plugged back into the formal spell, using the final elements to dismiss the magic. It faded like a long wave flowing back to the sea, and left Dayna with the same feeling she used to get after a good aerobics workout.

Only better. She opened her eyes and grinned at Jaime, and found Jaime grinning back.

᯽ ᯽ ᯽

"Jess," Jaime told her—again, "you did very well. You're on the right track, and you know it."

Jess shifted the backpack she carried and said nothing. Jaime was right, of course. It was simply too soon to ask Lady to trigger the changespell. She needed to practice on some intermediate spells before jumping to the big one. Still . . . she'd hoped to return to Anfeald able to prove Ander wrong. Even Carey thought it might be too much for her—he just wasn't as outspoken about it.

"Never mind, Jess," Dayna said. "We'll work on it again when we get a chance. Maybe they'll send the changespell team back to Anfeald again. It's really a better setup for doing that kind of intensive work."

"Yes," Jess said. There was no point in thinking about it now, when they were spending their last afternoon with Dayna. "Are we going to go to the village, now?"

"You still want to get your ears pierced?" Jaime asked, amusement in her voice. She fingered one of her own silver studs, and held a branch aside for the rest of them as they stepped out of the woods and on to the main road, only a few moments from the hold.

"I had Kymmet scrip changed to coin," Jess said, not

certain of Jaime's reaction. "This is a good place to get it done." More personal than the city practitioners, and less expensive, too.

"I'm sorry," Jaime said, but this time she outright snickered. "I just keep imaging Lady with great big hoop earrings."

Dayna giggled, while Jess snorted at the thought. "No," she said decisively. "Small ones . . . that blue stone. No one will see them unless they look."

"I can't help it," Jaime said, and snickered again.

"Uh-oh," Dayna said, stopping Jaime's levity short. Jess saw immediately what it was—someone lingering at the opening of Sherra's stout wooden gate. "I think vacation's over."

In a moment, they knew for sure. The figure turned out to be Katrie, one of Sherra's few men-at-arms and one of the first people Jaime had met in Camolen; Jess knew her from her courier days under Carey. She was a competent no-nonsense woman, who also enjoyed life, and whose loyalties ran strong. Tall, sturdy, very light blonde hair, her features were too strong to be beautiful, but Jess had always thought she would make a very handsome mare.

Now, she wasted no time. "Visitors coming," she said shortly—she was there to greet them, then. "The outlaws have struck again."

"Who?" Jess asked, thinking immediately of Carey.

"Group of Ninth Level Meditators just north of the border," Katrie told her. "Their regular supply convoy came today and discovered a hold full of hedgehogs clinging to their meditation beads. Some of the local Meditators are coming here to talk to Sherra about it."

"Meditators?" Dayna said, horror in her voice. "Since when did they ever do anyone any harm?"

"That," said Katrie grimly, resting her hand on the hilt of her knife, "is the point. I'm not supposed to know this—

and I'm not telling how I heard!—but since you're about to find out anyway, I'll pass it on. The outlaws have set up an ultimatum—the Council has to remove the mage lure blockade, or the outlaws will keep using the reverse changespell on the most innocent victims they can find."

"They must be desperate," Jaime murmured. "I bet Ernie finally told them the truth about mage lure."

"Thanks, Katrie," Dayna said, and took Jaime and Jess each by the arm, tugging them onward. Jess couldn't help it, that sudden grip, that preemptory tug—she reared back and tore loose, garnering Dayna's astonishment and Jaime's quick reaction.

"Easy, Jess," she said. "It's all right—"

And by then Jess knew it was, but she couldn't help the annoyed glare she sent at Dayna; she tossed her head to hide how upset she was, and slowly settled. Jaime, too, sent Dayna an annoyed look. "You ought to know better than that."

"All right, all right, I'm sorry." And clearly, she was—as well as embarrassed. This time only nodding, Dayna drew them alongside the tall, rough lumber fence. "Listen. I'll try to see you before you leave tonight, but I might not get a chance. You've got to think about what I said before. About us doing something. You can see what's happening—things are only going to get worse around here, and yeah, yeah, the Council will finally do something, but by then we'll have a whole *zoo* of changed people, and who knows how many of them we'll get back sane?"

Reluctantly, Jaime said, "I wish I didn't think you were right."

"But I am." Dayna didn't miss a beat. "Think about it. I'll be with the changespell team, but it's not like they can't get along without me. Shandy just barely keeps herself from patting me on the head, I swear. Ask Carey about it, why don't you—we'll need someone who can guide us, who really knows the country, and I don't think

Jess ever worked up in that area. And get back to me—you can send it through the Dispatch, all I need is one word—*yes*." She looked at Jaime, her eyes intent. "I can *do* this, Jay. I can find them—and I can blast 'em with enough raw magic to keep us safe. And I'm the *only* one who can."

Jaime gave Jess an unhappy look, but Jess, her anger at Dayna gone, nodded. "Yes," she said. "I'll talk to Carey."

❧ ❧ ❧

Jess sat on the bed in Carey's room, the first and largest in the second floor courier quarters. Carey was lounging against the window sill, and while he'd greeted Jess and Jaime at the spell booth and been cheerful enough through their late dinner, now he was a little distracted. The room to the door was open, as he always left it in the early evening; they'd already been interrupted twice—once by a courier who'd accidentally been scheduled for overlapping runs, and once by the man in charge of exercising the stallion.

Jess didn't mind. It was part of Carey's job, and who he was—and he cared enough about it to make sure his people could get in touch with him as easily as possible.

She hadn't brought up Dayna's proposal yet. He'd rested his hand lightly on the back of her neck on the way up here, and she'd been distracted thinking about it, and now he was looking at her like he could tell she was working her way up to something.

She played with the back of her baseball cap a moment, sliding the size adjustment strap back and forth in its clip. Then she decided she might as well just say it. Jaime might do it differently, but Jaime had gone to eat a private dinner in Arlen's quarters. "Dayna thinks we should go after the outlaws," she blurted, just as Carey was beginning to smile at her hesitation.

The smile vanished. "*Dayna* thinks *what*?"

Jess left the bed and joined him at the window, where the summer dusk was just falling—starting to get earlier again, and pointing at autumn. "It surprised us, too," she said. "But I want to do it."

"You want to do *what*? Charge off into the countryside with no notion of where you're going and what you're going to do when you get there?"

She frowned at him. "That's rude. I'm not stupid."

Carey groaned, and rubbed his eye in a weary gesture. "You're right, you're right. I'm sorry. But come on, Jess . . . you've got to admit that *sounded* a little stupid. But—well, never mind. What's going on?"

So Jess told him what Dayna had in mind, absently moving in closer to brush the smudge of dirt from his shoulder, to run her hand down his arm and take a closer look at the nasty cut he seemed to have inflicted on his hand while she was gone. When she would have moved in right next to him, putting their bodies in contact like any two close horse companions, he shifted away from her. It was enough to bring her gaze back up to his, for a long and questioning look, but she couldn't read the conflict in his eyes. "What do you think?" she said finally, not entirely sure, herself, just what she was asking about.

Carey cleared his throat. "I think Dayna's bitten off a little more than she can chew. If any of that was viable, the Council would be doing it."

"*They* didn't help Arlen last year," Jess said. "We did."

Carey ducked his head, crossed his arms over his chest. When he looked up again, it was with a little flip of his head, getting his dark blonde forelock out of his eyes. "True," he said. "But things were a little different. Arlen's time was running out. There's no reason we have to rush into this."

Jess looked at him a long moment. Then she said softly, "Willand has captured me and watched me beaten. She has burned Kymmet trying to kill me. She tried to tag you and Jaime with that dart. Dayna got a threat while she was at the farm. And now the outlaws are going after people who have nothing to do with any of this, and turning them into animals."

Carey closed his eyes. "All true," he said. "I just don't know that Dayna's way will get us anything but trouble. Suppose we fail? Then Willand has her hands on us all, and people are *still* being turned into animals. Sooner or later, their mage lure will run out. And then they'll die."

"Yes," Jess said. "Will that be soon enough?" After a long hesitation, she added, "We need you. But I can find maps, and I can show Dayna how to get where she wants to go, that way."

He shook his head at her, a faint grin on his face. "You've always been persuasive, Jess, in more ways than you know. But you sure are getting better with words."

"Then are you coming with us?"

"I don't know," Carey said. "And I'm not sure you *can* do it without me. It may not be fair, but if I don't want this to happen, it won't."

She hadn't considered that—hadn't thought *he* would consider it. "You'd tell Arlen?" Before Carey could answer, she heard a noise behind her, and turned to look.

And there was Ander, in the open doorway, his eyes narrowed and his voice suspicious. "Tell Arlen what?"

Jess frowned at him, and before the anger in Carey's eyes could make it to his mouth, said, "You're supposed to *knock*, Ander. Even when the door is open."

"If you weren't so close to him, he'd have been able to see past you to the door, and found me," Ander said.

"You're really pushing it," Carey growled.

"Maybe I am. But don't forget—I've got a stake in all this, too." He gave Jess a quick look, one she suddenly recognized as hurt, and then went on. "I was in that fire, too. And you're talking about people I . . . care about.

Deeply. So excuse me for coming to the party without an invitation, but I'm here, and I want to know what's going on."

Jess cast a quick glance at Carey, simmering in anger, and knew it would be best to separate the two men—one who thought he loved her, and one who'd declared his love a year ago and didn't seem to know what to do with it. But Ander was right. He'd been in that fire; he'd saved her life. He'd been with her through this entire thing.

Carey seemed, begrudgingly, to realize the same thing. Or perhaps he just wanted to maintain what control he could. "We're thinking about going after the outlaws. Dayna has a way, but the Council patted her on the head and sent her out to play."

"Thinking about going after them?" Ander asked pointedly. "Or arguing about going after them?"

"Some of both," Carey said, just as pointedly unconcerned about Ander's observation.

Ander gave them a sudden grin; it had a feral quality that made Jess blink. "I've had enough, myself. It's time to get back to work at Kymmet. Jess has Willsey scheduled to come down for work, and I have three babies who need ground handling they haven't managed to get yet. So if you go . . . I'm coming with you."

"I don't remember asking you," Carey said.

Ander's grin just broadened. "Sometimes, it doesn't pay to wait around. Sometimes you have to go get what you want—even if it means taking it from someone else who hasn't made up his mind yet."

Jess just frowned at him. She had the impression he wasn't talking about the outlaws at all.

❧ ❧ ❧

Carey stood out by the gate to the back pasture, where the broodmares lived. He had The Dun—whom Jess had never asked to see, and probably never would—and another older mare who had failed to conceive; he wondered if it was time to retire her. A third mare lost her foal to the windstorm, and Carey had put her back in training, hoping to console her with the activity.

A breeze whispered by his face, bringing with it the teasing scent of rain. It was a dark night, overcast and moonless, and he wasn't sure exactly what he was doing out here when he should have been sleeping instead. His body was no longer so forgiving about losing a night or two of sleep, and when tomorrow came, it wasn't going to go light on him just because he had circles under his eyes.

It was a big pasture. The mares spent most of their time at the far end of it, by a small cluster of trees. But they must have scented him, for he heard a snort—that was The Dun—and then another, from the mare he'd ingeniously named Socks. Soon he had them spotted—dark, slowly moving shapes against an only marginally lighter skyline. Without hurry, they ambled to the gate to find out what he was doing there.

"Looking for answers," he told them, only then realizing it was the truth. There were too many questions in his head . . . and most of them were about himself.

A year ago, headstrong and undeterred by the disapproval of almost everyone around him, Carey had ignored the Council, broken out of house arrest at Sherra's, and ridden to rescue Arlen. He hadn't thought about consequences. He hadn't wondered if he was doing it exactly right. He'd known it had to be done, he'd taken his best options, and he'd done it.

He suddenly wondered if he'd do the same thing today. "Would I?" he asked out loud to The Dun, who was searching his hands and arms for treats as they rested on top of the fence. In response, she licked his arm several times.

No wonder Jess had been puzzled. No wonder she didn't seem to understand why he was so careful around her. He wasn't the same person she'd come to know, both as horse and human. He was Carey a year after being irreparably touched by Calandre's twisted magic. A whole year of learning to accept his new limits, to plan his days so he could make it through them without falling on his face from fatigue, or simply being unable to function the next day. He was someone who now weighed everything he did before he did it.

Had he fallen into ruts of thinking that didn't do him any good? When had it been, anyway, that he'd gotten so concerned about whether or not it was fair to Jess, to draw her even closer, to do what he'd wanted to do ever since he'd been in *Ohio*, for Heavens' sake, and take her in his arms and show her how deeply he really felt about her? At first he'd been too sick to even think of such a thing. And somehow, by the time he was feeling more like himself, Jess was off in Kymmet, and he was wondering if she didn't need a little more room to grow.

He was an idiot. A burning in Ninth-Level Hells idiot, so wrapped up in learning to live with the limitations of his damaged body that he'd lost track of the bigger things, the more important things. The things that made him want to *live*.

And now Willand was threatening those things again—his friends, his own safety, his *Jess*—and he wasn't sure whether or not he wanted to do something about it? "I'm an idiot," he groaned out loud, resting his forehead on his arms. The Dun whuffled at his hair. Just like her daughter. It raised goosebumps on Carey's arms.

He looked back toward the hold—the back of the hill, from this pasture, a big dark lump rising in the night sky. There, on the second floor, Jess was sleeping, had probably gone to sleep wondering what was wrong with him, and why he had changed so much.

Well, he knew why he'd changed. And on a day-to-day basis, maybe it was the way he would have to live. But for the important things . . . there was still enough of the old Carey left to handle them.

✤ ✤ ✤

Jess whimpered in her sleep. *The rope lashed by her face*. She twitched, trying to escape. *Shammel's greasy-looking grin flickered before her*. She wouldn't let him! *The rope slashed the air and smacked dun haunches, ripping flesh with searing pain*. Escape, she had to—the scent of rain in her nose—hands reaching for her . . .

Jess shrieked in fury and terror and launched herself off the bed, ears flattened, teeth bared, hooves ready to . . . *hands* ready to . . . it was dark, where was she?

"Easy, Braveheart. It was just a dream."

Jess made a stricken sound and struggled to orient herself. Carey's voice, tender and reassuring. The dim outlines of the furniture in the borrowed room. The smell of impending rain on the cool currents of a breeze through the window. Arlen's. Safe.

"Carey," she said, her voice thick and her mouth struggling more than usual with the formation of the word.

"It's me," he said, moving up next to her in the dark, smelling of horse, his hair in need of a trim and in his eyes, though not enough to hide the shine of them. "I wanted to talk to you . . . I'm glad I came. Pretty bad dream, eh?"

"Yes," Jess said, still a little befuddled. "But . . . why . . . how . . ."

"The guest rooms are all keyed to me," Carey said. "I knocked, but you didn't answer, and then I heard—well, I was worried."

All right. It was the middle of the night, and she'd had a bad dream, but it was over now—it really was—

and Carey was here. She took a deep breath, and let it out slowly. "I'm all right."

"Want to talk about it?"

His voice had just the right combination of sympathy and concern, but she didn't want to talk about it. The beating haunted her too much already. "No," she murmured, looking away from him a moment—though his expression drew her back. She doubted he could make out the details of her own appearance, and thought he'd probably forgotten how well she could see in the dark. His face was alert concern and . . . tenderness. And something else, too, something she couldn't quite decipher, but that reminded her of Carey from days gone by.

She moved away from him and went to stand by the window, waking up enough to recall the thoughts that had made falling asleep in the first place so difficult. "I want to talk about something else."

"Okay," he said, shifting his weight off his stiff leg but sounding willing enough to listen. It only underscored what she was about to say.

"What we talked about earlier . . . Dayna's idea," Jess started, and waited for him to nod before continuing. "I said I could use a map if you didn't want to go. That's what I want to do." She never should have asked him, not with the things Calandre's spell had done to him. Finding the outlaws would be no simple thing, no mere morning's ride—and he couldn't do it, not even if he wanted to.

"What are you talking about? I never said I wouldn't—"

"I can use *here* spells to make sure I know where I am on the map," she continued, as if he hadn't spoken. This was hard enough. "Dayna will be guiding us, too. So we can do it. If you don't tell Arlen. You won't, will you?"

When she turned to look at him, she saw a frown. He

shook his head, and said, "No. I have no intention of telling Arlen. I'm not so sure he wouldn't agree with Dayna, but it's not fair to put him in that position, not with his Council obligations."

"I brought a horse," Jess said, "but Jaime will need a horse from the stable." She didn't mention Ander, although she knew he would be coming. But Ander was healthy, and a superb archer. He could watch out for himself.

"Jaime can have a horse," Carey said, though his voice had gone odd. "Jess, you're not just deciding to do this even if I don't want to, are you? You're deciding to do it *without* me."

How was she supposed to answer that one? And why did it make her want to cry? Even though she knew he wouldn't be able to see, Jess turned away. She closed her eyes and tilted her head back to catch the breeze, free to come in at night when the hold's cooling spells weren't in effect. Definitely rain. Even in her distress she hoped for it, and an end to the drought.

"Jess," Carey said, moving up behind her until he was so close she could feel the warmth of his body through the night shift she wore. Yes, he definitely smelled like horse. His hand landed on her shoulder, warm, with just the right pressure to reassure her instead of spook her. "What's going on here? I'm right, aren't I? You want to leave me out of this one." She was sure she heard the hurt this time.

"No," she said. "I mean, yes . . . I mean . . . I worry!"

"Worry," he repeated flatly.

"Yes. Because of . . . since . . ." She gave up, and finally added, most fiercely, "I won't let anything happen to you!"

The sudden silence was very loud, and seemed very long to Jess. Then—

"Ohhh, that's it. You think I can't handle it anymore." He didn't sound hurt any longer, but understanding also brought a touch of anger. He used his hold on her shoulder to turn her around to face him, although she complied only reluctantly. "I've got news for you, Jess. I'm the one who makes up my mind about what I can and can't do, not you. And I've already decided to come with you."

Jess blinked surprise. "You have?" And then, "But . . . so much riding. For *days*, Carey. I don't want to see you hurt!"

His hand fell away from her shoulder. "If I can stand it, then so can you. But it's my decision. Not yours. You of all people should understand that. You're not very happy when people try to make decisions about what *you* can do—like your pal Ander, telling you that Lady can't manage the changespell stone."

"That makes me mad," Jess admitted, and then suddenly truly understood what she had been doing. "I *was* doing what he does to me!" More puzzled, she added, "I didn't even see it. All I wanted was to make sure you were all right. I . . . wanted to protect you."

Carey sighed. "I know," he said. "Believe me, I know." He moved up next to her so they were shoulder to shoulder but facing opposite directions. "When something's so very important . . . it's easy to do the wrong thing, just because you want so much to do the *right* thing, you don't think quite straight."

"Yes," she murmured, and suddenly realized he was talking about himself. "The wrong thing?" she asked, leaning into his shoulder a little. "What was the wrong thing?" Behind her, the smell of rain grew thick, and she heard the first hesitant patter of droplets against the window sill.

She felt more than saw him shake his head. "I didn't give you enough credit, Jess. I knew what I wanted—and you'd better believe I wanted it!—and I tried to protect you from making the wrong decision. I think I just ended up confusing you."

She thought she knew, then, what he was talking about,

and she closed her eyes and thought of thunderstorms instead of the gentle but steady rain now falling outside. She thought of Carey, and all the hot, demanding sensations of an aroused mare in heat. It wasn't like that now; that was a thunderstorm compared to this rain. She thought the rain would last longer.

Jess stepped back until the small of her back pressed up against the window, and slid between Carey and sill. It was a tight squeeze. There, she nibbled his neck, a delicate version of equine flirting. She nibbled all the way up to his ear, and he groaned softly, a small and frustrated sound. "I remember the thunderstorm," she whispered.

His hands had settled on her hips; they tightened a moment, then moved up her back to tangle in her hair, and gently pull her head back—just enough so he could look into her eyes. For a moment, that's all they did, though Jess realized she was trembling a little, and wondered when that had started, and then felt that tremble resonate through Carey. He took a deep breath, untangling one hand from her hair so his fingers, a little unsteady, were free to brush across her lips.

And then he kissed her. Less volatile, less needy than when she'd put him up against the tack shed, but slow and deep, while his hands moved across her shoulders and traced tingling little paths on her back beneath her hair. She began to lose track of what she'd been thinking; she was, suddenly, nothing but feeling. The thin shift sliding between them, the bristle of the short hair at the nape of his neck and then the tense muscles of his back beneath her hands; the way the little fluttery thrill traveled up and down her spine and settled lower.

When he lifted his lips from hers, she made a small noise of protest, but it was only to return the favor of nibbling at her ear for a moment, which she decided she liked just as much. After he'd nibbled that ear, and kissed his way across her face to reach the other one, he pulled her in close, holding her tight. "I remember the thunderstorm, too," he said, his voice low and a little hoarse. "But I think this nice slow rain is going to be *much* more satisfying."

Chapter 12

Arlen, Jaime thought, was beginning to suspect something was up. She sat in the biggest chair in his quarters, her feet tucked under herself and the small cat in her lap, feeling grateful for the wizardly equivalent of air conditioning and trying to decide what it was she really wanted to do.

Jess seemed prepared to charge out after Willand with Dayna, and Carey, to Jaime's surprise, had agreed it might be for the best. And Ander was walking around with a look of determination set on his handsome features, not about to be left out. Now, they were waiting for her, waiting for Jaime's own decision. But Jaime still wasn't sure. Or rather, while part of her was entirely convinced that the Council would not manage to stop the outlaws before more innocent people suffered, and that Dayna's expedition was the right thing to do, she was also excruciatingly aware of the consequences of failure. The very thought of finding herself in Willand's hands again evoked a visceral fear that she couldn't do a thing to mitigate.

If they were going to do anything, they needed to quit deciding and just *do* it. *She* needed to quit deciding, and just do it. And she was as firmly stuck in indecision as she'd ever been in her life.

It would be easier if she could just ask Arlen what he thought—let someone else make the decisions she couldn't. She closed her eyes and thought about Arlen. She called to mind his strength and conviction, and the way he'd dealt with Renia, knowing the mage lure had made her strong enough—if not wise enough—to match his prowess.

She thought of how, an hour or so ago, while he was taking tea with her and chatting about new developments in the science of magic—a new road spell that was supposed to allow the surface to withstand dry spells better, and even some slight signs of success in weather control—he seemed to hesitate on the brink of asking what was on her mind. Once he even looked at her, shook his head, and muttered, "It's better if I don't know." Jaime quickly distracted him by asking about progress on the mage lure blockade. Arlen complied with details, as if he, too, was glad for the distraction.

One shipment had been discovered and destroyed. And on the morning of the fifth day, the news spread around the hold like Willand's fire through Kymmet—the outlaws had struck again. They'd taken the staff and students of a small short-term school and turned them into sheep. Unfamiliar with the school and preoccupied with her own concerns, it took Jaime a moment to understand that it was for precocious magic users, those whose talent came out early enough that the students had little control—over the magic, or over their own misuse of it. It was, she realized with a sick cold lump in her stomach, the equivalent of a preschool camp.

The outlaws had to be *stopped*. Dayna had to go, and she needed her friends to do it. They *had* to do this thing, no matter what small chance of success awaited them. Carey, Jess, Dayna, Ander—and Jaime. It was a decision already made, she realized, and simply not acknowledged.

At least, that's what she felt one moment. The next, she was convinced Dayna's plan was entirely folly, and that she wanted nothing to do with it. Fear, it seemed, held a very strong vote. She wished she'd asked Arlen about the plan when she'd had the chance.

Jaime stroked the cat and stared at Arlen's latest stitchery project, letting her mind go blank. What a relief. She'd think about her dilemma in another moment, perhaps, and she'd make a decision, she really would. But for now, there was just the cat in her lap and her eyes losing focus and her brain wandering . . .

A clunking noise from down the hall brought her back to here and now. It came from Arlen's workroom—nothing so strange about that. He and his apprentices were working on something this afternoon, and that often brought more activity on this floor.

The next moment, Jaime was alert and on the verge of alarm, her hand stilled on the cat's back and her body stiffened. Someone had cried out, she thought, from behind the closed door of the workroom. She nudged the cat out of her lap and went to pause at the threshold of the study, looking at the workroom door as if it could tell her anything.

There it was again. A cry of strained effort . . . it sounded like Natt. Jaime walked slowly to the workroom, her hand raised as though to knock—but she wouldn't. She would never interrupt Arlen at work. He knew what he was doing; there was nothing to worry about.

Cesna's short scream of fear startled Jaime away from the door, but she didn't miss the sound of someone falling—the tangled sounds of a stool hitting the floor, and a body with it. Jaime pounded on the door. "Arlen!"

It opened immediately. Natt stood before her, white-faced and sweating. Beyond him, Arlen was sprawled on the floor, with Cesna frantically trying to rouse him. His mouth was slack, and his skin gray, and Jaime didn't even ask for permission, but pushed past Natt to kneel beside Arlen and demand of Cesna, "What happened?"

"I'll try to raise Sherra," Natt told Cesna. "I don't know

if I can get her direct—I may have to go through the Dispatch."

"That'll take too long," Cesna said, fear in her eyes.

"I'll *try*," Natt said, and hurried across the hall to the apprentices' workroom.

"What *happened*?" Jaime repeated, resting her hand on Arlen's chest to feel a rise and fall that was far too shallow. "How is he hurt? We have to *do* something!"

Cesna sparked irritation at her. "There's nothing you can do. It was magic, and you're no wizard."

"Then *you* do something!" Jaime demanded.

Cesna looked away, closed her eyes and bit her lip. "I don't know how," she said, looking very young. "If only Natt can get Sherra here—"

Jaime took Arlen's hand; it was very cold, and clammy. "At least we can treat him for shock," she said, and ran back to her room to pull sheets and blankets from her bed, rushing the bundle back to the workroom. "Here," she said, flipping the bedding out to lie flat on the floor. "Roll him onto this—gotta get him off that cold floor."

Cesna didn't question her. She seemed glad enough to let someone older take charge, and together they got Arlen onto the bedding. Jaime flipped the remainder of the blankets back over him, leaning across him to snug them tight. "What happened?" she asked again. "What was he doing?"

This time, she got an answer. Strained with concern, Cesna said, "He . . . he asked Natt and I if we would help search that area Dayna was so interested in. He didn't think the Council had tried hard enough, and even though he wasn't supposed to try anything on his own, he thought that together . . . that if he had us linked . . . that he might at least find a *trace* of them."

"And did he?" Jaime asked, tucking soft wool around Arlen's shoulder even though it was already tucked, just so she could be doing something. She wasn't sure she wanted to hear the answer to this one.

Cesna nodded, then shook her head. "No, we hadn't, not yet. They must have felt him. They came after us—and . . ."

To Jaime's surprise, the girl's chin gave a sudden quiver; she realized the apprentice was about to fall apart on her. "Grow up!" she snapped, her voice harsher than she'd intended. "Arlen needs you now, and you won't do him a bit of good if you're crying over him."

Cesna's head came up; she glared at Jaime. "Natt and I couldn't hold the link," she said. "Not under the strain of attack. Whatever they did—whatever *Willand* did—he took it alone."

Jaime just stared at him a moment. She had her answer, without even asking. While she had been wondering whether circumstances had grown dire enough to risk taking her own shot at Willand and the outlaws, Arlen had defied his own Council and done just that.

And now look at him. This is what you're *facing*. But instead of feeding the fear that was always waiting within her, Jaime felt something else. She looked down at Arlen, who, even though they lived on a different worlds, was such a very important part of her life. Yet another special friend hurt by Willand's destructive touch.

Jaime smoothed the blanket over his chest, and pulled it up higher around his neck, running her hand over his hair, already grayed to excess by his earlier encounter with Willand and her mistress. She looked at Cesna, and said, "Enough is enough." The young wizard gave her a blank look, but Jaime didn't need her understanding. She knew what it meant to her. Decisions.

Enough is enough.

❧ ❧ ❧

Yes. That was the message Jaime sent to Dayna, sticking it in the hold's queue of messages for the Dispatch just like any other, where it waited its turn until Natt or Cesna sent the day's collection of correspondence. Messages to family members, requisitions to supply companies, business talk between wizards and couriers—and one short declaration of intent to charge off toward trouble.

The next incoming round brought her Dayna's reply. *Wait*.

Wait. While Sherra labored over Arlen, bringing him out of shock, but unable to rouse him from what Jaime could only call a coma. Just wait. That sounded like it was supposed to be easy enough, didn't it? Then why was Ander repairing arrows that were in perfectly good condition? And Carey, snarly enough to garner wide berth from his couriers, went over—and over—schedules that had been set for days. The grooms had given up on questioning Jaime, and now merely pointed her at the horses who needed clean stalls or grooming; they were distracted enough by their own concerns for Arlen that they didn't care what she did.

Jess also recruited Jaime into helping her clean and repair tack, all the while sitting with her hands in saddlesoap and a distracted, dreamy expression on her face. Jaime had a good idea what that expression was all about, but kept her thoughts, and her smile, to herself. It was the one bright point in the pall that had settled over the hold.

There was some fuss when Dayna went missing from Sherra's—but neither Cesna or Natt had the attention to spare to question any of them about it, and they never had to try out their carefully formulated professions of ignorance. To her own surprise, Jaime's resolve never wavered. Where before she'd been able to think of the outlaw wizards—aside from Willand—as merely desperate, they'd now gone beyond that. They'd attacked a preschool, and—Natt confirmed—they'd been standing behind Willand, bolstering her, in her attack upon Arlen. Suddenly Jaime could think of them as nothing but warped and twisted creatures who deserved all that was coming to them. Her last doubts about helping Dayna disappeared, and even her fear of Willand was helping to fuel her anger. She was *tired* of having this woman so rule her life.

By the fourth day, the tack was cleaned, the schedules were written, and even Ander had to admit there was nothing more to be done with the arrows. Jaime was eating lunch in the unnaturally quiet and grim atmosphere of the dining room when something tickled at her ears, and spread to the back of her throat. She coughed, and suddenly realized she was thinking, *I'm here*, though it certainly hadn't been generated by her own mental process.

I'm here. The process repeated itself three more times, just enough to annoy her severely. Dayna, of course. It had to be Dayna. Jaime finished her meal and went to find the others. Whether this venture was foolhardy and stupid, or whether it would ultimately be seen as heroic, it was about to start.

❧ ❧ ❧

"The nice thing about being in charge," Carey had said when he heard of Dayna's arrival, "is that I can send people on all sorts of odd jobs right when we want to be quiet about leaving." And he had. While Jess and Jaime shuffled gear—activity that drew no notice, considering their tack-cleaning binge—Carey arranged for the stable to be all but abandoned in the early hours of the evening.

Jess would have preferred to stay with him, but everyone else agreed it would attract less attention if they left the hold separately. So immediately after their meal, Jess went up to see Arlen, who had just that afternoon opened his eyes for the first time, although he hadn't spoken at all. Sherra, looking worn and concerned, couldn't say anything reassuring about his recovery. Jess had always known Arlen as the man who could make things happen, and found it hard to imagine Arlen *not* recovering; the thought of it troubled her. She knelt by his bed and placed her head on his chest for a few minutes, a wordless goodbye that left Sherra giving her a thoughtful and narrow-eyed stare.

And then, while the stable area was still full of people putting horses up for the evening, grooming and treating the odd assortment of scrapes and injuries a hard-working horse inevitably acquired, Jess and Ander took their horses out for exercise.

They didn't go far. They didn't know where Dayna was, but surely she was close; they spent their time riding the trails in the woods closest to the hold, not looking for her so much as presenting themselves to be seen. And *heard*, for they kept their pace at a walk. The horses would have plenty of work to do over the next couple of days, and the paths were just wide enough to ride side by side and talk.

Although, Jess thought as she eyed the cloudy sky just barely visible through the break in the canopy above them and wondered if it was going to rain again, *not* talking might be a good thing, too. Especially considering what Ander seemed to have on his mind. "Haven't seen much of you the past few days," he'd just said to her.

She gave up trying to see enough of the sky to predict the weather, but stayed where she was on the horse. Feet out of the stirrups, leaning backward over the low cantle of the saddle to rest her upper shoulders and head on the horse's haunches, she left the reins looped over the pommel and considered Ander's odd statement. The movement of the horse's body as it walked made her shoulders dip alternately beneath her, and stretched her back out. "I saw *you*," she concluded finally. "I was in the stable."

"I don't know how you do that," he said, referring to her position and a little crabby about it—because he wasn't flexible enough to do the same, she knew. He wouldn't expect an answer, so she didn't. After a moment, he said, "I meant in the evening. It's been the best time for going out, what with the rain. I'd have thought you'd have wanted to work on the changespell thing."

"You don't think I can do that," Jess observed, though she wasn't thinking about the changespell and their conflict over it. She was thinking of the time she'd spent with Carey. Time that Ander was asking about. Exciting and private time, when she finally saw the parts of Carey that had been hidden from her until now. His playful streak, and the way his eyes looked when he shared the fire he created inside her. She was learning how much power she had over him—and she liked it.

Ander didn't seem to notice her drifting thoughts. "Well, no . . . I don't think Lady can trigger the spell. But my opinion's never stopped you from trying something."

"No," she said, letting herself flex with her mare's movement and wondering if this was the time to tell Ander to let go.

"It doesn't matter," he said suddenly. "I don't care about the changespell one way or the other. I was really just trying to say I've missed seeing you. The hold couriers are nice enough, but I'm not one of theirs, and I'm not running jobs right now."

She'd never considered Ander as someone who'd have any trouble fitting in, not if he really wanted to. So this was about her, as she thought. And therefore, it was about her and Carey. She sat up, and wiggled her shoulders so her tunic would fall back into place. Then she said simply, "I've been with Carey."

His mouth tightened; in the cloudy day gloom beneath the trees, she couldn't quite make out the look in his eye. After a moment, he said, "I wondered."

And after another moment, he said, "Doesn't mean I'm giving up, Jess. I 'spect you know what I mean."

She might not have, as recently as a couple of months earlier. But Dun Lady's Jess was nothing if not a quick study, and she well remembered the feel of his arms around her while the flame roared above them and the water flowed around them. She merely said, "I'm sorry."

After that, they rode in silence. It was only a short time later that Jess heard a provocative whistle cut the air—the sort of noise she heard construction workers make at her in Columbus, when Jaime took her into the city. It was behind them, and they both twisted simultaneously to find Dayna standing in the middle of the path.

"Good thing I'm not a lost child," Dayna said. "Or the enemy."

"We weren't looking for a lost child or the enemy," Ander said, and sounded cheerful enough so that Jess gave him a second look. No, his eyes were still unhappy. This was for Dayna's sake. "I'll ride out to the edge of the woods and wait for Carey and Jaime. Do you want to wait here, or—"

"Oh, we'll come along," Dayna said. "I know it'll mean traveling after dark, but I think we should be well clear of this area by the time everyone knows *you're* missing, too."

Ander gave them a little half bow and turned his horse around, cantering off the other way.

"He's in an odd mood," Dayna said, and shrugged. She called over, "C'mon out, Katrie—and bring the horses!"

"Katrie?" Jess said, staring at the tall woman who emerged from a small scooped-out hollow in the rolling woods, leading a sturdy-looking chestnut with a spiky mane and a small, familiar-looking bay. Fahrvegnügen.

Dayna seemed uncommonly cheerful. "They sent her out looking for me when I didn't come back from my 'short pleasure ride.' She's good, so of course she found me. I decided to tell her what I was up to before using magic to send her on her way, and *she* decided she wanted to help. I figured we could use it."

"Yes," Jess said, nodding at the woman when she came up to them and handed Dayna Fahrvegnügen's reins. It would be good to have this woman with them. Just because Dayna intended to disable the outlaws' magic didn't mean they shouldn't have other ways to defend themselves.

"So what have they been saying?" Dayna asked, pulling herself awkwardly into the saddle. "About us, I mean. I'm betting they figure Willand got me, or Jenci."

"Nothing," Jess said. At Dayna's surprise, she hesitated, knowing Dayna had to learn of the attack on Arlen, and not knowing how to tell her. Jaime should tell her, or Carey. She said, "I don't think they wanted to tell us until they figured it out."

"Well, they're going to figure it out *now*," Dayna said. "Say, Jess, I've actually learned to canter on this horse. With her gaits, who couldn't! Let's see if we can catch up to Ander."

Jess doubted that, but there was no point in being too far behind. She turned her Kymmet mare—the sorrel's name was Lady, and she'd never been able to use it—around and put her to a canter. In a moment, she heard Dayna and Katrie pick up the gait and follow.

They met Carey and Jaime as dark was falling, and spent a few moments sorting out gear—and sorting out the current situation for Dayna, who took the news about Arlen with grim determination. Carey hadn't been able to bring more than the extra blankets and an extra pair of saddlebags, but fully intended to send Ander—who wouldn't be recognized—into the next small town to secure them more supplies. He had courier scrip aplenty, which the merchants would return to Arlen for coin or services. Assuming Sherra was letting him handle such things yet, at that, Arlen would surely know what they were up to—but by then, it would be too late.

Katrie's presence was greeted with some enthusiasm, but no one wasted much time on small talk. Instead they rode, intent on getting out of Anfeald without notice. Carey had a one-use commercial spellstone, and it cast a gentle and diffuse light to help dispel the dark night and its drizzly offering of rain, but it was miserable riding nonetheless. By the time they reached a stopping point, everyone had gotten a little crabby. They hobbled the horses, turned them loose to pick at the leaves and undergrowth, and huddled beneath the blankets, hoping the rain would let up enough so the thick wool wouldn't soak through.

Jess, snuggled in close to Carey, felt a lot less dismal than she thought the others looked. In a few days, perhaps, they would be facing more than just rain, fatigue, and soggy clothes—but for now, she was perfectly willing to put that aside, and watch the gentle rise and fall of Carey's chest as he slept.

⁂

Jess opened her eyes to find Carey already awake. She rested her face briefly on his upper arm and turned to see what the others were up to—and in doing so, discovered a host of aches she'd thought she'd put behind her. The bones she'd abused in the fire were full of weather pains, probably made all the worse for sleeping on the damp ground. At least it had quit raining—though she could hardly complain about rain, anyway. The gentle patter meant something special to her, more than just an end to the drought.

If she hurt, how must Carey feel? Jess gave him a quick anxious glance. He hadn't said anything yesterday, and she'd almost forgotten he was sure to have trouble with this trip. But now he just shrugged and gave her a rueful little grin. While she wanted to talk to him, first things came first. Slowly, stiffly, she climbed to her feet. Everyone else was just now waking, so she had the woods to herself, and she went to find a convenient bush.

When she returned, they were all on their feet, looking disgruntled and damp and bleary, with their hair sticking out at odd angles and sleep creases on their faces. Jaime and Dayna were stumbling off into the woods in the opposite direction from Jess, and Carey was sitting against a tree, rubbing the heels of his hands into his eyes. Every now and then, one of the trees would drip last night's rain down on them, big cold drops that the warm humidity of the morning did nothing to dispel.

No one was ready to talk about their situation, that was clear enough. Jess went off into the woods to track down their horses, which were making enough noise to keep the task from becoming too difficult. Along the way she shook the water off a sapling and onto her face, scrubbing it with her hands. There, that was a little better.

When she returned with a handful of horses in tow and several others following loosely, the others were sitting, waiting for her, still looking less than enthusiastic. Ander got up to help her tie the horses to trees, and when she went to sit down, Jaime offered her one of the peanut butter sandwiches Jess had packed, along with a mostly empty canteen.

"Time to figure out where we stand and what we need," Carey said, absently stretching his arm a couple of times as he talked. "We'll need to stop for supplies some time today—we just ate nearly all the food we have. We've got no grain for the horses—I just couldn't get it packed up without raising suspicions. We need to think about weapons, too."

"Why?" Jaime said. "We're using Dayna's raw magic, aren't we?"

"Not everyone in their new hideout is likely to be a wizard," Carey told her. "What if they've finally had some solid success with their changespells? Renia said they were planning to create enhanced guards."

Dayna winced. "I wish you hadn't thought of that."

"Better that he did," Ander said. "I've got my bow . . . assuming this rain doesn't mess with it too much."

Dayna reached for the gear at her side, and pulled out a small pouch. "I've got a little something," she said. "It's a backup against the wizards—and it took some doing to get it. This place is a bad influence on me. Before I got here, I never so much as stole change from a vending machine. Last year I broke Carey out of Sherra's house arrest, and this week, I stole this."

"What is it?" Jess asked through a mouthful of peanut butter, wondering what would fit in the small pouch and be worth the importance Dayna was obviously placing on it.

She gave a triumphant little smile. "Sherra's concentrated mage lure antidote."

Jess vaguely remembered it from their conversation in Siccawei; at the lack of response, Dayna's expression changed to a little scowl. "Don't you get it? This is full strength stuff. It counteracts the mage lure—not completely, but well enough. Take a normal dose without a healer working on you, and you might just hurt a whole hell of a lot, lose a few brain cells. Take a concentrated overdose, and what do you think will happen?"

"I'm not sure," Jaime said. "But . . . I think I like the sound of it."

"It's something for you guys to have in case you run into someone when I'm not around." She tossed it into the space between them, an offering. "There are some hollow darts in there, too. I got them from Katrie."

"Then we have to find a way to deliver them," Ander said. "I'd say the bow, but that's not something anyone else is going to use with much success. I'm thinking about one of those handbows the Landers have been using for sport hunting lately. I can rig some darts to the quarrels—it'll be crude, but at close range, it'll work just fine. Be hard to take a wizard by surprise that way, but better than nothing."

"We can get one," Carey agreed. "And don't forget—even if a wizard's shielded, it's possible to get through, especially with a puncturing weapon."

"True," Dayna conceded. "But it's not likely, unless the wizard's sending out a lot of offensive magic. That'll weaken a shield, all right."

Carey gave her a crooked and humorless grin. "I think we can count on offensive magic from any of the outlaws," he said. "So that gives us a crossbow, a couple of knives we don't want to get close enough to use, and the null wards I, mmmm, *borrowed* from Arlen."

"Null wards?" Jaime scratched her arm, frowning at the bug bite there. "Isn't there some little spell . . . ?"

"Sorry," Dayna said. "I don't think you want me using magic for things like bug repellent—someone'll hear it. Otherwise I would have kept us dry last night. I've got us each shielded from magical searches, and that was my last spell—and it sure won't hold up if I start tossing magic around." She shrugged at Jaime, who made a face at her, and continued. "Null wards are a sort of perimeter system that keeps magic from affecting anything inside them. You know, the same system used on Willand's prison rooms." She turned her attention to Carey. "I just hope these are industrial strength, Carey. We're going to be working with some potent and pissed-off wizards."

He frowned at her. "Industrial strength? That I don't know. They're war wards, stockpiled against border squabbles. Same sort of thing used to hold both Calandre and Willand last year, while they were still at the hollow where they were caught. Ought to be plenty strong enough."

That seemed to satisfy Dayna, who nodded. "That makes things a lot easier. We can pop the wizards into a warded room as soon as we catch them; I can keep raw magic stirred up long enough to get them there. If we stay together, we should be safe enough from them, until we get them all."

"I don't know." Ander frowned, ran his hand the length of his bow in an affectionate gesture. "If we're inside, I won't be much use against guards, if they have them."

"Don't forget me," Katrie said, the first thing Jess had heard her say all morning. Her short, strikingly blonde hair tousled and a smear of peanut butter she probably didn't know about by the side of her mouth, she still managed to look more alert than the rest of them put together. She sat with her legs crossed and her back straight. "I'm used to woods patrol and guarding open spaces, it's true—but if you're looking for close quarters weapons, I'm the best thing you've got. And I wouldn't be here if I didn't think I could help."

"She's right," Ander said.

"Besides," Katrie added, wiping at her cheek when Jess gestured to her and mimed doing so herself, "if you want my opinion, you don't *want* anything more in the way of weapons. Load yourself down with stuff you're not familiar with, and all it's going to do is get in your way when you find yourself in a pinch. You need to approach this place with strategy, and caution. Use what you have, which is Dayna's magic. Considering what we're going up against, it's as good a defense as you're going to get. And if I know Dayna, she wouldn't be here unless it was a pretty potent weapon."

Jaime tugged at a tiny sapling next to her knee, not looking at the rest of them. "I'm in," she said, "but I'm not sure I'm going to be of any use to you. Carey knows the area, and Ander's got his bow . . . no one's going to get their hands on Jess without magic, but me? I'm just good with horses," and she gave a wry grin, "and scared to death of Willand."

"Oh, shut up," Dayna said. "We've got days between here and there, and I need someone to keep me in line."

Jaime snorted, but a smile crept onto her face all the same. "Well," she said, "if we get there and it really just looks like I'll be in the way, park me somewhere, all right? I want to help, but my pride can stand it. And Katrie can make the call; hers is the best judgement we've got for this kind of thing."

Katrie looked surprised, but gratified. She said, "I can teach you to use the handbow, Jaime."

Jaime's eyes widened slightly; after a moment, she gave a definite nod. "Good," she said. "I want to be able to help."

"Sounds like a good idea to me," Carey said. "On to the more mundane things. As far as I can tell, this will take several days of travel—maybe more than you're expecting. I simply can't ride as hard as the rest of you."

"Don't bet on that," Dayna muttered. "A slow pace is fine with me. I need to be able to think of something besides saddle sores when I'm playing with raw magic."

Carey gave her a small smile. "True enough . . . but the longer we take to get there, the more chance they have to pick up on the signs we're coming."

"Like what?" Dayna demanded. "The outlaws'd have to be searching specifically for us. Sherra might figure out what we're up to—Arlen, too, if he comes out of it. But they're not going to broadcast this on the Dispatch—if they talk about it, they're using the highest level of protection, and my bet is they'll go to courier from now on."

Carey shrugged, and didn't respond to her directly. "We've got another half a day to the nearest village that's small enough so they won't have much interest in any Dispatch chatter about us—just in case—and large enough to be able to supply us."

When it came to discussions like this, Jess invariably

found herself listening more than anything else. But she knew when it was time to quit talking and get moving. "We should go now, talk later," she said. "There will be more rain . . . and we need slickers." Dayna hadn't brought one, nor had Katrie.

"Sounds good to me," Jaime said, squinting up though the branches even as a fat drop plopped on her forehead. "We're just going to get stiff all over again, sitting around like this."

Jess rose, and went to the combined pile of gear to pluck out Carey's saddle. It wasn't going to be an easy trip for him . . . but she could help him as best she could.

That he didn't protest when he saw what she was doing, but merely gave her a rueful smile of gratitude, said more to her than his words to the contrary—*I decide what I can and cannot do*—ever could.

ꕥ ꕥ ꕥ

The next day, Dayna took a hand in the navigating, telling Carey which general direction she wanted to go and letting him pick the best route to get there. Jaime watched the assurance her on friend's face and wondered if she looked the same, or if her fears were there for all the others to see. She was still full of resolve . . . for now. She couldn't help but nag herself with the possibility that all that resolve would melt away once she truly faced her enemy again.

When she wasn't worrying about herself, she worried about Arlen. Sherra hadn't known if he would use magic again, hadn't known how long it would take before he was himself again. She freely admitted that this kind of injury was rare, and the healing specialists had far too few cases in their knowledge base to predict Arlen's progress. He could snap out of it in a day . . . or linger in bed for months.

Every time she closed her eyes, Jaime thought of the

moment she'd seen him on the floor in his workroom, and the horrifyingly slack expression on his face. *Karen Ann Quinlan*, she thought, and wondered what Camolen policy was for sustaining life when the person within the body had fled.

That's ridiculous. He could be fine by now. She tried to think of Arlen as the strong man who had held his own against Renia, instead of the one she'd found on the workroom floor.

Failing that, she distracted herself by watching the byplay between Jess and Carey—it was obvious enough to her that the two had consummated their relationship, though if Ander realized it, he wasn't letting on, was still watching Jess as though he thought he might make her his, somehow.

But Carey had a new ease to his behavior around Jess, as though he'd given himself permission to touch her—to put his hand on her arm, to nudge her when he wanted her attention, to run his hand down the length of her hair. Nor, Jaime thought, would Carey have previously accepted the way Jess looked after him, taking care of his horse, saving him steps around their campfires.

It was a good thing, too. Jaime wasn't sure how long he'd be able to go on like this. There were lines of pain etched around his eyes, and sometimes she caught him, his mouth grim and his eyes hollow and empty, like all his effort was going into simply making it through the next hour, or the next day. And though his riding never faltered, on the ground he was stiff and limping, and slow to rise from rest.

The trip was easier once Ander had picked them up some supplies, and Carey made sure they were never too far from this or that tiny town—a precaution that did well by them when Jess's mare threw and twisted a shoe past any hope of resetting it. The days as a whole were easier for Jaime once Katrie introduced her to the handbow, which turned out to be what Jaime had seen in sports stores as a pistol crossbow. The handheld grip was eerily reminiscent of a pistol, given that this world had yet—and never would, if it was lucky—to invent the weapon. The bow was small and stout, and took enough pull that Jaime had to struggle with the spanner to cock it.

But struggle she did, and she practiced at every opportunity. The weapon had power, and Jaime's accuracy improved dramatically, although never at any great distance. When she thought of Arlen, and saw the image of his body sprawled across the stone floor, she practiced. When the thought of Willand started a trickle of fear between her shoulders, she practiced. After a few days of it, even though she knew she had a long way to go before becoming as proficient as Katrie, she no longer doubted her contribution to the group.

They'd been on the road four days when Dayna stopped them short. "This is it," she said. "This is where I hit the shield. I don't know how big it is, or have any idea where to find them within it."

"Time to blunder around?" Ander said, not looking happy about it.

"Not necessarily," Dayna said. "Once we get in a ways, I might be able to feel something. Or I could throw a little raw magic around, see if that upsets them enough to let a little signature leak out."

"They'll know we're here if you do that," Carey said, his face set in adamant disagreement. "We're headed straight for a rocky mess of woods, with a gorge backing it up. I've never been this way—mostly because no one's bothered to try to tame it—but the map makes it clear enough."

"Well, that's true," Dayna said. "They *will* hear me, no matter how slight the magic. But do you *want* to just blunder?"

"There are other ways," Katrie said. "If they have any sort of physical presence in the area, they'll leave signs. Think like someone who doesn't want to be found, why don't you. What better place than this? I'd say the closer to Carey's gorge, the better."

"It's not my gorge," Carey said, and Jaime thought it was his discomfort that gave his voice its snappish tone. He cast Jess a quick glance as she brought her horse up close to his, close enough to bump his knee—and, apparently, to bump his irritation away. He gave her a rueful smile, and continued on a much more congenial note. "But Katrie has a good point. Given that we don't want to use magic, and we don't want to blunder, my vote's for heading to the gorge."

No one disagreed, and that put Carey back in the lead. They were on a narrow track, plenty wide for one horse but not for two, and Jaime wondered just how long they'd be in this area before reaching the gorge. They were each carrying enough grain for another day, and food for perhaps another two. The horses were losing weight despite their efforts to make enough foraging time; they really should have had a pack horse, she thought.

But she kept it to herself. Everyone else here, with the probable exception of Dayna, already knew it. Jess had taken to going out and gathering piles of leafy branches simply so her horse wouldn't have to work so hard to find a meal, but Jaime thought doing it helped Jess more than it helped the mare she rode. On the other hand, the terrain was becoming significantly more rocky, and the trees more sparsely set; the normal shrubby undergrowth was still struggling back from its badly withered state. Here, maybe the horses could use all the help they could get.

Carey, Jess, Dayna, Katrie, Jaime, and Ander. That was the order in which they rode, and after they stopped for lunch and to let the horses pick, they returned to it.

Jaime was staring at Katrie's broad shoulders, automatically correcting the woman's slouch with her unspoken instructor's voice, when Carey gave a sharp shout and commotion broke out in the front of the line.

Jaime still couldn't see anything besides Katrie's suddenly tense back, and she turned her horse to the side of the trail to discover they'd run into a man—lanky, unimpressive of stature and clearly hard-worked, he stood just at the side of the trail, obviously uncertain whether to stay or to run.

Until Jess got a good look at him, and gave a cry of anger, a name Jaime couldn't decipher. The man bolted, turned rabbit and ran into the trees. Carey shouted for him to stop, while Jess's mare did a little dance, a clear reflection of Jess's indecisiveness, and desire to give chase.

"No, Jess!" Jaime shouted up to her, thinking of the rough terrain. "You'll lame the mare!"

She didn't know if Jess heard, or simply worked it out for herself, but she was suddenly on the ground, flinging her rein at Carey and darting into the trees after her quarry. Katrie, too, swung off her horse and joined the chase, though Jaime knew she would never catch up with Jess.

Without Katrie in her way, Jaime could see the action clearly, for the man was almost paralleling the trail, heading back the way they'd come. The fugitive, sprinting through the trees, looked over his shoulder to discover Jess. His arms pumped harder, frantically, but his stride was interrupted by the constant need to catch his balance on uneven ground.

And Jess moved up on him, her stride powerful, her feet hardly seeming to touch the ground. She absorbed the changes in footing that threw him, and drew perceptibly closer with each flash of her legs. As she neared him, he dodged, futile and worthless efforts that only lost him more ground. Jess matched his steps for a heartbeat, waited for the right moment, and jammed her shoulder into his.

Down he went, bouncing off a tree in the process. Jess stood over him as he cringed from her, then made a derisive noise; she tossed her head, and walked away. Katrie was upon them, then, and didn't hesitate when she got there. She hauled the man to his feet and back toward the waiting line of riders.

Jess was ahead of them, with enough lead to gather her reins and mount up, her body language shouting her disdain and hatred.

Who is this man? Jaime wasn't the only one who wanted to know. By the time Katrie got there, the horses were bunched up into an impossible knot on the trail, crowding around the man as though the animals themselves were going to pass judgement.

The man was bleeding from scrapes on his arms and the heels of his hands—Jaime had no doubt there was tree bark ground into those wounds. His forehead dripped blood, and his eyes still looked a little dazed.

"And who in the Lowest Hell are you?" Carey asked, almost conversationally.

"Benlan," Jess said. Her voice and face pronounced the man guilty, although only she knew of what.

"Renia talked about a Benlan," Jaime said suddenly. "One of the wizards."

"So she did," Carey said, and gave the man an unpleasant grin. "Can't use your magic or the others will catch you, is that it? Guess that more or less leaves you at our mercy."

"*I* know what to do with him," Jess said, letting her mare move forward a step. Benlan tried to back up, but Katrie's grip, his flesh white around the edges of her fingers, stopped him.

"Bloody Hells, who *are* you?" He tried to jerk his arm out of Katrie's grasp and failed. "What do you know of Renia?"

"Oh, let me introduce us," Dayna said, far too sweetly to be sincere. "This is Carey—"

Under his breath, Benlan said, "*Shit!*"

"—and the nice lady holding on to you is Katrie. I'm Dayna, that's Jaime, and way down at the end is Ander. I see you seem to recognize some of those names, how odd. Oh, and I almost forgot. The one who seems to have such an inexplicable hatred for you is Jess."

Benlan merely repeated his epithet, and didn't seem to be sure whether he should be glaring at them all or throwing himself at their mercy.

"I suppose you're doing what Renia was doing, running away," Carey said. "Only Arlen destroyed the travel site outside his hold, so you've had to walk out. Well, guess what. You're going to turn yourself around and walk right back in again."

The man didn't hesitate. "Not a chance."

Jess's mare moved forward another step. When the horse tossed her head, it bumped Benlan's arm.

"Now, now," Dayna said. "Don't hurt Benlan, Jess. We still might get some use out of him. Interesting, that name Benlan." She glanced at Jaime. "Did you know that on the other side of the Lorakans, there was once a king named Benlan? He was assassinated; it was all mixed up with mage lure. And here you are, with an antiquated name, and all mixed up with mage lure."

"How'd you—?" Jaime asked, startled.

Dayna shrugged. "I had some time to read while I was recovering from the drug," she said. She stared down at Benlan, and suddenly, she didn't really look like a small woman sitting on a small horse, not anymore. She looked dangerous. "Jess isn't the only one who has a grudge against you, you slimy outlaw. *Your* mage lure killed a friend of mine. *Your* mage lure put me through hell. Fortunately, Sherra's a damn fine wizard even without drugs to enhance her talent, and she got us all through it. She also worked up an antidote. The problem is, if you take it, even diluted to proper dosage, without a healer to guide you through the reaction, you . . . well." She shrugged. "You die."

Benlan merely looked impatient, as if he'd decided this group of people wasn't really a threat after all, and wanted to get on his way. His muddy brown eyes searched the trail beyond Ander, and didn't return to Dayna when she spoke up again.

"Of course, the antidote I have with me isn't even diluted. Ander," she said, "you have those darts, right?"

"Sure do," Ander said, cheerfully enough, as if he'd caught on to the play Dayna was directing. "You want 'em?"

Jaime decided she wanted a part, too. "Well, there's no way we can just let him go. He must think he has a way to get his hands on the mage lure without Ernie—ah, that's Dayton to you, Benlan—or he wouldn't be sneaking away from his friends. So he's not going to just quietly crawl away and die, he's going to continue being trouble."

"Are you crazy?" Benlan said, eyeing them all in turn and clearly not sure. "This is bigger than all of you. If you're heading for our hold, you're just going to die. And so will I, if they catch me hanging around. What's the problem, you need a guide? You can damn well look somewhere *else*."

Jess had been silent, watching her friends play out their roles. Now she looked down at the man, her disdain for him still plainly expressed in her flared nostrils and tense mouth. "We're looking at you."

"But—I—"

"It's true," said Carey. "We are."

"So here's the deal," Dayna said. "You take us to whatever hole your nasty friends are hiding in, and we *won't* kill you. If not . . ." She shrugged again. "I imagine the effects of that antidote on someone who's been taking mage lure as long as you have are going to be pretty nasty. We probably won't even hang around to watch." She smiled prettily at him, her features as pixieish as they'd ever been, her hair drawn back in a short ponytail, and her voice utterly convincing as she added, "Believe it, Benlan. Or die."

He just stared at her, then stared at all of them, as his silence stretched out. Then he shook his head. "Willand underestimated all of you," he said. "It still won't be enough—but all I can say is, I hope she gets what's coming to her."

"She will," Dayna said, self-assured. "If you're lucky, you'll live long enough to see it."

"Unless you try something stupid, like taking us around in circles instead of to your friends," Carey added. "Three of us are couriers, and the others have eyes. We'll notice. Besides, I think it's safe to say the place is within a day and a half of walking, or you'd look a lot more used up than you do."

"I'm feeling generous," Dayna said. "I'll give him two days. If we're not there by then, he's obviously not keeping his part of the bargain."

"Stop trying to impress me," Benlan said, sullen in defeat. "We'll be there before the day is over. Don't blame me for the consequences."

They made a rope harness for him and gave him to Katrie, letting him walk between Katrie and Dayna's horses. In short order he'd taken them off the main track—if you could even call it that—and on to a barely perceptible trail that wound along the side of a hill; it was, at least, much less rocky. Soon after that, Jaime almost ran her horse into Katrie's, taken by surprise when the woman stopped short.

"What's up?" she asked. "Someone need a bladder break up there?"

Katrie spoke back over her shoulder. "I'm not sure." Jaime couldn't see her face, but there was a frown in her voice, and Jaime knew there was *some*thing . . .

"Next time we're riding up front," she muttered to her horse, but then Katrie shot a single, sharp word over her shoulder.

"Rider!"

"There—" Ander, behind her, had heard, and was standing in his stirrups, looking down over the hill. Jaime followed his pointing hand and finally saw a black horse slipping and stumbling down a steep trail in the hillside ahead of them, disappearing and reappearing from behind trees. The horse was hardly helped in his efforts by the rider; even from here Jaime could see he was off-balance and bouncing around.

"Who is it, Benlan?" Dayna turned in her saddle to look at Benlan, who merely shrugged, and said something Jaime initially didn't understand, but was able to puzzle out. *Dayton*.

Ernie. "Where's he going?" she asked, more to herself than anyone else, but it was Dayna who answered.

"It doesn't matter where he's going—what matters is that we've got to get him!"

"Forget him," Ander said, loud enough to carry to the front of the line. "He's nobody; he doesn't even have magic. The peacekeepers can take care of him later."

"Are you kidding?" Jaime said, incredulous. "Ernie's the key to this whole thing! You'd better believe he knows how to get his hands on more mage lure. Let him go, and the whole thing could start all over again before the peacekeepers figure out what hole he's crawled into!"

"She's right." Dayna watched the black horse as it grew smaller, and more easily hidden by trees. "Someone's got to go after him." Jaime could hear the longing in her voice. This was the man who had shot Eric, Dayna's closest friend, and a man she'd already tried to kill once.

"Not you," Carey said from the front of the line, as if he, too, knew what Dayna was thinking. "You're the one with the raw magic—and the one who can't ride. It's got to be someone who can stay on a horse in this terrain, and still catch up with Ernie. And that means me. You don't need me as guide anymore, and I'm not going to be much use in a tussle. But I can outride that son of a bitch on my worst day."

"What about the tussle part?" Jaime protested. "That's sure to be part of it, Carey."

"Not if I can unhorse him," Carey said.

Jess glanced back at Jaime and said, "He won't be alone."

"Jess—" Carey started.

"Just *go*, dammit!" Dayna snapped. "He may ride like a sack of potatoes, but you still have to catch up to him before he hits a turn-off!"

Carey glanced at Jess, frowning, but Jaime could tell just from the set of Jess's shoulders that she wasn't going to change her mind. So, apparently, could he. Without saying anything else, he turned his horse off the trail and cut across the hill, striking out for the path Ernie had disappeared down.

Jess turned back to look at Dayna, and said, "He won't get away." She turned her horse off the trail to follow, giving the mare plenty of rein. Ahead of her, Carey rode like he was part of his horse, supporting it through the stumbles and giving it the freedom it needed to move swiftly through the shifting footing.

No, Jaime thought, watching Carey and Jess, as much—or more—partners as they'd ever been. Ernie wasn't likely to outride them, once he even figured out they were on his trail.

"So much for Ernie," Dayna said. Her expression was defiant enough that Jaime knew she was suddenly scared—and well she might be, finding herself at the head of the abruptly shrunken party, with the weight of their success settling firmly on her shoulders. "Let's get moving." Fahrvegnügen stepped out—hesitantly at first, and then with more assurance.

Jaime wished she could feel the same, but she'd caught a glimpse of Benlan's face, and thought she saw something new in the expression there. Something no longer quite so resigned.

She hoped she was imagining it.

Chapter 13

Dayna was faking it. Suddenly out in front, on a horse she could ride only because it was such a tractable and smooth-gaited animal, she no longer had anything to buffer herself from what she was trying to do—and the fact that she had drawn her friends into this danger as well as herself.

You had reasons for doing this, and they're still good reasons. And her friends weren't naive—they had reasons, too. They knew what the outlaws could do, had seen what Willand was willing to do. No one talked much about Arlen, but she knew they were all thinking about him.

The raw magic will work. It would work, and she wouldn't lose control of it, either. Just because everyone in Camolen had a knee-jerk reaction to the idea of using raw magic didn't mean it couldn't be done. She used it all the time, far more often than anyone, including herself, had suspected.

And what if they see you coming? Benlan had guided them for several hours since they'd left Carey and Jess behind, and though the turn-offs had been unexpected, now the trail was becoming clearer. They must be getting close. *What if some changed animal turned guard tears your throat out, and leaves the others to the outlaws?*

"What if we do nothing and all end up as sheep, anyway?" she muttered, loudly enough so Katrie, riding behind her, said, "What?"

"Nothing," Dayna answered. She let her reins drape so Fahrvegnügen could pick out her own path—the horse was doing it anyway, no point in fooling herself—and twisted, holding onto pommel and cantle to keep her saddle-sore body steady in the saddle. Benlan stared back up at her, his sleepy-looking eyes more sullen than cowed. She didn't really like that. She put on the faking-it Dayna face and said, "Thinking bad thoughts, are you, Benlan?"

"What's the problem?" he asked. "I'm doing what you asked. I'm taking you to our little hold. I'm not even leading you in circles first."

"Why'd you leave them?" Dayna asked, as surprised at the question as he seemed to be. She'd intended to ask about the others, all right, but not quite so personally. She just wasn't cut out for the role of a tough guy.

He looked like he was about to fire off a sarcastic reply, but instead, after a moment, he said, "It was never my intent to hurt and threaten people. I got sick of it. I'm not the only one, but the others are too frightened to do anything about it. They figure they're in too deep to back out now."

"And you aren't?"

He scowled at her. "What are you looking for, some admission of guilt? Go to hell, lady. Pick the deepest one while you're at it."

"You're quite the asshole," she observed, or at least, her façade observed it. The inner Dayna would just as soon have stopped talking to him—although in the end, it was her inner self, the one who wanted to know all the details and maintain control over the situation, that persisted. "Just how many of you are there?"

He didn't answer.

Behind him, Katrie said, "I think you should remind him that we're going to tie him to a very visible tree just outside the hold, and that if we lose, he's not going to be happy with who finally comes out to untie him. Or, should I say, *they're* not going to be happy with *him.*"

Dayna looked at Benlan. The man was clearly tiring, had probably been walking—and unused to it—for nearly two days now. His footwear was soft and gave him little protection against the jutting roots and rocks of the trail, and his tunic was long sleeved and too heavy for summer, even though the worst of the heat seemed to have broken. Dayna let Katrie's statement sink in, and then lifted one fine eyebrow in a gesture she would never have admitted teaching herself just because Spock had done it.

"Ah, dammit," he muttered. He recovered from a stumble and directed his glare back up at her. No longer so sullen; that was good. "There's Jenci . . . and Emmy and Strovan and old Ludy—and the cook, of course."

"Strongarms?" Katrie prodded, while Dayna frowned at the list. Renia, of course, was dead, and they had Benlan here; she supposed that was a substantial enough group.

"A couple," Benlan said. "I'm not sure how good they are—they're certainly not civilized. We just got a few territorial animals and made our territory theirs. It was all we had time to do before things got out of hand. It's still a workable idea, and I'll fight for the patent on it."

"You're welcome to it." Dayna's emphasis got her point across fairly well; she wanted no part of the spell. "But don't change the subject. You forgot to mention Willand—where is she?"

His gaze flickered away from her, out to the woods and back again. "She's there," he said, and something in his voice was subtly different. "I just hate to think about her."

"You're a pretty bad liar," Katrie said. For the first time, she gave his harness rope a good swift tug, and he slipped and went down on his knees before her horse. Dayna was about to cry a warning, but Katrie had already stopped her mount, and Dayna did the same. Past Katrie, Ander moved his horse close up behind Jaime, frowning.

Katrie leaned over her horse's shoulder and looked down at Benlan. "You can still talk through a broken nose."

Still a little stunned by his fall, Benlan probably didn't mean to say what he did. "You're all full of shit. I ought to just turn around and walk out of here."

Dayna was surprised that Katrie could dismount so quickly, moving seamlessly to grab the front of Benlan's tunic, jerk him off the ground, and bounce her fist off his face. She let him drop to the ground and straightened as he keened a string of pained curses, his hands covering his face. "See?" she said, standing with one hand on her knife. "You *can* still talk with a broken nose."

"You bitch!" he wailed, sputtering blood. She kicked him, hard, and he lost all his air in a guttural grunt, falling to his side. Dayna gasped, a sound of protest. Of course Katrie had this in her; being tough was what she did. Dayna suddenly realized just how good she was at it.

"Remind me to keep you on my side," Ander said, taking his feet from his stirrups and stretching his legs, his bright blue eyes eyeing Katrie with new respect. Beside him, Jaime's expression was tight, but resolute. She met Dayna's gaze, and nodded slightly. She, too, wanted to know about Willand.

So that was all Dayna said to Benlan, once he seemed to be recovering from Katrie's attention. "Willand, Benlan."

He shot her a glance of hatred through tearing eyes, but kept his mouth shut.

"Now!" Katrie bellowed, so suddenly she startled them all. Then she bent over him and said, "No time to think of lies, you little bastard. Start talking by the time I count to three or I get mad again. One—"

"Out!" Benlan blurted, still spitting out what was left of his nosebleed. "At her cabin!"

"Her *cabin*?" Jaime said.

"She's too good for the rest of us," Benlan said, his

words bitter. "Says we distract her with our discussions—we do most of our work together. So she spends a lot of time in her cabin—" Probably without thinking, he waved his hand in the general direction they'd come from.

Jaime's head snapped up to look at Dayna, but Dayna just stared at her. She'd lost her sense of direction; the wave meant nothing to her. Jaime said, "That's where Ernie was headed!" in a voice filled with certainty—and with horror at that certainty. "We just sent Carey and Jess straight at Willand!"

Dayna felt like Katrie had just kicked *her*. "Maybe they caught up to him before. . . ." and just let it trail off.

Benlan was shaking his head. "No," he managed painfully. "It wasn't far from where we saw him."

"And you just let them ride right off to her," Katrie said, anger filling her voice, making her stern features even harder. "You *know* what she'll do to them!" She reached for him, and he tried to scrabble back away from her.

"No!" Jaime's command was loud and ringing. "We're not going to be like that. It was bad enough, beating him in the first place. Well, he talked, and we're not going to beat him again because we didn't like what we heard."

Katrie stepped away from him, shrugging—but her cold glance down at the cowering Benlan was a message clear enough. No more fooling around, no more patience with him—because she'd be just as pleased for an excuse to lay into him again.

Dayna couldn't fake it any more. She was as dazed as Benlan. *Carey and Jess had ridden straight at Willand.*

"It looks like I have some purpose in this group after all," Jaime said. "Besides just keeping Dayna in line, that is." She patted the crossbow pistol that sat tied on top of her saddlebags and blanket, and turned her horse off the trail to go around Ander.

"Jaime!" Dayna protested.

"Look," Jaime said. "Those wizards need to be stopped as badly as Willand does, and you need all the protection you can get at that hold—Ander and Katrie can give you that. I've got the shieldstone, I've got the antidote, and I'm not half bad with the handbow. I don't even have to get close to them."

This was a half truth. The regular quarrels might have some accuracy at a distance. The ones Ander had rigged with the hollow-tipped darts did not. "Jaime," Dayna said again, helplessly, and had the odd sensation of time and decisions slipping through her hands.

"This one was meant for me," Jaime said. "I've got to face up to that woman once and for all . . . even if it means I lose." And she nudged her horse onward, trotting back the way they'd come.

Dayna watched her go, and looked at the suddenly small group she and her remaining friends made. She stared down at Benlan, and abruptly the faking-it Dayna was back—only this time, she was more a part of Dayna than something she was merely wearing. "Get him to his feet," she said. "Let's go do our part."

Once Jess's mare struck the trail Ernie had taken, the ride turned from slipping and scrambling to something less challenging, and she rocked in the saddle as her mare tucked her haunches and went to work, understanding without further signal from Jess that the goal was to reach the bottom of this hill as quickly as possible. Jess crooned nonsense syllables of encouragement and kept her body and her balance out of the mare's way.

Ernie was in sight within moments, though he gave no sign of hearing them above the noise of his own progress—the clatter of hoof on trail rock and the slap of leaves against human and horseflesh. Jess was immersed in the same noises, listening to the gentle grunts of her horse, making sure they didn't turn to sounds of distress. The steep trail bottomed out and followed the curving base of the hill; narrow though it was, there was plenty of space for two experienced courier horses to turn loose a little speed, moving fast enough that leaves and whiplike branches left stinging marks.

They were almost upon him when Ernie finally turned and spotted them. Jess only glimpsed his face, but found the man's surprise unexpectedly gratifying. He hunched over his horse and used the ends of his long reins to whip it forward, not stopping even when he got the best the horse could give.

Now that they were on only a slight downhill, Carey blocked most of Ernie from Jess's sight, but she doubted the black gelding could keep this up for long, not the way Ernie was bouncing around on it, throwing its balance off at the most crucial of moments. With any luck the horse would trip and fall and that would be the end of this chase.

But he didn't. He picked up speed, until Jess's mare was in full gallop beneath her, while Jess ignored the branch welts on her arms and ducked against the leaves that rushed her face. It was folly, on a trail she didn't know. But neither she nor Carey would let this man go free.

Suddenly, the trail opened up around her, as if it were a creek emptying into a pond. Surprised, Jess lifted her head, and discovered they were in a clearing—and in the clearing was a cabin.

Standing in front of the cabin was Willand.

Jess pulled the mare up hard, setting her back on her haunches to reverse direction in a circle so small she almost spun around, flinging divots of dirt behind her; before her and then behind her, Carey's horse was fighting him, settling from a rear to do the same. *Shieldstone*, she reminded herself, while the mare sprinted away, and the leaves returned to slap her face, making thinking impossible and leaving her only with the doing, riding through the woods on a narrow path with tree trunks brushing up against her legs and her back tingling like a giant target.

Carey would know what to do, in a moment they'd be safe enough, stop to think—

A giant cracking sound cut through the noise of her run; Jess flinched and her mare startled sideways to bounce off a tree with a grunt at the insult. She slowed the horse until they were prancing in place, waiting for the sky to fall but afraid to move in case *this* was the safe place. The woods were full of snapping, cracking branches, and the screech of wood against wood. The dying throes of a tree, she realized finally, trying to locate it and failing, until she turned the mare in tight circles on the trail, afraid to move forward or back until she knew where it was—and then, somewhere, it hit the ground in another rush of breaking branches, bounced, and settled.

That's when she saw she was alone.

"Carey!" she called, not realizing until she'd done it that she was only shouting her location to Willand, and then not caring. *"Ca-rey!"*

Silence. And then her answer, the faint staccato hoofbeats of a horse approaching at a gallop. Relief washed over her—until the riderless gelding came into sight, crashing off into the woods at the sight of her in its path, barely slowing at the closer press of the trees there.

Jess aimed the mare at the cabin again. Tired, the horse moved with less enthusiasm, and when the clearing popped up in front of them, Jess slowed her to a jigging trot, trying to make sense of what she saw, and to find Carey in the mess of it.

The downed tree that now blocked the path had been

chosen with some care—propped up by its crown and resting slantwise, it was big enough to be a significant obstacle, long enough so it wasn't easy to go around, thick enough so it wasn't easy to go under.

Just on the other side was Carey, looking like a rag doll that had been flung aside and left to lay. Except Willand was striding up to him, reaching for him—reaching for the spellstones around his neck. *The shieldstone!*

Her fingers crept up to the same stone, hanging from her braid and ever-clinking behind her ear. She'd gone up against Willand once before, armed only with a shieldstone—she'd taken the woman by surprise, and overcome her physically before the wizard could call magic to her aid.

It could happen again. She was unnoticed, trapped behind the fallen tree. But as impressive as the tree trunk was, it wasn't as high as the jumps she'd taken for fun. It wasn't as high as the banks this mare had launched herself up. Abruptly, Jess turned the mare, sent her back a few calmly trotted yards. Facing the tree again, she saw Willand running her hand down the side of Carey's face, examining him like something she'd just purchased. *No*.

Her cantered approach was quiet, as though the tree wasn't looming before them. Three calculated strides away, Jess set the mare back on her haunches and legged her into bounding collection, giving her the power she'd need—and then one final, startling *kick*—

The mare thrust herself upward, her ears flat back and her legs tucked tightly to her body. Clinging, the reins flung free, Jess felt the lurch as the mare's belly bumped wood, and then slid over the other side, breaking bark all the way. With no room for her hind legs to land, the mare fell forward, caught herself, stumbled, and headed, out of balance and out of control, at Willand.

Willand sprang back from Carey, and flung her hand out before her, as though to stop the thousand pounds of horseflesh pounding toward her. Jess, scrambling to regain her seat, clutching at the reins she'd all but lost, just barely realized what was really happening, what the wizard was really doing.

Flaunting Carey's spellstones. Holding them high, the shieldstone among them, while dire magic gathered around her and the other hand readied to sling it at Carey. *Stop, or else.*

Jess stopped. She wrenched the mare's head around, and the horse slung her head back and forth in protest, foam and spit flying. Willand stood her ground, the spellstones dangling from her hand, as Jess settled the mare, ending up sideways from her original course. She had to look over her shoulder to see Willand.

Willand, of course, was smiling.

Her extended freedom hadn't restored the soft lines of her youth, stolen from her by a year in captivity, but her confidence didn't seem to have suffered any. She crooked a finger at Jess. One finger, one joint, bent by mere degrees.

Jess, her gaze on Carey—who was stirring, clearly still stunned from his fall—turned the mare to face her enemy.

"No," said Willand. "Off."

Behind the wizard, Ernie had tied his horse in back of the cabin and was coming toward them. There was someone else, a figure standing just outside the cabin, and he followed Ernie. Jess looked at them, and looked at Carey, and then Willand.

"Off," said Willand, and pointed to the ground.

Slowly, Jess dismounted. She let the reins trail, knowing the mare was tired and probably hurting, and wouldn't go anywhere. Not that it mattered. She wouldn't be taking that jump again—and neither, did it seem, would Jess.

She discovered her knees weren't as steady as they should be.

And then Carey, his voice utterly weary, said, "*Damn.*"

Jess barely glanced at Willand for permission before she was on the ground beside Carey. "All right?" she asked, her voice low.

"Perfect," he said, looking up at Willand, and then back to Jess, catching her with his gaze to let her know he was all right, it was all right . . . *they* were all right. But Jess shook her head, not believing. Carey closed his eyes, and she knew she was right.

Slowly, painfully, he rolled over on his side and sat up. "Nothing broken," he said, as though they weren't standing at the feet of someone who'd tried to exact revenge on them all summer. "Must have actually remembered to roll when I fell."

"Try not to fall," she advised him for the future, and then hugged him tightly.

"You two always were big on the touching scenes," Ernie said from above them. Jess pulled away from Carey to give him the full force of her glare, but he was already looking at Willand. "Damn, I hate riding. You people need to invent cars."

"*We people* like the way things are," Willand said. She looked down at Jess and Carey and said, "With some small exceptions, which are about to be taken care of." She closed her eyes a moment, and when she opened them, she gave the hill a quick search. "You came alone. Too bad."

Jess said nothing. Dayna's spell would hold, she thought. The others were safe from detection, if only Willand didn't look too hard. . . .

Ernie was grinning at her. Jess hadn't remembered much about him. She hadn't remembered that his eyes were a pleasant and surprising blue, and that his features were surprisingly bland. But she remembered that grin, and she hated it. It must have shown in her face, because as he looked down on her, it only grew. "*Gotcha*, Jess, baby. You got a lot to own up for. True, I've found a place for myself on this oddball little world of yours—but I had a damn fine place in the world I came from, too. Somebody's got to pay for all I went through when I got here. I decided it might as well be you."

"You could have walked away from that parking lot," Carey said, his voice rasping on a growl that could have been pain, could have been anger. He was on his knees now, shoving one foot in front of himself so he could rise—but Willand put her hand out, and he settled there, instead. Jess eyed him, finding the angry scrapes and swelling bruises from his fall, but nothing worse. She, too, was on her knees, sitting back on her heels, looking like she was settled in, and not like she could explode into movement any time she wanted.

She could. She *would*. She looked at Carey to tell him so, and he gave her the slightest shake of his head. *When, if not now?* When would they ever have a better chance, before Willand toyed with them?

She saw it in his eyes, then. It wasn't the timing. It was him. He couldn't do it, couldn't force his body further past the limits he'd already been pushing for days. His eyes were hazel anger, and frustration . . . and truth.

Ernie had missed the entire byplay, focused in on his little world of revenge. Behind him, the third person, moving closer, turned out to be Shammel. Ernie wasn't paying attention to that, either. "*You* could have done the smart thing and just given me that gold," he snapped, his nondescript features turning ugly with emotion. "You were out of your league, you dumb-ass jockey—and you still *are*."

"Now, now," Willand said. "That's a waste of energy, Dayton. Leave them to me. That's why you gave me the mage lure, isn't it? So I could walk out of that prison house and amuse you with these two. Well, and a few of their friends, but I have no doubt if these two are here, the friends aren't far away. We'll take care of them in due time."

"Don't count on it," Carey muttered.

Willand made an offhand gesture at him, and Carey grunted as though struck, his head rocking backward. In a moment, blood trickled from his mouth. Jess tensed inside her deceptively relaxed pose and wondered *when*. When she should move . . . when she should take the chance—and when would it become too late.

"Watch out for the mare," Shammel said, sounding lazy. "She's a little unpredictable."

"She's our concern," Ernie growled at him. "Keep your place."

"I am, I am," Shammel said, not sounding the least intimidated. "You called me here because you want me to take a run for you—through the blockade. Hell of a dangerous trip, and a long one, too . . . and I have—*had*—no idea of taking you up on it. You don't have enough gold to make it worth my while."

"I will," Ernie said, unperturbed, his gaze not leaving his captives. "Soon enough."

"Let me put it this way, then. I can't *carry* enough gold to make it worth my while. The mare though . . . the woman. Jess. I took a liking to her. I'd do it, for her."

"She's not going to be a woman much longer," Willand said. "Now that I have her here again, it won't take long before I figure out how to spell her back to a horse—and keep her that way."

Shammel snorted. "No, she won't be much good to me like that. Although . . ." He looked at Jess, his black eyes touching her the same as if he'd used his hands. She remembered his touch when she was captive, right after he'd beaten her. His hands had followed the lines of her body, caressing her—

"No!" she flared. "I am not for you." And she couldn't help it, she looked at Carey—even though she sensed it was the wrong thing to do just then.

Ernie nearly crowed with delight. "Oh, that's it, is it? You been riding her every way you can, Carey? Did you have to tell her *whoa* to get her to stand still for it? Does she *neigh* for you when you touch her right?"

"You shit-eating *bastard*," Carey snarled, and on the battle cry of the last word, launched himself at Ernie.

"No!" Jess cried, thinking of nothing but Carey—not Willand, not escape, just keeping Carey from being hurt. But by the time she moved, Ernie had already met Carey's stumbling charge and countered it, knocking him to the ground and kicking him, sending him rolling away from Ernie's boot, again and again, until too many solid kicks landed and he just curled around himself and took the next one with an agonized groan.

No! Jess flung herself at Ernie's back, teeth bared—and was blindsided, knocked flat on her back by Shammel. She struggled against him, bucking beneath him, her cap flying and her hair in her face.

"That is *enough*," Willand said, her voice ringing, and carrying enough command to stop them all. "*Men*," she snorted, striding over to stand between where Ernie had stopped kicking Carey and where Shammel sat on Jess. "Have you got it out of your system, now?"

Panting, Jess twisted to look at Willand, finding her with her hands on her hips and her expression impatient and exasperated.

"Good," Willand said, when no one answered. "Because you'd *better*. I have plans for both of them. Shammel, she's going to be a horse. That's the way I want it, and that's the way it's going to be. I might, however—because it amuses me—consider a negotiation, in exchange for a reduction in your job fee. You bring the mage lure back, and I'll let you have her—*as a horse*."

"But—"

"Shut *up*! With a little more time, I can modify it so she turns human when she comes into heat. I assume from the drool I saw coming from your mouth that that's what you *want*?"

Shammel hesitated, as if waiting for a *but*. When it didn't come, he nodded, and added a leering grin as he looked down at Jess. "You shouldn't have messed with me, sweetheart." He reached for the side of her head, ignoring the glare she gave him. Sifting through her hair, he came up with her spellstones, and let them trickle through his fingers until he found the traditionally lapis shieldstone. It was separate from the others, on its own tiny braid. Shammel cut it with a jerk of his knife and displayed it to Willand.

"Fine. Dayton, drag him over here beside her. I only want to cast this spell once. And Shammel, unless you want to take an unexpected nap, you'd better get off her."

Carey, his head lolling as Ernie dragged him by his arms, landed beside Jess with a thump; she craned her head to look at him, desperately trying to see how badly he was hurt. Shammel leaned over her, looking greasier than ever at close range, and forced her head back to look at him, cruel fingers at her chin. "Take a good look at him, sweetheart," he said. "It's the last time you'll see him through human eyes." Then he climbed off her hips, unmindful of stepping on her on the way.

Instantly, Jess started to her feet, but saw Willand, standing above them, her hands poised and her lips mouthing some mnemonic phrase. She twisted aside, throwing herself over Carey as if she could protect him from the spell. She had an instant's impression of the sharp smell of his blood, the tang of his sweat, and the sweeter, nearly obscured odor beneath it all that had always been simply *him*. Then her cheek pressed against his, and her hair swept over them both like a dark dun curtain of night.

଒ ଓ ଒

"I *really* think you should get off your horses now," Benlan said, his diction blunted by his inability to breathe through his nose. It was a swollen blob on his face, with dried blood crusting his nostrils, smearing rust across his cheek. He no longer offered Katrie any resistance, or Dayna any backtalk. And this was the second time he'd repeated the advice in the last several minutes.

Dayna looked around. The terrain didn't seem to be getting any rougher—it had, in fact, flattened considerably, although Benlan had assured them they were close to the gorge, and even closer to the crude log hold that served the wizards.

"There's no reason not to," Katrie said. "If he's lying, we'll know soon enough. And I have to admit, I'd feel more comfortable, and less like a target, if I was on foot."

"The shields ought to protect us from casual notice," Dayna said, but it wasn't an argument. She'd be glad for a little walking, she thought, assuming she still *could* walk, after all these days on horseback. Stiffly, she dismounted, and the others followed suit—although Ander was slow at it, and clearly reluctant. He hadn't said much since Jess and Carey had split off from the group, although Dayna knew he was angry that Jaime had acted so quickly, and left to ride back to them before Ander could convince her *he* was the one to go.

They haltered and tied the horses, and stood together in a small, uncertain group. "Are we really that close?" Dayna asked Benlan, and he only nodded miserably in reply. She took a deep breath and said, "Alright, then. They'll have detection spells, I'm sure, but we shouldn't trigger them, not with the shields. If they think something's up and go looking for us, that'll be another story. There's no way my spells are going to stand up against theirs this close."

Katrie gave Benlan a hard look. "Is there anything else we should know about?" she asked. "And do I need to remind you that you'll be right outside the hold, tied and helpless? You leave out something that trips us up, it'll be the outlaws coming out to deal with you afterward."

He shook his head, a weary gesture. "No," he said tonelessly. "There's nothing. Don't worry, I'm not stupid. I'm better off with you, and I know it. I'd be a lot happier if that wasn't the case, because you're not going to win this."

"Thank you very much Mr. Cheerleader," Dayna snapped. "As a pep talk, that was unequalled. Now, *is there anything else we should know about?*"

He gave it a moment of thought. "It's a crude place. The only thing that keeps the weather out is the spells we put on it. There's just one main room in the house, and the bathroom is a pithouse out back—hangs right over the gorge. The barn isn't much better, but it's bigger, and that's where we spend most of our time. Emmy and Ludy are still set on making something of the changespell—as if they can keep this the legitimate business venture it started out to be—so the barn's full of their efforts. Jenci stays off to himself, and Strovan is busy licking Jenci's boots." He shrugged. "There's not much more than that, to it. Cinny, the cook, stays in the house—she's the one who makes sure we have what we need, and she's busy enough with it. She also doesn't have any real idea what this has turned into." His eyes lit with a final spark of defiance. "She's a nice person—there's no reason to harm her."

Katrie shrugged. "She stays out of our way, we won't." She gave Dayna a thoughtful look. "You're running this thing," she said. "But if it was me, I'd go in slow. We know how many of them there are—there's no reason not to wait until they're all in one place. We can just set the null wards around the building and invoke them, and leave it like that."

"That'd save a lot of trouble," Dayna said. She wouldn't even have to throw raw magic at them, if they could pull it off without being seen. "It might not work, though. If I do end up having to use the magic, though, you'll have to trigger the null wards. Can you do it?"

Katrie scoffed. "Those things are made so the lowliest rank of peacekeeper can trigger them. You *do* have them, don't you? They weren't in Carey's saddlebags?"

Dayna had an instant of panic, even though she *knew* she'd taken charge of the wards at the beginning of the journey. Yes, she had them. No, Carey hadn't ridden off with them. She took a deep breath and nodded at Katrie. She had to keep herself together better than *this*.

But Katrie hadn't noticed her moment of panic. She was eyeing Ander, her face full of unforgiving speculation. "Look," she said. "I know you don't want to be here—I know you wanted to go help Jess. But this is the way it's turned out, and if you're going to be part of this, we need *all* of you here. Quit mooning about Jess—and Carey—and put your mind on *us*. We're all worried about them. But if we don't make it out of here, we can't do anything to help them."

His bright blue eyes reflected surprise, and then his mustache quirked to the side over his mouth. "All right," he said. "That's fair."

She nodded. "Good. Dayna, do you want me to take the lead with our guide, here, until we spot them?"

Dayna kept her mouth tightly closed on the gibberish that threatened to spill out. *Yes! Take the lead! Take over! Be in charge and let the decisions be on* your *head!* Instead, she merely waved Katrie ahead, a gracious and queenly gesture. *I should get an Oscar for this.*

They walked quietly through the woods—at least, as

quietly as one stumbling, haltered captive and two neophyte guerrillas could move—one armed with a bow he'd only ever used on targets and game. Only Katrie seemed in her element, which didn't surprise Dayna in the least. She only wished she could hand over her raw magic to Katrie and watch from a safe distance.

But she couldn't. And when the hold—not so very far from the horses, after all—came into view, it was time to reach down and reengage that façade of confidence she'd been leaning on earlier. She closed her eyes and took a deep breath, searching for the anger she'd felt when she'd heard about Jess's kidnapping . . . the sheep . . . the Meditators . . . She thought about Rorke's twisted body, and about the threats she and her friends had received.

"Dayna?" Ander asked, his voice low and close. "You ready for this?"

She snapped her eyes open and looked up at him. "Yes," she said, and she was.

For a while, though, they simply watched the hold. It was dilapidated, long abandoned by whoever had led the hermit's life to build it. The shingles were broken and thinning, the chinking dotted with generous gaps. The barn, also log, had sections that were never built to be airtight in the first place, and Dayna imagined she saw movement within. Cinny turned out to be a middle-aged woman, spare of frame and brisk of movement, who appeared once or twice in the doorway of the cabin—shaking out bedding, drawing water from the well by the door.

No one else made an appearance. It was late afternoon, so Dayna figured it was feasible that they were all in the barn, working, and would continue that way for a while longer. She exchanged a look with Katrie, who seemed to be waiting for Dayna to make decisions.

So she did. "Let's move a little closer," she said. "Katrie, when we settle down again, you can move ahead and start setting the wards. Just do your best—from the condition of that barn, I wouldn't be surprised if they can spot you right through the logs. I'll be ready to throw magic at them if you get in trouble—and I'll throw it at them when you signal you're ready to trigger the wards. Might as well make sure they can't interfere with that."

Katrie nodded as if it all sounded perfectly reasonable to her.

"Leave me here," Benlan said. "Tie me, but leave me here."

"There's no reason to bring him in any closer." Ander said it like he was trying to convince himself, standing hipshot behind a tree and frowning down at where Benlan was crouched beside the cover of a hazel bush.

"No," Dayna said, "there isn't. You're used to tying knots that have to hold horses and packs, Ander—you tie him."

Ander took the rope from Katrie and stripped the harness from Benlan in an impersonal way; his movements as he tied the man were efficient and just as impersonal. In minutes Benlan was well trussed, a nearly professional expression of misery etched on his swollen face. Ander gave him a pat on the shoulder—like he might have patted a horse—and an affable grin. "We'll be back for you."

"Yeah, right," Benlan muttered, but when Dayna glared at him, he clamped his mouth shut and looked the other way.

Carefully, they moved closer to the barn, crawling from tree to tree in such a dramatic manner that Dayna felt she was playing out a scene in a war movie—but this was no child's game. When they finally made it to the last big tree between them and the barn, she was shaky and sweating, and expecting to be struck by lightning at any moment.

But there they were, the three of them, lying on their

bellies in the woods. There was a rock under Dayna's hipbone and a leaf from a tiny seedling maple in her face, and she forced herself to ignore the small flying bug that was playing hide and seek in her nose. Katrie gave her a look—*now*?—and Dayna nodded.

And there was no turning back.

ꕥ ꕥ ꕥ

She opened her eyes. Just a crack, and the images flooded in. The colors . . . weren't right. Flat. She closed them again, groaning slightly. Her body felt out of true with itself, and she wasn't quite sure how to move it. Then a fly landed on her ear and she twitched it.

Lady. She was Lady. Not her choice, she could tell right away it hadn't been her choice. Never did she feel such disorientation when she'd reached for her Lady-shape on her own.

Whump! A booted foot bounced off her stomach, and she jerked her head up—or tried to. Someone had her tied, her head so close to the ground she could lift it only an inch. Eyes open, rolling in fear as she tried to take in the whole of her surroundings, Lady remembered where she was. And who had her.

Shammel bent over to grin in her face. "You know who's boss, now, eh?" He walked a tight circle around her, and Lady's ears followed his progress while her eyes searched for Carey. There he was, a fuzzy heap of human she couldn't move her head enough to focus on. She thought he was propped against a tree stump . . . she was sure he was alone.

Something came down on her side, a significant weight. She scraped her legs against the ground, trying to obtain footing that would never do her any good while her head was tied down. Straining, she lifted her head just enough to see that Shammel was sitting on her side. Just sitting there. Grinning at her.

But Willand came up and snapped something at him; Shammel replied in a rude tone, slowly rising from his living footstool. He came to her head, fussing with something by her chin.

It took her a moment to realize she was free. She surged upward, finding her feet in a violent movement that would have propelled her right over Shammel—if he hadn't jerked his arm, exploding pain across her sensitive nose. She flung her head up and danced backward a few steps. A chain—he had a *chain* across her nose.

Again, Willand's sharp command put a stop to it. Lady had a moment, then, to take stock. She was on the other side of the clearing from the fallen tree, not far from the cabin. Ernie sat in the doorway of the cabin, watching them, and Carey— Yes, that was a tree stump he leaned against, but his head sagged down on his chest. Was he still sleeping? Was he dead? She stretched her neck toward him, calling him, a low intense whicker that got no response.

She pawed the ground, demanding. *Take me to him!*

"Stop it," Shammel said, twitching the chain. She laid her ears back and pawed again, narrowly missing his foot. *Carey!*

"No, no . . . that's all right." Willand stood beside her, considering her from a short distance, her hands on her hips, resting on trousers that were obviously hand-me-downs, her hair drawn back in a practical and unflattering fashion. "Take her over there. I want her to have the full impact of the situation."

"She's a *horse*," Shammel said. His hand reached up and flicked at her braid, and for the first time, Lady realized she still had the spellstones. All but the shieldstone. There they were, and she could do nothing with them. Nothing.

Shammel led her to Carey. "She's not going to think about this like Jess would, you know."

"She'll understand," Willand said, pacing their progress. "It'll be enough."

Lady pulled against the lead as she neared Carey, ignoring the cut of the thin chain. She ran her nose over his hair—sweat, dust—and down his neck, trying to raise some response. She lipped his shirt—blood, and the smell of fear. She whuffled into his face, feeling the puff of his own breath come back into her nostrils. *Alive*.

And then she swung her head around to look at Willand, her ears back, her chin tight, her hatred clear. Willand laughed. "I told you," she said to Shammel. She moved closer to Lady, up near her head. "Yes, you damn meddling mare, I have him. And as soon as I finish figuring out the key to trapping you like that, I'll start on him. Calandre had—poor Calandre, her spirit's broken, did you know that? She'll never be good for anything, even if she *does* get out of confinement. But she had a good idea with her compost spell, and I think I'll do it again. Only slower. Much slower. And you can watch, Jess. You can watch, and you won't be able to do a damn thing about it." Willand smiled at that, looking smug and satisfied. "Then, of course, I'll finish tracking down the rest of you. I particularly look forward to dealing with Jaime."

"She's a *horse*," Shammel said again, his voice indicating what he thought of Willand's common sense, his gesture leaving slack in Lady's lead.

Faster than either of them could react, Lady's head flashed out, teeth bared, fastening on Willand's arm. She bit down hard and didn't let go.

Twisting, Willand rained fisted blows on her head, all of which hurt Willand more than Lady. "Get her *off*!" she cried. "Get her *off*!"

Shammel slapped the chain hard against Lady's nose, sending sparks of pain all the way up through her eyes. Lady held fast, grinding flesh. Finally Shammel grabbed her upper lip and *twisted*, overloading the sensitive nerves there—not so much with pain, but the shock of it. Lady felt Willand's arm slip through her teeth, leaving a scrap of her tunic behind.

Shammel released her nose and grabbed her ear, wrenching it down until Lady thought he was ripping it right off—she twisted her head to ease the cruel grip, and that's how he held her, head halfway to the ground, legs spraddled wide to accommodate.

Willand stood before her, holding her arm, tears of pain running down her face, and tears in her voice when she laughed. "Oh, no, Shammel. She's *much* more than just a horse. She'll see, and she'll *know*. She'll watch her Carey die."

⁂

Dayna sprawled on her stomach, propping herself up on her elbows as she peered through the thin brush to watch Katrie. She realized she was chewing her lip, stopped herself, and a few minutes later discovered she had bitten a nail to the quick. She looked up in surprise when Ander's hand landed on her shoulder. He crouched over her, keeping low.

"A few more minutes and we'll have them," he murmured, meeting her eyes for a moment before looking back out to where Katrie slunk to the third corner of the barn.

She shook her head. "I never expected it to be that easy. I still don't."

By the barn, Katrie froze and flattened, apparently in response to some noise inside the barn that Dayna couldn't hear. Dayna held her breath, and Ander's hand tightened on her shoulder. After a moment, when Katrie moved onward, Dayna let her breath out in a carefully silent sigh, and rested her forehead on her arms, breathing in the heady scent of the earth her nose almost touched.

"It'll be all right," Ander said.

Vaguely sensing he was reassuring himself as much for his own sake as for hers, she nodded, not lifting her head. Only a few more moments, surely. And then she'd feel the magic of the wards being triggered, and it would be over, and their wild gamble would meet with success.

There's still Willand. But this wasn't the time to think about that. Maybe instead she'd dare to look up now. Maybe she'd find Katrie about to place the fourth ward.

Beside her, Ander stiffened.

"What?" Dayna asked, bringing her head up. Katrie was frozen against the barn, but her attention was riveted not on the wizards inside, but on the *woods*. Ander twisted around, looking for whatever she'd seen, while Katrie's low, frantic hand motions made it clearer than ever that the problem was out *here*.

"I can't find—" Ander started, cut short by a piercing cry, startlingly close. Dayna stiffened as it ki-yi'd a measure, silenced, and started again, from a slightly different location. Up on her knees, she whirled to find it, until Ander cried, "There!" and pointed.

A small woman crouched in the woods, yelping alarm and then scuttling silently into a new position from which to eye them; she looked as frightened of them as Dayna was of her. Her gaze was accusing, her clothes dingy and torn, her short, scruffy yellowish hair dirty and uncombed.

"Cairndog, I think," Ander said, running his words together in the brief silence between her cries. "She won't hurt us—they're timid, and usually run in packs." He pitched a rock at the woman, who stopped in mid-yelp and vanished into the woods.

"She's got a big mouth," Dayna said, turning quickly to check on the barn. Katrie was as flat as she could get, tucked in beside the barn, and raised voices from within told Dayna why. They were coming out to check on their alarm system. She felt a spell click into place, not quite touching them—but Katrie was frozen, all slight movement stilled.

Katrie would be found, *they* would be found—and as she hesitated, the raw magic just out of reach, Ander hissed, "Do it, Dayna!"

What if she was wrong? What if it didn't work? What if—

The first figure appeared at the barn doorway, a tall and slightly gawky woman. So much for *what ifs*—no more time. Dayna pulled in the raw magic, gathered it and let it spin away from her, potential intact. It stirred through the area like invisible dust swirls, and the woman at the barn stumbled, grabbing a rough log for balance. From inside, a man's voice raised in anger.

Ander didn't hesitate. He was up and running for the barn, back to Dayna in three steps, and hauling her upward. She stumbled along behind him and finally caught her balance, just in time to skid to a halt by the corner of the barn, half her attention on her feet, half on the magic she was funneling through herself. The woman had staggered back into the barn without even noticing them, one hand to her head and the other keeping herself upright. Dayna knew the feeling.

Before them, Katrie's face was clenched in effort, her muscles trembling as she fought to break free of the spell that held her. Ander went for the ward in her hand, and found that he couldn't pry it from her fingers, as much as either of them tried to make the handoff. "Damn," he muttered, looking up at Dayna as he tugged the smooth, cut and polished brick of the ward and gave up, retrieving his bow. "We're going to have to go in there and get them under control before we can use this."

Don't distract me, Dayna thought, wishing she'd emphasized the need before they'd started. But Carey would have *known*.

Ander grabbed Dayna's shoulders and guided her into

the barn—he'd figured out that much, at least—stopping in the doorway to assess the situation. There was an elderly lady collapsed on the floor, with a middle-aged man, stout and balding, bent over her, shaking her, and obviously fighting the effects of the raw magic himself. A tall man and the gawky woman were arguing, their voices escalating into anger. Around them were makeshift tables with rickety legs; two of the three seats were merely log stumps. Papers were scattered everywhere.

At the end of the tables, up against the wall with a narrow aisle for access, were crated animals, some misshapen and missized—what remained of the original experiment. They, too, seemed to sense something was wrong, and were pacing in the crates, scratching at the corners.

The tall man was the first to see them, and he cut his argument off in mid word; his companion turned to see what he was looking at. Ander said, loud enough to grab everyone—and everything's—attention, "Yes, *we're* doing it. We got tired of you and we're here to stop you."

With a frown, the tall man muttered something at them, making a gesture he stopped in mid-movement.

"You can't," Ander said. His hands were casual on his bow, but there was an arrow nocked and ready. "Not as long as we're here. It's down to plain old force, and the first of you to try something is going find out just how much that hurts."

Dayna heard him as though through a fog, all her attention on the magic that tugged at her. She had to keep it under her control, just as much as she wanted and no more. . . .

"You can start by releasing our friend," Ander said.

"The intruder?" the man asked, jerking his head at the side of the barn. "We can't. It takes a spell to undo that spell."

"He's right," Dayna said distantly. "I can't affect magic

that's already been invoked . . . and he can't trigger the release while I'm doing this."

"*Whatever* you're doing, stop it!" the stout man said, looking up from the old woman. "I think you're killing her!"

"Ludy?" The other woman realized her colleague's status for the first time, turning with a little wail. "Ludy!" And she, too, knelt by the old woman. "Oh, please, stop! We'll give you our honor, we'll release your friend, but don't do this to her!"

"And you?" Ander said, looking pointedly at the tall man.

He shrugged.

"Please!" the woman cried, her hands traveling over the old woman's shoulders and arms, as though she could find something there to comfort or fix.

"You'll have to tame your friend here, first," Ander said, his voice hard. He lifted the bow slightly, placing enough tension on the string to bend the tips of the stave.

"Jenci," the stout man said, turning to the tall man with anger on his face. "This has gone far enough. They know where we are—we've *lost*."

"*Who* knows where we are?" Jenci said. "One small wizard, a man with a bow, and the woman we hold captive outside?"

"There are more of us," Ander said, adding in an offhand way, "We already have Benlan, and there are others, taking care of Ernie—er, Dayton—and Willand, right now."

We hope, Dayna thought. She closed her eyes, trying to convince herself she didn't feel faint, that the power of the raw magic wasn't too much for her. She heard the voices of heated conversation, but didn't take them in. Then the woman gave a little shriek, part anger, part alarm, and Dayna's eyes flew open to see the crates were open, and Jenci was leaping out of the way. Wolf, cairndog, a badger, some kind of bobcatlike creature—they leapt out of the crates without hesitation, heading for the door and unmindful of the fact she and Ander were standing in it, or that the three wizards on the floor were in the way.

The man and woman threw themselves over Ludy, and Ander jerked Dayna aside, losing his grasp on the nocked arrow. Dayna stumbled out of her carefully balanced state, and the raw magic boiled up around her, overflowing her tenuous constraint. The man cried out with pain, hands clutching at his head, and the woman fainted over Ludy. Jenci, staggering and barely on his feet, shoved past them all in the wake of the fleeing animals.

Dayna's knees gave out, and Ander, who was bolting past her to go after Jenci, made a nimble pivot to grab her. "No," he said, catching her around the waist and pulling her in close while he fumbled to find a better hold. His face was only inches away and he told her fiercely, "Hold on to that magic!"

"I can't . . ." Dayna whispered, filled with the roar of runaway raw magic, and buffeted by its waves.

Ander shoved her back up against the rough log doorway to make a quick, snatching change of grip; he got his hands under her arms and let her slide carefully to the floor, following her all the way down, and then crouching before her, as insistent as ever. "You *can*! There's no one else here to do it!"

We'll all die. . . . No Arlen to clean up after the wild surge of magic she'd once used to rescue Jess from the Lady form, no Sherra to heal them after the backlash of magic hit, when she couldn't hold on any longer and finally let go. *No*. They said raw magic couldn't be controlled; they said it was dangerous. *No*. She was going to have to prove them wrong.

She closed her eyes—they weren't focusing anyway—and grit her teeth and reached out with every bit of intractable, argumentative, hard-to-get-along-with

Dayna that she had. She made a net of herself, and threw it around the boil of magic, half-aware of Ander's encouragement, her fingers around his arms and clutching him like a lover.

"Atta girl," Ander breathed. "You *can* . . ."

Magic fought her, pummeled her, strained against her net . . . magic slowed, and grew sluggish, and gradually dissipated. Dayna let out her breath in a gasp, suddenly aware of the sweat trickling between her breasts and down her nose. When she opened her eyes, she found Ander grinning at her.

"Told you!" he said, taking her face between his hands and planting a resounding kiss on her forehead.

"Right. Then why do you look so relieved?" Dayna weakly arched an eyebrow at him, waiting for him to make a face and turn away, which he obligingly did—leaving her to close her eyes again and shudder at the death that had come so close.

"Now, how about some cooperation?" Ander was saying to the three wizards—although as Dayna recalled, only one of them was actually conscious. "We can do that again, anytime, and you can't get through her personal shields with any attack before she can turn your thoughts to mush again."

His answer was weary and miserable. "Give me a minute. I'll free your friend." After another moment, in a voice that hadn't quite worked its way up to an accusation, he said, "I think Ludy's dead."

"Blame that on your colleague," Ander said. "We were willing enough to be easy on you all—not a bad deal, considering the lives you've ruined."

The man didn't respond right away; when he did, it sounded less like an argument than something he was repeating to himself. "We were just trying to be the best we could. It all seemed so reasonable at first . . . we didn't realize Dayton was so . . . cruel. We didn't know he'd bring in Willand . . . and that Jenci would turn like he did." A long pause. "Dayton found out about the northern provinces' history of feuding . . . he was going to stir up trouble, and let Jenci sell the reverse changespell to the highest bidder."

"And after a suitable period, the reverse spell or a checkspell would be offered to the other side, right?" Ander said, and snorted without waiting for the answer. "At least Renia knew when she'd had enough, and got out."

"And died for it, too."

Dayna had had enough. She opened her eyes, shifting her bruised back away from the logs. "Quit whining. If you'd been content to stay where your natural talent put you, none of this would have happened. And since you *can* whine, you can work a little simple magic. Release Katrie, and do it now."

"Ah, that's our Dayna," Ander said, and probably felt he was well qualified to do so, after the group's long ride together. "Feeling better?"

Dayna smeared a hand across her face, wiping away sweat and a few stray tears she hadn't realized were there. "I guess I am," she said. "I was pretty distracted for a while, but as soon as I figure out who shoved my back against those damn log ends, *Ander*, there'll be hell to pay."

From outside, Katrie called, "I'm loose! You want me to set those wards?"

"Set, don't trigger," Dayna called back. "And check the cook!" She stood up, pulling her tunic back into place from where Ander's handling had turned it askew. As if she didn't realize the male wizard was watching her, waiting, she calmly smoothed her hair back, pulled the band from her ponytail, and gathered it up again. Then she set her hands on her hips and looked down at him. Beside him, over the body of the old woman, the remaining wizard stirred, making a pained noise. "You're Strovan, right? And she must be Emmy." At his surprised nod, she said, "Benlan told us quite a bit."

"Speaking of whom, I'd best go get him; we can stash him in here with the others." Ander gave her a questioning look—a *will you be all right* expression.

Dayna nodded. As Ander left, and Katrie came to stand in the doorway. "The cook's in the house," she said. "Scared to death. She's not going to bother us."

Strovan said, "You're premature to think you've won. Willand is still out there, and as soon as Jenci recovers from your . . . mind static, he'll probably join her."

"She's got a travel site set up at her cabin?" Dayna asked sharply. She told herself it didn't matter, that it would be hours before Jenci could perform the travel spell.

"At the edge of the clearing," Strovan said, readily, patting Emmy on the shoulder as the woman raised her head and looked blearily around. Then, as Dayna frowned at him, he said, "Oh, don't worry. You can have your friend set up the wards—no need to threaten us with that mind static to get us talking about Willand and Jenci. If those two hadn't gotten carried away, we could have pulled this project off. We'd have had the rights to a new spell, and the expertise in using it . . ."

"You're deluding yourself," Dayna said, trying to keep the snap out of her voice. He was, after all, cooperating—so far. Behind her, Katrie quietly left, and a moment later, the null wards kicked in. "The Council would have forbidden the spell as soon as inspections made it clear what the animals go through."

He blinked at her. "Why . . . your own good friend is a changed horse!"

"Exactly," Dayna said, and left it at that. If Jaime hadn't made it to the cabin in time, then she'd have a mess to deal with when she got there—which should be any time now, considering the hours that had passed between the time they'd spotted Ernie and the time Benlan had finally warned them, and then the time since Jaime had split off. She needed backup—and she certainly didn't need Jenci popping in to make things worse.

Dayna heard Katrie's surprised, "Ander?" and a moment later, Ander was in the doorway, catching himself on a log to slow his sprint, and breathing hard. "Jenci got there first," he said, quick run-together words between his panting. "You don't want to know . . . that man's a menace even without his magic."

"He killed Benlan?" Strovan scowled. "Benlan was harmless. There was simply no need—" He cut himself off, and climbed heavily to his feet. Running his hand over his bald head as though to smooth hair that wasn't there, he said, "If Jenci feels anything like I do, it's going to take him quite a while before he's up to anything as complex as a travel spell. If you have a horse—and you can *ride*—you can beat him there."

"The turn-off to Willand's cabin is *hours* away," Dayna said, frowning at him.

"No," Strovan said. "There's another way. Dayton can't ride any better than a wizard—he always took the long way."

Ander straightened, giving the wizard a sharp look. "The path here took a big northern loop," he said. "It's true, Dayna—I bet it's the *easiest* path, but it's hours longer than a straight line. What's between the two, one of those gorges?"

"Exactly," Strovan said, seeming relieved that Ander had picked up on it so quickly. "I know it can be ridden, though it's not easy, and it's not safe. But you can probably get there before Jenci does—assuming that's where he's going."

"We *have* to assume that," Dayna said. "We don't dare *not*. Ander—"

"Yes," he said. "I can do it. Strovan, get over here and get your pointing finger ready. I want to know just where to go."

"Never mind that," Dayna said. She might not be skilled enough to find a travel site she hadn't studied, and she might not be able to spell herself to Willand because of it, but she could darn well make a maplight spell for Ander, keyed to Jaime. "I'll get you there. Just go get your horse."

Chapter 14

Jaime couldn't remember when she'd been so acutely aware of the passage of time. After almost a week of riding, her horse was tired, and needed constant goading to keep its pace brisk—and brisk, aside from a few short canters, was the best she could do in this terrain. As it was, the horse stumbled far too often for her comfort.

But this wasn't about comfort. It was about getting to Jess and Carey, who were almost certainly in trouble. As often as she checked her watch, Jaime twisted to check the crossbow pistol tied to the top of her bedroll, and the short, capped quiver of bolts next to it.

When she at last came to the steep turn-off, she let the horse pick its own pace, wishing she had a crupper as the saddle slipped closer and closer to the horse's neck. As the path leveled out—or as level as it was going to get—she dismounted and reset the saddle, cinching it tight over horseflesh that was hot and dripping with sweat. She untied the handbow and slung the quiver across her chest, letting it settle just out of the way of her elbow.

Benlan had said it wasn't far from here, and as much as she felt the pressure to hurry, she was glad for her horse's fatigue. It wouldn't do to run right up on the cabin . . .

But the slower pace gave her more of a chance to think, and to realize what she was doing. *Riding right into Willand's hands.*

No. It didn't have to be that way. She had something to fight back with, this time. She had a shieldstone, she had doctored bolts, and she had her wits. And she had something else, too—a deep and festering need to stand up to this woman, to show her she had only been bent, not broken—that the emotional, frightened woman testifying against Willand had come back strong.

The problem was, she had to convince herself, first.

Well, there wasn't time for that. She'd just have to pretend. Especially since this seemed to be it. Just up ahead, through the trees that filled the slight curve of the path, she saw a fallen tree; beyond that, there was enough light to convince her there was a clearing.

Leave the horse here. Some sensible part of her mind was still functioning, at least enough to take care of that. If Dayna's shielding held, then Willand wouldn't detect her magically, at least not on a casual basis, but there was plenty enough opportunity to trip or stumble, or for her horse to snort its fatigue. She tied the animal just off the trail and stood by it a moment, loosening the girth, making sure the halter, slipped on over the bridle, was not going to rub the horse's cheek. That the rope was high enough it wouldn't get a front leg over—

Just go. Jaime left off her fussing, wiped her sweaty hands down the front of her shirt, and picked up the bow. Slowly and carefully, but without undue slinking—she didn't know how to do it properly and figured she'd just be more likely to trip up—she approached the downed tree. It was fresh; she could still smell the newly turned dirt and roots, and the sharp odor of sap from the bent and broken branches.

Sticking to the edge of the woods, she crept up to the thicker end of the trunk, hoping her booted legs would blend into the trees behind her as she peered over the top.

Yes, this was the clearing, cabin, Willand, Ernie, and all.

And yes, Jess and Carey were in trouble.

❧ ❧ ❧

Jaime. *Lady's head rose, taking in the scent of her friend. Her ears pricked forward, and then back, as the Jess-self warned her not to give Jaime away.* Jaime is here. *And with Jaime,* hope.

❧ ❧ ❧

Jaime rested her forehead against the tree trunk, seeing again in her mind's eye what she'd just observed. Jess—changed to Lady, and probably not by choice—tied to a tree near the cabin. She was tied up short, and by someone who knew not to take chances—she wore two halters with thick ropes, neither of which she had a chance of breaking. The ground around the tree was torn with her impatience and struggles. And someone, in a move they probably thought was quite funny, had put Jess's Baltimore Orioles cap on Lady's head.

Closer to her, close enough so she could see his tunic was half torn off and his tough riding pants sported a long rip up the thigh, Carey sprawled against a thick tree stump. She couldn't tell if he was dead or merely unconscious, nor what might have been done to him.

Willand was on the other side of Lady, sitting on another stump with paper propped against her knees and a pencil bouncing against the papers. She stared at Lady, her wide and deceptively bland eyes narrowed in thought. Working on a spell, no doubt. Too bad she was out of range of Lady's back feet—although someone, it seemed, to judge by the rust-stained bandage on Willand's carefully cradled left arm, had already had a go at the wizard.

Ernie was there, wandering around in restless movements just short of pacing, circling Carey's tree stump, eyeing Lady, and casting the occasional scowl at the third figure in the doorway, someone Jaime couldn't quite identify. She thought she'd seen him before, but . . .

"Is he ever going to wake up, or is he just going to die there?" Ernie said. "Maybe he was really hurt in that fall."

"And maybe you kicked him too hard," Willand said, distracted and barely audible; she rubbed her eyes. Then she looked over at Carey and said, "I do know you're awake, by the way."

"Burn in the lowest hell," Carey replied, in the same pleasant and conversational tone. Willand merely smiled.

Good. Now to let him know I'm here. . . . With Ernie hanging around, that wasn't going to be easy. But for once, Willand did her a favor.

"Dayton, I can't think with all that pacing." Willand was rubbing her eyes again; Jaime was struck by the sudden realization that the wizard might actually be feeling Dayna's raw magic. "Quit hovering; nothing's going to happen without you. Carey's much too smart to move. Go make friends with Shammel, why don't you. I'm sure you must have some business to discuss."

Ernie might have muttered—Jaime wasn't sure, and she doubted it was loud enough for Willand to hear, in any case. But in the midst of the mutter and scowl, he moved back to the cabin, disappearing inside. Jaime doubted he'd be there long.

So now was her chance. She looked down at the handbow and wondered if her aim was good enough to get a bolt near enough so Carey would notice it—without hitting him.

❧ ❧ ❧

Lady strained at the halter ropes, trying to focus on Carey. He'd spoken! He was awake! She nickered at him, but no one seemed to notice. Nor did they heed when she jerked her head up, surprised by the skipping arrival of something *in the sparse ground cover by Carey's knee.*

But Willand noticed the movement of the something, though she clearly had not seen what it was. She straightened on the stump, staring toward Carey, toward Jaime. No—distract her—can't kick—

No, but her bladder was full enough. Lady swung her haunches toward Willand, straddled the ground, and let loose, pretending not to notice Willand's cry of dismay at all. The rock Willand bounced off her side was little enough to pay for success, and Lady pretended not to notice that, either, although she swung her haunches away again after a moment.

Jaime was here. Carey was awake. Things would happen. Deep inside, Jess was stirring, the depths of her thoughts tugging at Lady. Spellstone. *She was helpless here as Lady, and equally unable to help.* Spellstone . . .

It was beyond her.

଄ ଄ ଄

Jaime let out a deep breath, the one she'd been holding for far too long. *Thank you, Lady.* Clever horse, distracting Willand with the one thing no one would think to suspect. And the look on Willand's face . . . she clamped a hand over her mouth and put her face against the tree, desperately trying not to break into hysterical giggles. *It's just nerves*—muffled snort of a giggle—*so stop it.*

After a moment, she did. She peered back over the tree to discover Carey leaning over his own leg, examining whatever cut or bruise hid under the tear in his pants. While he was at it, he snagged the arrow.

Then what was left? Carey and Lady knew she was there, Dayton and Shammel were as far away as they were likely to get . . . and Willand was distracted by what little of Dayna's raw magic reached this far, an advantage which Jaime could lose at any time.

Jaime reached down to the belt knife Carey had bought for her at the beginning of this journey. Her priority was Willand, but if she could cut Lady loose, the mare would do her best to keep Ernie and Shammel from interfering.

She spanned the miniature crossbow and inserted a dart-enhanced bolt—she'd have to be close to have any chance of hitting her target—and tugged the quiver around in front so she could easily snatch a second bolt. *Don't waste the raw magic, woman. Go.*

Jaime wasn't quite ready . . . but her body went anyway, crossing the road to the high point of the trunk and ducking under it. There was no point in trying to hide; as soon as Willand looked up, she would see Jaime. And if she wasn't badly incapacitated by the raw magic, she'd start lobbing spells—simple wind spells, or pinging pebbles off her, or even felling another tree on her.

So she just walked, the handbow low and next to her leg, her head high, moving out with casual strides. Carey saw her, exchanged a quick, grim look with her, and braced himself against the tree trunk. He didn't seem capable of getting up to join her, and she hadn't expected it. She just walked on, hoping Willand didn't have enough magic to raise a shield if she recognized the handbow.

Willand glanced up, and her expression of surprise changed quickly to a genuine laugh. "My heavens," she called, "are you *all* going to come after me? You're going to make my job easier than I expected."

"Don't count on it," Jaime said, not hesitating, her hand hovering over the knife as she tracked sideways, moving for Lady's head but wary of putting the horse between herself and Willand—and therefore putting Willand out of sight, even for an instant. The distance between them struck her as insurmountable.

"Ernie, Shammel," Willand called, raising her voice

very little. "Get out here." They immediately appeared in the doorway of the rough little cabin, and just as quickly, headed for Jaime. "No, you idiots," Willand said. "She's got a handbow. Split up, go to the other two."

And they did, at a run; Jaime hesitated. With Shammel now at Lady's head and armed with a wicked knife, there was no chance to free her. And Ernie hovered over Carey, who had shifted so he could watch Jaime. The unspoken threats were clear enough. Jaime looked at Carey, caught his eye; he nodded.

That, too, was clear enough. The priority now was Willand. Jaime took a deep breath and started walking.

"Think again," Willand said. She was standing, now, and had moved well away from Lady's haunches. "I don't even need to resort to magic to stop you, Jaime Cabot. Once your friends start screaming, you'll stop all on your own."

"You don't have magic to resort to," Jaime said, surprised at the calm in her own voice. "Dayna's seeing to that. That mage lure isn't all it's cracked up to be, is it?" There. Finally close enough for a sure hit. "Did you know that Sherra worked up an antidote for it? She did. It's got to be diluted, and administered with healers standing by, or it'll kill someone on mage lure." She raised the handbow. "I wouldn't have come without it."

If Willand was concerned, it didn't show. At least, not until she frowned, and murmured something, and nothing but a feeble wind stirred the dirt at Jaime's feet—while Willand herself grimaced in pain, her hand shooting to her temple. She instantly changed her tactics, her expression hardening in defiance, even as she spoke through gritted teeth. "Then you've got some decisions to make, don't you?" she said, her glance flicking to Ernie and Carey. "Dayton, he's yours."

ଓଃ ଛଓ ଓଃ

Lady danced around the tree, tugging at the halter, bumping into Shammel and hardly feeling the blow of the weighted quirt he brought down on her shoulder. "Get back, bitch!"

No, of far more importance was the tension that filled the air, the abrupt grin on Ernie's face, the way Carey seemed to gather himself, the knife that suddenly hovered between them.

Another mutter from Shammel; another blow. Blood trickled down Lady's shoulder and still she danced, jerkjerkjerk against the halter ropes, a little grunt and squeal of anger; she struck the tree with a slash of her front hoof, gouging bark.

These halters would never hold Jess, Jess with her clever human hands, Jess with her short silly face and no whiskers, who would slip right out of the halters. Spellstone! *Lady snorted an equine expletive.* Spellstone, dammit!

❧ ❧ ❧

"No!" Jaime cried, wincing at the background sound of Shammel's quirt on horseflesh, though her eyes were on Ernie and his knife. "Ernie, I'll kill her!"

Ernie looked at Willand, a question in his raised eyebrow, and very little concern.

"If you were going to do it, you would have done it already," Willand said, looking pointedly at the tremble of the crossbow.

Jaime glared at it, willing it to steady. *Shoot her, shoot her*, shoot *her*! But she didn't. This woman had tortured her, had proven her strength and her power. And she stood before Jaime with scorn on her face, still radiating that power. Jaime had none. She was frightened and weak, and had never killed anything in her life. Mark had killed, her sweet and gentle brother had killed a man, and still suffered the nightmares from it. Was it worth it to trade one nightmare for the other? *Yes!* railed a voice deep inside her. *Shoot her!*

"You don't have the nerve, Jaime. I could have told you that." Willand shook her head, a derisive motion. "I, on the other hand, do." And she nodded to Ernie.

Instantly, Carey's leg shot out, nailing Ernie just behind the knee. Even as he fell, Ernie aimed himself and his knife for Carey.

"*Carey!*" Jaime screamed, an echo of Lady's anguished equine cry. The dun was in a rampage, fighting the ropes so hard Jaime thought her neck would break, while Shammel whipped her and Carey—

Carey batted at the knife, and twisted oddly, grunting with effort. Ernie landed on top of him, and the sounds of the conflict were overwhelmed by Lady's fury.

Lady flung herself against the ropes, straining back and haunches in an instant of total effort, digging her feet in, churning up dirt and moss and making Shammel hop to avoid her, even as he moved in close enough to whip her. Her thoughts came in panting gulps, as much of an effort as her breathing. Careyknife *and* stopErnie *and* spellstonespellstonespellstone! *She saw nothing but her rage, a blur of tree and taut rope and falling lash—until she finally sagged, leaning all her weight against the ropes, her neck stretched, her body admitting defeat. She hung there, a balance of horse and rope and tree, and Shammel, grinning in victory, stepped back.*

Not spellstone. *Thinking spellstone didn't work. Raging against the ropes didn't work. Lady's sight went tunnel-vision narrow.* Jess, *she whispered deep inside herself.* Not spellstone. *What she wanted was* Jess.

Lady exploded into movement, startling Shammel and coming down hard on his foot, so he staggered back with a howl of pain. Jess! *Jess with the long dun hair, black stripe of bangs and centerline. Jess of the long, lean legs and tall standing body. Jess, without whiskers, without tail, without delicately swiveling ears.* Jess.

And suddenly her head was free, and her hair whipped in her face, and her sweat and blood trickled down bare flanks—and she was turning on Shammel, with his broken foot and the whip he'd dropped, attacking with a cry of very human triumph.

❧ ❧ ❧

Jaime stiffened with her fear for Carey, who was buried under Ernie with neither of them moving—and then Jess's voice rang through the clearing. Her voice, human outrage and victory mixed into a battle cry. "Jess," she murmured, a word full of satisfaction, and stepped back, turning so she could see both Willand and Lady.

Jess, launching herself at Shammel, who was already off balance, unable to bear weight on one foot. She knocked him flat, landing on him with all her momentum concentrated in her knees, so he made an agonized sound and retched and writhed beneath her. She flung the whip far away from him and left him, turning immediately to Carey. The grief at what she saw instantly converted to murderous wrath, and she fixed her dark fury on Willand.

At the same moment, Willand gave a cry of relief and joy, a sound so out of place that Jaime threw her a startled look, stepping back yet once again. The triumphant expression on Willand's face could mean nothing else. She had her magic back, and she was looking at Jess.

"Don't you touch her!" Jaime cried, watching the triumph turn to menacing concentration on Jess, as Willand's perfect lips started the murmur that came with her magic.

"Or *what*?" Willand said, those lips turning up in a sneer. "We've already been through this." And she made a simple gesture, stirring a sharp wind around Jaime's face, sharp enough to tug at her short hair and sting her eyes. With it came a strike of pain, racing down her legs like lightning to the ground. *Just like before*—pain flickered down her arms—*just like before*—Jaime whimpered in fear.

The attack galvanized Jess into motion. Naked, beyond rational thought, moving with innate graceful power, she launched herself toward Willand. Willand gave a quick mutter and a flick of her fingers—and Jess fell, tumbling only until she got her feet under her again. Singleminded, unstoppable, she aimed herself at Willand again.

And fell, rolling with a cry of pain as Willand gestured at her again—and again—

No more. Jaime's heart had had enough, even if her brain stood numb and her eyes blinked futilely against the tears of wind and pain and fear. She couldn't aim . . . but she knew where Willand was, all right, and how to make sure she didn't miss.

Jaime charged, carrying her own personal windstorm of suffering right along, her head ducked and her hand reaching, reaching—contact! *Dayna was right—right through the shields!* Jaime snared Willand's arm, jerked the woman in close and the pistol bow up into her side. And she pulled the trigger.

Willand jerked back with a small, astonished noise as the bolt tore into her body. She looked at Jaime in utter befuddlement, her hands fumbling ineffectively at the feathered end of the shaft sticking out of her body. She gave a twitch, a little grunt; with a hoarse, guttural cry, she arched backwards, spasming, teetering—and dead before she hit the ground, with blood at her nose and ears and mouth, and dark splotchy bruises blossoming on her skin.

The windstorm died.

ઉ༺ ༻ઉ ઉ༺

Ander ignored the maplight, and corrected his horse sharply when the beast wanted to follow the bright pinpoint. It might be pointing out the proper direction to reach Jaime, but it was also floating toward a vertical slab of rock there was no way to negotiate. "We'll get back to it," he muttered to the horse, who was far too experienced to simply ignore the light. Ander gave him a solid thump in the side, unapologetic as the horse wrung its tail and snapped its ears back. In another moment it was moving forward again, its attention on the narrow bit of traversable trail Ander had found.

The outlaws' hold was far above them, and a mile behind them. The gorge stretched beside them, a narrow, rock-filled river at its base, several stories down.

Ander wasn't at all certain he would find a way to get them there—or a way to get them out, once the maplight veered south again to find Jaime. The feeling in the pit of his stomach was a sickening preview of finding himself trapped here, knowing Jenci was probably on his way to Willand, and that Jaime and Carey—and *Jess*, dammit, *Jess*—would likely suffer under his hand.

If Willand hadn't gotten them all, already.

His horse stumbled, and slid a few feet, knocking Ander hard against the gorge rock jutting out beside him. His head rang so hard that the ride became something dim that his instincts directed, while he floundered for something to anchor his scattered thoughts on.

Jess, of course. She might think she'd chosen Carey, but that didn't stop him from feeling the way he did, from loving the way she moved, and the way her hair fell out the back of that odd black cap of hers, and the way she could boil an issue or question down to its most basic elements. *Yes*, she'd say, or *no*, or *damn straight*.

There. Ander blinked as his vision cleared, then clutched the horse's mane as he realized it was about to plunge several feet down sheer, crumbly slope. Then he had his balance back, and the horse was listening again, and they were a team.

They'd have to stay that way, he thought, if they were to have a chance at making it to that clearing before Jenci. *What if Strovan was wrong about how long it will be before Jenci can work travel magic? What if Willand already has them? What if I'm too late?*

Ander rode.

❦ ❦ ❦

Stunned, Jess lay awkwardly on the ground, realizing the pain was over, and that she was truly human. From Lady to Jess, on her own. *I did it*. She blinked at the scene before her, as Jaime staggered back from Willand, dropping the pistol bow. Jaime looked at her hands, and wiped them down the front of her tunic, turning away from the wizard's body. She was crying, Jess realized vaguely, struggling with the purity of the Lady-emotions that clung to her. Slowly, she got to her feet, and no magic stopped her this time.

For the first time, she felt the massive bruising on her shoulder, the stripes that ran from the center of her back, across her shoulder and onto the back of her upper arm. *Shammel*. Where—?

There he was, trying to crawl toward the back of the cabin, his movements jerky and furtive. Two horses were back there; Lady had smelled them. He'd have to be stopped . . . but he wasn't her priority. Jaime, standing and staring blankly at Willand, wasn't her priority.

Carey.

She went to him, or to the two of them, Ernie and Carey, only then realizing, as her mind cleared, the wrongness of what she saw. Neither of them had moved. Ernie was flopped on top of Carey, completely covering him, and in the center of his back, his shirt made an odd, rust-stained little peak. The knife lay on the ground beside them both.

Carey's leg twitched. Jess stared a moment. The knife was not in Carey. Ernie was not moving, Ernie was bleeding. It made no sense to her, but after an instant she tossed the need for sense away, and ran to the stump with a glad little cry that stirred Jaime out of her blank-eyed stupor.

Jess tugged at Ernie—and oh, how it pulled the welts on her back!—grabbing an arm and unceremoniously dumping him face first in the dirt. There was Carey, looking rumpled and flat and blinking wuzzily at her. "Jess," he said, wonder in his voice. "You're Jess."

Jess nodded, finding no words in the midst of her relief. She dropped down beside him and gently touched his shoulder.

After a moment, he scrounged up a grin, and it had a particularly cocky look, a look that reminded Jess of the Carey she had known before she'd ever been human. "Burn Calandre's damn spell," he said. "I win."

"Yes," Jess said, not entirely sure what he was talking about, but so glad to see that grin that it didn't matter.

"That being said, give me a hand." Carey got one elbow beneath him. "I don't think I'm quite ready to go anywhere—*ow!*—but sitting is better than lying here like one of Jaime's Ohio road kills."

"You look like a road kill," Jaime observed, coming up behind Carey and crouching to help him sit. Her hair stuck out at all angles, with bits of leaf here and there; without thinking, Jess reached over to pluck out a particularly big piece. Jaime gave her a rueful grin. "I'll have to live with myself," she said, "but somehow I think living with something I did will be a lot easier than living with something I was unable to do."

Jess just looked at her, not quite getting it, until Jaime gave a pointed glance at Willand. Then Jess said, realizing it for the first time, "You stood up to her. Even when she had magic, you stood up to her."

"Yes," Jaime said in quiet satisfaction. She tilted her head, touching her forehead to Jess's. "And you triggered that spell. Good job, Jess. Good job." She took a deep breath. "However things go from here, we can't forget those things. Now—where are your clothes?"

"I don't know," Jess said. "Somewhere."

"Someone better stop that greasy job-rider," Carey said, pointing at Shammel, who was just going out of sight around the cabin.

"He still has to get up on the horse," Jess said, and gave Carey a wicked smile. "I stepped on his foot. Hard."

"I'll get him," Jaime said. "Or I'll get the horses, anyway. If he thinks he can crawl all the way to the nearest town, he's welcome to try." She ran her fingers through her hair, dislodging a twig or two, and headed for the back of the cabin, unconcerned.

"Clothes might be good, Jess," Carey said. "I'm in no shape to see you without them."

But Jess had turned to Ernie, wondering if he might be yet alive; she rolled him over and discovered why he was not. The fletching of the pistol bow bolt stuck out of his torso, just below his breastbone, and angled up. She looked at Carey. "The arrow Jaime used to warn you?"

"Bolt. Yes. He's not using that shirt, Jess, and there's not all that much blood on it. Put it on, hmm?"

She eyed it distastefully. It closed down the front with fancy carved toggles, at least—she wouldn't have to pull it over his head. And it was a fine material, finer even than her own tunic. She looked at Carey, and he gave a little nod, confirming it; he really wanted her covered. "No breasts," she grumbled, starting in at the top toggle. It was one of the first lessons she'd learned, in Dayna's kitchen, with Dayna's borrowed bathrobe falling open and herself oblivious.

When she'd wrestled the shirt free from Ernie and

shrugged it carelessly on—it came just to her hips, and was tight enough over her chest that she fastened it with another grumble—Jaime was back, leading two horses and leaving behind her the barely audible string of Shammel's curses. "Ah, good," she said, looking at Jess. "That'll do for now. I'm going to tie these two by the fallen tree, and go after mine—she's not far."

"I doubt we'll ever see my Kefren again," Carey said ruefully.

Jaime shrugged. "He'll probably stick to the trail, so we might," she said. "We're going to have to start thinking about riding out of here, and looking for Dayna. I know she was using raw magic, but who knows if she was successful. This day's not over yet."

Carey groaned; it was a dramatic noise, but Jess, watching him, knew he'd had a bad fall, and knew he'd been beaten, and wondered how much more any one person could be expected to take. All the determination in the world wouldn't do him any good if he was hurt inside. Without saying anything, she went and sat down next to him, careful of her back and lining her legs up so they traveled the length of his, touching. He gave her a grin, not quite as cocky as the one before. "She's right," he said. "We can't just wait around here."

"We can find your spellstones," Jess said sensibly. "You've got a recall spell on them."

His brows rose a notch. "Good thinking," he said. "I don't think we can invoke it until we're free of the shielded area, though. And . . . I can't go without knowing about Dayna and Katrie . . . and even Ander."

"No," she said.

He rested a hand on her bare thigh and said nothing for a moment; then he looked at her, a quirky little smile on his face. "You did it," he said. "You triggered the spellstone. You're Jess again, and you did it all on your own."

"I got mad," Jess said. "I had to help you. There was no not-doing it."

"No, Braveheart, I suppose not." Carey moved his hand on her thigh, a gentle caress. "Not for you."

* * *

Jaime found them sitting that way when she returned with her horse, leaving the mare just on the other side of the fallen tree. It was, she thought, as intimate a non-embrace as she'd ever seen, and her throat tightened up a little at the sight of it. She suddenly realized she wanted Arlen's arms around her, and wondered with a renewed ache if he would be all right.

But she was also in take-charge-and-be-practical mode, so she cleared that throat, and let them know she was there—not that Jess hadn't known, for Jaime had seen the slight tilt of her head that meant her phantom horse ears had responded to the sound of approach. "There's got to be food in that cabin somewhere," she said. "And Jess's clothes . . . and maybe even some first-aid supplies." She frowned, coming alongside them now. "On second thought, probably not. Willand probably just spelled herself whole if she cut a finger."

"I doubt she was much good at *healing*," Carey said, his voice dry. "And I'm not sure you should go in there, at any rate. She might have the thing warded against intruders."

"That does sound more like her," Jaime admitted. "Well, I'll be careful. I won't go near anything that looks like it might be work. But I'm hungry, and we really should eat before we move out. I'd like to feed my horse, if I can find any grain behind the cabin—there's a shelter there, for wood and such. And Carey, we really need to take a look at you."

"I'm all right," he said. When she gave him her most skeptical look, he added, "Well, look, I hurt like the burning hells, and I could use a few stitches, but I'm not going to die on you."

Startled, Jess said, "No!" and Carey patted her leg.

"I won't," he reassured her. "Though I might not do you much good, either, if there's trouble to be handled for Dayna."

"I think you've done your share," Jaime said. "Now. Food."

Carefully, she poked her head in the shabby little cabin. It was dim, but it was clear that one side of the one-room structure was reserved for work, while on the other, there was a dry sink, complete with a cloth-wrapped half-loaf of bread, and some grapes, and cheese . . . the wine, Jaime decided prudently, they could do without. They had water on her horse.

She brought the food out. Jess had retrieved the halters and rope that had held Lady prisoner, and had removed the ropes, her eye on Shammel, who had managed to rise and was hopping from tree to tree, slowing moving away from the cabin. "If we let him go," she said as Jaime sat down next to them, ignoring Ernie's body behind her, and Willand's contorted form before her, just far enough away so she was out of focus when Jaime looked at her friends. "If we let him go, he'll die before he finds help."

"I think you're right," Jaime said. "And if he's smart, he'll figure it out. For now, I'm going to eat, and I think you should, too. You like grapes, right?"

"Grapes?" Jess said eagerly, and her lower lip quivered ever so slightly, just like Lady's when she smelled a treat. Jaime laughed and handed the bunch over, not expecting to see them again. Then Carey made a comment about their dining companions being dull company, and Jaime stuffed a slice of bread in his mouth, and Jess laughed right out loud.

And so they ate lunch, with death around them and fear behind them, and reveled in the fact they were able to do it at all. Jess in particular caught a case of the giggles. But dangling a grape above her mouth, and laughing too hard to try to catch it, she suddenly froze.

She looked around them, a frantic gesture, and got to her knees; the grapes fell to the ground unheeded. "Magic," she whispered.

Jaime didn't hesitate. It might be friendly and it might not, but she certainly wasn't going to take any chances. She lurched to her feet and went after the handbow, still lying in the dust where she'd dropped it.

She had the thing, discovered the spanner broken and barely functional, and was struggling to pull the bowstring back when the magic peaked, finally strong enough so she could feel it, too. She froze in mid-tug, trying to locate the results of the spell.

Jess had obviously already done so. She had moved in front of Carey, still on one knee but ready to shoot to her feet, the half-buttoned shirt gaping and hanging loose. Jaime followed her intense gaze, and discovered a man standing by the tree where Lady had been tied, and looking more surprised than dangerous at the sight of them—until he saw Willand's contorted body, and made a hissing sound between his teeth, turning back to them with anger in his face.

Jaime thought of Carey and Jess's shieldstones, no doubt sitting in Willand's dim work area, the one she'd been afraid to explore. And she realized that this man, threatened as Willand had been by the handbow and not hampered by Dayna's raw magic, would no doubt put up his own shields—physical ones. There was no use threatening him, not until she was ready to shoot. And she wouldn't be ready for that until she had the damn bow spanned.

She didn't even want him to see it. Using her body to shield it from his sight, she ran back to Carey and Jess, behind the stump. If it looked like she was cowering, all the better.

"Distract him," she muttered to Carey, struggling to span the thing while concealing the effort. Carey didn't have the chance.

"Stay away from us," Jess warned the man, who had stepped into the clearing and seemed torn between checking Willand's body and turning his wrath upon them. "I'll kill you."

"Will you?" he asked sharply, looking the raggedy trio up and down. Jess, barely clothed, Carey, in obvious need of what support he could get from the stump, and Jaime, hiding behind the other two. "I don't think so. Once I find out what happened here, I rather suspect it will be the other way around."

❦ ❦ ❦

Ander rode hard, harder than was safe and much harder than he'd ever ridden before, down into the small river in the bottom of the gorge. The horse took him through shallow rapids, slipping and sliding on moss and slime-covered rocks, its legs cut and bleeding, until the opposite bank gentled and he dared to take it. But after that, the horse didn't go far. It stumbled over nothing and came to a full stop, unable to move one step further.

Ander swung off and wrapped the reins high around the horse's throatlatch, sticking a loop of them through the crown of the bridle and around one ear where they couldn't be stepped on. He left the horse standing spraddle-legged in the path, and ran, picking up a steady lope of his own, his bow banging against his back and his booted feet thumping against the soil. In moments he saw the outline of a building against the trees, and a clearing beyond; by the time he slowed, he realized it was the back of a small cabin, with a sheltered hitching rail and the signs of recent horse.

He hit the back of the cabin and stopped, breathing

as lightly as his lungs would let him, pressed against the back corner of the structure, and listening.

"I said, *what happened to her*?"

That was Jenci, all right, and his temper sounded ragged. Ander, pulling the bow off his back and nocking an arrow, peeked carefully around the edge of the building.

Jenci was neither close nor facing the cabin; he was simply shouting loudly enough that it sounded so. He was instead closing in on the huddle of Jess, Carey, and Jaime; Ander's gaze skipped over the clearing, finding two bodies and the signs of struggle. One of them was clearly female. Willand? Ander inched along the side of the cabin, trying for silence, but wanting one of the trio to see him, to know he was there to help.

"You're going to tell me, by burning hells, or I'll rip it out of you!" Jenci stood before them and roared, while Jess hovered protectively before Carey, her expression defiant; Jaime seemed frozen with fear, and Carey looked badly used. Ander's gaze flickered again to Jess. Her shirt was someone else's; there was a tangle of halter and lead at her feet. He'd never seen quite that particular expression before—but whatever else it meant, it definitely meant trouble.

It seemed to surprise them all when Jaime spoke up. "Why should we tell you anything, when you're going to kill us?" she asked, more grit in her voice than showed on her face. Ander realized she was looking directly at him, had seen him—and was talking to *him*. He hesitated, bowstring half drawn, not quite able to shoot someone in the back.

"Because it'll mean an easier death!" Jenci snapped. "You may have a shieldstone, but your friends *don't*—and even at that, I've got plenty of ways to get through to you." He pointed at Jess, an abrupt movement that she flinched from, though she held her ground, tossing her head and glaring with renewed defiance. But the feel of magic intensified, and uncertainty crossed Jess's face.

Jaime jumped to her feet, revealing the handbow she desperately tried to span—was it damaged?—and then tossed away, holding the bolt in her bare hand. Jenci lashed a spell at her, at them all, a glow so blinding that Ander had to squint to see even the wizard's black silhouette. Jess's cry of fear tore through his heart.

No, he couldn't shoot a man in the back. But there was a way to change that. "*Jenci!*" he called, and then realized he had only an instant before the wizard spelled a physical shield. *He is not without weapons*, Ander told himself, and loosed the arrow as Jenci turned.

The blinding light flared and faded, and Ander was running to the stump before he could fully see what awaited him there.

Jaime lowered her arm from where it shielded her eyes and breathed, "Thank God," whatever that meant, looking down at the handbow bolt she clutched in her white-knuckled hand. Jess knelt by Carey, apparently unreassured by his nearly impatient insistence that he was all right. And once Ander had gotten a good look at Jess, he could look nowhere else.

She came to her feet easily, and stared back at him. She was naked beneath that shirt, by heavens, not a stitch on. As he forced himself to close his mouth, he realized what it meant. She'd been changed, and now she was Jess again. He was surprised at the swell of emotion in his throat, and the husky way his words came out. "Did you . . . ?"

"Yes," she said proudly. "They were going to hurt Carey."

He blinked at her; she'd actually done it. *They were going to hurt Carey*. Ander glanced away from her for the merest instant, to Carey's battered appearance. "It looks like they already did plenty."

"Not enough to keep me from killing Ernie," Carey

said dryly, his hand resting on the back of Jess's knee, a possessive gesture. Ander barely heard him; he was staring again.

She was beautiful. She'd always *been* beautiful to him, as exotic as her features and coloring were, as odd as her behavior could be . . . but he suddenly knew, finally, that she was Carey's. Or Carey was hers. Ander didn't know which—he just knew that the spell she'd struggled with for so long had been out of her reach, until she'd had to do it for Carey. He knew he was looking at someone that meant everything to him, and that *she* was out of *his* reach, and always had been.

Jess's expression grew puzzled, and she glanced down at herself, at the bloodied shirt that fell just below her hips and covered nothing of her thighs, and at the curves of her breasts that were only half covered by the loose material. Her expression cleared. "Oh, that's right," she said, her voice taking the same tone he'd heard her use when she reminisced about doing some sly thing in her Lady form. "*No breasts.*"

Chapter 15

The second time the travel site activated, Jess knew what it was right away—and this time, they all knew *where* it was, as well. They had plenty of time to array themselves around it, creating a welcoming committee that included Ander's drawn bow, Jaime's finally cocked handbow, and Jess, her borrowed shirt more securely buttoned, moving in from the side, exhausted but ready to defend them.

Carey was the first to recognize his old friend, even before the faint haze of can't-look-straight-at-it magic faded. "*Arlen!*"

Arlen! Jess straightened, alert with anticipation instead of alarm; Jaime's handbow sagged, pointing at the ground, her face lighting with hope. Only Ander hesitated, waiting until Arlen was well and truly *there* before turning his aim aside, slowly releasing the pull on the bowstring. Arlen gave him a look as pointed as the arrow, but said nothing—he didn't have the chance.

"Arlen!" Jaime cried. "Arlen, you're all right! How—" she started, and then shook her head. "I don't *care* how. I'm so glad to see you!" She seemed to hesitate, and then committed herself; she ran to Arlen, dropping the bow on the way, and threw her arms around him. Arlen held her closely, his chin resting on the top of her head. Jess recognized the expression on his face; she'd seen it on Carey's when he was reaching for her.

After a moment, Arlen cleared his throat. "I take it

everything's secure here?" Stepping toward the center of the clearing, he looked it over from one end to the other, Jaime tucked under his arm. He wasn't dressed as finely as he was wont, but instead wore tough, well-used gray pants with tall leather boots, and a short tunic made from the same material, reinforced with leather. And although his stride was firm, and his voice steady, his eyes were strained and set above dark circles of fatigue.

"Everything's fine," Carey told him. "At least, it is now. A few moments ago, we were wondering where to go from here."

"And how to get my clothes," Jess added.

Arlen glanced at her, smiling briefly. "I can see where that would be on your mind."

"What are you doing here?" Jaime asked, moving in closer to him. "Are you all right? Sherra said it was all right for you to come?"

"I'm all right," he said, reaching out to touch her arm with a smile of reassurance that quickly faded. "Or close enough to make no difference—and I don't answer to Sherra." Jess had the sneaking suspicion that that meant Sherra had said *no*, but Arlen didn't elucidate. He was giving Carey a look that meant trouble, hands on hips, weight back on one leg. "And I've got plenty of questions of my own, not the least of which is, just what did you think you were doing, trotting off to face down drug-enhanced wizards on your own?"

"Oh, come on," Carey said, shifting against the stump and bringing one careful knee up to rest his arm over. "You knew we were up to something, even before you got yourself blasted by the outlaws."

"I expected to be invited!" Arlen said, his eyes flashing sudden anger.

Carey only shrugged. "We thought that would put you in a bad spot, what with Council obligations hanging over you."

Swallowing irritation, Arlen said, "I don't suppose it would have made any difference in the end—you'd have gone on without me even if I *had* been invited, once I let Willand clobber me." He sighed, and dropped his hands to his sides. "I started making sense again the same evening you took off—not that anyone noticed you were gone until the next day, things were in such an uproar. Sherra returned to Siccawei a day later, and I've been searching for you ever since—unfortunately, I'm not quite up to strength, or I'd have found you before now. Those are handy little spells Dayna put on you, but not up to a good hard look."

"That's what she told us, but they did the job," Carey said, sitting on the stump, and looking even more worn than Arlen. "And how *did* you find us?"

"The outlaws' shield started to fray a little while ago, but I had nothing to home in on until I heard that last burst of magic. I traced the spell booth from it, and came. I won't be the last." He cocked his head, and Jess looked around, wondering what he heard that she hadn't, and if it meant danger. "Especially not after that," he added. "Dayna's realized she can ram through the shield from the inside—she's calling Sherra."

He closed his eyes a moment, then said, "There. I don't know Dayna direct, but I got through to Sherra. She'll pass on to Dayna that you're all right."

"More or less," Carey said. "Arlen, our shieldstones and Jess's clothes are in the cabin—it was Willand's—and for once we've been smart enough not to blunder into anything. If you'd check for wardspells, we can get them back again."

"For once," Arlen agreed. "Give me a moment. I want to see what's happened here." And he paced through the clearing, stopping to take in the sight of Willand's body, nodding to himself at what he saw. At Ernie's stiffening, half-clothed form, he raised an eye at Carey, who shrugged again. He examined the signs of struggle at Lady's tree, lifting and discarding, with some disdain, the quirt Shammel had left behind. He went to the other side of the clearing to run his hand down the length of the tree Willand had felled, and then returned to Carey's stump, in the approximate center of the clearing, and made a quick gesture that encompassed the hill before them.

Some distance up the hill, paralleling the trail Willand had blocked, a tree glowed orange and faded. "The missing one," Arlen said. "Who is it?"

"Shammel," Carey answered shortly. Arlen nodded, took a moment to assess Carey's hurts, and pronounced the most dramatic to be the slice on his arm, incurred when he'd blocked Ernie's knife. The rest, Arlen said, were muscle pulls and deep bruises, painful and slow healing, but not life threatening. Jess went to Carey then, and sat beside him.

"Get that look off your face," Carey told her, as Arlen finally went into the cabin, with Ander and Jaime hovering outside.

Jess frowned, trying to decide just what look Carey might mean, and he took her hand. "Look, Jess," he said. "I'm all right. All right, I hurt like the lowest hell. But I'm *alive*, and it was worth it. Don't you feel the same? I'm afraid to even look at what Shammel's done to you, but . . . damn, Jess, no one thought you could learn to trigger the changespell from Lady—not Ander, not Arlen . . . and sometimes, not even me. I should have known better."

"How could you know better?" Jess said, reasonable as ever. "*I* didn't know better." She eased her shoulder around within the oversize shirt, thankful so little of it was actually touching skin, for even that little was starting to stick to the drying, bloody welts. "Yes," she said. "It was worth this, to stop Willand and the outlaws. But I still feel sad to know you hurt. I can't help it."

Carey ran his thumb along each of her fingers in turn. "No, I suppose not. I guess I'm not real happy that you hurt, either. I guess . . . I've seen too much of that look in the last year. It even had *me* convinced I wasn't good for much any more."

"That's not true!" Jess protested immediately, tightening her hand down on his.

"No, it's not. I've got to be careful, I guess . . . but when it counts . . . when I *decide* to, I can still do what's needed."

That, Jess realized, was true. It had to be his decision, and she would have to learn to let him make those decisions. "Yes," she said, and leaned against his shoulder without thinking much about it; they pulled back from one another with startled and simultaneous noises of pain, and then Carey grinned at her, shaking his head.

"Right now," he said, the grin lingering, "I've decided that we should both just *watch* for a while."

"Clothes, Jess!" Jaime called, reaching into the cabin to accept the bundle from Arlen.

"No breasts," Jess whispered to Carey, as if in conspiracy. Carey laughed, and she knew he was thinking of the look on Ander's face when he realized how little Jess was wearing. She'd *never* understand it—she was naked when she was Lady, wasn't she?—but that didn't mean she had to remain stupid about it. Sly was better.

Jaime left the cabin and joined them at the stump, dropping the clothes in Jess's lap. "Put 'em on, Jess. You're killing Ander."

With Jaime standing between Jess and the cabin, and Ander looking unusually interested in whatever Arlen was up to inside, Jess quickly pulled on her breeches—but balked at the shirt, which was cut to fit and would rub against her whip welts. "It will *hurt*."

Jaime made a face. "I bet it will. Well, hang on to it. Someone'll come along and help before this is over." She moved aside, and it seemed to be a signal to the other two men, who didn't waste any time in joining them. Arlen arrived with Carey's spellstones dangling from his hand, and Jess's shieldstone as well. Carey tucked the chain of stones over his head in visible relief, and Jess let her shieldstone nestle in her hand, growing warm and sticky with the heat of her skin while Arlen sat down and started lobbing point-blank questions at them.

He started with their departure from Anfeald and didn't stop until he'd learned the details of their journey up until the time they'd separated, and then he questioned each of them in turn, so that when Ander responded, Jess heard for the first time what had happened with Dayna and the other wizards, and that Benlan was dead at Jenci's hand. When he spoke of the gorge, he kept his voice light, but when he told them his horse had given out on them, Jess exchanged a quick look with Jaime, and *knew*. It had been much more than a simple ride, it had been a ride many couriers wouldn't have lived through.

And he had done it to reach her. But he knew, now, that she was with Carey, and that there was no changing that. She'd seen it in his face, in the carefully blank expression in his eyes when, in talking about the ride, he looked at her.

He told Arlen about killing Jenci, and Arlen finally seemed to be out of questions. He stood, and looked around the clearing, and closed his eyes a moment. Then he said, "That's it then. I've cleared the others to come through. You've done your part—though I promise, what you've been through here will pale in comparison to the Council's reaction to it all. Believe me, I know. They're not happy when someone takes action against wizards without their sanction."

"Then they should have done it themselves," Jaime said sharply.

"Yes, you're right." Arlen rested his hand on top of

her head, a brief and affectionate touch. "Keep it in mind when they all start shouting at you at once. It'll make things easier."

Jaime made a grumbling noise, one that implied she'd have little tolerance for such shouting. Arlen drew her aside, leaving the others to sit together while he spoke softly to her, teasing a smile out of her. After that Jess caught snatches of words, like " . . . long-distance relationship," and " . . . hell of a commute," and, firmer than the rest, "We can do it." She smiled to herself.

Ander wasn't paying any attention to them. His face was pensive, glancing from Jess to Carey, as he asked, "What *now*?"

Jess heard the real question in his voice. *When do we get to go home? When can we just be couriers again, with no one out for our heads, and no one threatening to turn the whole of central Camolen into sheep.*

He wanted to go back to Kymmet, of course. Jess gave Carey a sudden startled look, and realized that while she, too, would go back to Kymmet, it would not be to stay. She'd gone there in the first place, a year ago, because she needed to learn about herself, and learn how to be Jess, without bcing overly dependent on Carey as she did it.

She'd listened and watched and read, trained horses, and tried to train herself. She and Lady had struggled with one another, fighting to stay separate so human did not confuse horse and horse did not control human. But that wasn't the answer. The answer was, she was not some *thing* that could be divided into parts. She was a whole, and each part had to reach for the other.

Carey was watching her, his hazel eyes solemn, as if he'd been able to tell her thoughts had wandered from the practical—putting on clothes and wishing for salve to soothe her back—to something deeper, and to decisions of her own. "Coming home?" he asked softly.

To me, he meant. Jess nodded, and replied just as softly, as if they were the only two in the clearing—for at the moment, they were the only two that mattered. "Damn straight."

She was a whole, now, and he was part of both her selves. She wasn't Jess, sometimes, or Lady others.

She was Dun Lady's Jess.

Author's Note

Authors take their neonatal ideas, massage and plump them, weave in subplots, and turn them into books. Along the way we grow to believe in our characters, and sweat and grow and cry with them. There are very few things as satisfying as typing the last few words of a book, and knowing you've told the story as best you can.

But then comes the important part, the reader's part. That's who we're writing *for*, after all. Long after I write those last words in *Changespell*, I'll wonder how they affect the people they're meant for . . . which is why my postal and current e-mail addresses are given below.

Doranna Durgin
PO Box 26207
Rochester, NY 14626
(SASE please)
doranna@sff.net

MERCEDES LACKEY

The Hottest Fantasy Writer Today!

URBAN FANTASY

Knight of Ghosts and Shadows with Ellen Guon
Elves in L.A.? It would explain a lot, wouldn't it? Eric Banyon really needed a good cause to get his life in gear—now he's got one. With an elven prince he must raise an army to fight against the evil elf lord who seeks to conquer all of California.

Summoned to Tourney with Ellen Guon
Elves in San Francisco? Where else would an elf go when L.A. got too hot? All is well there with our elf-lord, his human companion and the mage who brought them all together—until it turns out that San Francisco is doomed to fall off the face of the continent.

Born to Run with Larry Dixon
There are elves out there. And more are coming. But even elves need money to survive in the "real" world. The good elves in South Carolina, intrigued by the thrills of stock car racing, are manufacturing new, light-weight engines (with, incidentally, very little "cold" iron); the bad elves run a kiddie-porn and snuff-film ring, with occasional forays into drugs. *Children in Peril—Elves to the Rescue.* (Book I of the SERRAted Edge series.)

Wheels of Fire with Mark Shepherd
Book II of the SERRAted Edge series.

When the Bough Breaks with Holly Lisle
Book III of the SERRAted Edge series.

HIGH FANTASY

Bardic Voices: The Lark & The Wren
Rune could be one of the greatest bards of her world, but the daughter of a tavern wench can't get much in the way of formal training. So one night she goes up to play for the Ghost of Skull Hill. She'll either fiddle till dawn to prove her skill as a bard—or die trying....

The Robin and the Kestrel: Bardic Voices II
After the affairs recounted in *The Lark and The Wren*, Robin, a gypsy lass and bard, and Kestrel, semi-fugitive heir to a throne he does not want, have married their fortunes together and travel the open road, seeking their happiness where they may find it. This is their story. It is also the story of the Ghost of Skull Hill. Together, the Robin, the Kestrel, and the Ghost will foil a plot to drive all music forever from the land....

Bardic Choices: A Cast of Corbies with Josepha Sherman

If I Pay Thee Not in Gold with Piers Anthony
A new hardcover quest fantasy, co-written by the creator of the "Xanth" series. A marvelous adult fantasy that examines the war between the sexes and the ethics of desire! Watch out for bad puns!

BARD'S TALE

Based on the bestselling computer game, *The Bard's Tale.*™

Castle of Deception with Josepha Sherman

Fortress of Frost and Fire with Ru Emerson

Prison of Souls with Mark Shepherd

Also by Mercedes Lackey:

Reap the Whirlwind with C.J. Cherryh
Part of the Sword of Knowledge series.

The Ship Who Searched with Anne McCaffrey
The Ship Who Sang is not alone!

Wing Commander: Freedom Flight with Ellen Guon
Based on the bestselling computer game, *Wing Commander.*®

Join the Mercedes Lackey national fan club! For information send an SASE (business-size) to Queen's Own, P.O. Box 43143, Upper Montclair, NJ 07043.

Available at your local bookstore. If not, send this coupon and a check or money order for the cover price(s) to: Baen Books, Dept. BA, PO Box 1403, Riverdale NY 10471.

☐ Knight of Ghosts & Shadows • 69885-0 • $4.99
☐ Summoned to Tourney • 72122-4 • $4.99
☐ Born to Run • 72110-0 • $5.99
☐ Wheels of Fire • 72138-0 • $4.99
☐ When the Bough Breaks • 72156-9 • $5.99
The "Bardic Voices" series:
☐ The Lark & The Wren • 72099-6 • $5.99
☐ The Robin & The Kestrel • 87628-7 • $5.99
☐ Bardic Choices: A Cast of Corbies • 72207-7 • $5.99
☐ If I Pay Thee Not in Gold • 87623-6 • $5.99
☐ Castle of Deception • 72125-9 • $5.99
☐ Fortress of Frost & Fire • 72162-3 • $5.99
☐ Prison of Souls • 72193-3 • $5.99
☐ Reap the Whirlwind • 69846-X • $4.99
☐ The Ship Who Searched • 72129-1 • $5.99
☐ Wing Commander: Freedom Flight • 72145-3 • $4.99

Name: ______________________________

Address: ______________________________

____

Paksenarrion, a simple sheepfarmer's daughter, yearns for a life of adventure and glory, such as the heroes in songs and story. At age seventeen she runs away from home to join a mercenary company, and begins her epic life . . .

ELIZABETH MOON

"This is the first work of high heroic fantasy I've seen, that has taken the work of Tolkien, assimilated it totally and deeply and absolutely, and produced something altogether new and yet incontestably based on the master. . . . This is the real thing. Worldbuilding in the grand tradition, background thought out to the last detail, by someone who knows absolutely whereof she speaks. . . . Her military knowledge is impressive, her picture of life in a mercenary company most convincing."—**Judith Tarr**

About the author: Elizabeth Moon joined the U.S. Marine Corps in 1968 and completed both Officers Candidate School and Basic School, reaching the rank of 1st Lieutenant during active duty. Her background in military training and discipline imbue The Deed of Paksenarrion *with a gritty realism that is all too rare in most current fantasy.*